THE WRITINGS OF HERMAN MELVILLE

The Northwestern–Newberry Edition

VOLUME EIGHT

Israel Potter

This volume edited by
HARRISON HAYFORD
HERSHEL PARKER
G. THOMAS TANSELLE

Historical Note by
WALTER E. BEZANSON

Associates
RICHARD COLLES JOHNSON
BRIAN HIGGINS
ROBERT C. RYAN

Contributing Scholars
JOEL MYERSON
MARY K. MADISON
R. D. MADISON

Editorial Coordinator
ALMA A. MACDOUGALL

Israel Potter

His Fifty Years of Exile

HERMAN MELVILLE

NORTHWESTERN UNIVERSITY PRESS
and
THE NEWBERRY LIBRARY
Evanston and Chicago
1982

PUBLICATION OF *this edition of* THE WRITINGS OF HERMAN MELVILLE *has been made possible through the financial support of Northwestern University and its Research Committee and The Newberry Library. The research necessary to establish the text was undertaken under the Cooperative Research Program of the Office of Education. Northwestern University Press produced and published this edition and reserves all rights.*

LIBRARY OF CONGRESS CATALOG CARD NUMBER 82-81178

PRINTED IN THE UNITED STATES OF AMERICA

FIRST PAPERBACK PRINTING, 1982
SECOND PAPERBACK PRINTING, 1989
THIRD PAPERBACK PRINTING, 1993

CLOTH EDITION, ISBN 0-8101-0552-7
PAPER EDITION, ISBN 0-8101-0553-5

TO

His Highness

THE

𝕭𝖚𝖓𝖐𝖊𝖗-𝕳𝖎𝖑𝖑 𝕸𝖔𝖓𝖚𝖒𝖊𝖓𝖙

B IOGRAPHY, in its purer form, confined to the ended lives of the
true and brave, may be held the fairest meed of human virtue—one
given and received in entire disinterestedness—since neither can the
biographer hope for acknowledgment from the subject, nor the subject at all
avail himself of the biographical distinction conferred.

Israel Potter well merits the present tribute—a private of Bunker Hill,
who for his faithful services was years ago promoted to a still deeper privacy
under the ground, with a posthumous pension, in default of any during life,
annually paid him by the spring in ever-new mosses and sward.

I am the more encouraged to lay this performance at the feet of your
Highness, because, with a change in the grammatical person, it preserves,
almost as in a reprint, Israel Potter's autobiographical story. Shortly after his
return in infirm old age to his native land, a little narrative of his adventures,
forlornly published on sleazy gray paper, appeared among the peddlers,
written, probably, not by himself, but taken down from his lips by another.
But like the crutch-marks of the cripple by the Beautiful Gate, this blurred
record is now out of print. From a tattered copy, rescued by the merest
chance from the rag-pickers, the present account has been drawn, which,
with the exception of some expansions, and additions of historic and personal details, and one or two shiftings of scene, may, perhaps, be not unfitly
regarded something in the light of a dilapidated old tombstone retouched.

Well aware that in your Highness' eyes the merit of the story must be in its general fidelity to the main drift of the original narrative, I forbore anywhere to mitigate the hard fortunes of my hero; and particularly towards the end, though sorely tempted, durst not substitute for the allotment of Providence any artistic recompense of poetical justice; so that no one can complain of the gloom of my closing chapters more profoundly than myself.

Such is the work, and such the man, that I have the honor to present to your Highness. That the name here noted should not have appeared in the volumes of Sparks, may or may not be a matter for astonishment; but Israel Potter seems purposely to have waited to make his popular advent under the present exalted patronage, seeing that your Highness, according to the definition above, may, in the loftiest sense, be deemed the Great Biographer: the national commemorator of such of the anonymous privates of June 17, 1775, who may never have received other requital than the solid reward of your granite.

Your Highness will pardon me, if, with the warmest ascriptions on this auspicious occasion, I take the liberty to mingle my hearty congratulations on the recurrence of the anniversary day we celebrate, wishing your Highness (though indeed your Highness be somewhat prematurely gray) many returns of the same, and that each of its summer's suns may shine as brightly on your brow as each winter snow shall lightly rest on the grave of Israel Potter.

> Your Highness'
> Most devoted and obsequious,
> THE EDITOR.

JUNE 17th, 1854.

Contents

ix

EDITORIAL APPENDIX

Israel Potter

Chapter I

The Birthplace of Israel

THE TRAVELLER who at the present day is content to travel in the good old Asiatic style, neither rushed along by a locomotive, nor dragged by a stage-coach; who is willing to enjoy hospitalities at far-scattered farmhouses, instead of paying his bill at an inn; who is not to be frightened by any amount of loneliness, or to be deterred by the roughest roads or the highest hills; such a traveller in the eastern part of Berkshire, Mass., will find ample food for poetic reflection in the singular scenery of a country, which, owing to the ruggedness of the soil and its lying out of the track of all public conveyances, remains almost as unknown to the general tourist as the interior of Bohemia.

Travelling northward from the township of Otis, the road leads for twenty or thirty miles towards Windsor, lengthwise upon that long broken spur of heights which the Green Mountains of Vermont send into Massachusetts. For nearly the whole of the distance, you have the continual sensation of being upon some terrace in the moon. The feeling of the plain or the valley is never yours; scarcely the feeling of the earth. Unless by a sudden precipitation of the road you find yourself plunging into some gorge; you pass on, and on, and on, upon the crests or slopes of pastoral mountains, while far below, mapped out in its beauty, the valley of the Housatonic lies endlessly along at your feet. Often, as your horse gaining

3

some lofty level tract, flat as a table, trots gayly over the almost deserted and sodded road, and your admiring eye sweeps the broad landscape beneath, you seem to be Boótes driving in heaven. Save a potato field here and there, at long intervals, the whole country is either in wood or pasture. Horses, cattle and sheep are the principal inhabitants of these mountains. But all through the year lazy columns of smoke rising from the depths of the forest, proclaim the presence of that half-outlaw, the charcoal-burner; while in early spring added curls of vapor show that the maple sugar-boiler is also at work. But as for farming as a regular vocation, there is not much of it here. At any rate, no man by that means accumulates a fortune from this thin and rocky soil; all whose arable parts have long since been nearly exhausted.

Yet during the first settlement of the country, the region was not unproductive. Here it was that the original settlers came, acting upon the principle well-known to have regulated their choice of site, namely, the high land in preference to the low, as less subject to the unwholesome miasmas generated by breaking into the rich valleys and alluvial bottoms of primeval regions. By degrees, however, they quitted the safety of this sterile elevation, to brave the dangers of richer though lower fields. So that at the present day, some of those mountain townships present an aspect of singular abandonment. Though they have never known aught but peace and health, they, in one lesser aspect at least, look like countries depopulated by plague and war. Every mile or two a house is passed untenanted. The strength of the frame-work of these ancient buildings enables them long to resist the encroachments of decay. Spotted gray and green with the weather-stain, their timbers seem to have lapsed back into their woodland original, forming part now of the general picturesqueness of the natural scene. They are of extraordinary size, compared with modern farm-houses. One peculiar feature is the immense chimney, of light gray stone, perforating the middle of the roof like a tower.

On all sides are seen the tokens of ancient industry. As stone abounds throughout these mountains, that material was, for fences, as ready to the hand as wood, besides being much more durable. Consequently the landscape is intersected in all directions with walls of uncommon neatness and strength.

The number and length of these walls is not more surprising than the size of some of the blocks comprising them. The very Titans seemed to have been at work. That so small an army as the first settlers must needs have been, should have taken such wonderful pains to inclose so ungrateful a soil;

that they should have accomplished such herculean undertakings with so slight prospect of reward; this is a consideration which gives us a significant hint of the temper of the men of the Revolutionary era.

Nor could a fitter country be found for the birthplace of the devoted patriot, Israel Potter.

To this day the best stone-wall builders, as the best wood-choppers, come from those solitary mountain towns; a tall, athletic, and hardy race, unerring with the axe as the Indian with the tomahawk; at stone-rolling, patient as Sisyphus, powerful as Samson.

In fine clear June days, the bloom of these mountains is beyond expression delightful. Last visiting these heights ere she vanishes, Spring, like the sunset, flings her sweetest charms upon them. Each tuft of upland grass is musked like a bouquet with perfume. The balmy breeze swings to and fro like a censer. On one side the eye follows for the space of an eagle's flight, the serpentine mountain chains, southwards from the great purple dome of Taconic—the St. Peter's of these hills—northwards to the twin summits of Saddleback, which is the two-steepled natural cathedral of Berkshire; while low down to the west the Housatonic winds on in her watery labyrinth, through charming meadows basking in the reflected rays from the hill-sides. At this season the beauty of every thing around you populates the loneliness of your way. You would not have the country more settled if you could. Content to drink in such loveliness at all your senses, the heart desires no company but nature.

With what rapture you behold, hovering over some vast hollow of the hills, or slowly drifting at an immense height over the far sunken Housatonic valley, some lordly eagle, who in unshared exaltation looks down equally upon plain and mountain. Or you behold a hawk sallying from some crag, like a Rhenish baron of old from his pinnacled castle, and darting down towards the river for his prey. Or perhaps, lazily gliding about in the zenith, this ruffian fowl is suddenly beset by a crow, who with stubborn audacity pecks at him, and spite of all his bravery, finally persecutes him back to his stronghold. The otherwise dauntless bandit, soaring at his topmost height, must needs succumb to this sable image of death. Nor are there wanting many smaller and less famous fowl, who without contributing to the grandeur, yet greatly add to the beauty of the scene. The yellow bird flits like a winged jonquil here and there; like knots of violets the blue birds sport in clusters upon the grass; while hurrying from the pasture to the grove, the red robin seems an incendiary putting torch to the trees. Meanwhile the air is vocal with their hymns, and your own soul joys in the general joy. Like a stranger in an orchestra, you cannot help singing yourself when all around you raise such hosannas.

But in autumn, those gay northerners, the birds, return to their southern plantations. The mountains are left bleak and sere. Solitude settles down upon them in drizzling mists. The traveller is beset, at perilous turns, by dense masses of fog. He emerges for a moment into more penetrable air; and passing some gray, abandoned house, sees the lofty vapors plainly eddy by its desolate door; just as from the plain, you may see it eddy by the pinnacles of distant and lonely heights. Or, dismounting from his frightened horse, he leads him down some scowling glen, where the road steeply dips among grim rocks, only to rise as abruptly again; and as he warily picks his way, uneasy at the menacing scene, he sees some ghost-like object looming through the mist at the roadside; and wending towards it, beholds a rude white stone, uncouthly inscribed, marking the spot where, some fifty or sixty years ago, some farmer was upset in his wood-sled, and perished beneath the load.

In winter this region is blocked up with snow. Inaccessible and impassable, those wild, unfrequented roads, which in August are overgrown with high grass, in December are drifted to the arm-pit with the white fleece from the sky. As if an ocean rolled between man and man, intercommunication is often suspended for weeks and weeks.

Such, at this day, is the country which gave birth to our hero: prophetically styled Israel by the good Puritans, his parents, since for more than forty years, poor Potter wandered in the wild wilderness of the world's extremest hardships and ills.

How little he thought, when, as a boy, hunting after his father's stray cattle among these New England hills, he himself like a beast should be hunted through half of Old England, as a runaway rebel. Or, how could he ever have dreamed, when involved in the autumnal vapors of these mountains, that worse bewilderments awaited him three thousand miles across the sea, wandering forlorn in the coal-fogs of London. But so it was destined to be. This little boy of the hills, born in sight of the sparkling Housatonic, was to linger out the best part of his life a prisoner or a pauper upon the grimy banks of the Thames.

Chapter 2

The Youthful Adventures of Israel

IMAGINATION will easily picture the rural days of the youth of Israel. Let us pass on to a less immature period.

It appears that he began his wanderings very early; moreover, that ere, on just principles throwing off the yoke of his king, Israel, on equally excusable grounds, emancipated himself from his sire. He continued in the enjoyment of parental love till the age of eighteen, when, having formed an attachment for a neighbor's daughter—for some reason, not deemed a suitable match by his father—he was severely reprimanded, warned to discontinue his visits, and threatened with some disgraceful punishment in case he persisted. As the girl was not only beautiful, but amiable—though, as will be seen, rather weak—and her family respectable as any, though unfortunately but poor, Israel deemed his father's conduct unreasonable and oppressive; particularly as it turned out that he had taken secret means to thwart his son with the girl's connections, if not with the girl herself, so as to place almost insurmountable obstacles to an eventual marriage. For it had not been the purpose of Israel to marry at once, but at a future day, when prudence should approve the step. So, oppressed by his father, and bitterly disappointed in his love, the desperate boy formed the determination to quit them both, for another home and other friends.

It was on Sunday, while the family were gone to a farm-house church near by, that he packed up as much of his clothing as might be contained in a handkerchief, which, with a small quantity of provision, he hid in a piece of woods in the rear of the house. He then returned, and continued in the house till about nine in the evening, when, pretending to go to bed, he passed out of a back door, and hastened to the woods for his bundle.

It was a sultry night in July; and that he might travel with the more ease on the succeeding day, he lay down at the foot of a pine tree, reposing himself till an hour before dawn, when, upon awaking, he heard the soft, prophetic sighing of the pine, stirred by the first breath of the morning. Like the leaflets of that evergreen, all the fibres of his heart trembled within him; tears fell from his eyes. But he thought of the tyranny of his father, and what seemed to him the faithlessness of his love; and shouldering his bundle, arose, and marched on.

His intention was to reach the new countries to the northward and westward, lying between the Dutch settlements on the Hudson, and the Yankee settlements on the Housatonic. This was mainly to elude all search. For the same reason, for the first ten or twelve miles, shunning the public roads, he travelled through the woods; for he knew that he would soon be missed and pursued.

He reached his destination in safety; hired out to a farmer for a month through the harvest; then crossed from the Hudson to the Connecticut. Meeting here with an adventurer to the unknown regions lying about the head waters of the latter river, he ascended with this man in a canoe, paddling and poling for many miles. Here again he hired himself out for three months; at the end of that time to receive for his wages, two hundred acres of land lying in New Hampshire. The cheapness of the land was not alone owing to the newness of the country, but to the perils investing it. Not only was it a wilderness abounding with wild beasts, but the widely scattered inhabitants were in continual dread of being, at some unguarded moment, destroyed or made captive by the Canadian savages, who, ever since the French war, had improved every opportunity to make forays across the defenceless frontier.

His employer proving false to his contract in the matter of the land, and there being no law in the country to force him to fulfil it, Israel,—who however brave-hearted, and even much of a dare-devil upon a pinch, seems, nevertheless, to have evinced, throughout many parts of his career, a singular patience and mildness,—was obliged to look round for other means of livelihood, than clearing out a farm for himself in the wilderness. A party of royal surveyors were at this period surveying the unsettled regions bordering the Connecticut River to its source. At fifteen shillings per month, he engaged himself to this party as assistant chain-bearer, little thinking that the day was to come when he should clank the king's chains in a dungeon, even as now he trailed them a free ranger of the woods. It was midwinter; the land was surveyed upon snow-shoes. At the close of the day, fires were kindled with dry hemlock, a hut thrown up, and the party ate and slept.

Paid off at last, Israel bought a gun and ammunition, and turned hunter. Deer, beaver, &c., were plenty. In two or three months he had many skins to show. I suppose it never entered his mind, that he was thus qualifying himself for a marksman of men. But thus were tutored those wonderful shots who did such execution at Bunker's Hill; these, the hunter-soldiers, whom Putnam bade wait till the white of the enemy's eye was seen.

With the result of his hunting he purchased a hundred acres of land, further down the river, toward the more settled parts; built himself a log hut, and in two summers, with his own hands, cleared thirty acres for sowing. In the winter seasons he hunted and trapped. At the end of the two years, he sold back his land—now much improved—to the original owner, at an advance of fifty pounds. He conveyed his skins and furs to Charlestown, on the Connecticut (sometimes called No. 4), where he trafficked them away for Indian blankets, pigments, and other showy articles adapted to the business of a trader among savages. It was now winter again. Putting his goods on a hand-sled, he started towards Canada, a peddler in the wilderness, stopping at wigwams instead of cottages. One fancies that, had it been summer, Israel would have travelled with a wheelbarrow, and so trundled his wares through the primeval forests, with the same indifference as porters roll their barrows over the flagging of streets. In this way was bred that fearless self-reliance and independence which conducted our forefathers to national freedom.

This Canadian trip proved highly successful. Selling his glittering goods at a great advance, he received in exchange valuable peltries and furs at a corresponding reduction. Returning to Charlestown, he disposed of his return cargo again at a very fine profit. And now, with a light heart and a heavy purse, he resolved to visit his sweetheart and parents, of whom, for three years, he had had no tidings.

They were not less astonished than delighted at his reappearance; he had been numbered with the dead. But his love still seemed strangely coy; willing, but yet somehow mysteriously withheld. The old intrigues were still on foot. Israel soon discovered, that though rejoiced to welcome the return of the prodigal son—so some called him—his father still remained

inflexibly determined against the match, and still inexplicably counter-
mined his wooing. With a dolorous heart he mildly yielded to what
seemed his fatality; and more intrepid in facing peril for himself, than in
endangering others by maintaining his rights (for he was now one-and-
twenty), resolved once more to retreat, and quit his blue hills for the bluer
billows.

A hermitage in the forest is the refuge of the narrow-minded misan-
thrope; a hammock on the ocean is the asylum for the generous distressed.
The ocean brims with natural griefs and tragedies; and into that watery
immensity of terror, man's private grief is lost like a drop.

Travelling on foot to Providence, Rhode Island, Israel shipped on board
a sloop, bound with lime to the West Indies. On the tenth day out, the
vessel caught fire, from water communicating with the lime. It was impossible to extinguish the flames. The boat was hoisted out, but owing to long
exposure to the sun, it needed continual baling to keep it afloat. They had
only time to put in a firkin of butter and a ten-gallon keg of water. Eight in
number, the crew entrusted themselves to the waves, in a leaky tub, many
leagues from land. As the boat swept under the burning bowsprit, Israel
caught at a fragment of the flying-jib, which sail had fallen down the stay,
owing to the charring, nigh the deck, of the rope which hoisted it. Tanned
with the smoke, and its edge blackened with the fire, this bit of canvas
helped them bravely on their way. Thanks to kind Providence, on the
second day they were picked up by a Dutch ship, bound from Eustatia to
Holland. The castaways were humanely received, and supplied with every
necessary. At the end of a week, while unsophisticated Israel was sitting in
the main-top, thinking what should befall him in Holland, and wondering
what sort of unsettled, wild, country it was, and whether there was any
deer-shooting or beaver-trapping there; lo! an American brig, bound from
Piscataqua to Antigua, comes in sight. The American took them aboard and
conveyed them safely to her port. There Israel shipped for Porto Rico; from
thence, sailed to Eustatia.

Other rovings ensued; until at last, entering on board a Nantucket ship,
he hunted the leviathan off the Western Islands and on the coast of Africa,
for sixteen months; returning at length to Nantucket with a brimming hold.
From that island he sailed again on another whaling voyage, extending, this
time, into the great South Sea. There, promoted to be harpooner, Israel,
whose eye and arm had been so improved by practice with his gun in the
wilderness, now further intensified his aim, by darting the whale-lance; still,
unwittingly, preparing himself for the Bunker Hill rifle.

In this last voyage, our adventurer experienced to the extreme, all the hardships and privations of the whaleman's life on a long voyage to distant and barbarous waters; hardships and privations unknown at the present day, when science has so greatly contributed, in manifold ways, to lessen the sufferings, and add to the comforts of sea-faring men. Heartily sick of the ocean, and longing once more for the bush, Israel, upon receiving his discharge at Nantucket at the end of the voyage, hied straight back for his mountain home.

But if hopes of his sweetheart winged his returning flight, such hopes were not destined to be crowned with fruition. The dear, false girl, was another's.

Chapter 3

Israel Goes to the Wars; and Reaching Bunker Hill in Time to
Be of Service There, Soon After Is Forced to Extend His
Travels across the Sea into the Enemy's Land

LEFT TO IDLE LAMENTATIONS, Israel might now have planted
deep furrows in his brow. But stifling his pain, he chose rather to
plough, than be ploughed. Farming weans man from his sorrows.
That tranquil pursuit tolerates nothing but tranquil meditations. There, too,
in mother earth, you may plant and reap; not, as in other things, plant and
see the planting torn up by the roots. But if wandering in the wilderness;
and wandering upon the waters; if felling trees; and hunting, and ship-
wreck; and fighting with whales, and all his other strange adventures, had
not as yet cured poor Israel of his now hopeless passion; events were at hand
for ever to drown it.

It was the year 1774. The difficulties long pending between the colonies
and England, were arriving at their crisis. Hostilities were certain. The
Americans were preparing themselves. Companies were formed in most of
the New England towns; whose members, receiving the name of minutemen, stood ready to march anywhere at a minute's warning. Israel, for the
last eight months, sojourning as a laborer on a farm in Windsor, enrolled
himself in the regiment of Colonel John Patterson of Lenox, afterwards
General Patterson.

The battle of Lexington was fought on the 18th of April, 1775; news of
it arrived in the county of Berkshire on the 20th, about noon. The next

morning at sunrise, Israel swung his knapsack, shouldered his musket, and with Patterson's regiment, was on the march, quickstep, towards Boston.

Like Putnam, Israel received the stirring tidings at the plough. But although not less willing than Putnam, to fly to battle at an instant's notice; yet—only half an acre of the field remaining to be finished—he whipped up his team and finished it. Before hastening to one duty, he would not leave a prior one undone; and ere helping to whip the British, for a little practice' sake, he applied the gad to his oxen. From the field of the farmer, he rushed to that of the soldier, mingling his blood with his sweat. While we revel in broadcloth, let us not forget what we owe to linsey-woolsey.

With other detachments from various quarters, Israel's regiment remained encamped for several days in the vicinity of Charlestown. On the sixteenth of June, one thousand Americans, including the regiment of Patterson, were set about fortifying Bunker's Hill. Working all through the night, by dawn of the following day, the redoubt was thrown up. But every one knows all about the battle. Suffice it, that Israel was one of those marksmen whom Putnam harangued as touching the enemy's eyes. Forbearing as he was with his oppressive father and unfaithful love, and mild as he was on the farm; Israel was not the same at Bunker Hill. Putnam had enjoined the men to aim at the officers; so Israel aimed between the golden epaulettes, as, in the wilderness, he had aimed between the branching antlers. With dogged disdain of their foes, the English grenadiers marched up the hill with sullen slowness; thus furnishing still surer aims to the muskets which bristled on the redoubt. Modest Israel was used to aver, that considering his practice in the woods, he could hardly be regarded as an inexperienced marksman; hinting, that every shot which the epauletted grenadiers received from his rifle, would, upon a different occasion, have procured him a deer-skin. And like stricken deers the English, rashly brave as they were, fled from the opening fire. But the marksmen's ammunition was expended; a hand-to-hand encounter ensued. Not one American musket in twenty had a bayonet to it. So, wielding the stock right and left, the terrible farmers, with hats and coats off, fought their way among the furred grenadiers; knocking them right and left, as seal hunters on the beach, knock down with their clubs the Shetland seal. In the dense crowd and confusion, while Israel's musket got interlocked, he saw a blade horizontally menacing his feet from the ground. Thinking some fallen enemy sought to strike him at the last gasp, dropping his hold on his musket, he wrenched at the steel, but found that though a brave hand held it, that hand was powerless for ever. It was some British officer's laced sword-arm, cut from the trunk in the act of fighting; refusing to yield up its blade, to the last. At that moment another sword was aimed at Israel's head, by a living officer. In an instant the blow was parried by kindred steel, and the assailant fell by a brother's weapon, wielded by alien hands. But Israel did not come off unscathed. A cut on the right arm near the elbow, received in parrying the officer's blow; a long slit across the chest; a musket-ball buried in his hip, and another mangling him near the ankle of the same leg, were the tokens of intrepidity which our Sicinius Dentatus carried from this memorable field. Nevertheless, with his comrades he succeeded in reaching Prospect Hill, and from thence was conveyed to the hospital at Cambridge. The bullet was extracted, his lesser wounds were dressed, and after much suffering from the fracture of the bone near the ankle, several pieces of which were extracted by the surgeon, ere long, thanks to the high health and pure blood of the farmer, Israel rejoined his regiment when they were throwing up intrenchments on Prospect Hill. Bunker Hill was now in possession of the foe, who in turn had fortified it.

On the third of July, Washington arrived from the South to take the command. Israel witnessed his joyful reception by the huzzaing companies.

The British now quartered in Boston suffered greatly from the scarcity of provisions. Washington took every precaution to prevent their receiving a supply. Inland, all aid could easily be cut off. To guard against their receiving any by water, from tories and other disaffected persons, the general equipped three armed vessels to intercept all traitorous cruisers. Among them was the brigantine Washington, of ten guns, commanded by Captain Martindale. Seamen were hard to be had. The soldiers were called upon to volunteer for these vessels. Israel was one who so did; thinking that as an experienced sailor he should not be backward in a juncture like this, little as he fancied the new service assigned.

Three days out of Boston harbor, the brigantine was captured by the enemy's ship Foy, of twenty guns. Taken prisoner with the rest of the crew, Israel was afterwards put on board the frigate Tartar, with immediate sailing orders for England. Seventy-two were captives in this vessel. Headed by Israel, these men—half way across the sea—formed a scheme to take the ship, but were betrayed by a renegade Englishman. As ringleader, Israel was put in irons, and so remained till the frigate anchored at Portsmouth. There he was brought on deck; and would have met perhaps some terrible fate, had it not come out during the examination, that the Englishman had been a deserter from the army of his native country, ere proving a traitor to his adopted one. Relieved of his irons, Israel was placed in the marine hospital on shore, where half of the prisoners took the small-pox, which swept off a third of their number. Why talk of Jaffa?

From the hospital the survivors were conveyed to Spithead, and thrust on board a hulk. And here in the black bowels of the ship, sunk low in the sunless sea, our poor Israel lay for a month, like Jonah in the belly of the whale.

But one bright morning, Israel is hailed from the deck. A bargeman of the commander's boat is sick. Known for a sailor, Israel for the nonce is appointed to pull the absent man's oar.

The officers being landed, some of the crew propose, like merry Englishmen as they are, to hie to a neighboring ale-house, and have a cosy pot or two together. Agreed. They start, and Israel with them. As they enter the ale-house door, our prisoner is suddenly reminded of still more imperative calls. Unsuspected of any design, he is allowed to leave the party for a moment. No sooner does Israel see his companions housed, than putting speed into his feet, and letting grow all his wings, he starts like a deer. He runs four miles (so he afterwards affirmed) without halting. He sped towards London; wisely deeming that once in that crowd detection would be impossible.

Ten miles, as he computed, from where he had left the bargemen, leisurely passing a public house of a little village on the road-side, thinking himself now pretty safe—hark, what is this he hears?—

"Ahoy! what ship?"

"No ship," says Israel, hurrying on.

"Stop."

"If you will attend to your business, I will endeavor to attend to mine," replies Israel coolly. And next minute he lets grow his wings again; flying, one dare say, at the rate of something less than thirty miles an hour.

"Stop thief!" is now the cry. Numbers rushed from the road-side houses. After a mile's chase, the poor panting deer is caught.

Finding it was no use now to prevaricate, Israel boldly confesses himself a prisoner-of-war. The officer, a good fellow as it turned out, had him escorted back to the inn; where, observing to the landlord, that this must needs be a true-blooded Yankee, he calls for liquors to refresh Israel after his run. Two soldiers are then appointed to guard him for the present. This was towards evening; and up to a late hour at night, the inn was filled with strangers crowding to see the Yankee rebel, as they politely termed him. These honest rustics seemed to think that Yankees were a sort of wild creatures, a species of a 'possum or kangaroo. But Israel is very affable with them. That liquor he drank from the hand of his foe, has perhaps warmed his heart towards all the rest of his enemies. Yet this may not be wholly so. We shall see. At any rate, still he keeps his eye on the main chance—escape. Neither the jokes nor the insults of the mob does he suffer to molest him. He is cogitating a little plot to himself.

It seems that the good officer—not more true to the king his master than indulgent towards the prisoner which that same loyalty made—had left orders that Israel should be supplied with whatever liquor he wanted that night. So, calling for the can again and again, Israel invites the two soldiers to drink and be merry. At length, a wag of the company proposes that Israel should entertain the public with a jig; he (the wag) having heard, that the Yankees were extraordinary dancers. A fiddle is brought in, and poor Israel takes the floor. Not a little cut to think that these people should so unfeelingly seek to be diverted at the expense of an unfortunate prisoner, Israel, while jigging it up and down, still conspires away at his private plot, resolving ere long to give the enemy a touch of certain Yankee steps, as yet undreamed of in their simple philosophy. They would not permit any cessation of his dancing till he had danced himself into a perfect sweat, so that the drops fell from his lank and flaxen hair. But Israel, with much of the gentleness of the dove, is not wholly without the wisdom of the serpent. Pleased to see the flowing bowl, he congratulates himself that his own state of perspiration prevents it from producing any intoxicating effect upon him.

Late at night the company break up. Furnished with a pair of handcuffs, the prisoner is laid on a blanket spread upon the floor at the side of the bed in which his two keepers are to repose. Expressing much gratitude for the blanket, with apparent unconcern, Israel stretches his legs. An hour or two passes. All is quiet without.

The important moment had now arrived. Certain it was, that if this chance were suffered to pass unimproved, a second would hardly present itself. For early, doubtless, on the following morning, if not some way prevented, the two soldiers would convey Israel back to his floating prison, where he would thenceforth remain confined until the close of the war; years and years, perhaps. When he thought of that horrible old hulk, his nerves were restrung for flight. But intrepid as he must be to compass it, wariness too was needed. His keepers had gone to bed pretty well under the influence of the liquor. This was favorable. But still, they were full-grown, strong men; and Israel was handcuffed. So Israel resolved upon strategy first; and if that failed, force afterwards. He eagerly listened. One of the drunken soldiers muttered in his sleep, at first lowly, then louder and louder,—"Catch 'em! Grapple 'em! Have at 'em! Ha—long cutlasses! Take that, runaway!"

"What's the matter with ye, Phil?" hiccoughed the other, who was not yet asleep. "Keep quiet, will ye? Ye ain't at Fontenoy now."

"He's a runaway prisoner, I say. Catch him, catch him!"

"Oh, stush with your drunken dreaming," again hiccoughed his comrade, violently nudging him. "This comes o' carousing."

Shortly after, the dreamer with loud snores fell back into dead sleep. But by something in the sound of the breathing of the other soldier, Israel knew that this man remained uneasily awake. He deliberated a moment what was best to do. At length he determined upon trying his old plea. Calling upon the two soldiers, he informed them that urgent necessity required his immediate presence somewhere in the rear of the house.

"Come, wake up here, Phil," roared the soldier who was awake; "the fellow here says he must step out; cuss these Yankees; no better edication than to be gettin' up on nateral necessities at this time o'night. It ain't nateral; it's unnateral. D—n ye, Yankee, don't ye know no better?"

With many more denunciations, the two now staggered to their feet, and clutching hold of Israel, escorted him down stairs, and through a long, narrow, dark entry, rearward, till they came to a door. No sooner was this unbolted by the foremost guard, than, quick as a flash, manacled Israel, shaking off the grasp of the one behind him, butts him sprawling backwards into the entry; when, dashing in the opposite direction, he bounces the other head over heels into the garden, never using a hand; and then, leaping over the latter's head, darts blindly out into the midnight. Next moment he was at the garden wall. No outlet was discoverable in the gloom. But a fruit-tree grew close to the wall. Springing into it desperately, handcuffed as he was, Israel leaps atop of the barrier, and without pausing to see where he is, drops himself to the ground on the other side, and once more lets grow all his wings. Meantime, with loud outcries, the two baffled drunkards grope deliriously about in the garden.

After running two or three miles, and hearing no sound of pursuit, Israel reins up to rid himself of the handcuffs, which impede him. After much painful labor he succeeds in the attempt. Pressing on again with all speed, day broke, revealing a trim-looking, hedged, and beautiful country, soft, neat, and serene, all colored with the fresh early tints of the spring of 1776.

Bless me, thought Israel, all of a tremble, I shall certainly be caught now; I have broken into some nobleman's park.

But, hurrying forward again, he came to a turnpike road, and then knew that, all comely and shaven as it was, this was simply the open country of England; one bright, broad park, paled in with white foam of the sea. A copse skirting the road was just bursting out into bud. Each unrolling leaf was in very act of escaping from its prison. Israel looked at the budding leaves, and round on the budding sod, and up at the budding dawn of the day. He was so sad, and these sights were so gay, that Israel sobbed like a child, while thoughts of his mountain home rushed like a wind on his heart. But conquering this fit, he marched on, and presently passed nigh a field, where two figures were working. They had rosy cheeks, short sturdy legs, showing the blue stocking nearly to the knee, and were clad in long, coarse, white frocks, and had on coarse, broad-brimmed straw hats. Their faces were partly averted.

"Please, ladies," half roguishly says Israel, taking off his hat, "does this road go to London?"

At this salutation, the two figures turned in a sort of stupid amazement, causing an almost corresponding expression in Israel, who now perceived that they were men, and not women. He had mistaken them, owing to their frocks, and their wearing no pantaloons, only breeches hidden by their frocks.

"Beg pardon, lads, but I thought ye were something else," said Israel again.

Once more the two figures stared at the stranger, and with added boorishness of surprise.

"Does this road go to London, gentlemen?"

"Gentlemen—egad!" cried one of the two.

"Egad!" echoed the second.

Putting their hoes before them, the two frocked boors now took a good long look at Israel, meantime scratching their heads under their plaited straw hats.

"Does it, gentlemen? Does it go to London? Be kind enough to tell a poor fellow, do."

"Yees goin' to Lunnun, are yees? Weel—all right—go along."

And without another word, having now satisfied their rustic curiosity, the two human steers, with wonderful phlegm, applied themselves to their hoes; supposing, no doubt, that they had given all requisite information.

Shortly after, Israel passed an old, dark, mossy-looking chapel, its roof all plastered with the damp yellow dead leaves of the previous autumn, showered there from a close cluster of venerable trees, with great trunks, and overstretching branches. Next moment he found himself entering a village. The silence of early morning rested upon it. But few figures were seen. Glancing through the window of a now noiseless public-house, Israel saw a table all in disorder, covered with empty flagons, and tobacco-ashes, and long pipes; some of the latter broken.

After pausing here a moment, he moved on, and observed a man over the way standing still and watching him. Instantly Israel was reminded that he had on the dress of an English sailor, and that it was this probably which had arrested the stranger's attention. Well knowing that his peculiar dress exposed him to peril, he hurried on faster to escape the village; resolving at the first opportunity to change his garments. Ere long, in a secluded place about a mile from the village, he saw an old ditcher tottering beneath the weight of a pick-axe, hoe and shovel, going to his work; the very picture of poverty, toil and distress. His clothes were tatters.

Making up to this old man, Israel, after a word or two of salutation, offered to change clothes with him. As his own clothes were prince-like compared to the ditcher's, Israel thought that however much his proposition might excite the suspicion of the ditcher, yet self-interest would prevent his communicating the suspicions. To be brief, the two went behind a hedge, and presently Israel emerged, presenting the most forlorn appearance conceivable; while the old ditcher hobbled off in an opposite direction, correspondingly improved in his aspect; though it was rather ludicrous than otherwise, owing to the immense bagginess of the sailor-trousers flapping about his lean shanks, to say nothing of the spare voluminousness of the pea-jacket. But Israel—how deplorable, how dismal his plight! Little did he ween that these wretched rags he now wore, were but suitable to that long career of destitution before him; one brief career of adventurous wanderings: and then, forty torpid years of pauperism. The coat was all patches. And no two patches were alike, and no one patch was the color of the original cloth. The stringless breeches gaped wide open at the knee; the long woollen stockings looked as if they had been set up at some time for a target. Israel looked suddenly metamorphosed from youth to old age; just like an old man of eighty he looked. But indeed, dull dreary adversity was now in store for him; and adversity, come it at eighteen or eighty, is the true old age of man. The dress befitted the fate.

From the friendly old ditcher, Israel learned the exact course he must steer for London; distant now between seventy and eighty miles. He was also apprised by his venerable friend, that the country was filled with soldiers, on the constant look-out for deserters whether from the navy or army, for the capture of whom a stipulated reward was given, just as in Massachusetts at that time for prowling bears.

Having solemnly enjoined his old friend not to give any information, should any one he meet inquire for such a person as Israel, our adventurer walked briskly on, less heavy of heart, now that he felt comparatively safe in disguise.

Thirty miles were travelled that day. At night Israel stole into a barn, in hopes of finding straw or hay for a bed. But it was spring; all the hay and straw were gone. So after groping about in the dark, he was fain to content himself with an undressed sheep-skin. Cold, hungry, foot-sore, weary, and impatient for the morning dawn, Israel drearily dozed out the night.

By the first peep of day coming through the chinks of the barn, he was up and abroad. Ere long finding himself in the suburbs of a considerable village, the better to guard against detection he supplied himself with a rude crutch, and feigning himself a cripple, hobbled straight through the town, followed by a perverse-minded cur, which kept up a continual, spiteful, suspicious bark. Israel longed to have one good rap at him with his crutch, but thought it would hardly look in character for a poor old cripple to be vindictive.

A few miles further, and he came to a second village. While hobbling through its main street, as through the former one, he was suddenly stopped by a genuine cripple, all in tatters too, who, with a sympathetic air, inquired after the cause of his lameness.

"White swelling," says Israel.

"That's just my ailing," wheezed the other; "but you're lamer than me," he added with a forlorn sort of self-satisfaction, critically eyeing Israel's limp as once more he stumped on his way, not liking to tarry too long.

"But halloo, what's your hurry, friend?" seeing Israel fairly departing— "where 're you going?"

"To London," answered Israel, turning round, heartily wishing the old fellow any where else than present.

"Going to limp to Lunnun, eh? Well, success to ye."

"As much to you, sir," answers Israel politely.

Nigh the opposite suburbs of this village, as good fortune would have it, an empty baggage-wagon bound for the metropolis turned into the main road from a side one. Immediately Israel limps most deplorably, and begs the driver to give a poor cripple a lift. So up he climbs; but after a time, finding the gait of the elephantine draught-horses intolerably slow, Israel craves permission to dismount, when, throwing away his crutch, he takes nimbly to his legs, much to the surprise of his honest friend, the driver.

The only advantage, if any, derived from his trip in the wagon, was, when passing through a third village—but a little distant from the previous one—Israel, by lying down in the wagon, had wholly avoided being seen.

The villages surprised him by their number and proximity. Nothing like this was to be seen at home. Well knowing that in these villages he ran much more risk of detection than in the open country, he henceforth did his best to avoid them, by taking a roundabout course whenever they came in sight from a distance. This mode of travelling not only lengthened his journey, but put unlooked-for obstacles in his path—walls, ditches and streams.

Not half an hour after throwing away his crutch, he leaped a great ditch nineteen feet wide, and of undiscoverable muddy depth. I wonder if the old cripple would think me the lamer one now, thought Israel to himself, arriving on the hither side.

Chapter 4

Further Wanderings of the Refugee, with Some Account of a
Good Knight of Brentford Who Befriended Him

A T NIGHTFALL on the third day, Israel had arrived within sixteen
miles of the capital. Once more he sought refuge in a barn. This
time he found some hay, and flinging himself down procured a
tolerable night's rest.

Bright and early he arose refreshed, with the pleasing prospect of reaching his destination ere noon. Encouraged to find himself now so far from his
original pursuers, Israel relaxed in his vigilance; and about ten o'clock while
passing through the town of Staines suddenly encountered three soldiers.
Unfortunately in exchanging clothes with the ditcher, he could not bring
himself to include his shirt in the traffic; which shirt was a British navy
shirt; a bargeman's shirt; and though hitherto he had crumpled the blue
collar out of sight, yet, as it appeared in the present instance, it was not
thoroughly concealed. At any rate, keenly on the look-out for deserters, and
made acute by hopes of reward for their apprehension, the soldiers spied the
fatal collar, and in an instant laid violent hands on the refugee.

"Hey lad!" said the foremost soldier, a corporal, "you are one of his
majesty's seamen! come along with ye."

So, unable to give any satisfactory account of himself, he was made
prisoner on the spot, and soon after found himself handcuffed and locked up
in the Round House of the place, a prison so called, appropriated to runa-

ways, and those convicted of minor offences. Day passed dinnerless and supperless in this dismal durance, and night came on.

Israel had now been three days without food, except one two-penny loaf. The cravings of hunger now became sharper; his spirits, hitherto arming him with fortitude, began to forsake him. Taken captive once again upon the very brink of reaching his goal, poor Israel was on the eve of falling into helpless despair. But he rallied, and considering that grief would only add to his calamity, sought with stubborn patience to habituate himself to misery, but still hold aloof from despondency. He roused himself, and began to bethink him how to be extricated from this labyrinth.

Two hours sawing across the grating of the window, ridded him of his handcuffs. Next came the door, secured luckily with only a hasp and padlock. Thrusting the bolt of his handcuffs through a small window in the door, he succeeded in forcing the hasp and regaining his liberty about three o'clock in the morning.

Not long after sunrise, he passed nigh Brentford, some six or seven miles from the capital. So great was his hunger that downright starvation seemed before him. He chewed grass, and swallowed it. Upon first escaping from the hulk, six English pennies was all the money he had. With two of these he had bought a small loaf the day after fleeing the inn. The other four still remained in his pocket, not having met with a good opportunity to dispose of them for food.

Having torn off the collar of his shirt, and flung it into a hedge, he ventured to accost a respectable carpenter at a pale fence, about a mile this side of Brentford, to whom his deplorable situation now induced him to apply for work. The man did not wish himself to hire, but said that if he (Israel), understood farming or gardening, he might perhaps procure work from Sir John Millet, whose seat, he said, was not remote. He added that the knight was in the habit of employing many men at that season of the year; so he stood a fair chance.

Revived a little by this prospect of relief, Israel starts in quest of the gentleman's seat, agreeably to the directions received. But he mistook his way, and proceeding up a gravelled and beautifully decorated walk, was terrified at catching a glimpse of a number of soldiers thronging a garden. He made an instant retreat before being espied in turn. No wild creature of the American wilderness could have been more panic struck by a fire-brand, than at this period hunted Israel was by a red coat. It afterwards appeared that this garden was the Princess Amelia's.

Taking another path, ere long he came to some laborers shovelling gravel. These proved to be men employed by Sir John. By them he was directed towards the house, when the knight was pointed out to him, walking bareheaded in the inclosure with several guests. Having heard the rich man of England charged with all sorts of domineering qualities, Israel felt no little misgiving in approaching to an audience with so imposing a stranger. But screwing up his courage, he advanced; while seeing him coming all rags and tatters, the group of gentlemen stood in some wonder awaiting what so singular a phantom might want.

"Mr. Millet," said Israel, bowing towards the bareheaded gentleman.

"Ha,—who are you, pray?"

"A poor fellow, sir, in want of work."

"A wardrobe too, I should say," smiled one of the guests, of a very youthful, prosperous, and dandified air.

"Where's your hoe?" said Sir John.

"I have none, sir."

"Any money to buy one?"

"Only four English pennies, sir."

"*English* pennies. What other sort would you have?"

"Why China pennies to be sure," laughed the youthful gentleman. "See his long, yellow hair behind; he looks like a Chinaman. Some broken-down Mandarin. Pity he's no crown to his old hat; if he had, he might pass it round, and make eight pennies of his four."

"Will you hire me, Mr. Millet?" said Israel.

"Ha! that's queer again," cried the knight.

"Hark ye fellow," said a brisk servant, approaching from the porch, "this is Sir John Millet."

Seeming to take pity on his seeming ignorance, as well as on his undisputable poverty, the good knight now told Israel that if he would come the next morning, he would see him supplied with a hoe, and moreover would hire him.

It would be hard to express the satisfaction of the wanderer, at receiving this encouraging reply. Emboldened by it, he now returns towards a baker's he had spied, and bravely marching in, flings down all four pennies, and demands bread. Thinking he would not have any more food till next morning, Israel resolved to eat only one of the pair of two-penny loaves. But having demolished one, it so sharpened his longing, that yielding to the irresistible temptation, he bolted down the second loaf to keep the other company.

After resting under a hedge, he saw the sun far descended, and so prepared himself for another hard night. Waiting till dark, he crawled into an old carriage-house, finding nothing there but a dismantled old phaeton. Into this he climbed, and curling himself up like a carriage-dog, endeavored to sleep. But unable to endure the constraint of such a bed, got out, and stretched himself on the bare boards of the floor.

No sooner was light in the east, than he hastened to await the commands of one, who, his instinct told him, was destined to prove his benefactor. On his father's farm accustomed to rise with the lark, Israel was surprised to discover as he approached the house, that no soul was astir. It was four o'clock. For a considerable time he walked back and forth before the portal, ere any one appeared. The first riser was a man-servant of the household, who informed Israel that seven o'clock was the hour the people went to their work. Soon after, he met an hostler of the place, who gave him permission to lie on some straw in an outhouse. There he enjoyed a sweet sleep till awakened at seven o'clock, by the sounds of activity around him.

Supplied by the overseer of the men with a large iron fork and a hoe, he followed the hands into the field. He was so weak, he could hardly support his tools. Unwilling to expose his debility, he yet could not succeed in concealing it. At last to avoid worse imputations, he confessed the cause. His companions regarded him with compassion, and exempted him from the severer toil.

About noon, the knight visited his workmen. Noticing that Israel made little progress, he said to him, that though he had long arms and broad shoulders, yet he was feigning himself to be a very weak man, or otherwise must in reality be so.

Hereupon one of the laborers standing by, informed the gentleman how it was with Israel; when immediately the knight put a shilling into his hands, and bade him go to a little road-side inn, which was nearer than the house, and buy him bread and a pot of beer. Thus refreshed he returned to the band, and toiled with them till four o'clock, when the day's work was over.

Arrived at the house, he there again saw his employer, who after attentively eyeing him without speaking, bade a meal be prepared for him; when the maid presenting a smaller supply than her kind master deemed necessary, she was ordered to return and bring out the entire dish. But aware of the danger of sudden repletion of heavy food to one in his condition, Israel, previously recruited by the frugal meal at the inn, partook but sparingly. The repast was spread on the grass, and being over, the good knight again looking inquisitively at Israel, ordered a comfortable bed to be laid in the barn; and here Israel spent a capital night.

After breakfast, next morning, he was proceeding to go with the laborers to their work, when his employer approaching him with a benevolent air, bade him return to his couch, and there remain till he had slept his fill, and was in a better state to resume his labors.

Upon coming forth again a little after noon, he found Sir John walking alone in the grounds. Upon discovering him, Israel would have retreated, fearing that he might intrude; but beckoning him to advance, the knight, as Israel drew nigh, fixed on him such a penetrating glance, that our poor hero quaked to the core. Neither was his dread of detection relieved by the knight's now calling in a loud voice for one from the house. Israel was just on the point of fleeing, when overhearing the words of the master to the servant who now appeared, all dread departed:

"Bring hither some wine!"

It presently came; by order of the knight the salver was set down on a green bank near by, and the servant retired.

"My poor fellow," said Sir John, now pouring out a glass of wine, and handing it to Israel, "I perceive that you are an American; and, if I am not mistaken, you are an escaped prisoner of war. But no fear—drink the wine."

"Mr. Millet," exclaimed Israel aghast, the untasted wine trembling in his hand, "Mr. Millet, I——"

"*Mr.* Millet—there it is again. Why don't you say *Sir John* like the rest?"

"Why, sir—pardon me—but somehow, I can't. I've tried; but I can't. You won't betray me for that?"

"Betray—poor fellow! Hark ye, your history is doubtless a secret which you would not wish to divulge to a stranger; but whatever happens to you, I pledge you my honor I will never betray you."

"God bless you for that, Mr. Millet."

"Come, come; call me by my right name. I am not Mr. Millet. *You* have said *Sir* to me; and no doubt you have a thousand times said *John* to other people. Now can't you couple the two? Try once. Come. Only *Sir* and then *John*—*Sir John*—that's all."

"John—I can't—Sir, sir!—your pardon. I didn't mean that."

"My good fellow," said the knight looking sharply upon Israel, "tell me, are all your countrymen like you? If so, it's no use fighting them. To that effect, I must write to his Majesty myself. Well, I excuse you from Sir Johnning me. But tell me the truth, are you not a sea-faring man, and lately a prisoner of war?"

Israel frankly confessed it, and told his whole story. The knight listened with much interest; and at its conclusion, warned Israel to beware of the soldiers; for owing to the seats of some of the royal family being in the neighborhood, the red-coats abounded hereabouts.

"I do not wish unnecessarily to speak against my own countrymen," he added, "I but plainly speak for your good. The soldiers you meet prowling on the roads, are not fair specimens of the army. They are a set of mean, dastardly banditti; who, to obtain their fee, would betray their best friends. Once more, I warn you against them. But enough; follow me now to the house, and as you tell me you have exchanged clothes before now, you can do it again. What say you? I will give you coat and breeches for your rags."

Thus generously supplied with clothes, and other comforts by the good knight, and implicitly relying upon the honor of so kind-hearted a man, Israel cheered up, and in the course of two or three weeks had so fattened his flanks, that he was able completely to fill Sir John's old buckskin breeches, which at first had hung but loosely about him.

He was assigned to an occupation which removed him from the other workmen. The strawberry bed was put under his sole charge. And often, of mild, sunny afternoons, the knight, genial and gentle with dinner, would stroll bareheaded to the pleasant strawberry bed, and have nice little confidential chats with Israel; while Israel, charmed by the patriarchal demeanor of this true Abrahamic gentleman, with a smile on his lip, and tears of gratitude in his eyes, offered him, from time to time, the plumpest berries of the bed.

When the strawberry season was over, other parts of the grounds were assigned him. And so six months elapsed, when, at the recommendation of Sir John, Israel procured a good berth in the garden of the Princess Amelia.

So completely now had recent events metamorphosed him in all outward things, that few suspected him of being any other than an Englishman. Not even the knight's domestics. But in the princess's garden, being obliged to work in company with many other laborers, the war was often a topic of discussion among them. And "the d—d Yankee rebels" were not seldom the object of scurrilous remark. Ill could the exile brook in silence such insults upon the country for which he had bled, and for whose honored sake he was that very instant a sufferer. More than once, his indignation came very nigh getting the better of his prudence. He longed for the war to end, that he might but speak a little bit of his mind.

Now the superintendent of the garden was a harsh, overbearing man. The workmen with tame servility endured his worst affronts. But Israel, bred among mountains, found it impossible to restrain himself when made the undeserved object of pitiless epithets. Ere two months went by, he quitted the service of the princess, and engaged himself to a farmer in a small village not far from Brentford. But hardly had he been here three weeks, when a rumor again got afloat, that he was a Yankee prisoner of war.

Whence this report arose he could never discover. No sooner did it reach the ears of the soldiers, than they were on the alert. Luckily Israel was apprised of their intentions in time. But he was hard pushed. He was hunted after with a perseverance worthy a less ignoble cause. He had many hairbreadth escapes. Most assuredly he would have been captured, had it not been for the secret good offices of a few individuals, who, perhaps, were not unfriendly to the American side of the question, though they durst not avow it.

Tracked one night by the soldiers to the house of one of these friends, in whose garret he was concealed: he was obliged to force the skuttle, and running along the roof, passed to those of adjoining houses to the number of ten or twelve, finally succeeding in making his escape.

Chapter 5

Israel in the Lion's Den

HARASSED DAY AND NIGHT, hunted from food and sleep, driven from hole to hole like a fox in the woods; with no chance to earn an hour's wages; he was at last advised by one whose sincerity he could not doubt, to apply, on the good word of Sir John Millet, for a berth as laborer in the King's Gardens at Kew. There, it was said, he would be entirely safe, as no soldier durst approach those premises to molest any soul therein employed. It struck the poor exile as curious, that the very den of the British lion, the private grounds of the British King, should be commended to a refugee as his securest asylum.

His nativity carefully concealed, and being personally introduced to the chief gardener by one who well knew him; armed too with a line from Sir John, and recommended by his introducer as uncommonly expert at horticulture; Israel was soon installed as keeper of certain less private plants and walks of the park.

It was here, to one of his near country retreats, that, coming from perplexities of state—leaving far behind him the dingy old bricks of St. James—George the Third was wont to walk up and down beneath the long arbors formed by the interlockings of lofty trees.

More than once, raking the gravel, Israel through intervening foliage would catch peeps in some private but parallel walk, of that lonely figure, not more shadowy with overhanging leaves than with the shade of royal meditations.

Unauthorized and abhorrent thoughts will sometimes invade the best human heart. Seeing the monarch unguarded before him; remembering that the war was imputed more to the self-will of the King than to the willingness of parliament or the nation; and calling to mind all his own sufferings growing out of that war, with all the calamities of his country; dim impulses, such as those to which the regicide Ravaillac yielded, would shoot balefully across the soul of the exile. But thrusting Satan behind him, Israel vanquished all such temptations. Nor did these ever more disturb him, after his one chance conversation with the monarch.

As he was one day gravelling a little bye-walk; wrapped in thought, the King turning a clump of bushes, suddenly brushed Israel's person.

Immediately Israel touched his hat—but did not remove it—bowed, and was retiring; when something in his air arrested the King's attention.

"You aint an Englishman,—no Englishman—no no."

Pale as death, Israel tried to answer something; but knowing not what to say, stood frozen to the ground.

"You are a Yankee—a Yankee," said the King again in his rapid and half-stammering way.

Again Israel assayed to reply, but could not. What could he say? Could he lie to a King?

"Yes, yes,—you are one of that stubborn race,—that very stubborn race. What brought you here?"

"The fate of war, sir."

"May it please your Majesty," said a low cringing voice, approaching, "this man is in the walk against orders. There is some mistake, may it please your majesty. Quit the walk, blockhead," he hissed at Israel.

It was one of the junior gardeners who thus spoke. It seems that Israel had mistaken his directions that morning.

"Slink, you dog," hissed the gardener again to Israel; then aloud to the king, "A mistake of the man, I assure your majesty."

"Go you away—away with ye, and leave him with me," said the king.

Waiting a moment, till the man was out of hearing, the king again turned upon Israel.

"Were you at Bunker Hill?—that bloody Bunker Hill—eh, eh?"

"Yes, sir."

"Fought like a devil—like a very devil, I suppose?"

"Yes, sir."

"Helped flog—helped flog my soldiers?"

"Yes, sir; but very sorry to do it."

"Eh?—eh?—how's that?"

"I took it to be my sad duty, sir."

"Very much mistaken—very much mistaken indeed. Why do ye sir me?—eh? I'm your king—your king."

"Sir," said Israel firmly, but with deep respect, "I have no king."

The king darted his eye incensedly for a moment; but without quailing, Israel, now that all was out, still stood with mute respect before him. The king, turning suddenly, walked rapidly away from Israel a moment, but presently returning with a less hasty pace, said, "You are rumored to be a spy—a spy, or something of that sort—aint you? But I know you are not—no, no. You are a runaway prisoner-of-war, eh? You have sought this place to be safe from pursuit, eh? eh? Is it not so?—eh? eh? eh?"

"Sir, it is."

"Well, ye're an honest rebel—rebel, yes, rebel. Hark ye, hark. Say nothing of this talk to any one. And hark again. So long as ye remain here at Kew, I shall see that you are safe—safe."

"God bless your majesty!"

"Eh?"

"God bless your noble majesty!"

"Come—come—come," smiled the king in delight, "I thought I could conquer ye—conquer ye."

"Not the king, but the king's kindness, your majesty."

"Join my army—army."

Sadly looking down, Israel silently shook his head.

"You won't? Well, gravel the walk then—gravel away. Very stubborn race—very stubborn race indeed—very—very—very."

And still growling, the magnanimous lion departed.

How the monarch came by his knowledge of so humble an exile, whether through that swift insight into individual character said to form one of the miraculous qualities transmitted with a crown, or whether some of the rumors prevailing outside of the garden had come to his ear, Israel could never determine. Very probably, though, the latter was the case, inasmuch as some vague shadowy report of Israel not being an Englishman, had a little previous to his interview with the king, been communicated to several of the inferior gardeners. Without any impeachment of Israel's fealty to his country, it must still be narrated, that from this his familiar audience with George the Third, he went away with very favorable views of that monarch. Israel now thought that it could not be the warm heart of the king, but the cold heads of his lords in council, that persuaded him so tyrannically to persecute America. Yet hitherto the precise contrary of this had been Israel's opinion, agreeably to the popular prejudice throughout New England.

Thus we see what strange and powerful magic resides in a crown, and how subtly that cheap and easy magnanimity, which in private belongs to most kings, may operate on good-natured and unfortunate souls. Indeed, had it not been for the peculiar disinterested fidelity of our adventurer's patriotism, he would have soon sported the red coat; and perhaps under the immediate patronage of his royal friend, been advanced in time to no mean rank in the army of Britain. Nor in that case would we have had to follow him, as at last we shall, through long, long years of obscure and penurious wandering.

Continuing in the service of the king's gardener at Kew, until a season came when the work of the garden required a less number of laborers; Israel, with several others, was discharged; and the day after, engaged himself for a few months to a farmer in the neighborhood where he had been last employed. But hardly a week had gone by, when the old story of his being a rebel, or a runaway prisoner, or a Yankee! or a spy, began to be revived with added malignity. Like bloodhounds, the soldiers were once more on the track. The houses where he harbored were many times searched; but thanks to the fidelity of a few earnest well-wishers, and to his own unsleeping vigilance and activity, the hunted fox still continued to elude apprehension. To such extremities of harassment, however, did this incessant pursuit subject him, that in a fit of despair he was about to surrender himself, and submit to his fate, when Providence seasonably interposed in his favor.

Chapter 6

Israel Makes the Acquaintance of Certain Secret Friends of America, One of Them Being the Famous Author of the "Diversions of Purley." These Despatch Him on a Sly Errand across the Channel

AT THIS PERIOD, though made the victims indeed of British oppression, yet the colonies were not totally without friends in Britain. It was but natural that when Parliament itself held patriotic and gifted men, who not only recommended conciliatory measures, but likewise denounced the war as monstrous; it was but natural that throughout the nation at large there should be many private individuals cherishing similar sentiments; and some who made no scruple clandestinely to act upon them.

Late one night while hiding in a farmer's granary, Israel saw a man with a lantern approaching. He was about to flee, when the man hailed him in a well-known voice, bidding him have no fear. It was the farmer himself. He carried a message to Israel from a gentleman of Brentford, to the effect, that the refugee was earnestly requested to repair on the following evening to that gentleman's mansion.

At first Israel was disposed to surmise that either the farmer was playing him false, or else his honest credulity had been imposed upon by evil-minded persons. At any rate, he regarded the message as a decoy, and for half an hour refused to credit its sincerity. But at length he was induced to think a little better of it. The gentleman giving the invitation was one Squire Woodcock, of Brentford, whose loyalty to the king, had been under suspicion; so at least the farmer averred. This latter information was not without its effect.

At nightfall on the following day, being disguised in strange clothes by the farmer, Israel stole from his retreat, and after a few hours' walk, arrived before the ancient brick house of the Squire; who opening the door in person, and learning who it was that stood there, at once assured Israel in the most solemn manner, that no foul play was intended. So the wanderer suffered himself to enter, and be conducted to a private chamber in the rear of the mansion, where were seated two other gentlemen, attired, in the manner of that age, in long laced coats, with smallclothes, and shoes with silver buckles.

"I am John Woodcock," said the host, "and these gentlemen are Horne Tooke and James Bridges. All three of us are friends to America. We have heard of you for some weeks past, and inferring from your conduct, that you must be a Yankee of the true blue stamp, we have resolved to employ you in a way which you cannot but gladly approve; for surely, though an exile, you are still willing to serve your country; if not as a sailor or soldier, yet as a traveller?"

"Tell me how I may do it?" demanded Israel, not completely at ease.

"At that in good time," smiled the Squire. "The point is now—do you repose confidence in my statements?"

Israel glanced inquiringly upon the Squire; then upon his companions; and meeting the expressive, enthusiastic, candid countenance of Horne Tooke—then in the first honest ardor of his political career—turned to the Squire, and said, "Sir, I believe what you have said. Tell me now what I am to do?"

"Oh, there is just nothing to be done to-night," said the Squire; "nor for some days to come perhaps, but we wanted to have you prepared."

And hereupon he hinted to his guest rather vaguely of his general intention; and that over, begged him to entertain them with some account of his adventures since he first took up arms for his country. To this Israel had no objections in the world, since all men love to tell the tale of hardships endured in a righteous cause. But ere beginning his story, the Squire refreshed him with some cold beef, laid in a snowy napkin, and a glass of Perry, and thrice during the narration of the adventures, pressed him with additional draughts.

But after his second glass, Israel declined to drink more, mild as the beverage was. For he noticed, that not only did the three gentlemen listen with the utmost interest to his story, but likewise interrupted him with questions and cross-questions in the most pertinacious manner. So this led him to be on his guard, not being absolutely certain yet, as to who they might really be, or what was their real design. But as it turned out, Squire Woodcock and his friends only sought to satisfy themselves thoroughly, before making their final disclosures, that the exile was one in whom implicit confidence might be placed.

And to this desirable conclusion they eventually came; for upon the ending of Israel's story, after expressing their sympathies for his hardships, and applauding his generous patriotism in so patiently enduring adversity, as well as singing the praises of his gallant fellow-soldiers of Bunker Hill; they openly revealed their scheme. They wished to know, whether Israel would undertake a trip to Paris, to carry an important message—shortly to be received for transmission through them—to Doctor Franklin, then in that capital.

"All your expenses shall be paid, not to speak of a compensation besides," said the Squire; "will you go?"

"I must think of it," said Israel, not yet wholly confirmed in his mind. But once more he cast his glance on Horne Tooke, and his irresolution was gone.

The Squire now informed Israel that, to avoid suspicions, it would be necessary for him to remove to another place until the hour at which he should start for Paris. They enjoined upon him the profoundest secrecy; gave him a guinea, with a letter for a gentleman in White Waltham, a town some miles from Brentford, which point they begged him to reach as soon as possible, there to tarry for further instructions.

Having informed him of thus much, Squire Woodcock asked him to hold out his right foot.

"What for?" said Israel.

"Why, would you not like to have a pair of new boots against your return?" smiled Horne Tooke.

"Oh yes; no objections at all," said Israel.

"Well then, let the boot-maker measure you," smiled Horne Tooke.

"Do *you* do it, Mr. Tooke," said the Squire, "you measure men's parts better than I."

"Hold out your foot, my good friend," said Horne Tooke—"there—now let's measure your heart."

"For that, measure me round the chest," said Israel.

"Just the man we want," said Mr. Bridges, triumphantly.

"Give him another glass of wine, Squire," said Horne Tooke.

Exchanging the farmer's clothes for still another disguise, Israel now set out immediately, on foot, for his destination, having received minute direc-

tions as to his road; and arriving in White Waltham on the following morning, was very cordially received by the gentleman to whom he carried the
letter. This person, another of the active English friends of America, possessed a particular knowledge of late events in that land. To him Israel was
indebted for much entertaining information. After remaining some ten days
at this place, word came from Squire Woodcock, requiring Israel's immediate return, stating the hour at which he must arrive at the house,
namely, two o'clock on the following morning. So, after another night's
solitary trudge across the country, the wanderer was welcomed by the same
three gentlemen as before, seated in the same room.

"The time has now come," said Squire Woodcock. "You must start this
morning for Paris. Take off your shoes."

"Am I to steal from here to Paris on my stocking-feet?" said Israel,
whose late easy good living at White Waltham had not failed to bring out
the good-natured and mirthful part of him, even as his prior experiences had
produced, for the most part, something like a contrary result.

"Oh no," smiled Horne Tooke, who always lived well; "we have
seven-league-boots for you. Don't you remember my measuring you?"

Hereupon going to the closet, the Squire brought out a pair of new
boots. They were fitted with false heels. Unscrewing these, the Squire
showed Israel the papers concealed beneath. They were of a fine tissuey
fibre, and contained much writing in a very small compass. The boots—it
need hardly be said—had been particularly made for the occasion.

"Walk across the room with them," said the Squire, when Israel had
pulled them on.

"He'll surely be discovered," smiled Horne Tooke. "Hark, how he
creaks."

"Come, come, it's too serious a matter for joking," said the Squire.
"Now my fine fellow, be cautious, be sober, be vigilant, and above all
things be speedy."

Being furnished now with all requisite directions, and a supply of
money, Israel taking leave of Mr. Tooke and Mr. Bridges, was secretly
conducted down stairs by the Squire, and in five minutes' time was on his
way to Charing Cross in London; where taking the post-coach for Dover,
he thence went in a packet to Calais, and in fifteen minutes after landing,
was being wheeled over French soil towards Paris. He arrived there in
safety, and freely declaring himself an American, the peculiarly friendly
relations of the two nations at that period, procured him kindly attentions
even from strangers.

Chapter 7

*After a Curious Adventure upon the Pont Neuf, Israel Enters
the Presence of the Renowned Sage, Dr. Franklin, Whom He
Finds Right Learnedly and Multifariously Employed*

FOLLOWING THE DIRECTIONS given him at the place where the
diligence stopped, Israel was crossing the Pont Neuf, to find Doctor
Franklin, when he was suddenly called to by a man standing on one
side of the bridge, just under the equestrian statue of Henry IV.

The man had a small, shabby-looking box before him on the ground,
with a box of blacking on one side of it, and several shoe-brushes upon the
other. Holding another brush in his hand, he politely seconded his verbal
invitation by gracefully flourishing the brush in the air.

"What do you want of me, neighbor?" said Israel, pausing in somewhat
uneasy astonishment.

"Ah Monsieur," exclaimed the man, and with voluble politeness he ran
on with a long string of French, which of course was all Greek to poor
Israel. But what his language failed to convey, his gestures now made very
plain. Pointing to the wet muddy state of the bridge, splashed by a recent
rain, and then to the feet of the wayfarer, and lastly to the brush in his hand,
he appeared to be deeply regretting that a gentleman of Israel's otherwise
imposing appearance, should be seen abroad with unpolished boots, offering at the same time to remove their blemishes.

"Ah Monsieur, Monsieur," cried the man, at last running up to Israel.
And with tender violence he forced him towards the box, and lifting this

unwilling customer's right foot thereon, was proceeding vigorously to work, when suddenly illuminated by a dreadful suspicion, Israel, fetching the box a terrible kick, took to his false heels and ran like mad over the bridge.

Incensed that his politeness should receive such an ungracious return, the man pursued; which but confirming Israel in his suspicions, he ran all the faster, and thanks to his fleetness, soon succeeded in escaping his pursuer.

Arrived at last at the street and the house, to which he had been directed; in reply to his summons, the gate, very strangely of itself, swung open; and much astonished at this unlooked-for sort of enchantment, Israel entered a wide vaulted passage leading to an open court within. While he was wondering that no soul appeared, suddenly he was hailed from a dark little window, where sat an old man cobbling shoes, while an old woman standing by his side, was thrusting her head into the passage, intently eyeing the stranger. They proved to be the porter and portress; the latter of whom, upon hearing his summons, had invisibly thrust open the gate to Israel, by means of a spring communicating with the little apartment.

Upon hearing the name of Doctor Franklin mentioned, the old woman, all alacrity, hurried out of her den, and with much courtesy showed Israel across the court, up three flights of stairs, to a door in the rear of the spacious building. There she left him while Israel knocked.

"Come in," said a voice.

And immediately Israel stood in the presence of the venerable Doctor Franklin.

Wrapped in a rich dressing-gown—a fanciful present from an admiring Marchesa—curiously embroidered with algebraic figures like a conjuror's robe, and with a skull-cap of black satin on his hive of a head, the man of gravity was seated at a huge claw-footed old table, round as the zodiac. It was covered with printed papers; files of documents; rolls of MSS.; stray bits of strange models in wood and metal; odd-looking pamphlets in various languages; and all sorts of books; including many presentation-copies; embracing history, mechanics, diplomacy, agriculture, political economy, metaphysics, meteorology, and geometry. The walls had a necromantic look; hung round with barometers of different kinds; drawings of surprising inventions; wide maps of far countries in the New World, containing vast empty spaces in the middle, with the word D E S E R T diffusely printed there, so as to span five-and-twenty degrees of longitude with only two syllables,—which printed word however bore a vigorous pen-mark, in the Doctor's hand, drawn straight through it, as if in summary repeal of it; crowded topographical and trigonometrical charts of various parts of

Europe; with geometrical diagrams, and endless other surprising hangings and upholstery of science.

The chamber itself bore evident marks of antiquity. One part of the rough-finished wall was sadly cracked; and covered with dust, looked dim and dark. But the aged inmate, though wrinkled as well, looked neat and hale. Both wall and sage were compounded of like materials,—lime and dust; both, too, were old; but while the rude earth of the wall had no painted lustre to shed off all fadings and tarnish, and still keep fresh without, though with long eld its core decayed: the living lime and dust of the sage was frescoed with defensive bloom of his soul.

The weather was warm; like some old West India hogshead on the wharf, the whole chamber buzzed with flies. But the sapient inmate sat still and cool in the midst. Absorbed in some other world of his occupations and thoughts, these insects, like daily cark and care, did not seem one whit to annoy him. It was a goodly sight to see this serene, cool and ripe old philosopher, who by sharp inquisition of man in the street, and then long meditating upon him, surrounded by all these queer old implements, charts and books, had grown at last so wondrous wise. There he sat, quite motion-less among those restless flies; and, with a sound like the low noon murmur of foliage in the woods, turning over the leaves of some ancient and tattered folio, with a binding dark and shaggy as the bark of any old oak. It seemed as if supernatural lore must needs pertain to this gravely ruddy personage; at least far foresight, pleasant wit, and working wisdom. Old age seemed in no-wise to have dulled him, but to have sharpened; just as old dinner-knives—so they be of good steel—wax keen, spear-pointed, and elastic as whale-bone with long usage. Yet though he was thus lively and vigorous to behold, spite of his seventy-two years (his exact date at the time) somehow, the incredible seniority of an antediluvian seemed his. Not the years of the calendar wholly, but also the years of sapience. His white hairs and mild brow, spoke of the future as well as the past. He seemed to be seven score years old; that is, three-score and ten of prescience added to three score and ten of remem-brance, makes just seven score years in all.

But when Israel stepped within the chamber, he lost the complete effect of all this; for the sage's back, not his face, was turned to him.

So, intent on his errand, hurried and heated with his recent run, our courier entered the room, inadequately impressed, for the time, by either it or its occupant.

"Bon jour, bon jour, monsieur," said the man of wisdom, in a cheerful voice, but too busy to turn round just then.

"How do you do, Doctor Franklin," said Israel.

"Ah! I smell Indian corn," said the Doctor, turning round quickly on his chair. "A countryman; sit down, my good sir. Well, what news? Special?"

"Wait a minute, sir," said Israel, stepping across the room towards a chair.

Now there was no carpet on the floor, which was of dark-colored wood, set in lozenges, and slippery with wax, after the usual French style. As Israel walked this slippery floor, his unaccustomed feet slid about very strangely, as if walking on ice, so that he came very near falling.

"'Pears to me you have rather high heels to your boots," said the grave man of utility, looking sharply down through his spectacles; "Don't you know that it's both wasting leather and endangering your limbs, to wear such high heels? I have thought at my first leisure, to write a little pamphlet against that very abuse. But pray, what are you doing now? Do your boots pinch you, my friend, that you lift one foot from the floor that way?"

At this moment, Israel having seated himself, was just putting his right foot across his left knee.

"How foolish," continued the wise man, "for a rational creature to wear tight boots. Had nature intended rational creatures should so do, she would have made the foot of solid bone, or perhaps of solid iron, instead of bone, muscle, and flesh.—But,—I see. Hold!"

And springing to his own slippered feet, the venerable sage hurried to the door and shot-to the bolt. Then drawing the curtain carefully across the window looking out across the court to various windows on the opposite side, bade Israel proceed with his operations.

"I was mistaken this time," added the Doctor, smiling, as Israel produced his documents from their curious recesses—"your high heels, instead of being idle vanities, seem to be full of meaning."

"Pretty full, Doctor," said Israel, now handing over the papers. "I had a narrow escape with them just now."

"How? How's that?" said the sage, fumbling the papers eagerly.

"Why, crossing the stone bridge there over the *Seen*"—

"*Seine*"—interrupted the Doctor, giving the French pronunciation—"Always get a new word right in the first place, my friend, and you will never get it wrong afterwards."

"Well, I was crossing the bridge there, and who should hail me, but a suspicious looking man, who, under pretence of seeking to polish my boots, wanted slyly to unscrew their heels, and so steal all these precious papers I've brought you."

"My good friend," said the man of gravity, glancing scrutinizingly upon his guest, "have you not in your time, undergone what they call hard times? Been set upon, and persecuted, and very ill entreated by some of your fellow-creatures?"

"That I have, Doctor; yes indeed."

"I thought so. Sad usage has made you sadly suspicious, my honest friend. An indiscriminate distrust of human nature is the worst consequence of a miserable condition, whether brought about by innocence or guilt. And though want of suspicion more than want of sense, sometimes leads a man into harm: yet too much suspicion is as bad as too little sense. The man you met, my friend, most probably, had no artful intention; he knew just nothing about you or your heels; he simply wanted to earn two sous by brushing your boots. Those blacking-men regularly station themselves on the bridge."

"How sorry I am then that I knocked over his box, and then ran away. But he didn't catch me."

"How? surely, my honest friend, you,—appointed to the conveyance of important secret despatches—did not act so imprudently as to kick over an innocent man's box in the public streets of the capital, to which you had been especially sent?"

"Yes, I did, Doctor."

"Never act so unwisely again. If the police had got hold of you, think of what might have ensued."

"Well, it was not very wise of me, that's a fact, Doctor. But, you see, I thought he meant mischief."

"And because you only thought he *meant* mischief, *you* must straightway proceed to *do* mischief. That's poor logic. But think over what I have told you now, while I look over these papers."

In half an hour's time, the Doctor, laying down the documents, again turned towards Israel, and removing his spectacles very placidly, proceeded in the kindest and most familiar manner to read him a paternal detailed lesson upon the ill-advised act he had been guilty of, upon the Pont Neuf; concluding by taking out his purse, and putting three small silver coins into Israel's hands, charging him to seek out the man that very day, and make both apology and restitution for his unlucky mistake.

"All of us, my honest friend," continued the Doctor, "are subject to making mistakes; so that the chief art of life, is to learn how best to remedy mistakes. Now one remedy for mistakes is honesty. So pay the man for the damage done to his box. And now, who are you, my friend? My correspondents here mention your name—Israel Potter—and say you are an

American, an escaped prisoner of war, but nothing further. I want to hear your story from your own lips."

Israel immediately began, and related to the Doctor all his adventures up to the present time.

"I suppose," said the Doctor, upon Israel's concluding, "that you desire to return to your friends across the sea?"

"That I do, Doctor," said Israel.

"Well, I think, I shall be able to procure you a passage."

Israel's eyes sparkled with delight. The mild sage noticed it, and added: "But events in these times are uncertain. At the prospect of pleasure never be elated; but, without depression, respect the omens of ill. So much my life has taught me, my honest friend."

Israel felt as though a plum-pudding had been thrust under his nostrils, and then as rapidly withdrawn.

"I think it is probable that in two or three days I shall want you to return with some papers to the persons who sent you to me. In that case you will have to come here once more, and then, my good friend, we will see what can be done towards getting you safely home again."

Israel was pouring out torrents of thanks when the Doctor interrupted him.

"Gratitude, my friend, cannot be too much towards God, but towards man, it should be limited. No man can possibly so serve his fellow, as to merit unbounded gratitude. Over gratitude in the helped person, is apt to breed vanity or arrogance in the helping one. Now in assisting you to get home—if indeed I shall prove able to do so—I shall be simply doing part of my official duty as agent of our common country. So you owe me just nothing at all, but the sum of these coins I put in your hand just now. But that, instead of repaying to me hereafter, you can, when you get home, give to the first soldier's widow you meet. Don't forget it, for it is a debt, a pecuniary liability, owing to me. It will be about a quarter of a dollar, in the Yankee currency. A quarter of a dollar, mind. My honest friend, in pecuniary matters always be exact as a second-hand; never mind with whom it is, father or stranger, peasant or king, be exact to a tick of your honor."

"Well, Doctor," said Israel, "since exactness in these matters is so necessary, let me pay back my debt in the very coins in which it was loaned. There will be no chance of mistake then. Thanks to my Brentford friends, I have enough to spare of my own, to settle damages with the boot-black of the bridge. I only took the money from you, because I thought it would not look well to push it back after being so kindly offered."

"My honest friend" said the Doctor, "I like your straightforward dealing. I will receive back the money."

"No interest, Doctor, I hope," said Israel.

The sage looked mildly over his spectacles upon Israel, and replied, "My good friend, never permit yourself to be jocose upon pecuniary matters. Never joke at funerals, or during business transactions. The affair between us two, you perhaps deem very trivial, but trifles may involve momentous principles. But no more at present. You had better go immediately and find the boot-black. Having settled with him, return hither, and you will find a room ready for you near this, where you will stay during your sojourn in Paris."

"But I thought I would like to have a little look round the town, before I go back to England," said Israel.

"Business before pleasure, my friend. You must absolutely remain in your room, just as if you were my prisoner, until you quit Paris for Calais. Not knowing now at what instant I shall want you to start, your keeping to your room is indispensable. But when you come back from Brentford again, then, if nothing happens, you will have a chance to survey this celebrated capital ere taking ship for America. Now go directly, and pay the boot-black. Stop, have you the exact change ready? Don't be taking out all your money in the open street."

"Doctor," said Israel, "I am not so simple."

"But you knocked over the box."

"That, Doctor, was bravery."

"Bravery in a poor cause, is the height of simplicity, my friend.—Count out your change. It must be French coin, not English, that you are to pay the man with.—Ah, that will do—those three coins will be enough. Put them in a pocket separate from your other cash. Now go, and hasten to the bridge."

"Shall I stop to take a meal any where, Doctor, as I return? I saw several cook-shops as I came hither."

"Cafés and restaurants, they are called here, my honest friend. Tell me, are you the possessor of a liberal fortune?"

"Not very liberal," said Israel.

"I thought as much. Where little wine is drunk, it is good to dine out occasionally at a friend's; but where a poor man dines out at his own charge, it is bad policy. Never dine out that way, when you can dine in. Do not stop on the way at all, my honest friend, but come directly back hither, and you shall dine at home, free of cost, with me."

"Thank you very kindly, Doctor."

And Israel departed for the Pont Neuf. Succeeding in his errand thither, he returned to Doctor Franklin, and found that worthy envoy waiting his attendance at a meal, which according to the Doctor's custom, had been sent from a neighboring restaurant. There were two covers; and without attendance the host and guest sat down. There was only one principal dish, lamb boiled with green peas. Bread and potatoes made up the rest. A decanter-like bottle of uncolored glass, filled with some uncolored beverage, stood at the venerable envoy's elbow.

"Let me fill your glass," said the sage.

"It's white wine, aint it?" said Israel.

"White wine of the very oldest brand; I drink your health in it, my honest friend."

"Why, it's plain water," said Israel, now tasting it.

"Plain water is a very good drink for plain men," replied the wise man.

"Yes," said Israel, "but Squire Woodcock gave me perry, and the other gentleman at White Waltham gave me port, and some other friends have given me brandy."

"Very good, my honest friend; if you like perry and port and brandy, wait till you get back to Squire Woodcock, and the gentleman at White Waltham, and the other friends, and you shall drink perry and port and brandy. But while you are with me, you will drink plain water."

"So it seems, Doctor."

"What do you suppose a glass of port costs?"

"About three pence English, Doctor."

"That must be poor port. But how much good bread will three pence English purchase?"

"Three penny rolls, Doctor."

"How many glasses of port do you suppose a man may drink at a meal?"

"The gentleman at White Waltham drank a bottle at a dinner."

"A bottle contains just thirteen glasses—that's thirty-nine pence, supposing it poor wine. If something of the best, which is the only sort any sane man should drink, as being the least poisonous, it would be quadruple that sum, which is one hundred and fifty-six pence, which is seventy-eight two-penny loaves. Now, do you not think that for one man to swallow down seventy-eight two-penny rolls at one meal is rather extravagant business?"

"But he drank a bottle of wine; he did not eat seventy-eight two-penny rolls, Doctor."

"He drank the money worth of seventy-eight loaves, which is drinking the loaves themselves; for money is bread."

"But he has plenty of money to spare, Doctor."

"To have to spare, is to have to give away. Does the gentleman give much away?"

"Not that I know of, Doctor."

"Then he thinks he has nothing to spare; and thinking he has nothing to spare, and yet prodigally drinking down his money as he does every day, it seems to me that that gentleman stands self-contradicted, and therefore is no good example for plain sensible folks like you and me to follow. My honest friend, if you are poor, avoid wine as a costly luxury; if you are rich, shun it as a fatal indulgence. Stick to plain water. And now, my good friend, if you are through with your meal, we will rise. There is no pastry coming. Pastry is poisoned bread. Never eat pastry. Be a plain man, and stick to plain things. Now, my friend, I shall have to be private until nine o'clock in the evening, when I shall be again at your service. Meantime you may go to your room. I have ordered the one next to this to be prepared for you. But you must not be idle. Here is Poor Richard's Almanac, which in view of our late conversation, I commend to your earnest perusal. And here, too, is a Guide to Paris, an English one, which you can read. Study it well, so that when you come back from England if you should then have an opportunity to travel about Paris, to see its wonders, you will have all the chief places made historically familiar to you. In this world, men must provide knowledge before it is wanted, just as our countrymen in New England get in their winter's fuel one season, to serve them the next."

So saying, this homely sage, and household Plato, showed his humble guest to the door, and standing in the hall, pointed out to him the one which opened into his allotted apartment.

Chapter 8

Which Has Something to Say about Dr. Franklin and the Latin Quarter

THE FIRST, both in point of time and merit, of American envoys was famous not less for the pastoral simplicity of his manners than for the politic grace of his mind. Viewed from a certain point, there was a touch of primeval orientalness in Benjamin Franklin. Neither is there wanting something like his scriptural parallel. The history of the patriarch Jacob is interesting not less from the unselfish devotion which we are bound to ascribe to him, than from the deep worldly wisdom and polished Italian tact, gleaming under an air of Arcadian unaffectedness. The diplomatist and the shepherd are blended; a union not without warrant; the apostolic serpent and dove. A tanned Machiavelli in tents.

Doubtless, too, notwithstanding his eminence as lord of the moving manor, Jacob's raiment was of homespun; the economic envoy's plain coat and hose, who has not heard of?

Franklin all over is of a piece. He dressed his person as his periods; neat, trim, nothing superfluous, nothing deficient. In some of his works his style is only surpassed by the unimprovable sentences of Hobbes of Malmsbury, the paragon of perspicuity. The mental habits of Hobbes and Franklin in several points, especially in one of some moment, assimilated. Indeed, making due allowance for soil and era, history presents few trios more akin, upon the whole, than Jacob, Hobbes, and Franklin; three labyrinth-minded, but plain-spoken Broadbrims, at once politicians and philosophers; keen observers of the main chance; prudent courtiers; practical magians in linsey woolsey.

In keeping with his general habitudes, Doctor Franklin while at the French Court did not reside in the aristocratical faubourgs. He deemed his worsted hose and scientific tastes more adapted in a domestic way to the other side of the Seine, where the Latin Quarter, at once the haunt of erudition and economy, seemed peculiarly to invite the philosophical Poor Richard to its venerable retreats. Here, of grey, chilly, drizzly November mornings, in the dark-stoned quadrangle of the time-honored Sorbonne, walked the lean and slippered metaphysician,—oblivious for the moment that his sublime thoughts and tattered wardrobe were famous throughout Europe,—meditating on the theme of his next lecture; at the same time, in the well-worn chambers overhead, some clayey-visaged chemist in ragged robe-de-chambre, and with a soiled green flap over his left eye, was hard at work stooping over retorts and crucibles, discovering new antipathies in acids, again risking strange explosions similar to that whereby he had already lost the use of one optic; while in the lofty lodging-houses of the neighboring streets, indigent young students from all parts of France, were ironing their shabby cocked hats, or inking the whity seams of their small-clothes, prior to a promenade with their pink-ribboned little grizzets in the Garden of the Luxembourg.

Long ago the haunt of rank, the Latin Quarter still retains many old buildings whose imposing architecture singularly contrasts with the unassuming habits of their present occupants. In some parts its general air is dreary and dim; monastic and theurgic. In those lonely narrow ways—long-drawn prospectives of desertion—lined with huge piles of silent, vaulted, old iron-grated buildings of dark grey stone, one almost expects to encounter Paracelsus or Friar Bacon turning the next corner, with some awful vial of Black-Art elixir in his hand.

But all the lodging-houses are not so grim. Not to speak of many of comparatively modern erection, the others of the better class, however stern in exterior, evince a feminine gayety of taste, more or less, in their furnishings within. The embellishing, or softening, or screening hand of woman is to be seen all over the interiors of this metropolis. Like Augustus Cæsar with respect to Rome, the Frenchwoman leaves her obvious mark on Paris. Like the hand of nature, you know it can be none else but hers. Yet sometimes she overdoes it, as nature in the peony; or underdoes it, as nature in the bramble; or—what is still more frequent—is a little slatternly about it, as nature in the pig-weed.

In this congenial vicinity of the Latin Quarter, and in an ancient building something like those last alluded to, at a point midway between the Palais des Beaux Arts and the College of the Sorbonne, the venerable American Envoy pitched his tent when not passing his time at his country retreat at Passy. The frugality of his manner of life did not lose him the good opinion even of the voluptuaries of the showiest of capitals, whose very iron railings are not free from gilt. Franklin was not less a lady's man, than a man's man, a wise man, and an old man. Not only did he enjoy the homage of the choicest Parisian literati, but at the age of seventy-two he was the caressed favorite of the highest born beauties of the Court; who through blind fashion having been originally attracted to him as a famous *savan*, were permanently retained as his admirers by his Plato-like graciousness of good-humor. Having carefully weighed the world, Franklin could act any part in it. By nature turned to knowledge, his mind was often grave, but never serious. At times he had seriousness—extreme seriousness—for others, but never for himself. Tranquillity was to him instead of it. This philosophical levity of tranquillity, so to speak, is shown in his easy variety of pursuits. Printer, postmaster, almanac maker, essayist, chemist, orator, tinker, statesman, humorist, philosopher, parlor-man, political economist, professor of housewifery, ambassador, projector, maxim-monger, herb-doctor, wit:—Jack of all trades, master of each and mastered by none—the type and genius of his land. Franklin was everything but a poet. But since a soul with many qualities, forming of itself a sort of handy index and pocket congress of all humanity, needs the contact of just as many different men, or subjects, in order to the exhibition of its totality; hence very little indeed of the sage's multifariousness will be portrayed in a simple narrative like the present. This casual private intercourse with Israel, but served to manifest him in his far lesser lights; thrifty, domestic, dietarian, and, it may be, didactically waggish. There was much benevolent irony, innocent mischievousness, in the wise man. Seeking here to depict him in his less exalted habitudes, the narrator feels more as if he were playing with one of the sage's worsted hose, than reverentially handling the honored hat which once oracularly sat upon his brow.

So, then, in the Latin Quarter lived Doctor Franklin. And accordingly in the Latin Quarter tarried Israel for the time. And it was into a room of a house in this same Latin Quarter that Israel had been directed when the sage had requested privacy for a while.

Chapter 9

Israel Is Initiated into the Mysteries of Lodging-houses in the Latin Quarter

CLOSING THE DOOR upon himself, Israel advanced to the middle of the chamber, and looked curiously round him.

A dark tessellated floor, but without a rug; two mahogany chairs, with embroidered seats, rather the worse for wear; one mahogany bed, with a gay but tarnished counterpane; a marble wash-stand, cracked, with a china vessel of water, minus the handle. The apartment was very large; this part of the house, which was a very extensive one, embracing the four sides of a quadrangle, having, in a former age, been the hotel of a nobleman. The magnitude of the chamber made its stinted furniture look meagre enough.

But in Israel's eyes, the marble mantel (a comparatively recent addition) and its appurtenances, not only redeemed the rest, but looked quite magnificent and hospitable in the extreme. Because, in the first place, the mantel was graced with an enormous old-fashioned square mirror, of heavy plate glass, set fast, like a tablet, into the wall. And in this mirror was genially reflected the following delicate articles:—First, two bouquets of flowers inserted in pretty vases of porcelain; second, one cake of white soap; third, one cake of rose-colored soap (both cakes very fragrant); fourth, one wax candle; fifth, one china tinder-box; sixth, one bottle of Eau de Cologne; seventh, one paper of loaf sugar, nicely broken into sugar-bowl size; eighth, one silver teaspoon; ninth, one glass tumbler; tenth, one glass decanter of cool pure water; eleventh, one sealed bottle containing a richly hued liquid, and marked "Otard."

"I wonder now what O-t-a-r-d is?" soliloquised Israel, slowly spelling the word. "I have a good mind to step in and ask Dr. Franklin. He knows everything. Let me smell it. No, it's sealed; smell is locked in. Those are pretty flowers. Let's smell them: no smell again. Ah, I see—sort of flowers in women's bonnets—sort of calico flowers. Beautiful soap. This smells anyhow—regular soap-roses—a white rose and a red one. That long-necked bottle there looks like a crane. I wonder what's in that? Hallo! E-a-u—d-e—C-o-l-o-g-n-e. I wonder if Dr. Franklin understands that? It looks like his white wine. This is nice sugar. Let's taste. Yes, this is very nice sugar, sweet as—yes, it's sweet as sugar; better than maple sugar, such as they make at home. But I'm crunching it too loud, the Doctor will hear me. But here's a teaspoon. What's this for? There's no tea, nor tea-cup; but here's a tumbler, and here's drinking water. Let me see. Seems to me, putting this and that and the other thing together, it's a sort of alphabet that spells something. Spoon, tumbler, water, sugar,——brandy—that's it. O-t-a-r-d is brandy. Who put these things here? What does it all mean? Don't put sugar here for show, don't put a spoon here for ornament, nor a jug of water. There is only one meaning to it, and that is a very polite invitation from some invisible person to help myself, if I like, to a glass of brandy and sugar, and if I don't like, let it alone. That's my reading. I have a good mind to ask Doctor Franklin about it, though, for there's just a chance I may be mistaken, and these things here be some other person's private property, not at all meant for me to help myself from. Co-logne, what's that?—never mind. Soap: soap's to wash with. I want to use soap, anyway. Let me see—no, there's no soap on the wash-stand. I see, soap is not given gratis here in Paris, to boarders. But if you want it, take it from the marble, and it will be charged in the bill. If you don't want it let it alone, and no charge. Well, that's fair, anyway. But then to a man who could not afford to use soap, such beautiful cakes as these lying before his eyes all the time, would be a strong temptation. And now that I think of it, the O-t-a-r-d looks rather tempting too. But if I don't like it now, I can let it alone. I've a good mind to try it. But it's sealed. I wonder now if I am right in my understanding of this alphabet? Who knows? I'll venture one little sip, anyhow. Come cork. Hark!"

There was a rapid knock at the door.

Clapping down the bottle, Israel said, "Come in."

It was the man of wisdom.

"My honest friend," said the Doctor, stepping with venerable briskness into the room, "I was so busy during your visit to the Pont Neuf, that I did not have time to see that your room was all right. I merely gave the order, and heard that it had been fulfilled. But it just occurred to me, that as the landladies of Paris have some curious customs which might puzzle an entire stranger, my presence here for a moment might explain any little obscurity. Yes, it is as I thought," glancing towards the mantel.

"Oh, Doctor, that reminds me; what is O-t-a-r-d, pray?"

"Otard is poison."

"Shocking."

"Yes, and I think I had best remove it from the room forthwith," replied the sage, in a business-like manner putting the bottle under his arm; "I hope you never use Cologne, do you?"

"What—what is that, Doctor?"

"I see. You never heard of the senseless luxury— a wise ignorance. You smelt flowers upon your mountains. You won't want this, either;" and the Cologne bottle was put under the other arm. "Candle—you'll want that. Soap—you want soap. Use the white cake."

"Is that cheaper, Doctor?"

"Yes, but just as good as the other. You don't ever munch sugar, do you? It's bad for the teeth. I'll take the sugar." So the paper of sugar was likewise dropped into one of the capacious coat pockets.

"Oh, you better take the whole furniture, Doctor Franklin. Here, I'll help you drag out the bedstead."

"My honest friend," said the wise man, pausing solemnly, with the two bottles, like swimmer's bladders under his arm-pits; "my honest friend, the bedstead you will want; what I propose to remove, you will not want."

"Oh, I was only joking, Doctor."

"I knew that. It's a bad habit, except at the proper time, and with the proper person. The things left on the mantel were there placed by the landlady to be used if wanted; if not, to be left untouched. To-morrow morning, upon the chambermaid's coming in to make your bed, all such articles as remained obviously untouched, would have been removed; the rest would have been charged in the bill, whether you used them up completely or not."

"Just as I thought. Then why not let the bottles stay, Doctor, and save yourself all this trouble?"

"Ah! why indeed. My honest friend, are you not my guest? It were unhandsome in me to permit a third person superfluously to entertain you under what, for the time being, is my own roof."

These words came from the wise man in the most graciously bland and flowing tones. As he ended, he made a sort of conciliatory half bow towards Israel.

Charmed with his condescending affability, Israel, without another word, suffered him to march from the room, bottles and all. Not till the first impression of the venerable envoy's suavity had left him, did Israel begin to surmise the mild superiority of successful strategy which lurked beneath this highly ingratiating air.

"Ah," pondered Israel, sitting gloomily before the rifled mantel, with the empty tumbler and tea-spoon in his hand, "it's sad business to have a Doctor Franklin lodging in the next room. I wonder if he sees to all the boarders this way. How the O-t-a-r-d merchants must hate him, and the pastry-cooks too. I wish I had a good pie to pass the time. I wonder if they ever make pumpkin pies in Paris? So, I've got to stay in this room all the time. Somehow I'm bound to be a prisoner, one way or another. Never mind, I'm an ambassador. That's satisfaction. Hark! The Doctor again.— Come in."

No venerable doctor; but in tripped a young French lass, bloom on her cheek, pink ribbons in her cap, liveliness in all her air, grace in the very tips of her elbows. The most bewitching little chambermaid in Paris. All art, but the picture of artlessness.

"Monsieur! pardon!"

"Oh, I pardong ye freely," said Israel. "Come to call on the Ambassador?"

"Monsieur, is de—de—" but, breaking down at the very threshold in her English, she poured out a long ribbon of sparkling French, the purpose of which was to convey a profusion of fine compliments to the stranger, with many tender inquiries as to whether he was comfortably roomed, and whether there might not be something, however trifling, wanting to his complete accommodation. But Israel understood nothing, at the time, but the exceeding grace, and trim, bewitching figure of the girl.

She stood eyeing him for a few moments more, with a look of pretty theatrical despair; and, after vaguely lingering a while, with another shower of incomprehensible compliments and apologies, tripped like a fairy from the chamber. Directly she was gone, Israel pondered upon a singular glance of the girl. It seemed to him that he had, by his reception, in some way, unaccountably disappointed his beautiful visitor. It struck him very strangely that she had entered all sweetness and friendliness, but had retired as if slighted, with a sort of disdainful and sarcastic levity, all the more stinging from its apparent politeness.

Not long had she disappeared, when a noise in the passage apprised him that, in her hurried retreat, the girl must have stumbled against something. The next moment, he heard a chair scraping in the adjacent apartment, and there was another knock at the door.

It was the man of wisdom this time.

"My honest friend, did you not have a visitor, just now?"

"Yes, Doctor, a very pretty girl called upon me."

"Well, I just stopped in to tell you of another strange custom of Paris. That girl is the chambermaid; but she does not confine herself altogether to one vocation. You must beware of the chambermaids of Paris, my honest friend. Shall I tell the girl, from you, that, unwilling to give her the fatigue of going up and down so many flights of stairs, you will, for the future waive her visits of ceremony?"

"Why, Doctor Franklin, she is a very sweet little girl."

"I know it, my honest friend; the sweeter, the more dangerous. Arsenic is sweeter than sugar. I know you are a very sensible young man; not to be taken in by an artful Ammonite; and so, I think I had better convey your message to the girl forthwith."

So saying, the sage withdrew, leaving Israel once more gloomily seated before the rifled mantel, whose mirror was not again to reflect the form of the charming chambermaid.

"Every time he comes in he robs me," soliloquised Israel, dolefully; "with an air all the time, too, as if he were making me presents. If he thinks me such a very sensible young man, why not let me take care of myself?"

It was growing dusk, and Israel lighting the wax candle, proceeded to read in his Guide-book.

"This is poor sight-seeing," muttered he, at last, "sitting here all by myself, with no company but an empty tumbler, reading about the fine things in Paris, and I, myself, a prisoner in Paris. I wish something extraordinary would turn up now; for instance, a man come in and give me ten thousand pounds. But here's 'Poor Richard;' I am a poor fellow myself; so let's see what comfort he has for a comrade."

Opening the little pamphlet, at random, Israel's eyes fell on the following passages: he read them aloud—

"'So what signifies wishing and hoping for better times? We may make these times better, if we bestir ourselves. Industry need not wish, and he that lives upon

hopes will die fasting, as Poor Richard says. There are no gains, without pains.
Then help, hands, for I have no lands, as Poor Richard says.' Oh confound all
this wisdom! It's a sort of insulting to talk wisdom to a man like me. It's
wisdom that's cheap, and it's fortune that's dear. That ain't in Poor Richard;
but it ought to be," concluded Israel, suddenly slamming down the pamphlet.

He walked across the room, looked at the artificial flowers, and the
rose-colored soap, and again went to the table and took up the two books.

"So here is the 'Way to Wealth,' and here is the 'Guide to Paris.' Wonder
now whether Paris lies on the Way to Wealth? if so, I am on the road. More
likely though, it's a parting-of-the-ways. I shouldn't be surprised if the
Doctor meant something sly by putting these two books in my hand.
Somehow, the old gentleman has an amazing sly look—a sort of mild
slyness—about him, seems to me. His wisdom seems a sort of sly, too. But
all in honor, though. I rather think he's one of those old gentlemen who say
a vast deal of sense, but hint a world more. Depend upon it, he's sly, sly, sly.
Ah, what's this Poor Richard says: 'God helps them that help themselves.'
Let's consider that. Poor Richard ain't a Dunker, that's certain, though he
has lived in Pennsylvania. 'God helps them that help themselves.' I'll just
mark that saw, and leave the pamphlet open to refer to again.—Ah!"

At this point, the Doctor knocked, summoning Israel to his own apartment. Here, after a cup of weak tea, and a little toast, the two had a long,
familiar talk together; during which, Israel was delighted with the unpretending talkativeness, serene insight, and benign amiability of the sage. But,
for all this, he could hardly forgive him for the Cologne and Otard depreda-
tions.

Discovering that, in early life, Israel had been employed on a farm, the
man of wisdom at length turned the conversation in that direction; among
other things, mentioning to his guest a plan of his (the Doctor's) for yoking
oxen, with a yoke to go by a spring instead of a bolt; thus greatly facilitating
the operation of hitching on the team to the cart. Israel was very much
struck with the improvement; and thought that, if he were home, upon his
mountains, he would immediately introduce it among the farmers.

Chapter 10

Another Adventurer Appears upon the Scene

ABOUT HALF-PAST TEN O'CLOCK, as they were thus conversing, Israel's acquaintance, the pretty chambermaid, rapped at the door, saying, with a titter, that a very rude gentleman in the passage of the court, desired to see Doctor Franklin.

"A very rude gentleman?" repeated the wise man in French, narrowly looking at the girl, "that means, a very fine gentleman who has just paid you some energetic compliment. But let him come up, my girl," he added patriarchically.

In a few moments, a swift coquettish step was heard, followed, as if in chase, by a sharp and manly one. The door opened. Israel was sitting so that, accidentally his eye pierced the crevice made by the opening of the door, which, like a theatrical screen, stood for a moment, between Doctor Franklin, and the just entering visitor. And behind that screen, through the crack, Israel caught one momentary glimpse of a little bit of by-play between the pretty chambermaid and the stranger. The vivacious nymph appeared to have affectedly run from him on the stairs—doubtless in freakish return for some liberal advances—but had suffered herself to be overtaken at last ere too late; and on the instant Israel caught sight of her, was with an insincere air of rosy resentment, receiving a roguish pinch on the arm, and a still more roguish salute on the cheek.

The next instant both disappeared from the range of the crevice; the girl departing whence she had come; the stranger—transiently invisible as he advanced behind the door,—entering the room. When Israel now perceived him again, he seemed, while momentarily hidden, to have undergone a complete transformation.

He was a rather small, elastic, swarthy man, with an aspect as of a disinherited Indian Chief in European clothes. An unvanquishable enthusiasm, intensified to perfect sobriety, couched in his savage, self-possessed eye. He was elegantly and somewhat extravagantly dressed as a civilian; he carried himself with a rustic, barbaric jauntiness, strangely dashed with a superinduced touch of the Parisian *salon*. His tawny cheek, like a date, spoke of the tropic. A wonderful atmosphere of proud friendlessness and scornful isolation invested him. Yet was there a bit of the poet as well as the outlaw in him, too. A cool solemnity of intrepidity sat on his lip. He looked like one who of purpose sought out harm's way. He looked like one who never had been, and never would be, a subordinate.

Israel thought to himself that seldom before had he seen such a being. Though dressed à-la-mode, he did not seem to be altogether civilized.

So absorbed was our adventurer by the person of the stranger, that a few moments passed ere he began to be aware of the circumstance, that Dr. Franklin and this new visitor having saluted as old acquaintants, were now sitting in earnest conversation together.

"Do as you please; but I will not bide a suitor much longer," said the stranger in bitterness. "Congress gave me to understand that, upon my arrival here, I should be given immediate command of the *Indien;* and now, for no earthly reason that I can see, you Commissioners have presented her, fresh from the stocks at Amsterdam, to the King of France, and not to me. What does the King of France with such a frigate? And what can I *not* do with her? Give me back the 'Indien,' and in less than one month, you shall hear glorious or fatal news of Paul Jones."

"Come, come, Captain," said Doctor Franklin, soothingly, "tell me now, what would you do with her, if you had her?"

"I would teach the British that Paul Jones, though born in Britain, is no subject to the British King, but an untrammelled citizen and sailor of the universe; and I would teach them, too, that if they ruthlessly ravage the American coasts their own coasts are vulnerable as New Holland's. Give me the *Indien*, and I will rain down on wicked England like fire on Sodom."

These words of bravado were not spoken in the tone of a bravo, but a prophet. Erect upon his chair, like an Iroquois, the speaker's look was like that of an unflickering torch.

His air seemed slightly to disturb the old sage's philosophic repose, who, while not seeking to disguise his admiration of the unmistakable spirit of the man, seemed but ill to relish his apparent measureless boasting.

As if both to change the subject a little, as well as put his visitor in better mood—though indeed it might have been but covertly to play with his enthusiasm—the man of wisdom now drew his chair confidentially nearer to the stranger's, and putting one hand in a very friendly, conciliatory way upon his visitor's knee, and rubbing it gently to and fro there, much as a lion-tamer might soothingly manipulate the aggravated king of beasts, said in a winning manner:—"Never mind at present, Captain, about the '*Indien*' affair. Let that sleep a moment. See now, the Jersey privateers do us a great deal of mischief by intercepting our supplies. It has been mentioned to me, that if you had a small vessel—say, even your present ship, the 'Ranger,'— then, by your singular bravery, you might render great service, by follow- ing those privateers where larger ships durst not venture their bottoms; or, if but supported by some frigates from Brest at a proper distance, might draw them out, so that the larger vessels could capture them."

"Decoy-duck to French frigates!—Very dignified office, truly!" hissed Paul in a fiery rage. "Doctor Franklin, whatever Paul Jones does for the cause of America, it must be done through unlimited orders: a separate, supreme command; no leader and no counsellor but himself. Have I not already by my services on the American coast shown that I am well worthy all this? Why then do you seek to degrade me below my previous level? I will mount, not sink. I live but for honor and glory. Give me then some- thing honorable and glorious to do, and something famous to do it with. Give me the *Indien*."

The man of wisdom slowly shook his head.

"Everything is lost through this shillyshallying, timidity called pru- dence," cried Paul Jones, starting to his feet; "to be effectual, war should be carried on like a monsoon; one changeless determination of every particle towards the one unalterable aim. But in vacillating councils, statesmen idle about like the cats' paws in calms. My God, why was I not born a Czar!"

"A Nor-wester rather. Come, come, Captain," added the sage, "sit down; we have a third person present, you see,"—pointing towards Israel, who sat rapt at the volcanic spirit of the stranger.

Paul slightly started, and turned inquiringly upon Israel, who, equally owing to Paul's own earnestness of discourse, and Israel's motionless bearing—had thus far remained undiscovered.

"Never fear, Captain," said the sage, "this man is true blue; a secret courier, and an American born. He is an escaped prisoner of war."

"Ah, captured in a ship?" asked Paul eagerly;—"what ship? None of mine! Paul Jones never was captured."

"No, sir, in the brigantine Washington, out of Boston," replied Israel; "We were cruising to cut off supplies to the English."

"Did your shipmates talk much of me?" demanded Paul, with a look as of a parading Sioux demanding homage to his gew-gaws; "what did they say of Paul Jones?"

"I never heard the name before this evening," said Israel.

"What? Ah—brigantine Washington—let me see; that was before I had outwitted the Solebay frigate, fought the Milford, and captured the Mellish and the rest off Louisbergh. You were long before the news, my lad," he added with a sort of compassionate air.

"Our friend here gave you a rather blunt answer," said the wise man, sagely mischievous, and addressing Paul.

"Yes. And I like him for it. My man, will you go a cruise with Paul Jones? You fellows, so blunt with the tongue, are apt to be sharp with the steel. Come, my lad, return with me to Brest. I go in a few days."

Fired by the contagious spirit of Paul, Israel, forgetting all about his previous desire to reach home, sparkled with response to the summons. But Doctor Franklin interrupted him.

"Our friend here," said he to the Captain, "is at present engaged for very different duty."

Much other conversation followed, during which Paul Jones again and again expressed his impatience at being unemployed, and his resolution to accept of no employ unless it gave him supreme authority; while in answer to all this, Dr. Franklin, not uninfluenced by the uncompromising spirit of his guest, and well knowing that however unpleasant a trait in conversation, or in the transaction of civil affairs, yet in war, this very quality was invaluable, as projectiles and combustibles, finally assured Paul, after many complimentary remarks, that he would immediately exert himself to the utmost to procure for him some enterprise which should come up to his merits.

"Thank you for your frankness," said Paul; "frank myself, I love to deal with a frank man. You, Doctor Franklin, are true, and deep; and so you are frank."

The sage sedately smiled, a queer incredulity just lurking in the corner of his mouth.

"But how about our little scheme for new modelling ships-of-war?" said the Doctor, shifting the subject; "it will be a great thing for our infant navy, if we succeed. Since our last conversation on that subject, Captain, at odds and ends of time, I have thought over the matter, and have begun a little skeleton of the thing here, which I will show you. Whenever one has a new idea in anything mechanical, it is best to clothe it with a body as soon as possible. For you can't improve so well on ideas, as you can on bodies."

With that, going to a little drawer, he produced a small basket, filled with a curious looking unfinished frame-work of wood, and several bits of wood unattached. It looked like a nursery basket containing broken odds and ends of playthings.

"Now look here, Captain, though the thing is but begun at present, yet there is enough to show that *one* idea at least of yours is not feasible."

Paul was all attention, as if having unbounded confidence in whatever the sage might suggest; while Israel looked on, quite as interested as either; his heart swelling with the thought of being privy to the consultations of two such men; consultations, too, having ultimate reference to such momentous affairs as the freeing of nations.

"If," continued the Doctor, taking up some of the loose bits and piling them along on one side of the top of the frame; "if the better to shelter your crew in an engagement, you construct your rail in the manner proposed—as thus—then, by the excessive weight of the timber, you will too much interfere with the ship's centre of gravity. You will have that too high."

"Ballast in the hold in proportion," said Paul.

"Then you will sink the whole hull too low. But here, to have less smoke in time of battle, especially on the lower decks, you proposed a new sort of hatchway. But that won't do. See here now, I have invented certain ventilating pipes—they are to traverse the vessel thus"—laying some toilette pins along—"the current of air to enter here and be discharged there. What do you think of that? But now about the main things—fast sailing, driving little to leeward, and drawing little water. Look now at this keel. I whittled it only night before last, just before going to bed. Do you see now how"—

At this crisis, a knock was heard at the door, and the chambermaid reappeared, announcing that two gentlemen were that moment crossing the court below to see Doctor Franklin.

"The Duke de Chartres, and Count D'Estaing," said the Doctor, "they appointed for last night but did not come. Captain, this has something indirectly to do with your affair. Through the Duke, Count D'Estaing has spoken to the King about the secret expedition, the design of which you first threw out. Call early to-morrow, and I will inform you of the result."

With his tawny hand Paul pulled out his watch, a small, richly jewelled lady's watch.

"It is so late, I will stay here to-night," he said; "Is there a convenient room?"

"Quick," said the Doctor, "it might be ill-advised of you to be seen with me just now. Our friend here will let you share his chamber. Quick, Israel, and show the Captain thither."

As the door closed upon them in Israel's apartment, Doctor Franklin's door closed upon the Duke and the Count. Leaving the latter to their discussion of profound plans for the timely befriending of the American cause, and the crippling of the power of England on the seas, let us pass the night with Paul Jones and Israel in the neighboring room.

Chapter 11

Paul Jones in a Reverie

G OD HELPS THEM that help themselves.' That's a clincher. That's been my experience. But I never saw it in words before. What pamphlet is this? 'Poor Richard,' hey!"

Upon entering Israel's room, Captain Paul, stepping towards the table and spying the open pamphlet there, had taken it up, his eye being immediately attracted to the passage previously marked by our adventurer.

"A rare old gentleman is 'Poor Richard,'" said Israel in response to Paul's observations.

"So he seems, so he seems;" answered Paul, his eye still running over the pamphlet again; "why, 'Poor Richard' reads very much as Doctor Franklin speaks."

"He wrote it," said Israel.

"Aye? Good. So it is, so it is; it's the wise man all over. I must get me a copy of this, and wear it around my neck for a charm. And now about our quarters for the night. I am not going to deprive you of your bed, my man. Do you go to bed and I will doze in the chair here. It's good as dozing in the crosstrees."

"Why not sleep together," said Israel, "see, it is a big bed. Or perhaps you don't fancy your bed-fellow, Captain?"

"When, before the mast, I first sailed out of Whitehaven to Norway," said Paul, coolly, "I had for hammock-mate a full-blooded Congo. We had a white blanket spread in our hammock. Every time I turned in I found the Congo's black wool worked in with the white worsted. By the end of the voyage the blanket was of a pepper-and-salt look, like an old man's turning head. So it's not because I am notional at all, but because I don't care to, my lad. Turn in and go to sleep. Let the lamp burn. I'll see to it. There, go to sleep."

Complying with what seemed as much a command as a request, Israel, though in bed, could not fall into slumber, for thinking of the little circumstance that this strange swarthy man, flaming with wild enterprises, sat in full suit in the chair. He felt an uneasy misgiving sensation, as if he had retired, not only without covering up the fire, but leaving it fiercely burning with spitting faggots of hemlock.

But his natural complaisance induced him at least to feign himself asleep; whereupon Paul, laying down "Poor Richard," rose from his chair, and, withdrawing his boots, began walking rapidly but noiselessly to and fro, in his stockings, in the spacious room, wrapped in Indian meditations. Israel furtively eyed him from beneath the coverlid, and was anew struck by his aspect, now that Paul thought himself unwatched. Stern, relentless purposes, to be pursued to the points of adverse bayonets, and the muzzles of hostile cannon, were expressed in the now rigid lines of his brow. His ruffled right hand was clutched by his side, as if grasping a cutlass. He paced the room as if advancing upon a fortification. Meantime a confused buzz of discussion came from the neighboring chamber. All else was profound midnight tranquillity. Presently, passing the large mirror over the mantel, Paul caught a glimpse of his person. He paused, grimly regarding it, while a dash of pleased coxcombry seemed to mingle with the otherwise savage satisfaction expressed in his face. But the latter predominated. Soon, rolling up his sleeve, with a queer wild smile, Paul lifted his right arm, and stood thus for an interval, eyeing its image in the glass. From where he lay, Israel could not see that side of the arm presented to the mirror, but he saw its reflection, and started at perceiving there, framed in the carved and gilded wood, certain large intertwisted cyphers covering the whole inside of the arm, so far as exposed, with mysterious tatooings. The design was wholly unlike the fanciful figures of anchors, hearts, and cables, sometimes decorating small portions of seamen's bodies. It was a sort of tattooing such as is seen only on thorough-bred savages—deep blue, elaborate, labyrinthine, cabalistic. Israel remembered having beheld, on one of his early voyages, something similar on the arm of a New Zealand warrior, once met, fresh from battle, in his native village. He concluded that on some similar early voyage Paul must have undergone the manipulations of some pagan artist.

Covering his arm again with his laced coat-sleeve, Paul glanced ironically at the hand of the same arm, now again half muffled in ruffles, and ornamented with several Parisian rings. He then resumed his walking with a prowling air, like one haunting an ambuscade; while a gleam of the consciousness of possessing a character as yet unfathomed, and hidden power to back unsuspected projects, irradiated his cold white brow, which, owing to the shade of his hat in equatorial climates, had been left surmounting his swarthy face, like the snow topping the Andes.

So at midnight, the heart of the metropolis of modern civilization was secretly trod by this jaunty barbarian in broad-cloth; a sort of prophetical ghost, glimmering in anticipation upon the advent of those tragic scenes of the French Revolution which levelled the exquisite refinement of Paris with the blood-thirsty ferocity of Borneo; showing that broaches and finger-rings, not less than nose-rings and tattooing, are tokens of the primeval savageness which ever slumbers in human kind, civilised or uncivilised.

Israel slept not a wink that night. The troubled spirit of Paul paced the chamber till morning; when, copiously bathing himself at the wash-stand, Paul looked care-free and fresh as a day-break hawk. After a closeted consultation with Doctor Franklin, he left the place with a light and dandified air, switching his gold-headed cane, and throwing a passing arm round all the pretty chambermaids he encountered, kissing them resoundingly, as if saluting a frigate. All barbarians are rakes.

Chapter 12

Recrossing the Channel, Israel Returns to the Squire's Abode—His Adventures There

ON THE THIRD DAY, as Israel was walking to and fro in his room, having removed his courier's boots, for fear of disturbing the Doctor, a quick sharp rap at the door announced the American envoy. The man of wisdom entered, with two small wads of paper in one hand, and several crackers and a bit of cheese in the other. There was such an eloquent air of instantaneous dispatch about him, that Israel involuntarily sprang to his boots, and, with two vigorous jerks, hauled them on, and then seizing his hat, like any bird, stood poised for his flight across the channel.

"Well done, my honest friend," said the Doctor; "you have the papers in your heel, I suppose."

"Ah," exclaimed Israel, perceiving the mild irony; and in an instant his boots were off again; when, without another word, the Doctor took one boot, and Israel the other, and forthwith both parties proceeded to secrete the documents.

"I think I could improve the design," said the sage, as, notwithstanding his haste, he critically eyed the screwing apparatus of the boot. "The vacancy should have been in the standing part of the heel, not in the lid. It should go with a spring, too, for better dispatch. I'll draw up a paper on false-heels one of these days, and send it to a private reading, at the Institute.

64

But no time for it now. My honest friend, it is now half-past ten o'clock. At half-past eleven, the diligence starts from the Place-du-Carrousel for Calais. Make all haste till you arrive at Brentford. I have a little provender here for you to eat in the diligence, as you will not have time for a regular meal. A day-and-night courier should never be without a cracker in his pocket. You will probably leave Brentford in a day or two after your arrival there. Be wary, now, my good friend; heed well, that, if you are caught with these papers on British ground, you will involve both yourself and our Brentford friends in fatal calamities. Kick no man's box, never mind whose, in the way. Mind your own box. You can't be too cautious, but don't be too suspicious. God bless you, my honest friend. Go!"

And, flinging the door open for his exit, the Doctor saw Israel dart into the entry, vigorously spring down the stairs, and disappear with all celerity, across the court into the vaulted way.

The man of wisdom stood mildly motionless, a moment, with a look of sagacious, humane meditation on his face, as if pondering upon the chances of the important enterprise: one which, perhaps, might in the sequel affect the weal or woe of nations yet to come. Then suddenly clapping his hand to his capacious coat-pocket, dragged out a bit of cork with some hens' feathers, and hurrying to his room, took out his knife, and proceeded to whittle away at a shuttle-cock of an original scientific construction, which, at some prior time he had promised to send to the young Dutchess D'Abrantes, that very afternoon.

Safely reaching Calais, at night, Israel stepped almost from the diligence into the packet, and, in a few moments, was cutting the water. As on the diligence he took an outside and plebeian seat, so, with the same secret motive of preserving unsuspected the character assumed, he took a deck passage in the packet. It coming on to rain violently, he stole down into the forecastle, dimly lit by a solitary swinging lamp, where were two men industriously smoking, and filling the narrow hole with soporific vapors. These induced strange drowsiness in Israel, and he pondered how best he might indulge it, for a time, without imperilling the precious documents in his custody.

But this pondering in such soporific vapors had the effect of those mathematical devices, whereby restless people cipher themselves to sleep. His languid head fell to his breast. In another moment, he drooped half-lengthwise upon a chest, his legs outstretched before him.

Presently he was awakened by some intermeddlement with his feet. Starting to his elbow, he saw one of the two men in the act of slyly slipping

off his right boot, while the left one, already removed, lay on the floor, all
ready against the rascal's retreat. Had it not been for the lesson learned on
the Pont Neuf, Israel would instantly have inferred that his secret mission
was known, and the operator some designed diplomatic knave or other,
hired by the British Cabinet, thus to lie in wait for him, fume him into
slumber with tobacco, and then rifle him of his momentous despatches. But
as it was, he recalled Doctor Franklin's prudent admonitions against the
indulgence of premature suspicions.

"Sir," said Israel very civilly, "I will thank you for that boot which lies
on the floor, and, if you please, you can let the other stay where it is."

"Excuse me," said the rascal, an accomplished, self-possessed prac-
titioner in his thievish art; "I thought your boots might be pinching you,
and only wished to ease you a little."

"Much obliged to ye for your kindness, sir," said Israel; "but they don't
pinch me at all. I suppose, though, you think that they wouldn't pinch *you*
either; your foot looks rather small. Were you going to try 'em on, just to
see how they fitted?"

"No," said the fellow, with sanctimonious seriousness; "but with your
permission I should like to try them on, when we get to Dover. I couldn't
try them well walking on this tipsy craft's deck, you know."

"No," answered Israel, "and the beach at Dover ain't very smooth
either. I guess, upon second thought, you had better not try 'em on at all.
Besides, I am a simple sort of a soul,—eccentric they call me,—and don't
like my boots to go out of my sight. Ha! ha!"

"What are you laughing at?" said the fellow testily.

"Odd idea! I was just looking at those sad old patched boots there on
your feet, and thinking to myself what leaky fire-buckets they would be to
pass up a ladder on a burning building. It would hardly be fair now to swop
my new boots for those old fire-buckets, would it?"

"By plunko!" cried the fellow, willing now by a bold stroke to change
the subject, which was growing slightly annoying; "by plunko, I believe we
are getting nigh Dover. Let's see."

And so saying, he sprang up the ladder to the deck. Upon Israel following, he found the little craft half becalmed, rolling on short swells almost in
the exact middle of the channel. It was just before the break of the morning;
the air clear and fine; the heavens spangled with moistly twinkling stars.
The French and English coasts lay distinctly visible in the strange starlight;
the white cliffs of Dover resembling a long gabled block of marble houses.
Both shores showed a long straight row of lamps. Israel seemed standing in

the middle of the crossing of some wide stately street in London. Presently a breeze sprang up, and ere long our adventurer disembarked at his destined port, and directly posted on for Brentford.

The following afternoon, having gained unobserved admittance into the house, according to preconcerted signals, he was sitting in Squire Wood-cock's closet, pulling off his boots and delivering his despatches.

Having looked over the compressed tissuey sheets, and read a line par-ticularly addressed to himself, the Squire turning round upon Israel, con-gratulated him upon his successful mission; placed some refreshment before him, and apprised him that, owing to certain suspicious symptoms in the neighborhood, he (Israel) must now remain concealed in the house for a day or two, till an answer should be ready for Paris.

It was a venerable mansion, as was somewhere previously stated, of a wide and rambling disorderly spaciousness, built, for the most part, of weather-stained old bricks, in the goodly style called Elizabethan. As with-out, it was all dark russet bricks; so within, it was nothing but tawny oak panels.

"Now, my good fellow," said the Squire, "my wife has a number of guests, who wander from room to room, having the freedom of the house. So I shall have to put you very snugly away, to guard against any chance of discovery."

So saying, first locking the door, he touched a spring nigh the open fire-place, whereupon one of the black sooty stone jambs of the chimney started ajar, just like the marble gate of a tomb. Inserting one leg of the heavy tongs in the crack, the Squire pried this cavernous gate wide open.

"Why, Squire Woodcock, what is the matter with your chimney?" said Israel.

"Quick, go in."

"Am I to sweep the chimney?" demanded Israel; "I didn't engage for that."

"Pooh, pooh, this is your hiding-place. Come, move in."

"But where does it go to, Squire Woodcock? I don't like the looks of it."

"Follow me. I'll show you."

Pushing his florid corpulence into the mysterious aperture, the elderly Squire led the way up a steep stairs of stone, hardly two feet in width, till they reached a little closet, or rather cell, built into the massive main wall of the mansion, and ventilated and dimly lit by two little sloping slits, ingeni-ously concealed without, by their forming the sculptured mouths of two griffins cut in a great stone tablet decorating that external part of the dwelling. A mattress lay rolled up in one corner, with a jug of water, a flask of wine, and a wooden trencher containing cold roast beef and bread.

"And I am to be buried alive here?" said Israel, ruefully looking round.

"But your resurrection will soon be at hand," smiled the Squire; "two days at the furthest."

"Though to be sure I was a sort of prisoner in Paris, just as I seem about to be made here," said Israel, "yet Doctor Franklin put me in a better jug than this, Squire Woodcock. It was set out with bouquets and a mirror, and other fine things. Besides, I could step out into the entry whenever I wanted."

"Ah, but my hero, that was in France, and this is in England. There you were in a friendly country: here you are in the enemy's. If you should be discovered in my house, and your connection with me became known, do you know that it would go very hard with me; very hard indeed?"

"Then for your sake, I am willing to stay wherever you think best to put me," replied Israel.

"Well then, you say you want bouquets and a mirror. If those articles will at all help to solace your seclusion, I will bring them to you."

"They really would be company; the sight of my own face particularly."

"Stay here, then. I will be back in ten minutes."

In less than that time, the good old Squire returned, puffing and panting, with a great bunch of flowers, and a small shaving glass.

"There," said he, putting them down; "now keep perfectly quiet; avoid making any undue noise, and on no account descend the stairs, till I come for you again."

"But when will that be?" asked Israel.

"I will try to come twice each day while you are here. But there is no knowing what may happen. If I should not visit you till I come to liberate you—on the evening of the second day, or the morning of the third—you must not be at all surprised, my good fellow. There is plenty of food and water to last you. But mind, on no account descend the stone-stairs, till I come for you."

With that, bidding his guest adieu, he left him.

Israel stood glancing pensively around for a time. By-and-by, moving the rolled mattress under the two air-slits, he mounted, to try if aught were visible beyond. But nothing was to be seen but a very thin slice of blue sky peeping through the lofty foliage of a great tree planted near the side-portal of the mansion; an ancient tree, coeval with the ancient dwelling it guarded.

Sitting down on the mattress, Israel fell into a reverie.

Poverty and liberty, or plenty and a prison, seem to be the two horns of the constant dilemma of my life, thought he. Let's look at the prisoner.

And taking up the shaving glass, he surveyed his lineaments.

"What a pity I didn't think to ask for razors and soap. I want shaving very badly. I shaved last in France. How it would pass the time here. Had I a comb now and a razor, I might shave and curl my hair, and keep making a continual toilet all through the two days, and look spruce as a robin when I get out. I'll ask the squire for the things this very night when he drops in. Hark! ain't that a sort of rumbling in the wall? I hope there ain't any oven next door, if so, I shall be scorched out. Here I am, just like a rat in the wainscot. I wish there was a low window to look out of. I wonder what Doctor Franklin is doing now, and Paul Jones? Hark! there's a bird singing in the leaves. Bell for dinner, that."

And for pastime, he applied himself to the beef and bread, and took a draught of the wine and water.

At last night fell. He was left in utter darkness. No squire.

After an anxious, sleepless night, he saw two long flecks of pale grey light slanted into the cell from the slits, like two long spears. He rose, rolled up his mattress, got upon the roll, and put his mouth to one of the griffins' mouths. He gave a low, just audible whistle, directing it towards the foliage of the tree. Presently there was a slight rustling among the leaves, then one solitary chirrup, and in three minutes a whole chorus of melody burst upon his ear.

"I've waked the first bird" said he to himself, with a smile, "and he's waked all the rest. Now then for breakfast. That over, I dare say the squire will drop in."

But the breakfast was over, and the two flecks of pale light had changed to golden beams, and the golden beams grew less and less slanting, till they straightened themselves up out of sight altogether. It was noon and no squire.

He's gone a hunting before breakfast, and got belated, thought Israel.

The afternoon shadows lengthened. It was sunset; no squire.

He must be very busy trying some sheep-stealer in the hall, mused Israel. I hope he won't forget all about me till to-morrow.

He waited and listened; and listened and waited.

Another restless night; no sleep; morning came. The second day passed like the first, and the night. On the third morning the flowers lay shrunken by his side. Drops of wet oozing through the air-slits, fell dully on the stone floor. He heard the dreary beatings of the tree's leaves against the mouths of the griffins, bedashing them with the spray of the rain-storm without. At intervals a burst of thunder rolled over his head, and lightning flashing down through the slits, lit up the cell with a greenish glare, followed by sharp splashings and rattlings of the redoubled rain-storm.

This is the morning of the third day, murmured Israel to himself; he said he would at the furthest come to me on the morning of the third day. This is it. Patience, he will be here yet. Morning lasts till noon.

But owing to the murkiness of the day, it was very hard to tell when noon came. Israel refused to credit that noon had come and gone, till dusk set plainly in. Dreading he knew not what, he found himself buried in the darkness of still another night. However patient and hopeful hitherto, fortitude now presently left him. Suddenly, as if some contagious fever had seized him, he was afflicted with strange enchantments of misery, undreamed of till now.

He had eaten all the beef, but there was bread and water sufficient to last by economy, for two or three days to come. It was not the pang of hunger then, but a nightmare originating in his mysterious incarceration, which appalled him. All through the long hours of this particular night, the sense of being masoned up in the wall, grew, and grew, and grew upon him, till again and again he lifted himself convulsively from the floor; as if vast blocks of stone had been laid on him; as if he had been digging a deep well, and the stone work with all the excavated earth had caved in upon him, where he burrowed ninety feet beneath the clover. In the blind tomb of the midnight he stretched his two arms sideways, and felt as if coffined at not being able to extend them straight out, on opposite sides, for the narrowness of the cell. He seated himself against one side of the wall, crosswise with the cell, and pushed with his feet at the opposite wall. But still mindful of his promise in this extremity, he uttered no cry. He mutely raved in the darkness. The delirious sense of the absence of light was soon added to his other delirium as to the contraction of space. The lids of his eyes burst with impotent distension. Then he thought the air itself was getting unbearable. He stood up at the griffin slits, pressing his lips far into them till he moulded his lips there, to suck the utmost of the open air possible.

And continually, to heighten his frenzy, there recurred to him again and again what the Squire had told him as to the origin of the cell. It seemed that this part of the old house, or rather this wall of it, was extremely ancient, dating far beyond the era of Elizabeth, having once formed portion of a religious retreat belonging to the Templars. The domestic discipline of this order was rigid and merciless in the extreme. In a side wall of their second-story chapel, horizontal and on a level with the floor, they had an internal vacancy left, exactly of the shape and average size of a coffin. In this place, from time to time, inmates convicted of contumacy were confined; but, strange to say, not till they were penitent. A small hole, of the girth of one's wrist, sunk like a telescope three feet through the masonry into the cell, served at once for ventilation, and to push through food to the prisoner. This hole opening into the chapel also enabled the poor solitaire, as intended, to overhear the religious services at the altar; and, without being present, take part in the same. It was deemed a good sign of the state of the sufferer's soul, if from the gloomy recesses of the wall, was heard the agonized groan of his dismal response. This was regarded in the light of a penitent wail from the dead; because the customs of the order ordained, that when any inmate should be first incarcerated in the wall, he should be committed to it in the presence of all the brethren; the chief reading the burial service as the live body was sepulchred. Sometimes several weeks elapsed ere the disentombment. The penitent being then usually found numb and congealed in all his extremities, like one newly stricken with paralysis.

This coffin-cell of the Templars had been suffered to remain in the demolition of the general edifice, to make way for the erection of the new, in the reign of Queen Elizabeth. It was enlarged somewhat, and altered, and additionally ventilated, to adapt it for a place of concealment in times of civil dissension.

With this history ringing in his solitary brain, it may readily be conceived what Israel's feelings must have been. Here, in this very darkness, centuries ago, hearts, human as his, had mildewed in despair; limbs, robust as his own, had stiffened in immovable torpor.

At length, after what seemed all the prophetic days and years of Daniel, morning broke. The benevolent light entered the cell, soothing his frenzy, as if it had been some smiling human face—nay, the Squire himself, come at last to redeem him from thrall. Soon his dumb ravings entirely left him, and gradually, with a sane, calm mind, he revolved all the circumstances of his condition.

He could not be mistaken; something fatal must have befallen his friend. Israel remembered the Squire's hinting, that in case of the discovery of his clandestine proceedings, it would fare extremely hard with him. Israel was forced to conclude that this same unhappy discovery had been made; that owing to some untoward misadventure, his good friend had been carried off a State-prisoner to London. That prior to his going, the Squire had not apprised any member of his household that he was about to leave behind him a prisoner in the wall; this seemed evident from the circumstance that, thus far, no soul had visited that prisoner. It could not be otherwise. Doubtless, the Squire, having no opportunity to converse in private with his relatives or friends at the moment of his sudden arrest, had been forced to keep his secret, for the present, for fear of involving Israel in still worse calamities. But would he leave him to perish piece-meal in the wall? All surmise was baffled in the unconjecturable possibilities of the case. But some sort of action must speedily be determined upon. Israel would not additionally endanger the Squire, but he could not in such uncertainty consent to perish where he was. He resolved at all hazards to escape: by stealth and noiselessly, if possible; by violence and outcry, if indispensable.

Gliding out of the cell, he descended the stone stairs, and stood before the interior of the jamb. He felt an immovable iron knob; but no more. He groped about gently for some bolt or spring. When before he had passed through the passage with his guide, he had omitted to notice by what precise mechanism the jamb was to be opened from within, or whether, indeed, it could at all be opened except from without.

He was about giving up the search in despair, after sweeping with his two hands every spot of the wall-surface around him, when chancing to turn his whole body a little to one side, he heard a creak, and saw a thin lance of light. His foot had unconsciously pressed some spring laid in the floor. The jamb was ajar. Pushing it open, he stood at liberty in the Squire's closet.

Chapter 13

His Escape from the House, with Various Adventures Following

H E STARTED at the funereal aspect of the room, into which, since
he last stood there, undertakers seemed to have stolen. The cur-
tains of the window were festooned with long weepers of crape.
The four corners of the red cloth on the round table were knotted with
crape.

Knowing nothing of these mournful customs of the country, nevertheless, Israel's instinct whispered him, that Squire Woodcock lived no more
on this earth. At once, the whole three days' mystery was made clear. But
what was now to be done? His friend must have died very suddenly; most
probably, struck down in a fit, from which he never more rose. With him
had perished all knowledge of the fact that a stranger was immured in the
mansion. If discovered then, prowling here in the inmost privacies of a
gentleman's abode, what would befal the wanderer, already not unsuspected in the neighborhood of some underhand guilt as a fugitive? If he
adhered to the strict truth, what could he offer in his own defence without
convicting himself of acts, which, by English tribunals, would be accounted
flagitious crimes? Unless, indeed, by involving the memory of the deceased
Squire Woodcock in his own self-acknowledged proceedings, so ungenerous a charge should result in an abhorrent refusal to credit his extraordinary

73

tale, whether as referring to himself or another; and so throw him open to still more grievous suspicions?

While wrapped in these dispiriting reveries, he heard a step not very far off in the passage. It seemed approaching. Instantly he flew to the jamb, which remained unclosed; and disappearing within, drew the stone after him by the iron knob. Owing to his hurried violence, the jamb closed with a dull, dismal and singular noise. A shriek followed from within the room. In a panic, Israel fled up the dark stairs; and near the top, in his eagerness, stumbled, and fell back to the last step with a rolling din, which reverberated by the arch overhead smote through and through the wall, dying away at last indistinctly, like low muffled thunder among the clefts of deep hills. When raising himself instantly, not seriously bruised by his fall, Israel intently listened;—the echoing sounds of his descent were mingled with added shrieks from within the room. They seemed some nervous female's, alarmed by what must have appeared to her supernatural or at least unaccountable noises in the wall. Directly he heard other voices of alarm undistinguishably commingled, and then, they retreated together, and all again was still.

Recovering from his first amazement, Israel revolved these occurrences. No creature now in the house knows of the cell, thought he. Some woman,—the housekeeper, perhaps,—first entered the room alone. Just as she entered, the jamb closed. The sudden report made her shriek; then, afterwards, the noise of my fall prolonging itself, added to her fright, while her repeated shrieks brought every soul in the house to her; who, aghast at seeing her lying in a pale faint, it may be, like a corpse, in a room hung with crape for a man just dead, they also shrieked out; and then with blended lamentations they bore the fainting person away. Now this will follow; no doubt it *has* followed ere now:—they believe that the woman saw or heard the spirit of Squire Woodcock. Since I seem then to understand how all these strange events have occurred; since I seem to know that they have plain common causes; I begin to feel cool and calm again. Let me see. Yes. I have it. By means of the idea of the ghost prevailing among the frightened household; by that means, I will this very night make good my escape. If I can but lay hands on some of the late Squire's clothing—if but a coat and hat of his—I shall be certain to succeed. It is not too early to begin now. They will hardly come back to the room in a hurry. I will return to it, and see what I can find to serve my purpose. It is the Squire's private closet; hence it is not unlikely that here some at least of his clothing will be found.

With these thoughts, he cautiously sprung the iron under foot, peeped in, and seeing all clear, boldly re-entered the apartment. He went straight to a high, narrow door in the opposite wall. The key was in the lock. Opening the door, there hung several coats, small clothes, pairs of silk stockings, and hats of the deceased. With little difficulty Israel selected from these the complete suit in which he had last seen his once jovial friend. Carefully closing the door, and carrying the suit with him, he was returning towards the chimney, when he saw the Squire's silver-headed cane leaning against a corner of the wainscot. Taking this also, he stole back to his cell.

Slipping off his own clothing, he deliberately arrayed himself in the borrowed raiment; silk small-clothes and all; then put on the cocked hat, grasped the silver-headed cane in his right hand, and moving his small shaving glass slowly up and down before him, so as by piece-meal to take in his whole figure, felt convinced that he would well pass for Squire Wood-cock's genuine phantom. But after the first feeling of self-satisfaction with his anticipated success had left him, it was not without some superstitious embarrassment that Israel felt himself encased in a dead man's broadcloth; nay, in the very coat in which the deceased had no doubt fallen down in his fit. By degrees he began to feel almost as unreal and shadowy as the shade whose part he intended to enact.

Waiting long and anxiously till darkness came, and then till he thought it was fairly midnight, he stole back into the closet, and standing for a moment uneasily in the middle of the floor, thinking over all the risks he might run, he lingered till he felt himself resolute and calm. Then groping for the door, leading into the hall, put his hand on the knob and turned it. But the door refused to budge. Was it locked? The key was not in. Turning the knob once more, and holding it so, he pressed firmly against the door. It did not move. More firmly still, when suddenly it burst open with a loud crackling report. Being cramped, it had stuck in the sill. Less than three seconds passed, when, as Israel was groping his way down the long wide hall towards the large staircase at its opposite end, he heard confused hurry-ing noises from the neighboring rooms, and in another instant several per-sons, mostly in night-dresses, appeared at their chamber-doors, thrusting out alarmed faces, lit by a lamp held by one of the number, a rather elderly lady in widow's weeds, who, by her appearance, seemed to have just risen from a sleepless chair, instead of an oblivious couch. Israel's heart beat like a hammer; his face turned like a sheet. But bracing himself, pulling his hat lower down over his eyes, settling his head in the collar of his coat, he advanced along the defile of wildly staring faces. He advanced with a slow and stately step; looked neither to the right nor the left; but went solemnly forward on his now faintly illuminated way, sounding his cane on the floor as he passed. The faces in the doorways curdled his blood, by their rooted looks. Glued to the spot, they seemed incapable of motion. Each one was silent as he advanced towards him or her; but as he left each individual, one after another, behind, each in a frenzy shrieked out, "the Squire, the Squire!" As he passed the lady in the widow's weeds, she fell senseless and crosswise before him. But forced to be immutable in his purpose, Israel solemnly stepping over her prostrate form, marched deliberately on.

In a few minutes more he had reached the main door of the mansion, and withdrawing the chain and bolt, stood in the open air. It was a bright moonlight night. He struck slowly across the open grounds towards the sunken fields beyond. When midway across the grounds, he turned towards the mansion, and saw three of the front windows filled with white faces, gazing in terror at the wonderful spectre. Soon descending a slope, he disappeared from their view.

Presently he came to hilly land in meadow, whose grass having been lately cut, now lay dotting the slope in cocks; a sinuous line of creamy vapor meandered through the lowlands at the base of the hill; while beyond was a dense grove of dwarfish trees, with here and there a tall tapering dead trunk, peeled of the bark, and overpeering the rest. The vapor wore the semblance of a deep stream of water, imperfectly descried; the grove looked like some closely-clustering town on its banks, lorded over by spires of churches.

The whole scene magically reproduced to our adventurer the aspect of Bunker Hill, Charles River, and Boston town, on the well-remembered night of the 16th of June. The same season; the same moon; the same new-mown hay on the shaven sward; hay which was scraped together during the night to help pack into the redoubt so hurriedly thrown up.

Acted on as if by enchantment, Israel sat down on one of the cocks, and gave himself up to reverie. But, worn out by long loss of sleep, his reveries would have soon merged into slumber's still wilder dreams, had he not rallied himself, and departed on his way, fearful of forgetting himself in an emergency like the present. It now occurred to him that, well as his disguise had served him in escaping from the mansion of Squire Woodcock, that disguise might fatally endanger him if he should be discovered in it abroad. He might pass for a ghost at night, and among the relations and immediate friends of the gentleman deceased; but by day, and among indifferent persons, he ran no small risk of being apprehended for an entry-thief. He bitterly lamented his omission in not pulling on the Squire's clothes over his own, so that he might now have reappeared in his former guise.

As meditating over this difficulty, he was passing along, suddenly he saw a man in black standing right in his path, about fifty yards distant, in a field of some growing barley or wheat. The gloomy stranger was standing stock-still; one outstretched arm, with weird intimation pointing towards the deceased Squire's abode. To the brooding soul of the now desolate Israel, so strange a sight roused a supernatural suspicion. His conscience morbidly reproaching him for the terrors he had bred in making his escape from the house; he seemed to see in the fixed gesture of the stranger something more than humanly significant. But somewhat of his intrepidity returned; he resolved to test the apparition. Composing itself to the same deliberate stateliness with which it had paced the hall, the phantom of Squire Woodcock firmly advanced its cane, and marched straight forward towards the mysterious stranger.

As he neared him, Israel shrunk. The dark coat-sleeve flapped on the bony skeleton of the unknown arm. The face was lost in a sort of ghastly blank. It was no living man.

But mechanically continuing his course, Israel drew still nearer and saw—a scarecrow.

An Encounter of Ghosts

Not a little relieved by the discovery, our adventurer paused, more particularly to survey so deceptive an object, which seemed to have been constructed on the most efficient principles; probably by some broken down wax-figure costumer. It comprised the complete wardrobe of a scare-crow, namely: a cocked hat, bunged; tattered coat; old velveteen breeches; and long worsted stockings, full of holes; all stuffed very nicely with straw, and skeletoned by a frame-work of poles. There was a great flapped pocket to the coat—which seemed to have been some laborer's—standing invitingly open. Putting his hands in, Israel drew out the lid of an old tobacco-box, the broken bowl of a pipe, two rusty nails, and a few kernels of wheat. This reminded him of the Squire's pockets. Trying them, he produced a handsome handkerchief, a spectacle-case, with a purse containing some silver and gold, amounting to a little more than five pounds. Such is the difference between the contents of the pockets of scare-crows and the pockets of well-to-do squires. Ere donning his present habiliments, Israel had not omitted to withdraw his own money from his own coat, and put it in the pocket of his own waistcoat, which he had not exchanged.

Looking upon the scare-crow more attentively, it struck him that, mis-

erable as its wardrobe was, nevertheless here was a chance for getting rid of
the unsuitable and perilous clothes of the Squire. No other available opportunity might present itself for a time. Before he encountered any living
creature by daylight, another suit must somehow be had. His exchange with
the old ditcher, after his escape from the inn near Portsmouth, had
familiarized him with the most deplorable of wardrobes. Well, too, he
knew, and had experienced it, that for a man desirous of avoiding notice, the
more wretched the clothes the better. For who does not shun the scurvy
wretch, Poverty, advancing in battered hat and lamentable coat?

Without more ado, slipping off the Squire's raiment, he donned the
scarecrow's, after carefully shaking out the hay, which, from many alter-
nate soakings and bakings in rain and sun, had become quite broken up, and
would have been almost dust, were it not for the mildew which damped it.
But sufficient of this wretched old hay remained adhesive to the inside of the
breeches and coat sleeves, to produce the most irritating torment.

The grand moral question now came up, what to do with the purse?
Would it be dishonest under the circumstances to appropriate that purse?
Considering the whole matter, and not forgetting that he had not received
from the gentleman deceased the promised reward for his services as
courier, Israel concluded that he might justly use the money for his own. To
which opinion surely no charitable judge will demur. Besides, what should
he do with the purse, if not use it for his own? It would have been insane to
have returned it to the relations. Such mysterious honesty would have but
resulted in his arrest as a rebel, or rascal. As for the Squire's clothes, handkerchief, and spectacle-case, they must be put out of sight with all despatch.
So, going to a morass not remote, Israel sunk them deep down, and heaped
tufts of the rank sod upon them. Then returning to the field of corn, sat
down under the lee of a rock, about a hundred yards from where the
scarecrow had stood, thinking which way he now had best direct his steps.
But his late ramble coming after so long a deprivation of rest, soon
produced effects not so easy to be shaken off, as when reposing upon the
haycock. He felt less anxious too, since changing his apparel. So before he
was aware, he fell into deep sleep.

When he awoke, the sun was well up in the sky. Looking around he saw
a farm-laborer with a pitch-fork coming at a distance into view, whose steps
seemed bent in a direction not far from the spot where he lay. Immediately
it struck our adventurer that this man must be familiar with the scarecrow;
perhaps had himself fashioned it. Should he miss it then, he might make
immediate search, and so discover the thief so imprudently loitering upon
the very field of his operations.

Waiting until the man momentarily disappeared in a little hollow, Israel ran briskly to the identical spot where the scarecrow had stood; where, standing stiffly erect, pulling the hat well over his face, and thrusting out his arm, pointed steadfastly towards the Squire's abode, he awaited the event. Soon the man reappeared in sight, and marching right on, paused not far from Israel, and gave him an one earnest look, as if it were his daily wont to satisfy that all was right with the scarecrow. No sooner was the man departed to a reasonable distance, than, quitting his post, Israel struck across the fields towards London. But he had not yet quite quitted the field, when it occurred to him to turn round, and see if the man was completely out of sight; when, to his consternation, he saw the man returning towards him, evidently by his pace and gesture in unmixed amazement. The man must have turned round to look, before Israel had done so. Frozen to the ground, Israel knew not what to do. But, next moment it struck him, that this very motionlessness was the least hazardous plan in such a strait. Thrusting out his arm again towards the house, once more he stood stock-still, and again awaited the event.

It so happened that this time in pointing towards the house, Israel unavoidably pointed towards the advancing man. Hoping that the strangeness of this coincidence might, by operating on the man's superstition, incline him to beat an immediate retreat, Israel kept cool as he might. But the man proved to be of a braver metal than anticipated. In passing the spot where the scarecrow had stood, and perceiving, beyond the possibility of mistake, that by some unaccountable agency it had suddenly removed itself to a distance; instead of being terrified at this verification of his worst apprehensions, the man pushed on for Israel, apparently resolved to sift this mystery to the bottom.

Seeing him now determinately coming, with pitchfork valiantly presented, Israel, as a last means of practising on the fellow's fears of the supernatural, suddenly doubled up both fists, presenting them savagely towards him at a distance of about twenty paces; at the same time showing his teeth like a skull's, and demoniacally rolling his eyes. The man paused bewildered; looked all round him; looked at the springing grain; then across at some trees; then up at the sky; and satisfied at last by those observations, that the world at large had not undergone a miracle in the last fifteen minutes, resolutely resumed his advance; the pitchfork like a boarding-pike now aimed full at the breast of the object. Seeing all his stratagems vain, Israel now threw himself into the original attitude of the scarecrow, and once again stood immovable. Abating his pace by degrees almost to a mere creep, the man at last came within three feet of him, and

pausing, gazed amazed into Israel's eyes. With a stern and terrible expression
Israel resolutely returned the glance, but otherwise remained like a statue;
hoping thus to stare his pursuer out of countenance. At last the man slowly
presented one prong of his fork towards Israel's left eye. Nearer and nearer
the sharp point came; till no longer capable of enduring such a test, Israel
took to his heels with all speed, his tattered coat-tails streaming behind him.
With inveterate purpose the man pursued. Darting blindly on, Israel leaping
a gate, suddenly found himself in a field where some dozen laborers were at
work; who recognizing the scarecrow—an old acquaintance of theirs, as it
would seem—lifted all their hands as the astounding apparition swept by,
followed by the man with the pitchfork. Soon all joined in the chase; but
Israel proved to have better wind and bottom than any. Outstripping the
whole pack, he finally shot out of their sight in an extensive park, heavily
timbered in one quarter. He never saw more of these people.

Loitering in the wood till nightfall, he then stole out and made the best
of his way towards the house of that good-natured farmer in whose corn-
loft he had received his first message from Squire Woodcock. Rousing this
man up a little before midnight, he informed him somewhat of his recent
adventures, but carefully concealed his having been employed as a secret
courier, together with his escape from Squire Woodcock's. All he craved at
present was a meal. The meal being over, Israel offered to buy from the
farmer his best suit of clothes, and displayed the money on the spot.

"Where did you get so much money?" said his entertainer in a tone of
surprise; "your clothes here don't look as if you had seen prosperous times
since you left me. Why, you look like a scarecrow."

"That may well be," replied Israel very soberly. "But what do you say?
will you sell me your suit?—here's the cash."

"I don't know about it," said the farmer, in doubt; "let me look at the
money. Ha!—a silk purse come out of a beggar's pocket!—Quit the house,
rascal, you've turned thief."

Thinking that he could not swear to his having come by his money with
absolute honesty—since indeed the case was one for the most subtle
casuist—Israel knew not what to reply. This honest confusion confirmed
the farmer; who with many abusive epithets drove him into the road; telling
him that he might thank himself that he did not arrest him on the spot.

In great dolor at this unhappy repulse, Israel trudged on in the moonlight some three miles to the house of another friend, who also had once
succored him in extremity. This man proved a very sound sleeper. Instead
of succeeding in rousing him by his knocking, Israel but succeeded in rous-

ing his wife, a person not of the greatest amiability. Raising the sash, and seeing so shocking a pauper before her, the woman upbraided him with shameless impropriety in asking charity at dead of night, in a dress so improper too. Looking down at his deplorable velveteens, Israel discovered that his extensive travels had produced a great rent in one loin of the rotten old breeches, through which a whitish fragment protruded.

Remedying this oversight as well as he might, he again implored the woman to wake her husband.

"That I shan't!" said the woman morosely. "Quit the premises, or I'll throw something on ye."

With that, she brought some earthenware to the window, and would have fulfilled her threat, had not Israel prudently retreated some paces. Here he entreated the woman to take mercy on his plight, and since she would not waken her husband, at least throw to him (Israel) her husband's breeches, and he would leave the price of them, with his own breeches to boot, on the sill of the door.

"You behold how sadly I need them," said he; "for heaven's sake befriend me."

"Quit the premises!" reiterated the woman.

"The breeches, the breeches! here is the money," cried Israel, half furious with anxiety.

"Saucy cur," cried the woman, somehow misunderstanding him; "do you cunningly taunt me with *wearing* the breeches? begone!"

Once more, poor Israel decamped, and made for another friend. But here a monstrous bull-dog, indignant that the peace of a quiet family should be disturbed by so outrageous a tatterdemalion, flew at Israel's unfortunate coat, whose rotten skirts the brute tore completely off; leaving the coat razeed to a spencer, which barely came down to the wearer's waist. In attempting to drive the monster away, Israel's hat fell off, upon which the dog pounced with the utmost fierceness, and thrusting both paws into it, rammed out the crown, and went snuffling the wreck before him. Recovering the wretched hat, Israel again beat a retreat, his wardrobe sorely the worse for his visits. Not only was his coat a mere rag, but his breeches, clawed by the dog, were slashed into yawning gaps, while his yellow hair waved over the top of the crownless beaver, like a lonely tuft of heather on the Highlands.

In this plight the morning discovered him dubiously skirmishing on the outskirts of a village.

"Ah! what a true patriot gets for serving his country!" murmured Israel.

But soon thinking a little better of his case, and seeing yet another house which had once furnished him with an asylum, he made bold to advance to the door. Luckily he this time met the man himself, just emerging from bed. At first the farmer did not recognize the fugitive; but upon another look, seconded by Israel's plaintive appeal, beckoned him into the barn, where directly our adventurer told him all he thought prudent to disclose of his story; ending by once more offering to negotiate for breeches and coat. Having ere this, emptied and thrown away the purse which had played him so scurvy a trick with the first farmer; he now produced three crown-pieces.

"Three crown-pieces in your pocket, and no crown to your hat!" said the farmer.

"But I assure you, my friend," rejoined Israel, "that a finer hat was never worn, until that confounded bull-dog ruined it."

"True," said the farmer. "I forgot that part of your story. Well, I have a tolerable coat and breeches which I will sell you for your money."

In ten minutes more, Israel was equipped in a grey coat of coarse cloth, not much improved by wear, and breeches to match. For half-a-crown more, he procured a highly respectable-looking hat.

"Now, my kind friend," said Israel, "can you tell me where Horne Tooke, and John Bridges live?"

Our adventurer thought it his best plan to seek out one or other of those gentlemen, both to report proceedings, and learn confirmatory tidings concerning Squire Woodcock, touching whose fate he did not like to inquire of others.

"Horne Tooke? What do you want with Horne Tooke?" said the farmer: "He was Squire Woodcock's friend, wasn't he? The poor Squire! Who would have thought he'd have gone off so suddenly. But apoplexy comes like a bullet."

I was right, thought Israel to himself. "But where does Horne Tooke live?" he demanded again.

"He once lived in Brentford, and wore a cassock there. But I hear he's sold out his living, and gone in his surplice to study law in Lunnon."

This was all news to Israel, who, from various amiable remarks he had heard from Horne Tooke at the Squire's, little dreamed he was an ordained clergyman. Yet a good-natured English clergyman translated Lucian; another, equally good-natured, wrote Tristram Shandy; and a third, an ill-natured appreciator of good-natured Rabelais, died a dean; not to speak of others. Thus ingenious and ingenuous are some of the English clergy.

"You can't tell me, then, where to find Horne Tooke?" said Israel, in perplexity.

"You'll find him, I suppose, in Lunnon."

"What street and number?"

"Don't know. Needle in a haystack."

"Where does Mr. Bridges live?"

"Never heard of any Bridges, except Lunnon bridges, and one Molly Bridges in Bridewell."

So Israel departed; better clothed, but no wiser than before.

What to do next? He reckoned up his money, and concluded he had plenty to carry him back to Doctor Franklin in Paris. Accordingly, taking a turn to avoid the two nearest villages, he directed his steps towards London, where, again taking the post coach for Dover, he arrived on the channel shore just in time to learn that the very coach in which he rode brought the news to the authorities there that all intercourse between the two nations was indefinitely suspended. The characteristic taciturnity and formal stolidity of his fellow-travellers—all Englishmen, mutually unacquainted with each other, and occupying different positions in life—having prevented his sooner hearing the tidings.

Here was another accumulation of misfortunes. All visions but those of eventual imprisonment or starvation vanished from before the present realities of poor Israel Potter. The Brentford gentleman had flattered him with the prospect of receiving something very handsome for his services as courier. That hope was no more. Doctor Franklin had promised him his good offices in procuring him a passage home to America. Quite out of the question now. The sage had likewise intimated that he might possibly see him some way remunerated for his sufferings in his country's cause. An idea no longer to be harbored. Then Israel recalled the mild man of wisdom's words—"At the prospect of pleasure never be elated; but without depression respect the omens of ill." But he found it as difficult now to comply, in all respects, with the last section of the maxim, as before he had with the first.

While standing wrapped in afflictive reflections on the shore, gazing towards the unattainable coast of France, a pleasant-looking cousinly stranger, in seaman's dress, accosted him, and, after some pleasant conversation, very civilly invited him up a lane into a house of rather secret entertainment. Pleased to be befriended in this his strait, Israel yet looked inquisitively upon the man, not completely satisfied with his good intentions. But the other, with good-humored violence, hurried him up the lane into the inn, when, calling for some spirits, he and Israel very affectionately drank to each other's better health and prosperity.

"Take another glass," said the stranger, affably.

Israel, to drown his heavy-heartedness, complied. The liquor began to take effect.

"Ever at sea?" said the stranger, lightly.

"Oh, yes; been a whaling."

"Ah!" said the other, "happy to hear that, I assure you. Jim! Bill!" And beckoning very quietly to two brawny fellows, in a trice Israel found himself kidnapped into the naval service of the magnanimous old gentleman of Kew Gardens—his Royal Majesty, George III.

"Hands off!" said Israel, fiercely, as the two men pinioned him.

"Reglar game-cock," said the cousinly-looking man. "I must get three guineas for cribbing him. Pleasant voyage to ye, my friend," and, leaving Israel a prisoner, the crimp, buttoning his coat, sauntered leisurely out of the inn.

"I'm no Englishman," roared Israel, in a foam.

"Oh! that's the old story," grinned his gaolers. "Come along. There's no Englishmen in the English fleet. All foreigners. You may take their own word for it."

To be short, in less than a week Israel found himself at Portsmouth, and, ere long, a fore-topman in his majesty's ship of the line, "Unprincipled," scudding before the wind down channel, in company with the "Undaunted," and the "Unconquerable;" all three haughty Dons bound to the East Indian waters as reinforcements to the fleet of Sir Edward Hughes.

And now, we might shortly have to record our adventurer's part in the famous engagement off the coast of Coromandel, between Admiral Suffren's fleet and the English squadron, were it not that fate snatched him on the threshold of events, and, turning him short round whither he had come, sent him back congenially to war against England, instead of on her behalf. Thus repeatedly and rapidly were the fortunes of our wanderer planted, torn up, transplanted, and dropped again, hither and thither, according as the Supreme Disposer of sailors and soldiers saw fit to appoint.

Chapter 14

In Which Israel Is Sailor under Two Flags, and in Three Ships,
and All in One Night

AS RUNNING down channel at evening, Israel walked the crowded main-deck of the seventy-four, continually brushed by a thousand hurrying wayfarers, as if he were in some great street in London, jammed with artisans, just returning from their day's labor, novel and painful emotions were his. He found himself dropped into the naval mob without one friend; nay, among enemies, since his country's enemies were his own, and against the kith and kin of these very beings around him, he himself had once lifted a fatal hand. The martial bustle of a great man-of-war, on her first day out of port, was indescribably jarring to his present mood. Those sounds of the human multitude disturbing the solemn natural solitudes of the sea, mysteriously afflicted him. He murmured against that untowardness which, after condemning him to long sorrows on the land, now pursued him with added griefs on the deep. Why should a patriot, leaping for the chance again to attack the oppressor, as at Bunker Hill, now be kidnapped to fight that oppressor's battles on the endless drifts of the Bunker Hills of the billows? But like many other repiners, Israel was perhaps a little premature with upbraidings like these.

Plying on between Scilly and Cape Clear, the Unprincipled—which vessel somewhat outsailed her consorts—fell in, just before dusk, with a large revenue cutter close to, and showing signals of distress. At the moment, no other sail was in sight.

Cursing the necessity of pausing with a strong fair wind at a juncture like this, the officer-of-the-deck shortened sail, and hove to; hailing the cutter, to know what was the matter. As he hailed the small craft from the lofty poop of the bristling seventy-four, this lieutenant seemed standing on the top of Gibraltar, talking to some lowland peasant in a hut. The reply was, that in a sudden flaw of wind, which came nigh capsizing them, not an hour since, the cutter had lost all four foremast men by the violent jibing of a boom. She wanted help to get back to port.

"You shall have one man," said the officer-of-the-deck, morosely.

"Let him be a good one then, for heaven's sake," said he in the cutter; "I ought to have at least two."

During this talk, Israel's curiosity had prompted him to dart up the ladder from the main-deck, and stand right in the gangway above, looking out on the strange craft. Meantime the order had been given to drop a boat. Thinking this a favorable chance, he stationed himself so that he should be the foremost to spring into the boat; though crowds of English sailors, eager as himself for the same opportunity to escape from foreign service, clung to the chains of the as yet imperfectly disciplined man-of-war. As the two men who had been lowered in the boat hooked her, when afloat, along to the gangway, Israel dropped like a comet into the stern-sheets, stumbled forward, and seized an oar. In a moment more, all the oarsmen were in their places, and with a few strokes, the boat lay alongside the cutter.

"Take which of them you please," said the lieutenant in command, addressing the officer in the revenue-cutter, and motioning with his hand to his boat's crew, as if they were a parcel of carcasses of mutton, of which the first pick was offered to some customer. "Quick and choose. Sit down, men"—to the sailors. "Oh, you are in a great hurry to get rid of the king's service, ain't you? Brave chaps indeed!—Have you chosen your man?"

All this while the ten faces of the anxious oarsmen looked with mute longings and appealings towards the officer of the cutter; every face turned at the same angle, as if managed by one machine. And so they were. One motive.

"I take the freckled chap with the yellow hair—him;" pointing to Israel.

Nine of the upturned faces fell in sullen despair, and ere Israel could spring to his feet, he felt a violent thrust in his rear from the toes of one of the disappointed behind him.

"Jump, dobbin!" cried the officer of the boat.

But Israel was already on board. Another moment, and the boat and cutter parted. Ere long night fell, and the man-of-war and her consorts were out of sight.

The revenue vessel resumed her course towards the nighest port, worked by but four men: the captain, Israel, and two officers. The cabin-boy was kept at the helm. As the only foremast man, Israel was put to it pretty hard. Where there is but one man to three masters, woe betide that lonely slave. Besides, it was of itself severe work enough to manage the vessel thus short of hands. But to make matters still worse, the captain and his officers were ugly-tempered fellows. The one kicked, and the others cuffed Israel. Whereupon, not sugared with his recent experiences, and maddened by his present hap, Israel seeing himself alone at sea, with only three men, instead of a thousand, to contend against, plucked up a heart, knocked the captain into the lee scuppers, and in his fury was about tumbling the first-officer, a small wash of a fellow, plump overboard, when the captain, jumping to his feet, seized him by his long yellow hair, vowing he would slaughter him. Meantime the cutter flew foaming through the channel, as if in demoniac glee at this uproar on her imperilled deck. While the consternation was at its height, a dark body suddenly loomed at a moderate distance into view, shooting right athwart the stern of the cutter. The next moment a shot struck the water within a boat's length.

"Heave to, and send a boat on board!" roared a voice almost as loud as the cannon.

"That's a war-ship," cried the captain of the revenue vessel, in alarm; "but she ain't a countryman."

Meantime the officers and Israel stopped the cutter's way.

"Send a boat on board, or I'll sink you," again came roaring from the stranger, followed by another shot, striking the water still nearer the cutter.

"For God's sake, don't cannonade us. I haven't got the crew to man a boat," replied the captain of the cutter. "Who are you?"

"Wait till I send a boat to you for that," replied the stranger.

"She's an enemy of some sort, that's plain," said the Englishman now to his officers; "we ain't at open war with France; she's some blood-thirsty pirate or other. What d' ye say, men," turning to his officers; "let's outsail her, or be shot to chips. We can beat her at sailing, I know."

With that, nothing doubting that his counsel would be heartily responded to, he ran to the braces to get the cutter before the wind, followed by one officer, while the other, for a useless bravado, hoisted the colors at the stern.

But Israel stood indifferent, or rather all in a fever of conflicting emotions. He thought he recognized the voice from the strange vessel.

"Come, what do ye standing there, fool? Spring to the ropes here!" cried the furious captain.

But Israel did not stir.

Meantime, the confusion on board the stranger, owing to the hurried lowering of her boat, with the cloudiness of the sky darkening the misty sea, united to conceal the bold manœuvre of the cutter. She had almost gained full headway ere an oblique shot, directed by mere chance, struck her stern, tearing the upcurved head of the tiller in the hands of the cabin-boy, and killing him with the splinters. Running to the stump, the captain huzzaed, and steered the reeling ship on. Forced now to hoist back the boat ere giving chase, the stranger was dropped rapidly astern.

All this while storms of maledictions were hurled on Israel. But their exertions at the ropes prevented his shipmates for the time from using personal violence. While observing their efforts, Israel could not but say to himself, "These fellows are as brave as they are brutal."

Soon the stranger was seen dimly wallowing along astern, crowding all sail in chase, while now and then her bow-gun, showing its red tongue, bellowed after them like a mad bull. Two more shots struck the cutter, but without materially damaging her sails, or the ropes immediately upholding them. Several of her less important stays were sundered, however; whose loose tarry ends lashed the air like scorpions. It seemed not improbable that owing to her superior sailing, the keen cutter would yet get clear.

At this juncture, Israel, running towards the captain, who still held the splintered stump of tiller, stood full before him, saying, "I am an enemy, a Yankee; look to yourself."

"Help here, lads, help," roared the captain, "a traitor, a traitor!"

The words were hardly out of his mouth when his voice was silenced for ever. With one prodigious heave of his whole physical force, Israel smote him over the taffrail into the sea, as if the man had fallen backwards over a teetering chair. By this time the two officers were hurrying aft. Ere meeting them midway, Israel, quick as lightning, cast off the two principal halyards, thus letting the large sails all in a tumble of canvass to the deck. Next moment one of the officers was at the helm, to prevent the cutter from capsizing by being without a steersman in such an emergency. The other officer and Israel interlocked. The battle was in the midst of the chaos of blowing canvass. Caught in a rent of the sail, the officer slipped and fell near the sharp iron edge of the hatchway. As he fell, he caught Israel by the most terrible part in which mortality can be grappled. Insane with pain, Israel dashed his adversary's skull against the sharp iron. The officer's hold relaxed; but himself stiffened. Israel made for the helmsman, who as yet knew not the issue of the late tussel. He caught him round the loins, bedding his fingers like grisly claws into his flesh, and hugging him to his heart. The man's ghost, caught like a broken cork in a gurgling bottle's neck, gasped with the embrace. Loosening him suddenly, Israel hurled him from him against the bulwarks. That instant another report was heard, followed by the savage hail—"You down sail at last, do ye? I'm a good mind to sink ye, for your scurvy trick. Pull down that dirty rag there, astern!"

With a loud huzza, Israel hauled down the flag with one hand, while with the other he helped the now slowly gliding craft from falling off before the wind.

In a few moments a boat was alongside. As its commander stepped to the deck, he stumbled against the body of the first-officer, which, owing to the sudden slant of the cutter in coming to the wind, had rolled against the side near the gangway. As he came aft, he heard the moan of the other officer, where he lay under the mizzen shrouds.

"What is all this?" demanded the stranger of Israel.

"It means that I am a Yankee impressed into the king's service; and for their pains I have taken the cutter."

Giving vent to his surprise, the officer looked narrowly at the body by the shrouds, and said, "this man is as good as dead; but we will take him to Captain Paul as a witness in your behalf."

"Captain Paul?—Paul Jones?" cried Israel.

"The same."

"I thought so. I thought that was his voice hailing. It was Captain Paul's voice that somehow put me up to this deed."

"Captain Paul is the devil for putting men up to be tigers. But where are the rest of the crew?"

"Overboard."

"What?" cried the officer; "come on board the Ranger. Captain Paul will use you for a broadside."

Taking the moaning man along with them, and leaving the cutter untenanted by any living soul, the boat now left her for the enemy's ship. But ere they reached it, the man had expired.

Standing foremost on the deck, crowded with three hundred men, as

Israel climbed the side, he saw, by the light of battle-lanthorns, a small, swart, brigandish-looking man, wearing a Scotch bonnet, with a gold band to it.

"You rascal," said this person, "why did your paltry smack give me this chase? Where's the rest of your gang?"

"Captain Paul," said Israel, "I believe I remember you. I believe I offered you my bed in Paris some months ago. How is Poor Richard?"

"God! Is this the courier? The Yankee courier? But how now; in an English revenue cutter?"

"Impressed, sir; that's the way."

"But where's the rest of them?" demanded Paul, turning to the officer.

Thereupon the officer very briefly told Paul what Israel had told him.

"Are we to sink the cutter, sir?" said the gunner, now advancing towards Captain Paul. "If it is to be done, now is the time. She is close under us, astern; a few guns pointed downwards, will settle her like a shotted corpse."

"No. Let her drift into Penzance, an anonymous earnest of what the white-squall in Paul Jones intends for the future."

Then giving directions as to the course of the ship, with an order for himself to be called at the first glimpse of a sail, Paul took Israel down with him into his cabin.

"Tell me your story now, my yellow lion. How was it all? Don't stand; sit right down there on the transom. I'm a democratic sort of sea-king. Plump on the wool-sack, I say, and spin the yarn. But hold; you want some grog first."

As Paul handed the flagon, Israel's eye fell upon his hand.

"You don't wear any rings now, Captain, I see. Left them in Paris for safety."

"Aye, with a certain marchioness there," replied Paul, with a dandyish look of sentimental conceit, which sat strangely enough on his otherwise grim and Fejee air.

"I should think rings would be somewhat inconvenient at sea," resumed Israel. "On my first voyage to the West Indies, I wore a girl's ring on my middle finger here, and it wasn't long before, what with hauling wet ropes, and what not, it got a kind of grown down into the flesh, and pained me very bad, let me tell you, it hugged the finger so."

"And did the girl grow as close to your heart, lad?"

"Ah, Captain, girls grow themselves off quicker than we grow them on."

"Some experience with the countesses as well as myself, eh? But the story; wave your yellow mane, my lion—the story."

So Israel went on, and told the story in all particulars.

At its conclusion, Captain Paul eyed him very earnestly. His wild, lonely heart, incapable of sympathizing with cuddled natures made hum-drum by long exemption from pain, was yet drawn towards a being, who in desperation of friendlessness, something like his own, had so fiercely waged battle against tyrannical odds.

"Did you go to sea young, lad?"

"Yes, pretty young."

"I went at twelve, from Whitehaven. Only so high," raising his hand some four feet from the deck. "I was so small, and looked so queer in my little blue jacket, that they called me the monkey. They'll call me something else before long. Did you ever sail out of Whitehaven?"

"No, Captain."

"If you had, you'd have heard sad stories about me. To this hour they say there that I,—blood-thirsty—coward dog that I am,—flogged a sailor, one Mungo Maxwell, to death. It's a lie, by heaven! I flogged him, for he was a mutinous scamp. But he died naturally, some time afterwards, and on board another ship. But why talk? They didn't believe the affidavits of others taken before London courts, triumphantly acquitting me; how then will they credit *my* interested words? If slander, however much a lie, once gets hold of a man, it will stick closer than fair fame, as black pitch sticks closer than white cream. But let 'em slander. I will give the slanderers matter for curses. When last I left Whitehaven, I swore never again to set foot on her pier, except, like Cæsar, at Sandwich, as a foreign invader. Spring under me, good ship; on you I bound to my vengeance!"

Men with poignant feelings, buried under an air of care-free self-command, are never proof to the sudden incitements of passion. Though in the main, they may control themselves, yet if they but once permit the smallest vent, then they may bid adieu to all self-restraint, at least for that time. Thus with Paul on the present occasion. His sympathy with Israel had prompted this momentary ebullition. When it was gone by, he seemed not a little to regret it. But he passed it over lightly, saying, "You see, my fine fellow, what sort of a bloody cannibal I am. Will you be a sailor of mine? A sailor of the captain who flogged poor Mungo Maxwell to death?"

"I will be very happy, Captain Paul, to be sailor under the man who will yet, I dare say, help flog the British nation to death."

"You hate 'em, do ye?"

"Like snakes. For months they've hunted me as a dog," half howled and half wailed Israel, at the memory of all he had suffered.

"Give me your hand, my lion; wave your wild flax again. By heaven, you hate so well, I love ye. You shall be my confidential man; stand sentry at my cabin door; sleep in the cabin; steer my boat; keep by my side whenever I land. What do you say?"

"I say I'm glad to hear you."

"You are a good, brave soul. You are the first among the millions of mankind that I ever naturally took to. Come, you are tired. There, go into that state-room for to-night—it's mine. You offered me your bed in Paris."

"But you begged off, Captain, and so must I. Where do you sleep?"

"Lad, I don't sleep half a night out of three. My clothes have not been off now for five days."

"Ah, Captain, you sleep so little and scheme so much, you will die young."

"I know it: I want to: I mean to. Who would live a doddered old stump? What do you think of my Scotch bonnet?"

"It looks well on you, Captain."

"Do you think so? A Scotch bonnet though, ought to look well on a Scotchman. I'm such by birth. Is the gold band too much?"

"I like the gold band, Captain. It looks something as I should think a crown might on a king."

"Aye."

"You would make a better looking king than George III."

"Did you ever see that old granny? Waddles about in farthingales, and carries a peacock fan, don't he? Did you ever see him?"

"Was as close to him as I am to you now, captain. In Kew Gardens it was, where I worked gravelling the walks. I was all alone with him, talking for some ten minutes."

"By Jove, what a chance! Had I but been there! What an opportunity for kidnapping a British king, and carrying him off in a fast-sailing smack to Boston, a hostage for American freedom. But what did you? Didn't you try to do something to him?"

"I had a wicked thought or two, captain; but I got the better of it. Besides, the king behaved handsomely towards me; yes, like a true man. God bless him for it. But it was before that, that I got the better of the wicked thought."

"Ah, meant to stick him, I suppose. Glad you didn't. It would have been very shabby. Never kill a king, but make him captive. He looks better as a led horse, than a dead carcass. I propose now, this trip, falling on the grounds of the Earl of Selkirk, a privy counsellor, and particular private friend of George III. But I won't hurt a hair of his head. When I get him on board here, he shall lodge in my best state-room, which I mean to hang with damask for him. I shall drink wine with him, and be very friendly; take him to America, and introduce his lordship into the best circles there; only I shall have him accompanied on his calls by a sentry or two disguised as valets. For the earl's to be on sale, mind; so much ransom; that is, the nobleman, Lord Selkirk, shall have a bodily price pinned on his coat-tail, like any slave up at auction in Charleston. But, my lad with the yellow mane, you very strangely draw out my secrets. And yet you don't talk. Your honesty is a magnet which attracts my sincerity. But I rely on your fidelity."

"I shall be a vice to your plans, Captain Paul. I will receive, but I won't let go, unless you alone loose the screw."

"Well said. To bed now; you ought to. I go on deck. Good-night, ace-of-hearts."

"That is fitter for yourself, Captain Paul; lonely leader of the suit."

"Lonely? Aye, but number one cannot but be lonely, my trump."

"Again I give it back. Ace-of-trumps may it prove to you, Captain Paul; may it be impossible for you ever to be taken. But for me—poor deuce, a trey, that comes in your wake—any king or knave may take me, as before now the knaves have."

"Tut, tut, lad; never be more cheery for another than for yourself. But a fagged body fags the soul. To hammock, to hammock! while I go on deck to clap on more sail to your cradle."

And they separated for that night.

Chapter 15

They Sail as Far as the Crag of Ailsa

NEXT MORNING Israel was appointed quarter-master; a sub-altern selected from the common seamen, and whose duty mostly stations him in the stern of the ship, where the captain walks. His business is to carry the glass on the look-out for sails; hoist or lower the colors; and keep an eye on the helmsman. Picked out from the crew for their superior respectability and intelligence, as well as for their excellent seamanship, it is not unusual to find the quarter-masters of an armed ship on peculiarly easy terms with the commissioned officers and captain. This berth, therefore, placed Israel in official contiguity to Paul, and without subjecting either to animadversion, made their public intercourse on deck almost as familiar as their unrestrained converse in the cabin.

It was a fine cool day in the beginning of April. They were now off the coast of Wales, whose lofty mountains, crested with snow, presented a Norwegian aspect. The wind was fair, and blew with a strange, bestirring power. The ship—running between Ireland and England, northwards, to-wards the Irish Sea, the inmost heart of the British waters—seemed, as she snortingly shook the spray from her bow, to be conscious of the dare-devil defiance of the soul which conducted her on this anomalous cruise. Sailing alone from out a naval port of France, crowded with ships-of-the-line, Paul Jones, in his small craft, went forth in single-armed championship against

94

the English host. Armed with but the sling-stones in his one shot-locker, like young David of old, Paul bearded the British giant of Gath. It is not easy, at the present day, to conceive the hardihood of this enterprise. It was a marching up to the muzzle. The act of one who made no compromise with the cannonadings of danger or death; such a scheme as only could have inspired a heart which held at nothing all the prescribed prudence of war, and every obligation of peace; combining in one breast the vengeful indignation and bitter ambition of an outraged hero, with the uncompunctuous desperation of a renegade. In one view, the Coriolanus of the sea; in another, a cross between the gentleman and the wolf.

As Paul stood on the elevated part of the quarter-deck, with none but his confidential quarter-master near him, he yielded to Israel's natural curiosity, to learn something concerning the sailing of the expedition. Paul stood lightly, swaying his body over the sea, by holding on to the mizzen-shrouds, an attitude not inexpressive of his easy audacity; while near by, pacing a few steps to and fro, his long spy glass now under his arm, and now presented at his eye, Israel, looking the very image of vigilant prudence, listened to the warrior's story. It appeared that on the night of the visit of the Duke de Chartres and Count D'Estaing to Doctor Franklin in Paris—the same night that Captain Paul and Israel were joint occupants of the neighboring chamber—the final sanction of the French king to the sailing of an American armament against England, under the direction of the Colonial Commissioner, was made known to the latter functionary. It was a very ticklish affair. Though swaying on the brink of avowed hostilities with England, no verbal declaration had as yet been made by France. Undoubtedly, this enigmatic position of things was highly advantageous to such an enterprise as Paul's.

Without detailing all the steps taken through the united efforts of Captain Paul and Doctor Franklin, suffice it that the determined rover had now attained his wish; the unfettered command of an armed ship in the British waters; a ship legitimately authorized to hoist the American colors; her commander having in his cabin-locker a regular commission as an officer of the American navy. He sailed without any instructions. With that rare insight into rare natures which so largely distinguished the sagacious Franklin, the sage well knew that a prowling *brave*, like Paul Jones, was, like the prowling lion, by nature a solitary warrior. "Let him alone;" was the wise man's answer to some statesman who sought to hamper Paul with a letter of instructions.

Much subtle casuistry has been expended upon the point, whether Paul

Jones was a knave or a hero, or a union of both. But war and warriors, like politics and politicians, like religion and religionists, admit of no metaphysics.

On the second day after Israel's arrival on board the Ranger, as he and Paul were conversing on the deck, Israel suddenly levelling his glass towards the Irish coast, announced a large sail bound in. The Ranger gave chase, and soon, almost within sight of her destination—the port of Dublin—the stranger was taken, manned, and turned round for Brest.

The Ranger then stood over, passed the Isle of Man towards the Cumberland shore, arriving within remote sight of Whitehaven about sunset. At dark she was hovering off the harbor, with a party of volunteers all ready to descend. But the wind shifted and blew fresh, with a violent sea.

"I won't call on old friends in foul weather," said Captain Paul to Israel. "We'll saunter about a little, and leave our cards in a day or two."

Next morning, in Glentinebay, on the south shore of Scotland, they fell in with a revenue wherry. It was the practice of such craft to board merchant vessels. The Ranger was disguised as a merchantman, presenting a broad drab-colored belt all round her hull; under the coat of a Quaker, concealing the intent of a Turk. It was expected that the chartered rover would come alongside the unchartered one. But the former took to flight, her two lug sails staggering under a heavy wind, which the pursuing guns of the Ranger pelted with a hail-storm of shot. The wherry escaped, spite the severe cannonade.

Off the Mull of Galloway, the day following, Paul found himself so nigh a large barley-freighted Scotch coaster, that, to prevent her carrying tidings of him to land, he dispatched her with the news, stern foremost, to Hades; sinking her, and sowing her barley in the sea, broadcast by a broadside. From her crew he learned that there was a fleet of twenty or thirty sail at anchor in Lochryan, with an armed brigantine. He pointed his prow thither; but at the mouth of the loch, the wind turned against him again, in hard squalls. He abandoned the project. Shortly after, he encountered a sloop from Dublin. He sunk her to prevent intelligence.

Thus, seeming as much to bear the elemental commission of Nature, as the military warrant of Congress, swarthy Paul darted hither and thither; hovering like a thunder-cloud off the crowded harbors; then, beaten off by an adverse wind, discharging his lightnings on uncompanioned vessels, whose solitude made them a more conspicuous and easier mark, like lonely trees on the heath. Yet all this while the land was full of garrisons, the embayed waters full of fleets. With the impunity of a Levanter, Paul skimmed his craft in the land-locked heart of the supreme naval power of earth; a torpedo-eel, unknowingly swallowed by Britain in a draught of old ocean, and making sad havoc with her vitals.

Seeing next a large vessel steering for the Clyde, he gave chase, hoping to cut her off. The stranger proving a fast sailer, the pursuit was urged on with vehemence, Paul standing, plank-proud, on the quarter-deck, calling for pulls upon every rope, to stretch each already half-burst sail to the uttermost.

While thus engaged, suddenly a shadow, like that thrown by an eclipse, was seen rapidly gaining along the deck, with a sharp defined line, plain as a seam of the planks. It involved all before it. It was the domineering shadow of the Juan Fernandez-like Crag of Ailsa. The Ranger was in the deep water which makes all round and close up to this great summit of the submarine Grampians.

The crag, more than a mile in circuit, is over a thousand feet high, eight miles from the Ayrshire shore. There stands the cone, lonely as a foundling, proud as Cheops. But, like the battered brains surmounting the Giant of Gath, its haughty summit is crowned by a desolate castle, in and out of whose arches the aerial mists eddy like purposeless phantoms, thronging the soul of some ruinous genius, who, even in overthrow, harbors none but lofty conceptions.

As the Ranger shot nigher under the crag, its height and bulk dwarfed both pursuer and pursued into nut-shells. The main-truck of the Ranger was nine hundred feet below the foundations of the ruin on the crag's top.

While the ship was yet under the shadow, and each seaman's face shared in the general eclipse, a sudden change came over Paul. He issued no more sultanical orders. He did not look so elate as before. At length he gave the command to discontinue the chase. Turning about, they sailed southward.

"Captain Paul," said Israel, shortly afterwards, "you changed your mind rather queerly about catching that craft. But you thought she was drawing us too far up into the land, I suppose."

"Sink the craft," cried Paul; "it was not any fear of her, nor of King George, which made me turn on my heel; it was yon cock of the walk."

"Cock of the walk?"

"Aye; cock of the walk of the sea; look,—yon Crag of Ailsa."

Chapter 16

They Look in at Carrickfergus, and Descend on Whitehaven

NEXT DAY, off Carrickfergus, on the Irish coast, a fishing boat, allured by the Quaker-like look of the incognito craft, came off in full confidence. Her men were seized, their vessel sunk. From them Paul learned that the large ship at anchor in the road, was the ship-of-war Drake, of twenty guns. Upon this he steered away, resolving to return secretly, and attack her that night.

"Surely, Captain Paul," said Israel to his commander, as about sunset they backed and stood in again for the land, "surely, sir, you are not going right in among them this way? Why not wait till she comes out?"

"Because, Yellow-hair, my boy, I am engaged to marry her to-night. The bride's friends won't like the match; and so, this very night, the bride must be carried away. She has a nice tapering waist, hasn't she, through the glass? Ah! I will clasp her to my heart."

He steered straight in like a friend; under easy sail, lounging towards the Drake, with anchor ready to drop, and grapnels to hug. But the wind was high; the anchor was not dropped at the ordered time. The Ranger came to a stand three biscuits' toss off the unmisgiving enemy's quarter, like a peaceful merchantman from the Canadas, laden with harmless lumber.

"I shan't marry her just yet," whispered Paul, seeing his plans for the time frustrated. Gazing in audacious tranquillity upon the decks of the enemy; and amicably answering her hail, with complete self-possession, he commanded the cable to be slipped, and then, as if he had accidentally parted his anchor, turned his prow on the seaward tack, meaning to return again immediately with the same prospect of advantage possessed at first. His plan being to crash suddenly athwart the Drake's bow, so as to have all her decks exposed point-blank to his musketry. But once more the winds interposed. It came on with a storm of snow; he was obliged to give up his project.

Thus, without any warlike appearance, and giving no alarm, Paul, like an invisible ghost, glided by night close to land, actually came to anchor, for an instant, within speaking-distance of an English ship-of-war; and yet came, anchored, answered hail, reconnoitered, debated, decided, and retired, without exciting the least suspicion. His purpose was chain-shot destruction. So easily may the deadliest foe—so he be but dexterous—slide, undreamed of, into human harbors or hearts. And not awakened conscience, but mere prudence, restrain such, if they vanish again without doing harm. At daybreak no soul in Carrickfergus knew that the devil, in a Scotch bonnet, had passed close that way over night.

Seldom has regicidal daring been more strangely coupled with octogenarian prudence, than in many of the predatory enterprises of Paul. It is this combination of apparent incompatibilities which ranks him among extraordinary warriors.

Ere daylight, the storm of the night blew over. The sun saw the Ranger lying midway over channel at the head of the Irish Sea; England, Scotland, and Ireland, with all their lofty cliffs, being simultaneously as plainly in sight beyond the grass-green waters, as the City Hall, St. Paul's, and the Astor House, from the triangular Park in New York. The three kingdoms lay covered with snow, far as the eye could reach.

"Ah, Yellow-hair," said Paul, with a smile, "they show the white flag, the cravens. And, while the white flag stays blanketing yonder heights, we'll make for Whitehaven, my boy. I promised to drop in there a moment ere quitting the country for good. Israel, lad, I mean to step ashore in person, and have a personal hand in the thing. Did you ever drive spikes?"

"I've driven the spike-teeth into harrows before now," replied Israel; "but that was before I was a sailor."

"Well then, driving spikes into harrows is a good introduction to driving spikes into cannon. You are just the man. Put down your glass; go to the carpenter, get a hundred spikes, put them in a bucket with a hammer, and bring all to me."

As evening fell, the great promontory of St. Bees Head, with its lighthouse, not far from Whitehaven, was in distant sight. But the wind became so light, that Paul could not work his ship in close enough at an hour as early as intended. His purpose had been to make the descent and retire ere break of day. But though this intention was frustrated, he did not renounce his plan, for the present would be his last opportunity.

As the night wore on, and the ship with a very light wind glided nigher and nigher the mark, Paul called upon Israel to produce his bucket for final inspection. Thinking some of the spikes too large, he had them filed down a little. He saw to the lanterns and combustibles. Like Peter the Great, he went into the smallest details, while still possessing a genius competent to plan the aggregate. But oversee as one may, it is impossible to guard against carelessness in subordinates. One's sharp eyes can't see behind one's back. It will yet be noted that an important omission was made in the preparations for Whitehaven.

The town contained, at that period, a population of some six or seven thousand inhabitants, defended by forts.

At midnight, Paul Jones, Israel Potter, and twenty-nine others, rowed in two boats to attack the six or seven thousand inhabitants of Whitehaven. There was a long way to pull. This was done in perfect silence. Not a sound was heard except the oars turning in the rowlocks. Nothing was seen except the two lighthouses of the harbor. Through the stilness and the darkness, the two deep-laden boats swam into the haven, like two mysterious whales from the Arctic Sea. As they reached the outer pier, the men saw each other's faces. The day was dawning. The riggers and other artisans of the shipping would before very long be astir. No matter.

The great staple exported from Whitehaven was then, and still is, coal. The town is surrounded by mines; the town is built on mines; its ships moor over mines. The mines honeycomb the land in all directions, and extend in galleries of grottoes for two miles under the sea. By the falling in of the more ancient collieries, numerous houses have been swallowed, as if by an earthquake; and a consternation spread like that of Lisbon, in 1755. So insecure and treacherous was the site of the place now about to be assailed by a desperado, nursed, like the coal, in its vitals.

Now, sailing on the Thames, nigh its mouth, of fair days, when the wind is favorable for inward bound craft, the stranger will sometimes see processions of vessels, all of similar size and rig, stretching for miles and miles, like a long string of horses tied two and two to a rope and driven to market. These are colliers going to London with coal.

About three hundred of these vessels now lay, all crowded together, in one dense mob, at Whitehaven. The tide was out. They lay completely helpless, clear of water, and grounded. They were sooty in hue. Their black yards were deeply canted, like spears, to avoid collision. The three hundred grimy hulls lay wallowing in the mud, like a herd of hippopotami asleep in the alluvium of the Nile. Their sailless, raking masts, and canted yards, resembled a forest of fish-spears thrust into those same hippopotamus hides. Partly flanking one side of the grounded fleet was a fort, whose batteries v ere raised from the beach. On a little strip of this beach, at the base of the fort, lay a number of small rusty guns, dismounted, heaped together in disorder, as a litter of dogs. Above them projected the mounted cannon.

Paul landed in his own boat at the foot of this fort. He dispatched the other boat to the north side of the haven, with orders to fire the shipping there. Leaving two men at the beach, he then proceeded to get possession of the fort.

"Hold on to the bucket, and give me your shoulder," said he to Israel.

Using Israel for a ladder, in a trice he scaled the wall. The bucket and the men followed. He led the way softly to the guard-house, burst in, and bound the sentinels in their sleep. Then arranging his force, ordered four men to spike the cannon there.

"Now, Israel, your bucket, and follow me to the other fort."

The two went alone about a quarter of a mile.

"Captain Paul," said Israel, on the way, "can we two manage the sentinels?"

"There are none in the fort we go to."

"You know all about the place, captain?"

"Pretty well informed on that subject, I believe. Come along. Yes, lad, I am tolerably well acquainted with Whitehaven. And this morning intend that Whitehaven shall have a slight inkling of *me*. Come on. Here we are."

Scaling the walls, the two involuntarily stood for an instant gazing upon the scene. The gray light of the dawn showed the crowded houses and thronged ships with a haggard distinctness.

"Spike and hammer, lad;—so,—now follow me along, as I go, and give me a spike for every cannon. I'll tongue-tie the thunderers. Speak no more!" and he spiked the first gun. "Be a mute," and he spiked the second. "Dumfounder thee," and he spiked the third. And so, on, and on, and on; Israel following him with the bucket, like a footman, or some charitable gentleman with a basket of alms.

"There, it is done. D'ye see the fire yet, lad, from the north? I don't."

"Not a spark, Captain. But day-sparks come on in the east."

"Forked flames into the hounds! What are they about? Quick, let us back to the first fort; perhaps something has happened, and they are there."

Sure enough, on their return from spiking the cannon Paul and Israel found the other boat back; the crew in confusion; their lantern having burnt out at the very instant they wanted it. By a singular fatality the other lantern, belonging to Paul's boat, was likewise extinguished. No tinder-box had been brought. They had no matches but sulphur matches. Loco-focos were not then known.

The day came on apace.

"Captain Paul," said the lieutenant of the second boat, "it is madness to stay longer. See!" and he pointed to the town, now plainly discernible in the grey light.

"Traitor, or coward!" howled Paul, "how came the lanterns out? Israel, my lion, now prove your blood. Get me a light—but one spark!"

"Has any man here a bit of pipe and tobacco in his pocket?" said Israel.

A sailor quickly produced an old stump of a pipe, with tobacco.

"That will do;" and Israel hurried away towards the town.

"What will the loon do with the pipe?" said one. "And where goes he?" cried another.

"Let him alone," said Paul.

The invader now disposed his whole force so as to retreat at an instant's warning. Meantime, the hardy Israel, long experienced in all sorts of shifts and emergencies, boldly ventured to procure, from some inhabitant of Whitehaven, a spark to kindle all Whitehaven's habitations in flames.

There was a lonely house standing somewhat disjoined from the town; some poor laborer's abode. Rapping at the door, Israel, pipe in mouth, begged the inmates for a light for his tobacco.

"What the devil," roared a voice from within; "knock up a man this time of night, to light your pipe? Begone!"

"You are lazy this morning, my friend," replied Israel; "it is daylight. Quick, give me a light. Don't you know your old friend? Shame! open the door."

In a moment a sleepy fellow appeared, let down the bar, and Israel, stalking into the dim room, piloted himself straight to the fire-place, raked away the cinders, lighted his tobacco, and vanished.

All was done in a flash. The man, stupid with sleep, had looked on bewildered. He reeled to the door; but dodging behind a pile of bricks, Israel had already hurried himself out of sight.

"Well done, my lion," was the hail he received from Paul, who, during his absence, had mustered as many pipes as possible, in order to communicate and multiply the fire.

Both boats now pulled to a favorable point of the principal pier of the harbor, crowded close up to a part of which lay one wing of the colliers.

The men began to murmur at persisting in an attempt impossible to be concealed much longer. They were afraid to venture on board the grim colliers, and go groping down into their hulls to fire them. It seemed like a voluntary entrance into dungeons and death.

"Follow me, all of you but ten by the boats," said Paul, without noticing their murmurs. "And now, to put an end to all future burnings in America, by one mighty conflagration of shipping in England. Come on, lads! Pipes and matches in the van!"

He would have distributed the men so as simultaneously to fire different ships at different points, were it not that the lateness of the hour rendered such a course insanely hazardous. Stationing his party in front of one of the windward colliers, Paul and Israel sprang on board.

In a twinkling, they had broken open a boatswain's locker, and, with great bunches of oakum, fine and dry as tinder, had leaped into the steerage. Here, while Paul made a blaze, Israel ran to collect the tar-pots, which being presently poured on the burning matches, oakum and wood, soon increased the flame.

"It is not a sure thing yet," said Paul, "we must have a barrel of tar."

They searched about until they found one: knocked out the head and bottom, and stood it like a martyr in the midst of the flames. They then retreated up the forward hatchway, while volumes of smoke were belched from the after one. Not till this moment did Paul hear the cries of his men, warning him that the inhabitants were not only actually astir, but crowds were on their way to the pier.

As he sprang out of the smoke towards the rail of the collier, he saw the sun risen, with thousands of the people. Individuals hurried close to the burning vessel. Leaping to the ground, Paul, bidding his men stand fast, ran to their front, and, advancing about thirty feet, presented his own pistol at now tumultuous Whitehaven.

Those who had rushed to extinguish what they had deemed but an accidental fire, were now paralyzed into idiotic inaction at the defiance of the incendiary; thinking him some sudden pirate or fiend dropped down from the moon.

While Paul thus stood guarding the incipient conflagration, Israel, without a weapon, dashed crazily towards the mob on the shore.

"Come back, come back," cried Paul.

"Not till I start these sheep, as their own wolves many a time started me!"

As he rushed bare-headed, like a madman, towards the crowd, the panic spread. They fled from unarmed Israel, further than they had from the pistol of Paul.

The flames now catching the rigging and spiralling around the masts, the whole ship burned at one end of the harbor, while the sun, an hour high, burned at the other. Alarm and amazement, not sleep, now ruled the world. It was time to retreat.

They re-embarked without opposition, first releasing a few prisoners, as the boats could not carry them.

Just as Israel was leaping into the boat, he saw the man at whose house he had procured the fire, staring like a simpleton at him.

"That was good seed you gave me," said Israel, "see what a yield;" pointing to the flames. He then dropped into the boat, leaving only Paul on the pier.

The men cried to their commander, conjuring him not to linger.

But Paul remained for several moments, confronting in silence the clamors of the mob beyond, and waving his solitary hand, like a disdainful tomahawk, towards the surrounding eminences, also covered with the affrighted inhabitants.

When the assailants had rowed pretty well off, the English rushed in great numbers to their forts, but only to find their cannon no better than so much iron in the ore. At length, however, they began to fire, having either brought down some ship's guns, or else mounted the rusty old dogs lying at the foot of the first fort.

In their eagerness they fired with no discretion. The shot fell short; they did not the slightest damage.

Paul's men laughed aloud, and fired their pistols in the air.

Not a splinter was made, not a drop of blood spilled throughout the affair. The intentional harmlessness of the result, as to human life, was only equalled by the desperate courage of the deed. It formed, doubtless, one feature of the compassionate contempt of Paul towards the town, that he took such paternal care of their lives and limbs.

Had it been possible to have landed a few hours earlier, not a ship nor a house could have escaped. But it was the lesson, not the loss, that told. As it was, enough damage had been done to demonstrate—as Paul had declared to the wise man in Paris—that the disasters caused by the wanton fires and assaults on the American coasts, could be easily brought home to the enemy's doors. Though, indeed, if the retaliators were headed by Paul Jones, the satisfaction would not be equal to the insult, being abated by the magnanimity of a chivalrous, however unprincipled a foe.

Chapter 17

*They Call at the Earl of Selkirk's; and Afterwards Fight the
Ship-of-war Drake*

THE Ranger now stood over the Solway Frith for the Scottish shore,
and at noon on the same day, Paul, with twelve men, including
two officers and Israel, landed on St. Mary's Isle, one of the seats of
the Earl of Selkirk.

In three consecutive days this elemental warrior either entered the harbors, or landed on the shores of each of the Three Kingdoms.

The morning was fair and clear. St. Mary's Isle lay shimmering in the
sun. The light crust of snow had melted, revealing the tender grass and
sweet buds of spring mantling the sides of the cliffs.

At once, upon advancing with his party towards the house, Paul augured
ill for his project from the loneliness of the spot. No being was seen. But
cocking his bonnet at a jaunty angle, he continued his way. Stationing the
men silently round about the house, followed by Israel, he announced his
presence at the porch.

A grey-headed domestic at length responded.

"Is the earl within?"

"He is in Edinburgh, sir."

"Ah—sure?—Is your lady within?"

"Yes, sir—who shall I say it is?"

"A gentleman who calls to pay his respects. Here, take my card."

And he handed the man his name, as a private gentleman, superbly engraved at Paris, on gilded paper.

Israel tarried in the hall while the old servant led Paul into a parlor.

Presently the lady appeared.

"Charming Madame, I wish you a very good morning."

"Who may it be, sir, that I have the happiness to see?" said the lady, censoriously drawing herself up at the too frank gallantry of the stranger.

"Madame, I sent you my card."

"Which leaves me equally ignorant, sir," said the lady coldly, twirling the gilded pasteboard.

"A courier dispatched to Whitehaven, charming Madame, might bring you more particular tidings as to who has the honor of being your visitor."

Not comprehending what this meant, and deeply displeased, if not vaguely alarmed at the characteristic manner of Paul, the lady, not entirely unembarrassed, replied, that if the gentleman came to view the isle, he was at liberty so to do. She would retire, and send him a guide.

"Countess of Selkirk," said Paul, advancing a step, "I call to see the earl. On business of urgent importance, I call."

"The earl is in Edinburgh," uneasily responded the lady, again about to retire.

"Do you give me your honor as a lady that it is as you say?"

The lady looked at him in dubious resentment.

"Pardon, Madame; I would not lightly impugn a lady's lightest word; but I surmised that, possibly, you might suspect the object of my call; in which case, it would be the most excusable thing in the world for you to seek to shelter from my knowledge the presence of the earl on the isle."

"I do not dream what you mean by all this," said the lady with decided alarm, yet even in her panic courageously maintaining her dignity, as she retired, rather than retreated, nearer the door.

"Madame," said Paul, hereupon waving his hand imploringly, and then tenderly playing with his bonnet with the golden band, while an expression poetically sad and sentimental stole over his tawny face; "it cannot be too poignantly lamented, that in the profession of arms, the officer of fine feelings and genuine sensibility should be sometimes necessitated to public actions which his own private heart cannot approve. This hard case is mine. The earl, Madame, you say is absent.—I believe those words. Far be it from my soul, enchantress, to ascribe a fault to syllables which have proceeded from so faultless a source."

This probably he said in reference to the lady's mouth, which was beautiful in the extreme.

He bowed very lowly, while the lady eyed him with conflicting and troubled emotions, but as yet all in darkness as to his ultimate meaning. But her more immediate alarm had subsided; seeing now, that the sailor-like extravagance of Paul's homage was entirely unaccompanied with any touch of intentional disrespect. Indeed, hyperbolical as were his phrases, his gestures and whole carriage were most heedfully deferential.

Paul continued: "The earl, Madame, being absent, and he being the sole object of my call, you can not labor under the least apprehension, when I now inform you, that I have the honor of being an officer in the American navy, who, having stopped at this isle to secure the person of the Earl of Selkirk as a hostage for the American cause, am, by your assurances, turned away from that intent; pleased, even in disappointment, since that disappointment has served to prolong my interview with the noble lady before me, as well as to leave her domestic tranquillity unimpaired."

"Can you really speak true?" said the lady in undismayed wonderment.

"Madame, through your window you will catch a little peep of the American colonial ship-of-war, Ranger, which I have the honor to command. With my best respects to your lord, and sincere regrets at not finding him at home, permit me to salute your ladyship's hand and withdraw."

But feigning not to notice this Parisian proposition, and artfully entrenching her hand, without seeming to do so, the lady, in a conciliatory tone, begged her visitor to partake of some refreshment ere he departed, at the same time thanking him for his great civility. But declining these hospitalities, Paul bowed thrice, and quitted the room.

In the hall he encountered Israel, standing all agape before a Highland target of steel, with a claymore and foil crossed on top.

"Looks like a pewter platter and knife and fork, Captain Paul."

"So they do, my lion; but come, curse it, the old cock has flown; fine hen, though, left in the nest; no use; we must away empty-handed."

"Why, ain't Mr. Selkirk in?" demanded Israel in roguish concern.

"Mr. Selkirk? Alexander Selkirk, you mean. No, lad, he's not on the Isle of St. Mary's; he's away off, a hermit, on the Isle of Juan Fernandes—the more's the pity; come."

In the porch they encountered the two officers. Paul briefly informed them of the circumstances; saying, nothing remained but to depart forthwith.

"With nothing at all for our pains?" murmured the two officers.

"What, pray, would you have?"

"Some pillage, to be sure—plate."

"Shame. I thought we were three gentlemen."

"So are the English officers in America; but they help themselves to plate whenever they can get it from the private houses of the enemy."

"Come, now, don't be slanderous," said Paul; "these officers you speak of are but one or two out of twenty, mere burglars and light-fingered gentry, using the king's livery but as a disguise to their nefarious trade. The rest are men of honor."

"Captain Paul Jones," responded the two, "we have not come on this expedition in much expectation of regular pay; but we *did* rely upon honorable plunder."

"Honorable plunder! That's something new."

But the officers were not to be turned aside. They were the most efficient in the ship. Seeing them resolute, Paul, for fear of incensing them, was at last, as a matter of policy, obliged to comply. For himself, however, he resolved to have nothing to do with the affair. Charging the officers not to allow the men to enter the house on any pretence, and that no search must be made, and nothing must be taken away, except what the lady should offer them upon making known their demand, he beckoned to Israel and retired indignantly towards the beach. Upon second thoughts, he dispatched Israel back, to enter the house with the officers, as joint receiver of the plate, he being, of course, the most reliable of the seamen.

The lady was not a little disconcerted on receiving the officers. With cool determination they made known their purpose. There was no escape. The lady retired. The butler came; and soon, several silver salvers, and other articles of value, were silently deposited in the parlor in the presence of the officers and Israel.

"Mister Butler," said Israel, "let me go into the dairy and help to carry the milk-pans."

But, scowling upon this rusticity, or roguishness—he knew not which—the butler, in high dudgeon at Israel's republican familiarity, as well as black as a thunder-cloud with the general insult offered to an illustrious household by a party of armed thieves, as he viewed them, declined any assistance. In a quarter of an hour the officers left the house, carrying their booty.

At the porch they were met by a red-cheeked, spiteful-looking lass, who, with her brave lady's compliments, added two child's rattles of silver and coral to their load.

Now, one of the officers was a Frenchman, the other a Spaniard.

The Spaniard dashed his rattle indignantly to the ground. The Frenchman took his very pleasantly, and kissed it, saying to the girl that he would long preserve the coral, as a memento of her rosy cheeks.

When the party arrived on the beach, they found Captain Paul writing with pencil on paper held up against the smooth tableted side of the cliff. Next moment he seemed to be making his signature. With a reproachful glance towards the two officers, he handed the slip to Israel, bidding him hasten immediately with it to the house and place it in Lady Selkirk's own hands.

The note was as follows:—

"MADAME,—

"After so courteous a reception, I am disturbed to make you no better return than you have just experienced from the actions of certain persons under my command. Actions, lady, which my profession of arms obliges me not only to brook, but, in a measure, to countenance. From the bottom of my heart, my dear lady, I deplore this most melancholy necessity of my delicate position. However unhandsome the desire of these men, some complaisance seemed due them from me, for their general good conduct and bravery on former occasions. I had but an instant to consider. I trust, that in unavoidably gratifying them, I have inflicted less injury on your ladyship's property than I have on my own bleeding sensibilities. But my heart will not allow me to say more. Permit me to assure you, dear lady, that when the plate is sold, I shall, at all hazards, become the purchaser, and will be proud to restore it to you, by such conveyance as you may hereafter see fit to appoint.

"From hence I go, Madame, to engage, to-morrow morning, his majesty's ship Drake, of twenty guns, now lying at Carrickfergus. I should meet the enemy with more than wonted resolution, could I flatter myself that, through this unhandsome conduct on the part of my officers, I lie not under the disesteem of the sweet lady of the Isle of St. Mary's. But unconquerable as Mars should I be, could I but dare to dream, that in some green retreat of her charming domain, the Countess of Selkirk offers up a charitable prayer for, my dear lady countess, one, who coming to take a captive, himself has been captivated.

"Your ladyship's adoring enemy,
"JOHN PAUL JONES."

How the lady received this super-ardent note, history does not relate. But history has not omitted to record, that after the return of the Ranger to

France, through the assiduous efforts of Paul in buying up the booty, piece by piece, from the clutches of those among whom it had been divided, and not without a pecuniary private loss to himself, equal to the total value of the plunder, the plate was punctually restored, even to the silver heads of two pepper-boxes; and, not only this, but the earl, hearing all the particulars, magnanimously wrote Paul a letter, expressing thanks for his politeness. In the opinion of the noble earl, Paul was a man of honor. It were rash to differ in opinion with such high-born authority.

Upon returning to the ship, she was instantly pointed over towards the Irish coast. Next morning Carrickfergus was in sight. Paul would have gone straight in; but Israel, reconnoitering with his glass, informed him that a large ship, probably the Drake, was just coming out.

"What think you, Israel, do they know who we are? Let me have the glass."

"They are dropping a boat now sir," replied Israel, removing the glass from his eye, and handing it to Paul.

"So they are—so they are. They don't know us. I'll decoy that boat alongside. Quick—they are coming for us—take the helm now yourself, my lion, and keep the ship's stern steadily presented towards the advancing boat. Don't let them have the least peep at our broadside."

The boat came on; an officer in its bow all the time eyeing the Ranger through a glass. Presently the boat was within hail.

"Ship ahoy! Who are you?"

"Oh, come alongside," answered Paul through his trumpet, in a rapid off-hand tone, as though he were a gruff sort of friend, impatient at being suspected for a foe.

In a few moments the officer of the boat stepped into the Ranger's gangway. Cocking his bonnet gallantly, Paul advanced towards him, making a very polite bow, saying: "Good morning, sir, good morning; delighted to see you. That's a pretty sword you have; pray, let me look at it."

"I see," said the officer, glancing at the ship's armament, and turning pale. "I am your prisoner."

"No—my guest," responded Paul, winningly. "Pray, let me relieve you of your—your—cane."

Thus humorously he received the officer's delivered sword.

"Now tell me, sir, if you please," he continued; "what brings out his majesty's ship Drake, this fine morning? Going a little airing?"

"She comes out in search of you; but when I left her side half an hour since, she did not know that the ship off the harbor was the one she sought."

"You had news from Whitehaven, I suppose, last night, eh?"

"Aye: express; saying that certain incendiaries had landed there early that morning."

"What?—what sort of men were they, did you say?" said Paul, shaking his bonnet fiercely to one side of his head, and coming close to the officer. "Pardon me," he added derisively, "I had forgot; you are my *guest*. Israel, see the unfortunate gentleman below, and his men forward."

The Drake was now seen slowly coming out under a light air, attended by five small pleasure-vessels, decorated with flags and streamers, and full of gaily-dressed people, whom motives similar to those which draw visitors to the circus, had induced to embark on their adventurous trip. But they little dreamed how nigh the desperate enemy was.

"Drop the captured boat astern," said Paul; "see what effect that will have on those merry voyagers."

No sooner was the empty boat descried by the pleasure-vessels, than forthwith surmising the truth, they with all diligence turned about and re-entered the harbor. Shortly after, alarm-smokes were seen extending along both sides of the channel.

"They smoke us at last, Captain Paul," said Israel.

"There will be more smoke yet before the day is done," replied Paul gravely.

The wind was right under the land; the tide unfavorable. The Drake worked out very slowly.

Meantime, like some fiery-heated duellist calling on urgent business at frosty daybreak, and long kept waiting at the door by the dilatoriness of his antagonist shrinking at the idea of getting up to be cut to pieces in the cold,—the Ranger, with a better breeze, impatiently tacked to and fro in the channel. At last, when the English vessel had fairly weathered the point, Paul, ranging ahead, courteously led her forth, as a beau might a belle in a ball-room—to mid-channel, and then suffered her to come within hail.

"She is hoisting her colors now, sir," said Israel.

"Give her the stars and stripes, then, my lad."

Joyfully running to the locker, Israel attached the flag to the halyards. The wind freshened. He stood elevated. The bright flag blew around him, a glorified shroud, enveloping him in its red ribbons and spangles, like up-springing tongues, and sparkles of flame.

As the colors rose to their final perch, and streamed in the air, Paul eyed them exultingly.

"I first hoisted that flag on an American ship, and was the first among men to get it saluted. If I perish this night, the name of Paul Jones shall live. Hark! they hail us."

"What ship are you?"

"Your enemy. Come on! What wants the fellow of more prefaces and introductions?"

The sun was now calmly setting over the green land of Ireland. The sky was serene; the sea smooth; the wind just sufficient to waft the two vessels steadily and gently. After the first firing, and a little manœuvering, the two ships glided on freely, side by side; in that mild air exchanging their deadly broadsides, like two friendly horsemen walking their steeds along a plain, chatting as they go. After an hour of this running fight, the conversation ended. The Drake struck. How changed from the big craft of sixty short minutes before! She seemed now, above deck, like a piece of wild western woodland into which choppers had been. Her masts and yards prostrate, and hanging in jack-straws; several of her sails ballooning out, as they dragged in the sea, like great lopped tops of foliage. The black hull and shattered stumps of masts, galled and riddled, looked as if gigantic woodpeckers had been tapping them.

The Drake was the larger ship; more cannon; more men. Her loss in killed and wounded was far the greater. Her brave captain and lieutenant were mortally wounded. The former died as the prize was boarded; the latter, two days after.

It was twilight; the weather still serene. No cannonade, nought that mad man can do, molests the stoical imperturbability of nature, when nature chooses to be still. This weather, holding on all through the following day, greatly facilitated the refitting of the ships. That done, the two vessels, sailing round the north of Ireland, steered towards Brest. They were repeatedly chased by English cruisers; but safely reached their anchorage in the French waters.

"A pretty fair four weeks' yachting, gentlemen," said Paul Jones, as the Ranger swung to her cable, while some French officers boarded her. "I bring two travellers with me, gentlemen," he continued. "Allow me to introduce you to my particular friend, Israel Potter, late of North America; and also to his Britannic Majesty's ship, Drake, late of Carrickfergus, Ireland."

This cruise made loud fame for Paul, especially at the court of France, whose king sent Paul a sword and a medal. But poor Israel, who also had conquered a craft, and all unaided too—what had he?

Chapter 18

The Expedition That Sailed from Groix

T HREE MONTHS after anchoring at Brest, through Dr. Franklin's
negotiations with the French king, backed by the bestirring ardor
of Paul, a squadron of nine vessels of various force were ready
in the road of Groix for another descent on the British coasts. These craft
were miscellaneously picked up; their crews a mongrel pack; the officers
mostly French, unacquainted with each other, and secretly jealous of Paul.
The expedition was full of the elements of insubordination and failure.
Much bitterness and agony resulted to a spirit like Paul's. But he bore up;
and though in many particulars the sequel more than warranted his misgiv-
ings, his soul still refused to surrender.

The career of this stubborn adventurer signally illustrates the idea, that
since all human affairs are subject to organic disorder; since they are created
in, and sustained by, a sort of half-disciplined chaos; hence, he who in great
things seeks success, must never wait for smooth water; which never was,
and never will be; but with what straggling method he can, dash with all his
derangements at his object, leaving the rest to Fortune.

Though nominally commander of the squadron, Paul was not so in
effect. Most of his captains conceitedly claimed independent commands.
One of them in the end proved a traitor outright; few of the rest were
reliable.

As for the ships, that commanded by Paul in person will be a good example of the fleet. She was an old Indiaman, clumsy and crank, smelling strongly of the savor of tea, cloves, and arrack, the cargoes of former voyages. Even at that day, she was, from her venerable grotesqueness, what a cocked hat is, at the present age, among ordinary beavers. Her elephantine bulk was houdahed with a castellated poop like the leaning tower of Pisa. Poor Israel, standing on the top of this poop, spy-glass at his eye, looked more an astronomer than a mariner; having to do, not with the mountains of the billows, but the mountains in the moon. Galileo on Fiesole. She was originally a single-decked ship; that is, carried her armament on one gun-deck. But cutting ports below, in her after part, Paul rammed out there six old eighteen pounders, whose rusty muzzles peered just above the water-line, like a parcel of dirty mulattoes from a cellar-way. Her name was the Duras; but, ere sailing, it was changed to that other appellation, whereby this sad old hulk became afterwards immortal. Though it is not unknown, that a compliment to Doctor Franklin was involved in this change of titles, yet the secret history of the affair will now for the first time be disclosed.

It was evening in the road of Groix. After a fagging day's work, trying to conciliate the hostile jealousy of his officers, and provide, in the face of endless obstacles (for he had to dance attendance on scores of intriguing factors and brokers ashore) the requisite stores for the fleet, Paul sat in his cabin in a half despondent reverie; while Israel, cross-legged at his commander's feet, was patching up some old signals.

"Captain Paul, I don't like our ship's name.—Duras? What's that mean?—Duras? Being cribbed up in a ship named Duras! a sort of makes one feel as if he were in durance vile."

"Gad, I never thought of that before, my lion. Duras—Durance vile. I suppose it's superstition, but I'll change it. Come, Yellow-mane, what shall we call her?"

"Well, Captain Paul, don't you like Doctor Franklin? Hasn't he been the prime man to get this fleet together? Let's call her the Doctor Franklin."

"Oh no, that will too publicly declare him just at present; and Poor Richard wants to be a little shady in this business."

"Poor Richard!—call her Poor Richard, then," cried Israel, suddenly struck by the idea.

"Gad, you have it," answered Paul, springing to his feet, as all trace of his former despondency left him;—"Poor Richard shall be the name, in honor to the saying, that 'God helps them that help themselves,' as Poor Richard says."

Now this was the way the craft came to be called the *Bon Homme Richard;* for it being deemed advisable to have a French rendering of the new title, it assumed the above form.

A few days after, the force sailed. Ere long, they captured several vessels; but the captains of the squadron proving refractory, events took so deplorable a turn, that Paul, for the present, was obliged to return to Groix. Luckily however, at this junction a cartel arrived from England with upwards of a hundred exchanged American seamen, who almost to a man enlisted under the flag of Paul.

Upon the resailing of the force, the old troubles broke out afresh. Most of her consorts insubordinately separated from the Bon Homme Richard. At length Paul found himself in violent storms beating off the rugged southeastern coast of Scotland, with only two accompanying ships. But neither the mutiny of his fleet, nor the chaos of the elements, made him falter in his purpose. Nay, at this crisis, he projected the most daring of all his descents.

The Cheviot Hills were in sight. Sundry vessels had been descried bound in for the Firth of Forth, on whose south shore, well up the Firth, stands Leith, the port of Edinburgh, distant but a mile or two from that capital. He resolved to dash at Leith, and lay it under contribution or in ashes. He called the captains of his two remaining consorts on board his own ship to arrange details. Those worthies had much of fastidious remark to make against the plan. After losing much time in trying to bring to a conclusion their sage deliberations, Paul by addressing their cupidity, achieved that which all appeals to their gallantry could not accomplish. He proclaimed the grand prize of the Leith lottery at no less a figure than £200,000; that being named as the ransom. Enough: the three ships entered the Firth, boldly and freely, as if carrying Quakers to a Peace-Congress.

Along both startled shores the panic of their approach spread like the cholera. The three suspicious crafts had so long lain off and on, that none doubted they were led by the audacious viking, Paul Jones. At five o'clock, on the following morning, they were distinctly seen from the capital of Scotland, quietly sailing up the bay. Batteries were hastily thrown up at Leith, arms were obtained from the castle at Edinburgh, alarm fires were kindled in all directions. Yet with such tranquillity of effrontery did Paul conduct his ships, concealing as much as possible their warlike character, that more than once his vessels were mistaken for merchantmen, and hailed by passing ships as such.

In the afternoon, Israel, at his station on the tower of Pisa, reported a boat with five men coming off to the Richard from the coast of Fife.

"They have hot oat-cakes for us," said Paul, "let 'em come. To encourage them, show them the English ensign, Israel, my lad."

Soon the boat was alongside.

"Well, my good fellows, what can I do for you this afternoon?" said Paul, leaning over the side with a patronizing air.

"Why, captain, we come from the Laird of Crokarky, who wants some powder and ball for his money."

"What would you with powder and ball, pray?"

"Oh! haven't you heard that that bloody pirate, Paul Jones, is somewhere hanging round the coasts?"

"Aye, indeed, but he won't hurt you. He's only going round among the nations, with his old hat, taking up contributions. So, away with ye; ye don't want any powder and ball to give him. He wants contributions of silver, not lead. Prepare yourselves with silver, I say."

"Nay, captain, the Laird ordered us not to return without powder and ball. See, here is the price. It may be the taking of the bloody pirate, if you let us have what we want."

"Well, pass 'em over a keg," said Paul laughing, but modifying his order by a sly whisper to Israel; "Oh, put up your price, it's a gift to ye."

"But ball, captain, what's the use of powder without ball?" roared one of the fellows from the boat's bow, as the keg was lowered in. "We want ball."

"Bless my soul, you bawl loud enough as it is. Away with ye, with what you have. Look to your keg, and hark ye, if ye catch that villain, Paul Jones, give him no quarter."

"But, captain, here," shouted one of the boatmen, "There's a mistake. This is a keg of pickles, not powder. Look," and poking into the bung-hole, he dragged out a green cucumber dripping with brine. "Take this back, and give us the powder."

"Pooh," said Paul, "the powder is at the bottom, pickled powder, best way to keep it. Away with ye, now, and after that bloody embezzler, Paul Jones."

This was Sunday. The ships held on. During the afternoon, a long tack of the Richard brought her close towards the shores of Fife, near the thriving little port of Kirkaldy.

"There's a great crowd on the beach, captain Paul," said Israel, looking through his glass. "There seems to be an old woman standing on a fish-barrel there, a sort of selling things at auction, to the people, but I can't be certain yet."

"Let me see," said Paul, taking the glass as they came nigher. "Sure enough, it's an old lady—an old quack-doctress, seems to me, in a black gown, too. I must hail her."

Ordering the ship to be kept on towards the port, he shortened sail within easy distance, so as to glide slowly by, and seizing the trumpet, thus spoke:—

"Old lady, ahoy! What are you talking about? What's your text?"

"The righteous shall rejoice when he seeth the vengeance. He shall wash his feet in the blood of the wicked."

"Ah, what a lack of charity. Now hear mine;—God helpeth them that help themselves, as Poor Richard says."

"Reprobate pirate, a gale shall yet come, to drive thee in wrecks from our waters."

"The strong wind of your hate fills my sails well. Adieu," waving his bonnet—"tell us the rest at Leith."

Next morning the ships were almost within cannon-shot of the town. The men to be landed were in the boats. Israel had the tiller of the foremost one, waiting for his commander to enter, when just as Paul's foot was on the gangway, a sudden squall struck all three ships, dashing the boats against them, and creating indiscribable confusion. The squall ended in a violent gale. Getting his men on board with all dispatch, Paul essayed his best to withstand the fury of the wind; but it blew adversely, and with redoubled power. A ship at a distance went down beneath it. The disappointed invader was obliged to turn before the gale, and renounce his project.

To this hour, on the shores of the Firth of Forth, it is the popular persuasion, that the Rev. Mr. Shirra's, of Kirkaldy, powerful intercession, was the direct cause of the elemental repulse experienced off the endangered harbor of Leith.

Through the ill qualities of Paul's associate captains: their timidity, incapable of keeping pace with his daring; their jealousy, blind to his superiority to rivalship—together with the general reduction of his force, now reduced, by desertion, from nine to three ships; and last of all, the enmity of seas and winds, the invader, driven, not by a fleet, but a gale, out of the Scottish waters, had the mortification in prospect of terminating a cruise, so formidable in appearance at the onset, without one added deed to sustain the reputation gained by former exploits. Nevertheless, he was not disheartened. He sought to conciliate fortune, not by despondency, but by resolution. And, as if won by his confident bearing, that fickle power suddenly went over to him from the ranks of the enemy, suddenly as plumed Marshal Ney to the stubborn standard of Napoleon from Elba, marching regenerated on Paris. In a word, luck—that's the word—shortly threw in Paul's way the great action of his life: the most extraordinary of all naval engagements; the unparalleled death-lock with the Serapis.

Chapter 19

They Fight the Serapis

THE BATTLE between the Bon Homme Richard and the Serapis stands in history as the first signal collision on the sea between the Englishman and the American. For obstinacy, mutual hatred, and courage, it is without precedent or subsequent in the story of ocean. The strife long hung undetermined, but the English flag struck in the end.

There would seem to be something singularly indicatory in this engagement. It may involve at once a type, a parallel, and a prophecy. Sharing the same blood with England, and yet her proved foe in two wars; not wholly inclined at bottom to forget an old grudge: intrepid, unprincipled, reckless, predatory, with boundless ambition, civilized in externals but a savage at heart, America is, or may yet be, the Paul Jones of nations.

Regarded in this indicatory light, the battle between the Bon Homme Richard and the Serapis—in itself so curious—may well enlist our interest.

Never was there a fight so snarled. The intricacy of those incidents which defy the narrator's extrication, is not ill figured in that bewildering intertanglement of all the yards and anchors of the two ships, which confounded them for the time in one chaos of devastation.

Elsewhere than here the reader must go who seeks an elaborate version of the fight, or, indeed, much of any regular account of it whatever. The writer is but brought to mention the battle, because he must needs follow, in all events, the fortunes of the humble adventurer whose life he records. Yet this necessarily involves some general view of each conspicuous incident in which he shares.

Several circumstances of the place and time served to invest the fight with a certain scenic atmosphere, casting a light almost poetic over the wild gloom of its tragic results. The battle was fought between the hours of seven and ten at night; the height of it was under a full harvest moon, in view of thousands of distant spectators crowding the high cliffs of Yorkshire.

From the Tees to the Humber, the eastern coast of Britain, for the most part, wears a savage, melancholy, and Calabrian aspect. It is in course of incessant decay. Every year the isle which repulses nearly all other foes, succumbs to the Attila assaults of the deep. Here and there the base of the cliffs is strewn with masses of rock, undermined by the waves, and tumbled headlong below; where, sometimes, the water completely surrounds them, showing in shattered confusion detached rocks, pyramids, and obelisks, rising half-revealed from the surf,—the Tadmores of the wasteful desert of the sea. Nowhere is this desolation more marked than for those fifty miles of coast between Flamborough Head and the Spurn.

Weathering out the gale which had driven them from Leith, Paul's ships, for a few days, were employed in giving chase to various merchantmen and colliers; capturing some, sinking others, and putting the rest to flight. Off the mouth of the Humber they ineffectually manœuvered with a view of drawing out a king's frigate, reported to be lying at anchor within. At another time a large fleet was encountered, under convoy of some ships of force. But their panic caused the fleet to hug the edge of perilous shoals very nigh the land, where, by reason of his having no competent pilot, Paul durst not approach to molest them. The same night he saw two strangers further out at sea, and chased them until three in the morning; when, getting pretty nigh, he surmised that they must needs be vessels of his own squadron, which, previous to his entering the Firth of Forth, had separated from his command. Daylight proved this supposition correct. Five vessels of the original squadron were now once more in company. About noon, a fleet of forty merchantmen appeared coming round Flamborough Head, protected by two English men-of-war, the Serapis and Countess of Scarborough. Descrying the five cruisers sailing down, the forty sail, like forty chickens, fluttered in a panic under the wing of the shore. Their armed protectors bravely steered from the land, making the disposition for battle. Promptly accepting the challenge, Paul, giving the signal to his consorts, earnestly pressed forward. But, earnest as he was, it was seven in the evening ere the

encounter began. Meantime his comrades, heedless of his signals, sailed
independently along. Dismissing them from present consideration, we
confine ourselves, for a while to the Richard and the Serapis, the grand
duellists of the fight.

The Richard carried a motley crew, to keep whom in order one hundred
and thirty-five soldiers—themselves a hybrid band—had been put on board,
commanded by French officers of inferior rank. Her armament was similarly heterogeneous; guns of all sorts and calibres; but about equal on the
whole to those of a thirty-two gun frigate. The spirit of baneful intermix-
ture pervaded this craft throughout.

The Serapis was a frigate of fifty guns, more than half of which individually exceeded in calibre any one gun of the Richard. She had a crew of
some three hundred and twenty trained man-of-war's men.

There is something in a naval engagement which radically distinguishes
it from one on the land. The ocean, at times, has what is called its *sea* and its
trough of the sea; but it has neither rivers, woods, banks, towns, nor mountains. In mild weather, it is one hammered plain. Stratagems,—like those of
disciplined armies, ambuscades—like those of Indians, are impossible. All is
clear, open, fluent. The very element which sustains the combatants, yields
at the stroke of a feather. One wind and one tide at one time operate upon all
who here engage. This simplicity renders a battle between two men-of-war,
with their huge white wings, more akin to the Miltonic contests of arch-
angels than to *the comparatively squalid* tussels of earth.

As the ships neared, a hazy darkness overspread the water. The moon
was not yet risen. Objects were perceived with difficulty. Borne by a soft
moist breeze over gentle waves, they came within pistol-shot. Owing to the
obscurity, and the known neighborhood of other vessels, the Serapis was
uncertain who the Richard was. Through the dim mist each ship loomed
forth to the other vast, but indistinct, as the ghost of Morven. Sounds of the
trampling of resolute men echoed from either hull, whose tight decks dully
resounded like drum-heads in a funeral march.

The Serapis hailed. She was answered by a broadside. For half an hour
the combatants deliberately manœuvered, continually changing their position, but always within shot fire. The Serapis—the better sailer of the
two—kept critically circling the Richard, making lounging advances now
and then, and as suddenly steering off; hate causing her to act not unlike a
wheeling cock about a hen, when stirred by the contrary passion. Meantime, though within easy speaking distance, no further syllable was exchanged; but an incessant cannonade was kept up.

At this point, a third party, the Scarborough, drew near, seemingly desirous of giving assistance to her consort. But thick smoke was now added to the night's natural obscurity. The Scarborough imperfectly discerned two ships, and plainly saw the common fire they made; but which was which, she could not tell. Eager to befriend the Serapis, she durst not fire a gun, lest she might unwittingly act the part of a foe. As when a hawk and a crow are clawing and beaking high in the air, a second crow flying near, will seek to join the battle, but finding no fair chance to engage, at last flies away to the woods; just so did the Scarborough now. Prudence dictated the step. Because several chance shot—from which of the combatants could not be known—had already struck the Scarborough. So, unwilling uselessly to expose herself, off went for the present this baffled and ineffectual friend.

Not long after, an invisible hand came and set down a great yellow lamp in the east. The hand reached up unseen from below the horizon, and set the lamp down right on the rim of the horizon, as on a threshold; as much as to say, Gentlemen warriors, permit me a little to light up this rather gloomy looking subject. The lamp was the round harvest moon; the one solitary foot-light of the scene. But scarcely did the rays from the lamp pierce that languid haze. Objects before perceived with difficulty, now glimmered ambiguously. Bedded in strange vapors, the great foot-light cast a dubious half demoniac glare across the waters, like the phantasmagoric stream sent athwart a London flagging in a night-rain from an apothecary's blue and green window. Through this sardonical mist, the face of the Man-in-the-Moon—looking right towards the combatants, as if he were standing in a trap-door of the sea, leaning forward leisurely with his arms complacently folded over upon the edge of the horizon,—this queer face wore a serious, apishly self-satisfied leer, as if the Man-in-the-Moon had somehow secretly put up the ships to their contest, and in the depths of his malignant old soul was not unpleased to see how well his charms worked. There stood the grinning Man-in-the-Moon, his head just dodging into view over the rim of the sea:—Mephistopheles prompter of the stage.

Aided now a little by the planet, one of the consorts of the Richard, the Pallas, hovering far outside the fight, dimly discerned the suspicious form of a lonely vessel unknown to her. She resolved to engage it, if it proved a foe. But ere they joined, the unknown ship—which proved to be the Scarborough—received a broadside at long gun's distance from another consort of the Richard, the Alliance. The shot whizzed across the broad interval like shuttlecocks across a great hall. Presently the battledores of both batteries were at work, and rapid compliments of shuttlecocks were very promptly exchanged. The adverse consorts of the two main belligerents fought with all the rage of those fiery seconds who in some desperate duels, make their principal's quarrel their own. Diverted from the Richard and the Serapis by this little by-play, the Man-in-the-Moon, all eager to see what it was, somewhat raised himself from his trap-door with an added grin on his face. By this time, off sneaked the Alliance, and down swept the Pallas, at close quarters engaging the Scarborough; an encounter destined in less than an hour to end in the latter ship's striking her flag.

Compared to the Serapis and the Richard, the Pallas and the Scarborough were as two pages to two knights. In their immature way they showed the same traits as their fully developed superiors.

The Man-in-the-Moon now raised himself still higher to obtain a better view of affairs.

But the Man-in-the-Moon was not the only spectator. From the high cliffs of the shore, and especially from the great promontory of Flamborough Head, the scene was witnessed by crowds of the islanders. Any rustic might be pardoned his curiosity in view of the spectacle presented. Far in the indistinct distance fleets of frightened merchantmen filled the lower air with their sails, as flakes of snow in a snow-storm by night. Hovering undeterminedly, in another direction, were several of the scattered consorts of Paul, taking no part in the fray. Nearer, was an isolated mist, investing the Pallas and Scarborough—a mist slowly adrift on the sea, like a floating isle, and at intervals irradiated with sparkles of fire and resonant with the boom of cannon. Further away, in the deeper water, was a lurid cloud, incessantly torn in shreds of lightning, then fusing together again, once more to be rent. As yet this lurid cloud was neither stationary nor slowly adrift, like the first mentioned one; but, instinct with chaotic vitality, shifted hither and thither, foaming with fire, like a valiant water-spout careering off the coast of Malabar.

To get some idea of the events enacting in that cloud, it will be necessary to enter it; to go and possess it, as a ghost may rush into a body, or the devils into the swine, which running down the steep place perished in the sea; just as the Richard is yet to do.

Thus far the Serapis and the Richard had been manœuvering and chasseing to each other like partners in a cotillon, all the time indulging in rapid repartee.

But finding at last that the superior managableness of the enemy's ship enabled him to get the better of the clumsy old Indiaman, the Richard, in taking position; Paul, with his wonted resolution, at once sought to neutralize this, by hugging him close. But the attempt to lay the Richard right across the head of the Serapis ended quite otherwise, in sending the enemy's jib-boom just over the Richard's great tower of Pisa, where Israel was stationed; who catching it eagerly, stood for an instant holding to the slack of the sail, like one grasping a horse by the mane prior to vaulting into the saddle.

"Aye, hold hard, lad," cried Paul, springing to his side with a coil of rigging. With a few rapid turns he knitted himself to his foe. The wind now acting on the sails of the Serapis forced her, heel and point, her entire length, cheek by jowl, alongside the Richard. The projecting cannon scraped; the yards interlocked; but the hulls did not touch. A long lane of darkling water lay wedged between, like that narrow canal in Venice which dozes between two shadowy piles, and high in air is secretly crossed by the Bridge of Sighs. But where the six yard-arms reciprocally arched overhead, three bridges of sighs were both seen and heard, as the moon and wind kept rising.

Into that Lethean canal,—pond-like in its smoothness as compared with the sea without—fell many a poor soul that night;—fell, for ever forgotten.

As some heaving rent coinciding with a disputed frontier on a volcanic plain, that boundary abyss was the jaws of death to both sides. So contracted was it, that in many cases the gun-rammers had to be thrust into the opposite ports, in order to enter to muzzles of their own cannon. It seemed more an intestine feud, than a fight between strangers. Or, rather, it was as if the Siamese Twins, oblivious of their fraternal bond, should rage in unnatural fight.

Ere long, a horrible explosion was heard, drowning for the instant the cannonade. Two of the old eighteen-pounders—before spoken of, as having been hurriedly set up below the main deck of the Richard—burst all to pieces, killing the sailors who worked them, and shattering all that part of the hull, as if two exploded steam-boilers had shot out of its opposite sides. The effect was like the fall of the walls of a house. Little now upheld the great tower of Pisa but a few naked crow stanchions. Thenceforth, not a few balls from the Serapis must have passed straight through the Richard without grazing her. It was like firing buck-shot through the ribs of a skeleton.

But, further forward, so deadly was the broadside from the heavy batteries of the Serapis,—levelled point-blank, and right down the throat and bowels, as it were, of the Richard—that it cleared everything before it. The men on the Richard's covered gun-deck ran above, like miners from the fire-damp. Collecting on the forecastle, they continued to fight with grenades and muskets. The soldiers also were in the lofty tops, whence they kept up incessant volleys, cascading their fire down as pouring lava from cliffs.

The position of the men in the two ships was now exactly reversed. For while the Serapis was tearing the Richard all to pieces below deck, and had swept that covered part almost of the last man; the Richard's crowd of musketry had complete control of the upper deck of the Serapis, where it was almost impossible for a man to remain unless as a corpse. Though in the beginning, the tops of the Serapis had not been unsupplied with marksmen, yet they had long since been cleared by the overmastering musketry of the Richard. Several, with leg or arm broken by a ball, had been seen going dimly downward from their giddy perch, like falling pigeons shot on the wing.

As busy swallows about barn-eaves and ridge-poles, some of the Richard's marksmen quitting their tops, now went far out on their yard-arms, where they overhung the Serapis. From thence they dropped hand-grenades upon her decks, like apples, which growing in one field fall over the fence into another. Others of their band flung the same sour fruit into the open ports of the Serapis. A hail-storm of aerial combustion descended and slanted on the Serapis, while horizontal thunder-bolts rolled crosswise through the subterranean vaults of the Richard. The belligerents were no longer, in the ordinary sense of things, an English ship, and an American ship. It was a co-partnership and joint-stock combustion-company of both ships; yet divided, even in participation. The two vessels were as two houses, through whose party-wall doors have been cut; one family (the Guelphs) occupying the whole lower story; another family (the Ghibelines) the whole upper story.

Meanwhile determined Paul flew hither and thither like the meteoric corposant-ball, which shiftingly dances on the tips and verges of ships' rigging in storms. Wherever he went, he seemed to cast a pale light on all faces. Blacked and burnt, his Scotch bonnet was compressed to a gun-wad on his head. His Parisian coat, with its gold-laced sleeve laid aside, disclosed to the full the blue tatooing on his arm, which sometimes in fierce gestures streamed in the haze of the cannonade, cabalistically terrific as the charmed standard of Satan. Yet his frenzied manner was less a testimony of his internal commotion than intended to inspirit and madden his men, some of whom seeing him, in transports of intrepidity stripped themselves to their trowsers, exposing their naked bodies to the as naked shot. The same was done on the Serapis, where several guns were seen surrounded by their buff crews as by fauns and satyrs.

At the beginning of the fray, before the ships interlocked, in the intervals of smoke which swept over the ships as mist over mountain-tops, affording open rents here and there—the gun-deck of the Serapis, at certain points, showed, congealed for the instant in all attitudes of dauntlessness, a gallery of marble statues—fighting gladiators.

Stooping low and intent, with one braced leg thrust behind, and one arm thrust forward, curling round towards the muzzle of the gun:—there was seen the *loader*, performing his allotted part; on the other side of the carriage, in the same stooping posture, but with both hands holding his long black pole, pike-wise, ready for instant use—stood the eager *rammer and sponger;* while at the breech, crouched the wary *captain of the gun*, his keen eye, like the watching leopard's, burning along the range; and behind, all tall and erect, the Egyptian symbol of death, stood the *matchman*, immovable for the moment, his long-handled match reversed. Up to their two long death-dealing batteries, the trained men of the Serapis stood and toiled in mechanical magic of discipline. They tended those rows of guns, as Lowell girls the rows of looms in a cotton factory. The Parcæ were not more methodical; Atropos not more fatal; the automaton chess-player not more irresponsible.

"Look, lad; I want a grenade, now, thrown down their main hatch-way. I saw long piles of cartridges there. The powder monkeys have brought them up faster than they can be used. Take a bucket of combustibles, and let's hear from you presently."

These words were spoken by Paul to Israel. Israel did as ordered. In a few minutes, bucket in hand, begrimed with powder, sixty-feet in air, he hung like Apollyon from the extreme tip of the yard over the fated abyss of the hatchway. As he looked down between the eddies of smoke into that slaughterous pit, it was like looking from the verge of a cataract down into the yeasty pool at its base. Watching his chance, he dropped one grenade with such faultless precision, that, striking its mark, an explosion rent the Serapis like a volcano. The long row of heaped cartridges was ignited. The fire ran horizontally, like an express on a railway. More than twenty men were instantly killed: nearly forty wounded. This blow restored the chances of battle, before in favor of the Serapis.

But the drooping spirits of the English were suddenly revived, by an event which crowned the scene by an act on the part of one of the consorts of the Richard, the incredible atrocity of which, has induced all humane minds to impute it rather to some incomprehensible mistake, than to the malignant madness of the perpetrator.

The cautious approach and retreat of a consort of the Serapis, the Scarborough, before the moon rose, has already been mentioned. It is now to be related how that, when the moon was more than an hour high, a consort of the Richard, the Alliance, likewise approached and retreated. This ship, commanded by a Frenchman, infamous in his own navy, and obnoxious in the service to which he at present belonged; this ship, foremost in insurgency to Paul hitherto, and which, for the most part had crept like a poltroon from the fray; the Alliance now was at hand. Seeing her, Paul deemed the battle at an end. But to his horror, the Alliance threw a broadside full into the stern of the Richard, without touching the Serapis. Paul called to her, for God's sake to forbear destroying the Richard. The reply was, a second, a third, a fourth broadside; striking the Richard ahead, astern, and amidships. One of the volleys killed several men and one officer. Meantime, like carpenters' augurs, and the sea-worm called remora, the guns of the Serapis were drilling away at the same doomed hull. After performing her nameless exploit, the Alliance sailed away, and did no more. She was like the great fire of London, breaking out on the heel of the great Plague. By this time, the Richard had received so many shot-holes low down in her hull, that like a sieve she began to settle.

"Do you strike?" cried the English captain.

"I have not yet begun to fight," howled sinking Paul.

This summons and response were whirled on eddies of smoke and flame. Both vessels were now on fire. The men of either knew hardly which to do; strive to destroy the enemy, or save themselves. In the midst of this, one hundred human beings, hitherto invisible strangers, were suddenly added to the rest. Five score English prisoners, till now confined in the Richard's hold, liberated in his consternation, by the master at arms, burst up the hatchways. One of them, the captain of a letter of marque, captured by Paul, off the Scottish coast, crawled through a port, as a burglar through a window, from the one ship to the other, and reported affairs to the English captain.

While Paul and his lieutenants were confronting these prisoners, the gunner, running up from below, and not perceiving his official superiors, and deeming them dead; believing himself now left sole surviving officer, ran to the tower of Pisa to haul down the colors. But they were already shot down and trailing in the water astern, like a sailor's towing shirt. Seeing the gunner there, groping about in the smoke, Israel asked what he wanted.

At this moment, the gunner, rushing to the rail, shouted "quarter! quarter!" to the Serapis.

"I'll quarter ye," yelled Israel, smiting the gunner with the flat of his cutlass.

"Do you strike?" now came from the Serapis.

"Aye, aye, aye!" involuntarily cried Israel, fetching the gunner a shower of blows.

"Do you strike?" again was repeated from the Serapis; whose captain, judging from the augmented confusion on board the Richard, owing to the escape of the prisoners, and also influenced by the report made to him by his late guest of the port-hole, doubted not that the enemy must needs be about surrendering.

"Do you strike?"

"Aye!—I strike *back*," roared Paul, for the first time now hearing the summons.

But judging this frantic response to come, like the others, from some unauthorized source, the English captain directed his boarders to be called; some of whom presently leaped on the Richard's rail; but, throwing out his tatooed arm at them with a sabre at the end of it, Paul showed them how boarders repelled boarders. The English retreated; but not before they had been thinned out again, like spring radishes, by the unfaltering fire from the Richard's tops.

An officer of the Richard, seeing the mass of prisoners delirious with sudden liberty and fright, pricked them with his sword to the pumps; thus keeping the ship afloat by the very blunder which had promised to have been fatal. The vessels now blazed so in the rigging, that both parties desisted from hostilities to subdue the common foe.

When some faint order was again restored upon the Richard, her chances of victory increased, while those of the English, driven under cover, proportionably waned. Early in the contest, Paul, with his own hand, had brought one of his largest guns to bear against the enemy's main-mast. That shot had hit. The mast now plainly tottered. Nevertheless, it seemed as if, in this fight, neither party could be victor. Mutual obliteration from the face of the waters seemed the only natural sequel to hostilities like these. It is, therefore, honor to him as a man, and not reproach to him as an officer, that, to stay such carnage, Captain Pearson, of the Serapis, with his own hands hauled down his colors. But just as an officer from the Richard swung himself on board the Serapis, and accosted the English captain, the first lieutenant of the Serapis came up from below inquiring whether the Richard had struck, since her fire had ceased.

So equal was the conflict that, even after the surrender, it could be, and was, a question to one of the warriors engaged (who had not happened to see the English flag hauled down) whether the Serapis had struck to the Richard, or the Richard to the Serapis. Nay, while the Richard's officer was

still amicably conversing with the English captain, a midshipman of the
Richard, in act of following his superior on board the surrendered vessel,
was run through the thigh by a pike in the hand of an ignorant boarder of
the Serapis. While equally ignorant, the cannons below deck were still thun-
dering away at the nominal conqueror from the batteries of the nominally
conquered ship.

But though the Serapis had submitted, there were two misanthropical
foes on board the Richard which would not so easily succumb,—fire and
water. All night the victors were engaged in suppressing the flames. Not
until daylight were the flames got under; but though the pumps were kept
continually going, the water in the hold still gained. A few hours after
sunrise the Richard was deserted for the Serapis and the other vessels of the
squadron of Paul. About ten o'clock, the Richard, gorged with slaughter,
wallowed heavily, gave a long roll, and blasted by tornadoes of sulphur,
slowly sunk, like Gomorrah, out of sight.

The loss of life in the two ships was about equal; one-half of the total
number of those engaged being either killed or wounded.

In view of this battle one may well ask—What separates the enlightened
man from the savage? Is civilization a thing distinct, or is it an advanced
stage of barbarism?

Chapter 20

The Shuttle

FOR A TIME BACK, across the otherwise blue-jean career of Israel, Paul Jones flits and re-flits like a crimson thread. One more brief intermingling of it, and to the plain old homespun we return.

The battle won, the squadron started for the Texel, where they arrived in safety. Omitting all mention of intervening harassments, suffice it, that after some months of inaction as to anything of a warlike nature, Paul and Israel (both from different motives, eager to return to America), sailed for that country in the armed ship Ariel; Paul as commander, Israel as quarter-master.

Two weeks out, they encountered by night, a frigate-like craft, supposed to be an enemy. The vessels came within hail, both showing English colors, with purposes of mutual deception, affecting to belong to the English navy. For an hour, through their speaking trumpets, the captains equivocally conversed. A very reserved, adroit, hoodwinking, statesman-like conversation, indeed. At last, professing some little incredulity as to the truthfulness of the stranger's statement, Paul intimated a desire that he should put out a boat and come on board to show his commission, to which the stranger very affably replied, that unfortunately his boat was exceedingly leaky. With equal politeness, Paul begged him to consider the danger attending a refusal, which rejoinder nettled the other, who suddenly retorted that he would answer for twenty guns, and that both himself and men were knock-down Englishmen. Upon this, Paul said that he would allow him exactly five minutes for a sober, second thought. That brief period passed, Paul, hoisting the American colors, ran close under the other ship's stern, and engaged her. It was about eight o'clock at night, that this strange quarrel was picked in the middle of the ocean. Why cannot men be peaceable on that great common? Or does nature in those fierce night-brawlers, the billows, set mankind but a sorry example?

After ten minutes' cannonading, the stranger struck, shouting out, that half his men were killed. The Ariel's crew hurraed. Boarders were called to take possession. At this juncture, the prize shifting her position so that she headed away, and to leeward of the Ariel, thrust her long spanker boom diagonally over the latter's quarter; when Israel, who was standing close by, instinctively caught hold of it—just as he had grasped the jib-boom of the Serapis—and, at the same moment, hearing the call to take possession, in the valiant excitement of the occasion, he leaped upon the spar, and made a rush for the stranger's deck, thinking, of course, that he would be immediately followed by the regular boarders. But the sails of the strange ship suddenly filled; she began to glide through the sea; her spanker-boom, not having at all entangled itself, offering no hindrance. Israel clinging midway along the boom, soon found himself divided from the Ariel, by a space impossible to be leaped. Meantime, suspecting foul play, Paul set every sail; but the stranger, having already the advantage, contrived to make good her escape, though perseveringly chased by the cheated conqueror.

In the confusion, no eye had observed our hero's spring. But, as the vessels separated more, an officer of the strange ship spying a man on the boom, and taking him for one of his own men, demanded what he did there.

"Clearing the signal halyards, sir," replied Israel, fumbling with the cord which happened to be dangling near by.

"Well, bear a hand and come in, or you will have a bow-chaser at you soon," referring to the bow guns of the Ariel.

"Aye, aye, sir," said Israel, and in a moment he sprang to the deck, and soon found himself mixed in among some two hundred English sailors of a large letter of marque. At once he perceived that the story of half the crew being killed was a mere hoax, played off for the sake of making an escape. Orders were continually being given to pull on this and that rope, as the ship crowded all sail in flight. To these orders Israel with the rest promptly responded, pulling at the rigging stoutly as the best of them; though heaven knows his heart sank deeper and deeper at every pull which thus helped once again to widen the gulf between him and home.

In intervals, he considered with himself what to do. Favored by the obscurity of the night and the number of the crew, and wearing much the same dress as theirs, it was very easy to pass himself off for one of them till morning. But daylight would be sure to expose him, unless some cunning plan could be hit upon. If discovered for what he was, nothing short of a prison awaited him upon the ship's arrival in port.

It was a desperate case; only as desperate a remedy could serve. One thing was sure, he could not hide. Some audacious parade of himself promised the only hope. Marking that the sailors, not being of the regular navy, wore no uniform; and perceiving that his jacket was the only garment on him which bore any distinguishing badge, our adventurer took it off, and privily dropped it overboard, remaining now in his dark blue woollen shirt, and blue cloth waistcoat.

What the more inspirited Israel to the added step now contemplated, was the circumstance, that the ship was not a Frenchman, or other foreigner, but her crew, though enemies, spoke the same language that he did.

So very quietly, at last, he goes aloft into the main-top, and sitting down on an old sail there, beside some eight or ten topmen, in an off-handed way asks one for tobacco.

"Give us a quid, lad," as he settled himself in his seat.

"Halloo," said the strange sailor, "who be you? Get out of the top! The fore and mizzen-top men won't let us go into their tops, and blame me if we'll let any of their gangs come here. So, away ye go."

"You're blind, or crazy, old boy," rejoined Israel. "I'm a top-mate; ain't I, lads?" appealing to the rest.

"There's only ten main-topmen belonging to our watch; if you are one, then there'll be eleven," said a second sailor. "Get out of the top!"

"This is too bad, maties," cried Israel, "to serve an old top-mate this way. Come, come, you are foolish. Give us a quid." And, once more, with the utmost sociability, he addressed the sailor next to him.

"Look ye," returned the other, "if you don't make away with yourself, you skulking spy from the mizzen, we'll drop you to deck like a jewel-block."

Seeing the party thus resolute, Israel, with some affected banter, descended.

The reason why he had tried the scheme—and, spite of the foregoing failure, meant to repeat it—was this: As customary in armed ships, the men were in companies, allotted to particular places and functions. Therefore, to escape final detection, Israel must some way get himself recognized as belonging to some one of those bands; otherwise, as an isolated nondescript,

discovery ere long would be certain; especially upon the next general mus-
ter. To be sure, the hope in question was a forlorn sort of hope; but it was
his sole one, and must therefore be tried.

Mixing in again for a while with the general watch, he at last goes on the
forecastle among the sheet-anchor-men there, at present engaged in critically discussing the merits of the late valiant encounter, and expressing their
opinion that by daybreak the enemy in chase would be hull-down out of
sight.

"To be sure she will," cried Israel, joining in with the group, "old
ballyhoo that she is, to be sure. But didn't we pepper her, lads? Give us a
chew of tobacco, one of ye? How many have we wounded, do ye know?
None killed that I've heard of. Wasn't that a fine hoax we played on 'em?
Ha! ha! But give us a chew."

In the prodigal fraternal patriotism of the moment, one of the old worthies freely handed his plug to our adventurer, who, helping himself, returned it, repeating the question as to the killed and wounded.

"Why," said he of the plug, "Jack Jewboy told me, just now, that there's
only seven men been carried down to the surgeon, but not a soul killed."

"Good, boys, good!" cried Israel, moving up to one of the gun-
carriages, where three or four men were sitting—"slip along, chaps, slip
along, and give a watchmate a seat with ye."

"All full here, lad; try the next gun."

"Boys, clear a place here," said Israel, advancing, like one of the family,
to that gun.

"Who the devil are *you*, making this row here?" demanded a stern-
looking old fellow, captain of the forecastle, "seems to me you make considerable noise. Are you a forecastleman?"

"If the bowsprit belongs here, so do I," rejoined Israel, composedly.

"Let's look at ye, then?" and seizing a battle-lantern, before thrust under
a gun, the old veteran came close to Israel before he had time to elude the
scrutiny.

"Take that!" said his examiner, and fetching Israel a terrible thump,
pushed him ignominiously off the forecastle as some unknown interloper
from distant parts of the ship.

With similar perseverance of effrontery, Israel tried other quarters of
the vessel. But with equal ill success. Jealous with the spirit of class, no social
circle would receive him. As a last resort, he dived down among the *holders*.

A group of them sat round a lantern, in the dark bowels of the ship, like
a knot of charcoal burners in a pine forest at midnight.

"Well, boys, what's the good word?" said Israel, advancing very cordially, but keeping as much as possible in the shadow.

"The good word is," rejoined a censorious old *holder*, "that you had best
go where you belong—on deck—and not be a skulking down here where
you *don't* belong. I suppose this is the way you skulked during the fight."

"Oh, you're growly to-night, shipmate," said Israel, pleasantly—
"supper sits hard on your conscience."

"Get out of the hold with ye," roared the other. "On deck, or I'll call the
master-at-arms."

Once more Israel decamped.

Sorely against his grain, as a final effort to blend himself openly with the
crew, he now went among the *waisters;* the vilest caste of an armed ship's
company; mere dregs and settlings—sea-Pariahs; comprising all the lazy, all
the inefficient, all the unfortunate and fated, all the melancholy, all the
infirm; all the rheumatical scamps, scape-graces, ruined prodigal sons, sooty
faces, and swineherds of the crew, not excluding those with dismal wardrobes.

An unhappy, tattered, moping row of them sat along dolefully on the
gun-deck, like a parcel of crest-fallen buzzards, exiled from civilized society.

"Cheer up, lads," said Israel, in a jovial tone, "homeward bound, you
know. Give us a seat among ye, friends."

"Oh, sit on your head!" answered a sullen fellow in the corner.

"Come, come, no growling; we're homeward-bound. Whoop, my
hearties!"

"Work-house bound, you mean," grumbled another sorry chap, in a
darned shirt.

"Oh, boys, don't be down-hearted. Let's keep up our spirits. Sing us a
song, one of ye, and I'll give the chorus."

"Sing if ye like, but I'll plug my ears for one," said still another sulky
varlet, with the toes out of his sea-boots; while all the rest with one roar of
misanthropy joined him.

But Israel, not to be daunted, began:

"'Cease, rude Boreas, cease your growling!'"

"And you cease your squeaking, will ye," cried a fellow in a banged
tarpaulin. "Did ye get a ball in the windpipe, that ye cough that way, worse
nor a broken-nosed old bellows? Have done with your groaning; it's worse
nor the death-rattle."

"Boys, is this the way you treat a watch-mate," demanded Israel reproachfully, "trying to cheer up his friends? Shame on ye, boys. Come, let's be sociable. Spin us a yarn, one of ye. Meantime, rub my back for me, another," and very confidently he leaned against his neighbor.

"Lean off me, will ye?" roared his friend, shoving him away.

"But who *is* this ere singing, leaning, yarn-spinning, chap? Who are ye? Be you a waister, or be you not?"

So saying, one of this peevish, sottish band staggered close up to Israel. But there was a deck above and a deck below, and the lantern swung in the distance. It was too dim to see with critical exactness.

"No such singing chap belongs to our gang, that's flat," he dogmatically exclaimed at last, after an ineffectual scrutiny. "Sail out of this!"

And with a shove, once more poor Israel was rejected.

Black-balled out of every club, he went disheartened on deck. So long, while night screened him at least, as he contented himself with promiscuously circulating, all was safe; it was the endeavor to fraternize with any one set which was sure to endanger him. At last, wearied out, he happened to find himself on the berth deck, where the watch below were slumbering. Some hundred and fifty hammocks were on that deck. Seeing one empty, he leaped in, thinking luck might yet some way befriend him. Here, at last, the sultry confinement put him fast asleep. He was wakened by a savage whiskerando of the other watch, who, seizing him by his waistband, dragged him most indecorously out, furiously denouncing him for a skulker.

Springing to his feet, Israel perceived from the crowd and tumult of the berth deck, now all alive with men leaping into their hammocks, instead of being full of sleepers quietly dosing therein, that the watches were changed. Going above, he renewed in various quarters his offers of intimacy with the fresh men there assembled; but was successively repulsed as before. At length, just as day was breaking, an irascible fellow, whose stubborn opposition our adventurer had long in vain sought to conciliate—this man suddenly perceiving, by the grey morning light, that Israel had somehow an alien sort of general look, very savagely pressed him for explicit information as to who he might be. The answers increased his suspicion. Others began to surround the two. Presently, quite a circle was formed. Sailors from distant parts of the ship drew near. One, and then another, and another, declared that they, in their quarters, too, had been molested by a vagabond claiming fraternity, and seeking to palm himself off upon decent society. In vain Israel protested. The truth, like the day, dawned clearer and clearer. More and more closely he was scanned. At length the hour for having all hands on deck arrived; when the other watch which Israel had first tried, reascending to the deck, and hearing the matter in discussion, they endorsed the charge of molestation and attempted imposture through the night, on the part of some person unknown, but who, likely enough, was the strange man now before them. In the end, the master-at-arms appeared with his bamboo, who, summarily collaring poor Israel, led him as a mysterious culprit to the officer of the deck; which gentleman having heard the charge, examined him in great perplexity, and, saying that he did not at all recognize that countenance, requested the junior officers to contribute their scrutiny. But those officers were equally at fault.

"Who the deuce *are* you?" at last said the officer of the deck, in added bewilderment. "Where did you come from? What's your business? Where are you stationed? What's your name? Who are you, any way? How did you get here? and where are you going?"

"Sir," replied Israel very humbly, "I am going to my regular duty, if you will but let me. I belong to the main top, and ought to be now engaged in preparing the top-gallant stu'n'-sail for hoisting."

"Belong to the main-top? Why, these men here say you have been trying to belong to the fore-top, and the mizen-top, and the forecastle, and the hold, and the waist, and every other part of the ship. This is extraordinary," he added, turning upon the junior officers.

"He must be out of his mind," replied one of them, the sailing-master.

"Out of his mind?" rejoined the officer of the deck. "He's out of all reason; out of all men's knowledge and memories! Why, no one knows him; no one has ever seen him before; no imagination, in the wildest flight of a morbid nightmare, has ever so much as dreamed of him. Who *are* you?" he again added, fierce with amazement. "What's your name? Are you down in the ship's books, or at all in the records of nature?"

"My name, sir, is Peter Perkins," said Israel, thinking it most prudent to conceal his real appellation.

"Certainly, I never heard that name before. Pray, see if Peter Perkins is down on the quarter-bills," he added to a midshipman. "Quick, bring the book here."

Having received it, he ran his fingers along the columns, and dashing down the book, declared that no such name was there.

"You are not down, sir. There is no Peter Perkins here. Tell me at once who are you?"

"It might be, sir," said Israel, gravely, "that seeing I shipped under the effects of liquor, I might, out of absent-mindedness like, have given in some other person's name instead of my own."

"Well, what name have you gone by among your shipmates since you've been aboard?"

"Peter Perkins, sir."

Upon this the officer turned to the men around, inquiring whether the name of Peter Perkins was familiar to them as that of a shipmate. One and all answered no.

"This won't do, sir," now said the officer. "You see it won't do. Who are you?"

"A poor persecuted fellow at your service, sir."

"*Who* persecutes you?"

"Every one, sir. All hands seem to be against me; none of them willing to remember me."

"Tell me," demanded the officer earnestly, "how long do you re-member yourself? Do you remember yesterday morning? You must have come into existence by some sort of spontaneous combustion in the hold. Or were you fired aboard from the enemy, last night, in a cartridge? Do you remember yesterday?"

"Oh yes, sir."

"What was you doing yesterday?"

"Well, sir, for one thing, I believe I had the honor of a little talk with yourself."

"With *me?*"

"Yes sir; about nine o'clock in the morning—the sea being smooth and the ship running, as I should think, about seven knots—you came up into the main-top, where I belong, and was pleased to ask my opinion about the best way to set a top gallant stu'n'-sail."

"He's mad! He's mad!" said the officer, with delirious conclusiveness. "Take him away, take him away—put him somewhere, master-at-arms. Stay, one test more. What mess do you belong to?"

"Number 12, sir."

"Mr. Tidds," to a midshipman, "send mess No. 12 to the mast."

Ten sailors replied to the summons, and arranged themselves before Israel.

"Men, does this man belong to your mess?"

"No, sir; never saw him before this morning."

"What are those men's names?" he demanded of Israel.

"Well, sir, I am so intimate with all of them," looking upon them with a kindly glance, "I never call them by their real names, but by nick-names. So, never using their real names, I have forgotten them. The nick-names that I know them by, are Towser, Bowser, Rowser, Snowser."

"Enough. Mad as a March hare. Take him away. Hold," again added the officer, whom some strange fascination still bound to the bootless investigation. "What's *my* name, sir?"

"Why, sir, one of my messmates here called you Lieutenant Williamson, just now, and I never heard you called by any other name."

"There's method in his madness," thought the officer to himself. "What's the captain's name?"

"Why, sir, when we spoke the enemy, last night, I heard him say, through his trumpet, that he was Captain Parker; and very likely he knows his own name."

"I have you now. That ain't the captain's real name."

"He's the best judge himself, sir, of what his name is, I should think."

"Were it not," said the officer, now turning gravely upon his juniors, "were it not, that such a supposition were on other grounds absurd, I should certainly conclude that this man, in some unknown way, got on board here from the enemy last night."

"How could he, sir?" asked the sailing-master.

"Heaven knows. But our spanker-boom geared the other ship, you know, in manœuvering to get headway."

"But supposing he *could* have got here that fashion, which is quite impossible under all the circumstances—what motive could have induced him voluntarily to jump among enemies?"

"Let him answer for himself," said the officer, turning suddenly upon Israel, with the view of taking him off his guard, by the matter of course assumption of the very point at issue.

"Answer, sir. Why did you jump on board here, last night, from the enemy?"

"Jump on board, sir, from the enemy? Why, sir, my station at general quarters is at gun No. 3, of the lower deck, here."

"He's cracked—or else I am turned—or all the world is;—take him away!"

"But where am I to take him, sir?" said the master-at-arms. "He don't seem to belong anywhere, sir. Where—where am I to take him?"

"Take him out of sight," said the officer, now incensed with his own perplexity. "Take him out of sight, I say."

"Come along, then, my ghost," said the master-at-arms. And, collaring the phantom, he led it hither and thither, not knowing exactly what to do with it.

Some fifteen minutes passed, when the captain coming from his cabin, and observing the master-at-arms leading Israel about in this indefinite style, demanded the reason of that procedure, adding that it was against his express orders for any new and degrading punishments to be invented for his men.

"Come here, master-at-arms. To what end do you lead that man about?"

"To no end in the world, sir. I keep leading him about because he has no final destination."

"Mr. officer of the deck, what does this mean? Who is this strange man? I don't know that I remember him. Who is he? And what is signified by his being led about?"

Hereupon, the officer of the deck, throwing himself into a tragical posture, set forth the entire mystery; much to the captain's astonishment, who at once indignantly turned upon the phantom.

"You rascal—don't try to deceive me. Who are you? and where did you come from last?"

"Sir, my name is Peter Perkins, and I last came from the forecastle, where the master-at-arms last led me, before coming here."

"No joking, sir, no joking."

"Sir, I'm sure it's too serious a business to joke about."

"Do you have the assurance to say, that you, as a regularly shipped man, have been on board this vessel ever since she sailed from Falmouth, ten months ago?"

"Sir, anxious to secure a berth under so good a commander, I was among the first to enlist."

"What ports have we touched at, sir?" said the captain, now in a little softer tone.

"Ports, sir, ports?"

"Yes, sir, *ports.*"

Israel began to scratch his yellow hair.

"What *ports*, sir?"

"Well, sir:—Boston, for one."

"Right there," whispered a midshipman.

"What was the next port, sir?"

"Why, sir, I was saying Boston was the *first* port, I believe; wasn't it?—and"—

"The *second* port, sir, is what I want."

"Well—New York."

"Right again," whispered the midshipman.

"And what port are we bound to, now?"

"Let me see—homeward-bound—Falmouth, sir."

"What sort of a place is Boston?"

"Pretty considerable of a place, sir."

"Very straight streets, ain't they?"

"Yes, sir; cow-paths, cut by sheep-walks, and intersected with hen-tracks."

"When did we fire the first gun?"

"Well, sir, just as we were leaving Falmouth, ten months ago—signal-gun, sir."

"Where did we fire the first *shotted* gun, sir?—and what was the name of the privateer we took upon that occasion?"

"'Pears to me, sir, at that time I was on the sick list. Yes, sir, that must have been the time; I had the brain fever, and lost my mind for a while."

"Master-at-arms, take this man away."

"Where shall I take him, sir?" touching his cap.

"Go, and air him on the forecastle."

So they resumed their devious wanderings. At last, they descended to the berth-deck. It being now breakfast-time, the master-at-arms, a good-humored man, very kindly introduced our hero to his mess, and presented him with breakfast; during which he in vain endeavored, by all sorts of subtle blandishments, to worm out his secret.

At length Israel was set at liberty; and whenever there was any important duty to be done, volunteered to it with such cheerful alacrity, and approved himself so docile and excellent a seaman, that he conciliated the approbation of all the officers, as well as the captain; while his general sociability served in the end, to turn in his favor the suspicious hearts of the mariners. Perceiving his good qualities, both as a sailor and man, the captain of the main-top applied for his admission into that section of the ship; where, still improving upon his former reputation, our hero did duty for the residue of the voyage.

One pleasant afternoon, the last of the passage, when the ship was nearing the Lizard, within a few hours' sail of her port, the officer of the deck, happening to glance upwards towards the main-top, descried Israel there, leaning very leisurely over the rail, looking mildly down where the officer stood.

"Well, Peter Perkins, you seem to belong to the main-top, after all."

"I always told you so, sir," smiled Israel, benevolently down upon him, "though, at first, you remember, sir, you would not believe it."

Chapter 21

Samson among the Philistines

AT LENGTH, as the ship, gliding on past three or four vessels at anchor in the roadstead—one, a man-of-war just furling her sails—came nigh Falmouth town, Israel, from his perch, saw crowds in violent commotion on the shore, while the adjacent roofs were covered with sightseers. A large man-of-war cutter was just landing its occupants, among whom were a corporal's guard and three officers, besides the naval lieutenant and boat's crew. Some of this company having landed, and formed a sort of lane among the mob, two trim soldiers, armed to the teeth, rose in the stern-sheets; and between them, a martial man of Patagonian stature, their ragged and handcuffed captive, whose defiant head overshadowed theirs, as St. Paul's dome its inferior steeples. Immediately the mob raised a shout, pressing in curiosity towards the colossal stranger; so that, drawing their swords, four of the soldiers had to force a passage for their comrades, who followed on, conducting the giant.

As the letter-of-marque drew still nigher, Israel heard the officer in command of the party ashore shouting, "To the castle! to the castle!" and so, surrounded by shouting throngs, the company moved on, preceded by the four drawn swords, ever and anon flourished at the rioters, towards a large grim pile on a cliff about a mile from the landing. Long as they were in sight, the bulky form of the captive was seen at times swayingly towering

142

over the flashing bayonets and cutlasses, like a great whale breaching amid a hostile retinue of sword-fish. Now and then, too, with barbaric scorn, he taunted them, with cramped gestures of his manacled hands.

When at last the vessel had gained her anchorage, opposite a distant detached warehouse, all was still; and the work of breaking out in the hold immediately commencing, and continuing till nightfall, absorbed all further attention for the present.

Next day was Sunday; and about noon Israel, with others, was allowed to go ashore for a stroll. The town was quiet. Seeing nothing very interesting there, he passed out, alone, into the fields along shore; and presently found himself climbing the cliff; whereon stood the grim pile before spoken of.

"What place is yon?" he asked of a rustic passing.

"Pendennis Castle."

As he stepped upon the short crisp sward under its walls, he started at a violent sound from within, as of the roar of some tormented lion. Soon the sound became articulate, and he heard the following words bayed out with an amazing vigor:—

"Brag no more, old England; consider you are but an island! Order back your broken battalions! home, and repent in ashes! Long enough have your hired tories across the sea forgotten the Lord their God, and bowed down to Howe and Knyphausen—the Hessian!——Hands off, red-skinned jackall! Wearing the king's plate,* as I do, I have treasures of wrath against you British."

Then came a clanking, as of a chain; many vengeful sounds, all confusedly together; with strugglings. Then again the voice:—

"Ye brought me out here, from my dungeon to this green—affronting yon Sabbath sun—to see how a rebel looks. But I show ye how a true gentleman and Christian can conduct in adversity. Back, dogs! Respect a gentleman and a Christian, though he *be* in rags and smell of bilge-water."

Filled with astonishment at these words, which came from over a massive wall, inclosing what seemed an open parade-space, Israel pressed forward; and soon came to a black archway, leading far within, underneath, to a grassy tract, through a tower. Like two boar's tusks, two sentries stood on guard at either side of the open jaws of the arch. Scrutinizing our adventurer a moment, they signed him permission to enter.

Arrived at the end of the arched-way, where the sun shone, Israel stood transfixed at the scene.

---

* Meaning, probably, certain manacles.

Like some baited bull in the ring, crouched the Patagonian-looking captive, hand-cuffed as before; the grass of the green trampled, and gored up all about him, both by his own movements and those of the people around. Except some soldiers and sailors, these seemed mostly town's-people, collected here out of curiosity. The stranger was outlandishly arrayed in the sorry remains of a half-Indian, half-Canadian sort of a dress, consisting of a fawn-skin jacket—the fur outside and hanging in ragged tufts—a half-rotten, bark-like belt of wampum; aged breeches of sagathy; bedarned worsted stockings to the knee; old moccasins riddled with holes, their metal tags yellow with salt-water rust; a faded red woollen bonnet, not unlike a Russian night-cap, or a portentous, ensanguined full-moon; all soiled, and stuck about with bits of half-rotted straw. He seemed just broken from the dead leaves in David's outlawed Cave of Adullam. Unshaven, beard and hair matted, and profuse as a corn-field beaten down by hail-storms, his whole marred aspect was that of some wild beast; but of a royal sort, and unsubdued by the cage.

"Aye, stare, stare! Though but last night dragged out of a ship's hold, like a smutty tierce; and this morning out of your littered barracks here, like a murderer; for all that, you may well stare at Ethan Ticonderoga Allen, the unconquered soldier, by ——! You Turks never saw a Christian before. Stare on! I am he, who, when your Lord Howe wanted to bribe a patriot to fall down and worship him by an offer of a major-generalship and five thousand acres of choice land in old Vermont—(Hah! three-times-three for glorious old Vermont, and my Green-Mountain-boys! Hurrah! Hurrah! Hurrah!) I am he, I say, who answered your Lord Howe, 'You, *you* offer *our* land? You are like the devil in Scripture, offering all the kingdoms in the world, when the d——d soul had not a corner-lot on earth!' Stare on!"

"Look you, rebel, you had best heed how you talk against General Lord Howe," here said a thin, wasp-waisted, epauleted officer of the castle, coming near and flourishing his sword like a schoolmaster's ferule.

"General Lord Howe? Heed how I talk of that toad-hearted king's lick-spittle of a scarlet poltroon; the vilest wriggler in God's worm-hole below? I tell you, that herds of red-haired devils are impatiently snorting to ladle Lord Howe with all his gang (you included) into the seethingest syrups of tophet's flames!"

At this blast, the wasp-waisted officer was blown backwards as from before the suddenly burst head of a steam-boiler.

Staggering away, with a snapped spine, he muttered something about its being beneath his dignity to bandy further words with a low-lived rebel.

"Come, come, Colonel Allen," here said a mild-looking man in a sort of clerical undress; "respect the day better than to talk thus of what lies beyond. Were you to die this hour, or what is more probable, be hung next week at Tower-wharf, you know not what might become, in eternity, of yourself."

"Reverend Sir," with a mocking bow; "when not better employed braiding my beard, I have a little dabbled in your theologies. And let me tell you, Reverend Sir," lowering and intensifying his voice: "that as to the world of spirits, of which you hint, though I know nothing of the mode or manner of that world, no more than do you, yet I expect when I shall arrive there, to be treated as well as any other gentleman of my merit. That is to say, far better than you British know how to treat an American officer and meek-hearted Christian captured in honorable war, by ——! Every one tells me as you yourself just breathed, and as, crossing the sea, every billow dinned into my ear—that I, Ethan Allen, am to be hung like a thief. If I am, the great Jehovah and the Continental Congress shall avenge me; while I, for my part, shall show you, even on the tree, how a Christian gentleman can die. Meantime, sir, if you are the clergyman you look, act out your consolatory function, by getting an unfortunate Christian gentleman about to die, a bowl of punch."

The good-natured stranger, not to have his religious courtesy appealed to in vain, immediately dispatched his servant, who stood by, to procure the beverage.

At this juncture, a faint rustling sound, as of the advance of an army with banners, was heard. Silks, scarfs, and ribbons fluttered in the background. Presently, a bright squadron of fair ladies drew nigh, escorted by certain outriding gallants of Falmouth.

"Ah," sighed a soft voice; "what a strange sash, and furred vest, and what leopard-like teeth, and what flaxen hair, but all mildewed;—is that he?"

"Yea, is it, lovely charmer," said Allen, like an Ottoman, bowing over his broad, bovine forehead, and breathing the words out like a lute; "it is he—Ethan Allen, the soldier; now, since ladies' eyes visit him, made trebly a captive."

"Why, he talks like a beau in a parlor; this wild, mossed American from the woods," sighed another fair lady to her mate; "but can this be he we came to see? I must have a lock of his hair."

"It is he, adorable Delilah; and fear not, even though incited by the foe, by clipping my locks, to dwindle my strength. Give me your sword, man," turning to an officer;—"Ah! I'm fettered. Clip it yourself, lady."

"No, no—I am"——

"Afraid, would you say? Afraid of the vowed friend and champion of all ladies all round the world? Nay, nay: come hither."

The lady advanced; and soon, overcoming her timidity, her white hand shone like whipped foam amid the matted waves of flaxen hair.

"Ah, this is like clipping tangled tags of gold-lace," cried she; "but see, it is half straw."

"But the wearer is no man-of-straw, lady; were I free, and you had ten thousand foes—horse, foot, and dragoons—how like a friend I could fight for you! Come, you have robbed me of my hair; let me rob your dainty hand of its price. What, afraid again?"

"No, not that; but"——

"I see, lady; I may do it, by your leave, but not by your word; the wonted way of ladies. There, it is done. Sweeter that kiss, than the bitter heart of a cherry."

When at length this lady left, no small talk was had by her with her companions about someway relieving the hard lot of so knightly an unfortunate. Whereupon a worthy, judicious gentleman, of middle-age, in attendance, suggested a bottle of good wine every day, and clean linen once every week. And these, the gentle Englishwoman—too polite and too good to be fastidious—did indeed actually send to Ethan Allen, so long as he tarried a captive in her land.

The withdrawal of this company was followed by a different scene.

A perspiring man in top-boots, a riding whip in his hand, and having the air of a prosperous farmer, brushed in, like a stray bullock, among the rest, for a peep at the giant; having just entered through the arch, as the ladies passed out.

"Hearing that the man who took Ticonderoga was here in Pendennis Castle, I've ridden twenty-five miles to see him; and to-morrow my brother will ride forty for the same purpose. So let me have first look. Sir," he continued, addressing the captive; "will you let me ask you a few plain questions, and be free with you?"

"Be free with me? with all my heart. I love freedom of all things. I'm ready to die for freedom; I expect to. So be free as you please. What is it?"

"Then, sir, permit me to ask what is your occupation in life;—in time of peace, I mean."

"You talk like a tax-gatherer;" rejoined Allen, squinting diabolically at him; "what is my occupation in life? Why, in my younger days I studied divinity, but at present I am a conjuror by profession."

Hereupon everybody laughed, equally at the manner as the words, and the nettled farmer retorted:—

"Conjurer, eh? well, you conjured wrong that time you were taken."

"Not so wrong, though, as you British did, that time I took Ticonderoga, my friend."

At this juncture the servant came with the punch, when his master bade him present it to the captive.

"No!—give it me, sir, with your own hands; and pledge me as gentleman to gentleman."

"I cannot pledge a state-prisoner, Colonel Allen; but I will hand you the punch with my own hands, since you insist upon it."

"Spoken and done like a true gentleman, sir; I am bound to you."

Then receiving the bowl into his gyved hands, the iron ringing against the china, he put it to his lips, and saying, "I hereby give the British nation credit for half a minute's good usage," at one draught emptied it to the bottom.

"The rebel gulps it down like a swilling hog at a trough;" here scoffed a lusty private of the guard, off duty.

"Shame to you!" cried the giver of the bowl.

"Nay, sir; his red coat is a standing blush to him, as it is to the whole scarlet-blushing British army." Then turning derisively upon the private: "you object to my way of taking things, do ye? I fear I shall never please ye. You objected to the way, too, in which I took Ticonderoga, and the way in which I meant to take Montreal. Selah! But, pray, now that I look at you, are not you the hero I caught dodging round, in his shirt, in the cattle-pen, inside the fort? It was the break of day, you remember."

"Come, Yankee," here swore the incensed private; "cease this, or I'll darn your old fawn-skins for ye, with the flat of this sword;" for a specimen, laying it lashwise, but not heavily, across the captive's back.

Turning like a tiger, the giant, catching the steel between his teeth, wrenched it from the private's grasp, and striking it with his manacles, sent it spinning like a juggler's dagger into the air; saying, "Lay your dirty coward's iron on a tied gentleman again, and these," lifting his handcuffed fists, "shall be the beetle of mortality to you!"

The now furious soldier would have struck him with all his force; but several men of the town interposed, reminding him that it were outrageous to attack a chained captive.

"Ah," said Allen, "I am accustomed to that, and therefore I am beforehand with them; and the extremity of what I say against Britain, is not

meant for you, kind friends, but for my insulters, present and to come."
Then recognizing among the interposers the giver of the bowl, he turned
with a courteous bow, saying, "Thank you again and again, my good sir;
you may not be the worse for this; ours is an unstable world; so that one
gentleman never knows when it may be his turn to be helped of another."

But the soldier still making a riot, and the commotion growing general,
a superior officer stepped up, who terminated the scene by remanding the
prisoner to his cell, dismissing the towns-people, with all strangers, Israel
among the rest, and closing the castle gates after them.

Chapter 22

Something Further of Ethan Allen; with Israel's Flight Towards the Wilderness

AMONG THE EPISODES of the Revolutionary War, none is stranger than that of Ethan Allen in England; the event and the man being equally uncommon.

Allen seems to have been a curious combination of a Hercules, a Joe Miller, a Bayard, and a Tom Hyer; had a person like the Belgian giants; mountain music in him like a Swiss; a heart plump as Cœur de Lion's. Though born in New England, he exhibited no trace of her character. He was frank; bluff; companionable as a Pagan; convivial; a Roman; hearty as a harvest. His spirit was essentially western; and herein is his peculiar Americanism; for the western spirit is, or will yet be (for no other is, or can be) the true American one.

For the most part, Allen's manner while in England, was scornful and ferocious in the last degree; however qualified by that wild, heroic sort of levity, which in the hour of oppression or peril, seems inseparable from a nature like his; the mode whereby such a temper best evinces its barbaric disdain of adversity; and how cheaply and waggishly it holds the malice, even though triumphant, of its foes! Aside from that inevitable egotism relatively pertaining to pine trees, spires, and giants, there were, perhaps, two special incidental reasons for the Titanic Vermonter's singular demeanor abroad. Taken captive while heading a forlorn hope before

Montreal, he was treated with inexcusable cruelty and indignity; something
as if he had fallen into the hands of the Dyaks. Immediately upon his capture
he would have been deliberately suffered to have been butchered by the
Indian allies, in cold blood on the spot, had he not, with desperate intrepidity, availed himself of his enormous physical strength, by twitching a
British officer to him, and using him for a living target, whirling him round
and round against the murderous tomahawks of the savages. Shortly afterwards, led into the town, fenced about by bayonets of the guard, the
commander of the enemy, one General Prescott, flourished his cane over the
captive's head, with brutal insults promising him a rebel's halter at Tyburn.
During his passage to England in the same ship wherein went passenger
Colonel Guy Johnson, the implacable tory, he was kept heavily ironed in the
hold, and in all ways treated as a common mutineer; or, it may be, rather as
a lion of Asia; which, though caged, was still too dreadful to behold without
fear and trembling; and consequent cruelty. And no wonder, at least for the
fear; for on one occasion, when chained hand and foot, he was insulted on
shipboard by an officer; with his teeth he twisted off the nail that went
through the mortise of his handcuffs, and so, having his arms at liberty,
challenged his insulter to combat. Often, as at Pendennis Castle, when no
other avengement was at hand, he would hurl on his foes such howling
tempests of anathema, as fairly to shock them into retreat. Prompted by
somewhat similar motives, both on shipboard and in England, he would
often make the most vociferous allusions to Ticonderoga, and the part he
played in its capture, well knowing, that of all American names, Ticonderoga was, at that period, by far the most famous and galling to Englishmen.

Parlor-men, dancing-masters, the graduates of the Abbé Bellegarde may
shrug their laced shoulders at the boisterousness of Allen in England. True,
he stood upon no punctilios with his jailers; for where modest gentleman-
hood is all on one side, it is a losing affair; as if my Lord Chesterfield should
take off his hat, and smile, and bow, to a mad bull, in hopes of a reciproca-
tion of politeness. When among wild beasts, if they menace you, be a wild
beast. Neither is it unlikely that this was the view taken by Allen. For,
besides the exasperating tendency to self-assertion which such treatment as
his must have bred on a man like him, his experience must have taught him,
that by assuming the part of a jocular, reckless, and even braggart barbarian,
he would better sustain himself against bullying turnkeys than by submis-
sive quietude. Nor should it be forgotten, that besides the petty details of
personal malice, the enemy violated every international usage of right and
decency, in treating a distinguished prisoner of war as if he had been a

Botany-Bay convict. If, at the present day, in any similar case between the same States, the repetition of such outrages would be more than unlikely, it is only because it is among nations as among individuals: imputed indigence provokes oppression and scorn; but that same indigence being risen to opulence, receives a politic consideration even from its former insulters.

As the event proved, in the course Allen pursued, he was right. Because, though at first nothing was talked of by his captors, and nothing anticipated by himself, but his ignominious execution, or, at the least, prolonged and squalid incarceration; nevertheless, these threats and prospects evaporated, and by his facetious scorn for scorn, under the extremest sufferings, he finally wrung repentant usage from his foes; and in the end, being liberated from his irons, and walking the quarter-deck where before he had been thrust into the hold, was carried back to America, and in due time at New York, honorably included in a regular exchange of prisoners.

It was not without strange interest that Israel had been an eye-witness of the scenes on the Castle Green. Neither was this interest abated by the painful necessity of concealing, for the present, from his brave countryman and fellow-mountaineer, the fact of a friend being nigh. When at last the throng was dismissed, walking towards the town with the rest, he heard that there were some forty or more other Americans, privates, confined on the cliff. Upon this, inventing a pretence, he turned back, loitering around the walls for any chance glimpse of the captives. Presently, while looking up at a grated embrasure in the tower, he started at a voice from it familiarly hailing him:—

"Potter, is that you? In God's name how came you here?"

At these words, a sentry below had his eye on our astonished adventurer. Bringing his piece to bear, he bade him stand. Next moment Israel was under arrest. Being brought into the presence of the forty prisoners, where they lay in litters of mouldy straw, strewn with gnawed bones, as in a kennel, he recognized among them one Singles, now Sergeant Singles, the man who, upon our hero's return home from his last Cape Horn voyage, he had found wedded to his mountain Jenny. Instantly a rush of emotions filled him. Not as when Damon found Pythias. But far stranger, because very different. For not only had this Singles been an alien to Israel (so far as actual intercourse went), but impelled to it by instinct, Israel had all but detested him, as a successful, and perhaps insidious rival. Nor was it altogether unlikely that Singles had reciprocated the feeling. But now, as if the Atlantic rolled, not between two continents, but two worlds—this, and the next— these alien souls, oblivious to hate, melted down into one.

At such a juncture, it was hard to maintain a disguise; especially when it involved the seeming rejection of advances like the sergeant's. Still, converting his real amazement into affected surprise, Israel, in presence of the sentries, declared to Singles that he (Singles) must labor under some unaccountable delusion; for he (Potter) was no Yankee rebel, thank Heaven, but a true man to his king; in short, an honest Englishman, born in Kent, and now serving his country, and doing what damage he might to her foes, by being first captain of a carronade on board a letter-of-marque, that moment in the harbor.

For a moment, the captive stood astounded; but observing Israel more narrowly, detecting his latent look, and bethinking him of the useless peril he had thoughtlessly caused to a countryman, no doubt unfortunate as himself, Singles took his cue, and pretending sullenly to apologize for his error, put on a disappointed and crest-fallen air. Nevertheless, it was not without much difficulty, and after many supplemental scrutinies and inquisitions from a board of officers before whom he was subsequently brought, that our wanderer was finally permitted to quit the cliff.

This luckless adventure not only nipped in the bud a little scheme he had been revolving, for materially befriending Ethan Allen and his comrades, but resulted in making his further stay at Falmouth perilous in the extreme. And as if this were not enough, next day, while hanging over the side, painting the hull, in trepidation of a visit from the castle soldiers, rumor came to the ship that the man-of-war in the haven purposed impressing one-third of the letter of marque's crew; though, indeed, the latter vessel was preparing for a second cruise. Being on board a private armed ship, Israel had little dreamed of its liability to the same governmental hardships with the meanest merchantman. But the system of impressment is no respecter either of pity or person.

His mind was soon determined. Unlike his shipmates, braving immediate and lonely hazard, rather than wait for a collective and ultimate one, he cunningly dropped himself overboard the same night, and after the narrowest risk from the muskets of the man-of-war's sentries (whose gangways he had to pass), succeeded in swimming to shore, where he fell exhausted, but recovering, fled inland; doubly hunted by the thought, that whether as an Englishman, or whether as an American, he would, if caught, be now equally subject to enslavement.

Shortly after the break of day, having gained many miles, he succeeded in ridding himself of his seaman's clothing, having found some mouldy old rags on the banks of a stagnant pond, nigh a rickety building, which looked like a poorhouse,—clothing not improbably, as he surmised, left there, on the bank, by some pauper suicide. Marvel not that he should, with avidity, seize these rags; what the suicides abandon the living hug.

Once more in beggar's garb, the fugitive sped towards London, prompted by the same instinct which impels the hunted fox to the wilderness; for solitudes befriend the endangered wild beast, but crowds are the security, because the true desert of persecuted man. Among the throngs of the capital, Israel for more than forty years was yet to disappear, as one entering at dusk into a thick wood. Nor did ever the German forest, nor Tasso's enchanted one, contain in its depths more things of horror than eventually were revealed in the secret clefts, gulfs, caves and dens of London.

But here we anticipate a page.

Chapter 23

Israel in Egypt

I T WAS a grey, lowering afternoon that, worn-out, half-starved, and
haggard, Israel arrived within some ten or fifteen miles of London,
and saw scores and scores of forlorn men engaged in a great brick-
yard.

For the most part, brick-making is all mud and mire. Where, abroad, the
business is carried on largely, as to supply the London Market, hordes of the
poorest wretches are employed; their grimy tatters naturally adapting them
to an employ where cleanliness is as much out of the question as with a
drowned man at the bottom of the lake in the Dismal Swamp.

Desperate with want, Israel resolved to turn brick-maker; nor did he
fear to present himself as a stranger; nothing doubting that to such a vocation, his rags would be accounted the best letters-of-introduction.

To be brief, he accosted one of the many surly overseers, or task-masters
of the yard, who with no few pompous airs, finally engaged him at six
shillings a week; almost equivalent to a dollar and a half. He was appointed
to one of the mills for grinding up the ingredients. This mill stood in the
open air. It was of a rude, primitive, Eastern aspect; consisting of a sort of
hopper, emptying into a barrel-shaped receptacle. In the barrel was a clumsy
machine turned round at its axis by a great bent beam, like a well-sweep,
only it was horizontal; to this beam, at its outer end, a spavined old horse

was attached. The muddy mixture was shovelled into the hopper by spavined-looking old men; while trudging wearily round and round the spavined old horse ground it all up till it slowly squashed out at the bottom of the barrel, in a doughy compound, all ready for the moulds. Where the dough squeezed out of the barrel, a pit was sunken, so as to bring the moulder here stationed down to a level with the trough, into which the dough fell. Israel was assigned to this pit. Men came to him continually, reaching down rude wooden trays, divided into compartments, each of the size and shape of a brick. With a flat sort of big ladle, Israel slapped the dough into the trays from the trough; then, with a bit of smooth board scraped the top even, and handed it up. Half buried there in the pit, all the time handing those desolate trays, poor Israel seemed some grave-digger, or church-yard man, tucking away dead little innocents in their coffins on one side, and cunningly disinterring them again to resurrectionists stationed on the other.

Twenty of these melancholy old mills were in operation. Twenty heart-broken old horses, rigged out deplorably in cast-off old cart harness, incessantly tugged at twenty great shaggy beams; while from twenty half-burst old barrels, twenty wads of mud, with a lava-like course, gouged out into twenty old troughs, to be slapped by twenty tattered men, into the twenty-times-twenty battered old trays.

Ere entering his pit for the first, Israel had been struck by the dismally devil-may-care gestures of the moulders. But hardly had he himself been a moulder three days, when his previous sedateness of concern at his unfortunate lot, began to conform to the reckless sort of half jolly despair expressed by the others. The truth indeed was, that this continual, violent, helter-skelter slapping of the dough into the moulds, begat a corresponding disposition in the moulder; who, by heedlessly slapping that sad dough, as stuff of little worth, was thereby taught, in his meditations, to slap, with similar heedlessness, his own sadder fortunes, as of still less vital consideration. To these muddy philosophers, men and bricks were equally of clay. What signifies who we be—dukes or ditchers? thought the moulders; all is vanity and clay. So slap, slap, slap; care-free and negligent; with bitter unconcern, these dismal desperadoes flapped down the dough. If this recklessness were vicious of them, be it so; but their vice was like that weed which but grows on barren ground; enrich the soil, and it disappears.

For thirteen weary weeks, lorded over by the taskmasters, Israel toiled in his pit. Though this condemned him to a sort of earthy dungeon, or grave-digger's hole while he worked; yet even when liberated to his meals, naught of a cheery nature greeted him. The yard was encamped, with all its endless rows of tented sheds, and kilns, and mills, upon a wild waste moor, belted round by bogs and fens. The blank horizon, like a rope, coiled round the whole.

Sometimes the air was harsh and bleak; the ridged and mottled sky looked scourged; or cramping fogs set in from sea, for leagues around, ferreting out each rheumatic human bone, and racking it; the sciatic limpers shivered; their aguish rags sponged up the mists. No shelter, though it hailed. The sheds were for the bricks. Unless, indeed, according to the phrase, each man was a "brick," which, in sober scripture, was the case; brick is no bad name for any son of Adam; Eden was but a brick-yard; what is a mortal but a few luckless shovelfuls of clay, moulded in a mould, laid out on a sheet to dry, and ere long quickened into his queer caprices by the sun? Are not men built into communities just like bricks into a wall? Consider the great wall of China: ponder the great populace of Pekin. As man serves bricks, so God him; building him up by billions into the edifices of his purposes. Man attains not to the nobility of a brick, unless taken in the aggregate. Yet is there a difference in brick, whether quick or dead; which, for the last, we now shall see.

All night long, men sat before the mouth of the kilns, feeding them with fuel. A dull smoke—a smoke of their torments—went up from their tops. It was curious to see the kilns under the action of the fire, gradually changing color, like boiling lobsters. When, at last, the fires would be extinguished, the bricks being duly baked, Israel often took a peep into the low vaulted ways at the base, where the flaming faggots had crackled. The bricks immediately lining the vaults would be all burnt to useless scrolls, black as charcoal, and twisted into shapes the most grotesque; the next tier would be a little less withered, but hardly fit for service; and gradually, as you went higher and higher along the successive layers of the kiln, you came to the midmost ones, sound, square, and perfect bricks, bringing the highest prices; from these the contents of the kiln gradually deteriorated in the opposite direction, upward. But the topmost layers, though inferior to the best, by no means presented the distorted look of the furnace-bricks. The furnace-bricks were haggard, with the immediate blistering of the fire—the midmost ones were ruddy with a genial and tempered glow—the summit ones were pale with the languor of too exclusive an exemption from the burden of the blaze.

These kilns were a sort of temporary temples constructed in the yard, each brick being set against its neighbor almost with the care taken by the mason. But as soon as the fire was extinguished, down came the kiln in a tumbled ruin, carted off to London, once more to be set up in ambitious edifices, to a true brick-yard philosopher, little less transient than the kilns.

Sometimes, lading out his dough, Israel could not but bethink him of what seemed enigmatic in his fate. He whom love of country made a hater of her foes—the foreigners among whom he now was thrown—he who, as soldier and sailor, had joined to kill, burn and destroy both them and theirs—here he was at last, serving that very people as a slave, better succeeding in making their bricks than firing their ships. To think that he should be thus helping, with all his strength, to extend the walls of the Thebes of the oppressor, made him half mad. Poor Israel! well-named—bondsman in the English Egypt. But he drowned the thought by still more recklessly spattering with his ladle: "What signifies who we be, or where we are, or what we do?" Slap-dash! "Kings as clowns are codgers—who ain't a nobody?" Splash! "All is vanity and clay."

Chapter 24

In the City of Dis

AT THE END of his brick-making, our adventurer found himself with a tolerable suit of clothes—somewhat darned—on his back, several blood-blisters in his palms, and some verdigris coppers in his pocket. Forthwith, to seek his fortune, he proceeded on foot to the capital, entering, like the king, from Windsor, from the Surrey side.

It was late on a Monday morning, in November—a Blue Monday—a Fifth of November—Guy Fawkes' Day!—very blue, foggy, doleful and gunpowdery, indeed, as shortly will be seen,—that Israel found himself wedged in among the greatest every-day crowd which grimy London presents to the curious stranger. That hereditary crowd—gulf-stream of humanity—which, for continuous centuries, has never ceased pouring, like an endless shoal of herring, over London Bridge.

At the period here written of, the bridge, specifically known by that name, was a singular and sombre pile, built by a cowled monk—Peter of Colechurch—some five hundred years before. Its arches had long been crowded at the sides with strange old rookeries of disproportioned and toppling height, converting the bridge at once into the most densely occupied ward, and most jammed thoroughfare of the town, while, as the skulls of bullocks are hung out for signs to the gateways of shambles, so the withered heads and smoked quarters of traitors, stuck on pikes, long crowned the Southwark entrance.

Though these rookeries, with their grisly heraldry, had been pulled down some twenty years prior to the present visit; still, enough of grotesque and antiquity clung to the structure at large, to render it the most striking of objects, especially to one like our hero, born in a virgin clime, where the only antiquities are the for ever youthful heavens and the earth.

On his route from Brentford to Paris, Israel had passed through the capital, but only as a courier. So that now, for the first, he had time to linger and loiter, and lounge—slowly absorb what he saw—meditate himself into boundless amazement. For forty years he never recovered from that surprise—never, till dead, had done with his wondering.

Hung in long, sepulchral arches of stone, the black, besmoked bridge seemed a huge scarf of crape, festooning the river across. Similar funereal festoons spanned it to the west, while eastward, towards the sea, tiers and tiers of jetty colliers lay moored, side by side, fleets of black swans.

The Thames, which far away, among the green fields of Berks, ran clear as a brook, here, polluted by continual vicinity to man, curdled on between rotten wharves, one murky sheet of sewerage. Fretted by the ill-built piers, awhile it crested and hissed, then shot balefully through the Erebus arches, desperate as the lost souls of the harlots, who, every night, took the same plunge. Meantime, here and there, like awaiting hearses, the coal-scows drifted along, poled broadside, pell-mell to the current.

And as that tide in the water swept all craft on, so a like tide seemed hurrying all men, all horses, all vehicles on the land. As ant-hills, the bridge arches crawled with processions of carts, coaches, drays, every sort of wheeled, rumbling thing, the noses of the horses behind touching the backs of the vehicles in advance, all bespattered with ebon mud, ebon mud that stuck like Jews' pitch. At times the mass, receiving some mysterious impulse far in the rear, away among the coiled thoroughfares out of sight, would start forward with a spasmodic surge. It seemed as if some squadron of centaurs, on the thither side of Phlegethon, with charge on charge, was driving tormented humanity, with all its chattels, across.

Whichever way the eye turned, no tree, no speck of any green thing was seen; no more than in smithies. All laborers, of whatsoever sort, were hued like the men in foundries. The black vistas of streets were as the galleries in coal mines; the flagging, as flat tomb-stones minus the consecration of moss; and worn heavily down, by sorrowful tramping, as the vitreous rocks in the cursed Gallipagos, over which the convict tortoises crawl.

As in eclipses, the sun was hidden; the air darkened; the whole dull, dismayed aspect of things, as if some neighboring volcano, belching its premonitory smoke, were about to whelm the great town, as Herculaneum and Pompeii, or the Cities of the Plain. And as they had been upturned in terror towards the mountain, all faces were more or less snowed, or spotted with soot. Nor marble, nor flesh, nor the sad spirit of man, may in this cindery City of Dis abide white.

On they passed; two-and-two, along the packed footpaths of the bridge; long-drawn, methodic, as funerals: some of the faces settled in dry apathy, content with their doom; others seemed mutely raving against it; while still others, like the spirits of Milton and Shelley in the prelatical Hinnom, seemed undeserving their fate, and despising their torture.

As retired at length, midway, in a recess of the bridge, Israel surveyed them, various individual aspects all but frighted him. Knowing not who they were; never destined, it may be, to behold them again; one after the other, they drifted by, uninvoked ghosts in Hades. Some of the wayfarers wore a less serious look; some seemed hysterically merry; but the mournful faces had an earnestness not seen in the others; because man, "poor player," succeeds better in life's tragedy than comedy.

Arrived, in the end, on the Middlesex side, Israel's heart was prophetically heavy; foreknowing, that being of this race, felicity could never be his lot.

For five days he wandered and wandered. Without leaving statelier haunts unvisited, he did not overlook those broader areas; hereditary parks and manors of vice and misery. Not by constitution disposed to gloom, there was a mysteriousness in those impulses which led him at this time to rovings like these. But hereby stoic influences were at work, to fit him at a soon-coming day, for enacting a part in the last extremities here seen; when by sickness, destitution, each busy ill of exile, he was destined to experience a fate, uncommon even to luckless humanity; a fate whose crowning qualities were its remoteness from relief and its depth of obscurity; London, adversity, and the sea, three Armageddons, which, at one and the same time, slay, and secrete their victims.

Chapter 25

Forty-five Years

F OR THE MOST PART, what befell Israel during his forty years'
wanderings in the London deserts, surpassed the forty years in the
natural wilderness of the outcast Hebrews under Moses.

In that London fog, went before him the ever-present cloud by day, but
no pillar of fire by the night, except the cold column of the monument; two
hundred feet beneath the mocking gilt flames on whose top, at the stone
base, the shiverer, of midnight, often laid down.

But these experiences, both from their intensity and his solitude, were
necessarily squalid. Best not enlarge upon them. For just as extreme suffering, without hope, is intolerable to the victim, so, to others, is its depiction,
without some corresponding delusive mitigation. The gloomiest and
truthfulest dramatist seldom chooses for his theme the calamities, however
extraordinary, of inferior and private persons; least of all, the pauper's;
admonished by the fact, that to the craped palace of the king lying in state,
thousands of starers shall throng; but few feel enticed to the shanty, where,
like a pealed knuckle-bone, grins the unupholstered corpse of the beggar.

Why at one given stone in the flagging does man after man cross yonder
street? What plebeian Lear or Œdipus; what Israel Potter cowers there by
the corner they shun? From this turning point then, we too cross over and
skim events to the end; omitting the particulars of the starveling's wran-

gling with rats for prizes in the sewers; or his crawling into an abandoned doorless house in St. Giles', where his hosts were three dead men, one pendant; into another of an alley nigh Houndsditch, where the crazy hovel, in phosphoric rottenness, fell sparkling on him one pitchy midnight, and he received that injury, which excluding activity for no small part of the future, was an added cause of his prolongation of exile; besides not leaving his faculties unaffected by the concussion of one of the rafters on his brain.

But these were some of the incidents not belonging to the beginning of his career. On the contrary, a sort of humble prosperity attended him for a time. Insomuch that once he was not without hopes of being able to buy his homeward passage, so soon as the war should end. But, as stubborn fate would have it, being run over one day at Holborn Bars, and taken into a neighboring bakery, he was there treated with such kindliness by a Kentish lass, the shop-girl, that in the end he thought his debt of gratitude could only be repaid by love. In a word, the money saved up for his ocean voyage was lavished upon a rash embarkation in wedlock.

Originally he had fled to the capital to avoid the dilemma of impressment or imprisonment. In the absence of other motives, the dread of those hardships would have fixed him there till the peace. But now, when hostilities were no more; so was his money. Some period elapsed ere the affairs of the two governments were put on such a footing as to support an American consul at London. Yet, when this came to pass, he could only embrace the facilities for a return here furnished, by deserting a wife and child; wedded and born in the enemy's land.

The peace immediately filled England and more especially London, with hordes of disbanded soldiers; thousands of whom, rather than starve, or turn highwaymen (which no few of their comrades did; stopping coaches at times in the most public streets), would work for such a pittance, as to bring down the wages of all the laboring classes. Neither was our adventurer the least among the sufferers. Driven out of his previous employ—a sort of porter in a river-side warehouse—by this sudden influx of rivals, destitute, honest men like himself, with the ingenuity of his race, he turned his hand to the village art of chair-bottoming. An itinerant, he paraded the streets with the cry of "old chairs to mend!" furnishing a curious illustration of the contradictions of human life; that he who did little but trudge, should be giving cosy seats to all the rest of the world. Meantime, according to another well-known Malthusian enigma in human affairs, his family increased. In all, eleven children were born to him in certain sixpenny garrets in Moorfields. One after the other, ten were buried.

When chair-bottoming would fail, resort was had to match-making. That business being overdone in turn, next came the collecting of old rags, bits of paper, nails, and broken glass. Nor was this the last step. From the gutter, he slid to the sewer. The slope was smooth. In poverty,

——"Facilis descensus Averni."

But many a poor soldier had sloped down there into the boggy canal of Avernus before him. Nay, he had three corporals and a sergeant for company.

But his lot was relieved by two strange things, presently to appear. In 1793 war again broke out; the great French war. This lighted London of some of its superfluous hordes, and lost Israel the subterranean society of his friends, the corporals and sergeant, with whom, wandering forlorn through the black kingdoms of mud, he used to spin yarns about sea prisoners in hulks, and listen to stories of the Black-hole of Calcutta; and often would meet other pairs of poor soldiers, perfect strangers, at the more public corners and intersections of sewers—the Charing-Crosses below; one soldier having the other by his remainder button, earnestly discussing the sad prospects of a rise in bread, or the tide; while through the grating of the gutters overhead, the rusty skylights of the realm, came the hoarse rumblings of bakers' carts, with splashes of the flood whereby these unsuspected gnomes of the city lived.

Encouraged by the exodus of the lost tribes of soldiers, Israel returned to chair-bottoming. And it was in frequenting Covent-Garden market, at early morning, for the purchase of his flags, that he experienced one of the strange alleviations hinted of above. That chatting with the ruddy, aproned, huckster-women, on whose moist cheeks yet trickled the dew of the dawn on the meadows; that being surrounded by bales of hay, as the raker by cocks and ricks in the field; those glimpses of garden produce, the blood-beets, with the damp earth still tufting the roots; that mere handling of his flags, and bethinking him of whence they must have come; the green hedges through which the wagon that brought them had passed; that trudging home with them as a gleaner with his sheaf of wheat; all this was inexpressibly grateful. In want and bitterness, pent in, perforce, between dingy walls, he had rural returns of his boyhood's sweeter days among them; and the hardest stones of his solitary heart (made hard by bare endurance alone), would feel the stir of tender but quenchless memories, like the grass of deserted flagging, upsprouting through its closest seams. Sometimes, when incited by some little incident, however trivial in itself, thoughts of home would—either by gradually working and working upon him, or else by an impetuous rush of recollection—overpower him for a time to a sort of hallucination.

Thus was it:—One fair half-day in the July of 1800, by good luck, he was employed, partly out of charity, by one of the keepers, to trim the sward in an oval inclosure within St. James' Park, a little green, but a three minutes' walk along the gravelled way, from the brick-besmoked and grimy Old Brewery of the palace, which gives its ancient name to the public resort on whose borders it stands. It was a little oval, fenced in with iron palings, between whose bars the imprisoned verdure peered forth, as some wild captive creature of the woods from its cage. And alien Israel there—at times staring dreamily about him—seemed like some amazed runaway steer, or trespassing Pequod Indian, impounded on the shores of Narragansett Bay, long ago; and back to New England our exile was called in his soul. For still working, and thinking of home; and thinking of home, and working amid the verdant quietude of this little oasis, one rapt thought begat another, till at last his mind settled intensely, and yet half humorously, upon the image of Old Huckleberry, his mother's favorite old pillion horse; and, ere long, hearing a sudden scraping noise (some hob-shoe without, against the iron paling), he insanely took it to be Old Huckleberry in his stall, hailing him (Israel) with his shod fore-foot clattering against the planks—his customary trick when hungry—and so, down goes Israel's hook, and with a tuft of white clover, impulsively snatched, he hurries away a few paces in obedience to the imaginary summons. But soon stopping midway, and forlornly gazing round at the inclosure, he bethought him that a far different oval, the great oval of the ocean, must be crossed ere his crazy errand could be done; and even then, Old Huckleberry would be found long surfeited with clover, since, doubtless, being dead many a summer, he must be buried beneath it. And many years after, in a far different part of the town, and in far less winsome weather too, passing with his bundle of flags through Red-Cross street, towards Barbican, in a fog so dense that the dimmed and massed blocks of houses, exaggerated by the loom, seemed shadowy ranges on ranges of midnight hills; he heard a confused pastoral sort of sounds; tramplings, lowings, halloos, and was suddenly called to by a voice, to head off certain cattle, bound to Smithfield, bewildered and unruly in the fog. Next instant he saw the white face—white as an orange blossom—of a black-bodied steer, in advance of the drove, gleaming ghost-like through the vapors; and presently, forgetting his limp, with rapid shout

and gesture, he was more eager, even than the troubled farmers, their own-
ers, in driving the riotous cattle back into Barbican. Monomaniac reminiscences were in him—"To the right, to the right!" he shouted, as, arrived at
the street corner, the farmers beat the drove to the left, towards Smithfield:
"To the right! you are driving them back to the pastures—to the right! that
way lies the barn-yard!" "Barn-yard?" cried a voice; "you are dreaming,
old man." And so, Israel, now an old man, was bewitched by the mirage of
vapors; he had dreamed himself home into the mists of the Housatonic
mountains; ruddy boy on the upland pastures again. But how different the
flat, apathetic, dead, London fog now seemed from those agile mists, which
goat-like, climbed the purple peaks, or in routed armies of phantoms, broke
down, pell-mell, dispersed in flight upon the plain; leaving the cattle-boy
loftily alone, clear-cut as a balloon against the sky.

In 1817, he once more endured extremity; this second peace again drifting its discharged soldiers on London, so that all kinds of labor were over-
stocked. Beggars, too, lighted on the walks like locusts. Timber-toed cripples stilted along, numerous as French peasants in *sabots*. And, as thirty years
before, on all sides, the exile had heard the supplicatory cry, not addressed to
him: "An honorable scar, your honor, received at Bunker-Hill, or Saratoga,
or Trenton, fighting for his most gracious Majesty, King George!" So now,
in presence of the still-surviving Israel, our Wandering Jew, the amended
cry was anew taken up, by a succeeding generation of unfortunates: "An
honorable scar, your honor, received at Corunna, or at Waterloo, or at
Trafalgar!" Yet not a few of these petitioners had never been outside of the
London Smoke; a sort of crafty aristocracy in their way, who, without
having endangered their own persons much if anything, reaped no insig-
nificant share, both of the glory and profit of the bloody battles they
claimed; while some of the genuine working heroes, too brave to beg, too
cut-up to work, and too poor to live, laid down quietly in corners and died.
And here it may be noted, as a fact nationally characteristic, that however
desperately reduced at times, even to the sewers, Israel, the American, never
sunk below the mud, to actual beggary.

Though henceforth elbowed out of many a chance threepenny job by
the added thousands who contended with him against starvation, nevertheless, somehow he continued to subsist, as those tough old oaks of the cliffs,
which though hacked at by hail-stones of tempests, and even wantonly
maimed by the passing woodman, still, however cramped by rival trees and
fettered by rocks, succeed, against all odds, in keeping the vital nerve of the
tap-root alive. And even towards the end, in his dismallest December, our

veteran could still at intervals feel a momentary warmth in his topmost boughs. In his Moorfields' garret, over a handful of re-ignited cinders (which the night before might have warmed some lord), cinders raked up from the streets, he would drive away dolor, by talking with his one only surviving, and now motherless child—the spared Benjamin of his old age—of the far Canaan beyond the sea; rehearsing to the lad those well-remembered adventures among New-England hills, and painting scenes of nestling happiness and plenty, in which the lowliest shared. And here, shadowy as it was, was the second alleviation hinted of above.

To these tales of the Fortunate Isles of the Free, recounted by one who had been there, the poor enslaved boy of Moorfields listened, night after night, as to the stories of Sinbad the Sailor. When would his father take him there? "Some day to come, my boy;" would be the hopeful response of an unhoping heart. And "would God it were to-morrow!" would be the impassioned reply.

In these talks Israel unconsciously sowed the seeds of his eventual return. For with added years, the boy felt added longing to escape his entailed misery, by compassing for his father and himself, a voyage to the Promised Land. By his persevering efforts he succeeded at last, against every obstacle, in gaining credit in the right quarter to his extraordinary statements. In short, charitably stretching a technical point, the American Consul finally saw father and son embarked in the Thames for Boston.

It was the year 1826; half a century since Israel, in early manhood, had sailed a prisoner in the Tartar frigate from the same port to which he now was bound. An octogenarian as he recrossed the brine, he showed locks besnowed as its foam. White-haired old ocean seemed as a brother.

Chapter 26

Requiescat in Pace

I T HAPPENED that the ship, gaining her port, was moored to the dock on a Fourth-of-July; and half-an-hour after landing, hustled by the riotous crowd near Faneuil Hall, the old man narrowly escaped being run over by a patriotic triumphal car in the procession, flying a broidered banner, inscribed with gilt letters:—

"BUNKER-HILL.
1775.
GLORY TO THE HEROES THAT FOUGHT!"

It was on Copp's Hill, within the city bounds, one of the enemy's positions during the fight, that our wanderer found his best repose that day. Sitting down here on a mound in the grave-yard, he looked off across Charles River towards the battle-ground, whose incipient monument, at that period, was hard to see, as a struggling sprig of corn in a chilly spring. Upon those heights, fifty years before, his now feeble hands had wielded both ends of the musket. There too he had received that slit upon the chest, which afterwards, in the affair with the Serapis, being traversed by a cutlass wound, made him now the bescarred bearer of a cross.

For a long time he sat mute, gazing blankly about him. The sultry July day was waning. His son sought to cheer him a little ere rising to return to

167

the lodging for the present assigned them by the ship-captain. "Nay," replied the old man, "I shall get no fitter rest than here by the mounds."

But from this true "Potters' Field," the boy at length drew him away; and encouraged next morning by a voluntary purse made up among the reassembled passengers, father and son started by stage for the country of the Housatonic. But the exile's presence in these old mountain townships proved less a return than a resurrection. At first, none knew him, nor could recall having heard of him. Ere long it was found, that more than thirty years previous, the last known survivor of his family in that region, a bachelor, following the example of three-fourths of his neighbors, had sold out and removed to a distant country in the west; where exactly, none could say.

He sought to get a glimpse of his father's homestead. But it had been burnt down long ago. Accompanied by his son, dim-eyed and dim-hearted, he next went to find the site. But the roads had years before been changed. The old road was now broused over by sheep; the new one ran straight through what had formerly been orchards. But new orchards, planted from other suckers, and in time grafted, throve on sunny slopes near by, where blackberries had once been picked by the bushel. At length he came to a field waving with buckwheat. It seemed one of those fields which himself had often reaped. But it turned out, upon inquiry, that but three summers since, a walnut grove had stood there. Then he vaguely remembered that his father had sometimes talked of planting such a grove, to defend the neighboring fields against the cold north wind; yet where precisely that grove was to have been, his shattered mind could not recall. But it seemed not unlikely that during his long exile, the walnut grove had been planted and harvested, as well as the annual crops preceding and succeeding it, on the very same soil.

Ere long, on the mountain side, he passed into an ancient natural wood, which seemed some way familiar, and midway in it, paused to contemplate a strange, mouldy pile, resting at one end against a sturdy beech. Though wherever touched by his staff, however lightly, this pile would crumble, yet here and there, even in powder, it preserved the exact look, each irregularly defined line, of what it had originally been—namely, a half-cord of stout hemlock (one of the woods least affected by exposure to the air), in a foregoing generation chopped and stacked up on the spot, against sledging-time; but, as sometimes happens in such cases, by subsequent oversight, abandoned to oblivious decay. Type now, as it stood there, of for ever arrested intentions, and a long life still rotting in early mishap.

"Do I dream?" mused the bewildered old man, "or what is this vision that comes to me, of a cold, cloudy morning, long, long ago, and I heaving yon elbowed log against the beech, then a sapling? Nay, nay; I can not be so old."

"Come away, father, from this dismal damp wood," said his son, and led him forth.

Blindly ranging to and fro, they next saw a man ploughing. Advancing slowly, the wanderer met him by a little heap of ruinous burnt masonry, like a tumbled chimney, what seemed the jams of the fire-place, now aridly stuck over here and there, with thin, clinging, round prohibitory mosses, like executors' wafers. Just as the oxen were bid stand, the stranger's plough was hitched over sideways, by sudden contact with some sunken stone at the ruin's base.

"There; this is the twentieth year my plough has struck this old hearth-stone. Ah, old man,—sultry day, this."

"Whose house stood here, friend?" said the wanderer, touching the half-buried hearth with his staff, where a fresh furrow overlapped it.

"Don't know; forget the name; gone West, though, I believe. You know 'em?"

But the wanderer made no response; his eye was now fixed on a curious natural bend or wave in one of the bemossed stone jambs.

"What are you looking at so, father?"

"'*Father!*' here," raking with his staff, "*my* father would sit, and here, my mother, and here I, little infant, would totter between, even as now, once again, on the very same spot, but in the unroofed air, I do. The ends meet. Plough away, friend."

Best followed now is this life, by hurrying, like itself, to a close.

Few things remain.

He was repulsed in efforts, after a pension, by certain caprices of law. His scars proved his only medals. He dictated a little book, the record of his fortunes. But long ago it faded out of print—himself out of being—his name out of memory. He died the same day that the oldest oak on his native hills was blown down.

Editorial Appendix

THE FIRST *of the three parts of this* APPENDIX *is a note on the composition, publication, reception, and later critical history of* Israel Potter, *contributed by Walter E. Bezanson, who also gave advice about the text and Related Document. The second, which records textual information, has been prepared by the three editors of the whole Melville Edition, Harrison Hayford, Hershel Parker, and G. Thomas Tanselle. It consists of a note on the textual history of* Israel Potter *and on the editorial principles of this Edition, followed by discussions of certain problematical readings, a list of emendations, a report of line-end hyphenation, and a full list of substantive variants between the* Putnam's Monthly Magazine *and* Putnam's *book editions. The third is a closely related document, Melville's basic source, prepared by R. D. Madison with the staff of the Edition.*

To insure uniform textual policy in all volumes of the Edition, the same three editors, Harrison Hayford, Hershel Parker, and G. Thomas Tanselle, participate in establishing the texts, writing textual commentary, and preparing textual lists for all volumes, except as otherwise noted; even when other textual editors are specifically named (as in the case of certain writings edited from manuscript), the final decisions still rest with one or more of these editors, as noted in individual volumes. Final responsibility for all aspects of every volume, including the HISTORICAL NOTE, *is exercised by the general editor of the Edition, Harrison Hayford.*

In the protracted preparation of Israel Potter *all three editors shared in the initial stage of determining the text, Harrison Hayford and G. Thomas Tanselle in the final stage. Harrison Hayford was the editor who supervised preparation of this volume. The editors were aided throughout by the Edition's bibliographical associate, Richard Colles Johnson, and in the initial stage very substantially by the first contributing scholar, Joel Myerson. In the later stages they were also aided by the Edition's editorial associate, Brian Higgins, by its manuscript associate, Robert C. Ryan, and by the additional contributing scholars, Mary K. Madison and R. D. Madison. The editorial coordinator was Alma A. MacDougall. Indispensable assistance was also given in the initial stage by Helen Baertschy of the Northwestern University Press and by these members of the Edition staff: Kermit Moyer, Barry Quarles, and Christopher Wallace. In the final stage Lynn Horth, Russell Reising, and Robert Sandberg also contributed substantially. At appropriate points in the* EDITORIAL APPENDIX *acknowledgment is made for generous assistance by other scholars.*

Historical Note

MELVILLE'S EIGHTH BOOK, *Israel Potter: His Fifty Years of Exile* (1855), began as a rewrite of an obscure little narrative entitled *Life and Remarkable Adventures of Israel R. Potter . . . ,* printed in Providence, Rhode Island, in 1824. A glance at the frontispiece and title page of the *Life* (reproduced below, pp. 286–87) will sufficiently suggest the popular style of this fugitive publication, and the central events of Potter's sad fall from Revolutionary hero to London peddler. Melville's *Israel Potter,* after its opening chapter, retells that tale, with close adherence to the language and events of the *Life,* and then, shaking free of the original narrative, alternately moves between invented episodes and historical sources unrelated to the *Life.*

Israel Potter is unique among Melville's books from *Typee* (1846) through *The Confidence-Man* (1857). It is the only full-length work to be published serially in a magazine, its nine installments running from July, 1854, through March, 1855, in *Putnam's Monthly,* the book appearing as soon as the March issue was distributed. It is the only one of the books to be offered in the guise of literal biography, the tale presuming to offer an accurate life-history of the man Israel Potter (1744–?1826) who indeed fought at Bunker Hill. It is also Melville's only fiction (setting aside the claims of *Billy Budd*) that can be classed as a historical novel, in this sense:

173

that the narrator in sustained sequences presents famous men of the American Revolution—Benjamin Franklin, John Paul Jones, Ethan Allen, and more briefly King George III and minor English supporters of the American cause—in situations which are a matter of historical record, such as Franklin in Paris, Jones on board the *Ranger* and the *Bon Homme Richard,* Allen in captivity at Falmouth, and the King at Kew Gardens. And finally *Israel Potter* is something of a stepchild among Melville's books—little known, not widely read, only intermittently in print, and until the mid-twentieth century exempted from sustained criticism. Since then, however, commentary has claimed that Melville found roots in his source for an original comedy of Yankee misfortunes which gave scope for all but his highest talents.

The idea of writing a book about the Rhode Island patriot and soldier who became a London beggar was in Melville's mind at least four and a half years before he is known to have begun writing it. The evidence for this, fragmentary but hard, is a casual disclosure penned in his European journal.[1] Late on Tuesday afternoon, December 18, 1849, Melville sat in his room at 25 Craven Street, London, jotting down the day's activities. It was raining miserably and after finding that the British Museum was closed he had given the day to wandering in the bookshops, cleaning up odds and ends in preparation for sailing home one week later, checking the reviews of *Redburn* (1849), and "looking over" the set of American proof sheets of *White-Jacket* (1850) before sending them as printer's copy for the English edition to Richard Bentley, his publisher, with whom he was to dine that night at six. Among the jottings, this:

> Thence among the old bookstores about Great Queen Street & Lincoln's Inn. Looked over a lot of ancient maps of London. Bought one (A.D. 1766) for 3 & 6 pence. I want to use it in case I serve up the Revolutionary narrative of the beggar.

The entry assures us that by the end of 1849 Melville had read the *Life and Remarkable Adventures,* probably owned a copy, and was thinking of working it up. If his statement in the book dedication is anything more than a contribution to the rhetoric of pathos, then what he owned was a "tattered copy, rescued by the merest chance from the rag-pickers". Did the purchaser, whether Melville or one of his family, pick it up as a birthday jest? Potter's

---

1. See the section on "Sources" at the end of the NOTE, where the documentation is explained. Quotations from Melville's letters follow the Davis-Gilman transcription (1960), retaining Melville's erratic spelling. All other documents are also quoted *literatim*.

birthday—August 1, prominently displayed on the frontispiece and repeated in the opening sentence of the narrative—was also Melville's. The
journal entry should be distinguished from travel impressions found elsewhere in the journal which eventually became absorbed into various fictions
by Melville, and even from passages treated consciously as story ideas;
rather we have here a defined project—reworking the *Life* for publication.
Although the project is a precise one, Melville is not sure at this point that
in fact he will do it—only "in case"; but he does hunt for and find a map.
And what are we to make of "serve up"? Has he already downgraded the
performance before beginning it? Not necessarily: the journal entries show
throw-away attitudes toward *Redburn* (though he hawkishly searched out
the reviews), and one might note that four months later, when he wrote to
Richard H. Dana, Jr., about his difficulties in trying "to cook the thing
up," the "thing" was the working manuscript of *Moby-Dick* (1851). Right
now he was gathering all he could from Europe, and could not say himself
where the pressures of circumstance and imagination would take him.

We can distinguish four environments which affected *Israel Potter* almost as much as book sources. London was one, and the purchase of the
map suggests that in 1849 Melville expected to do much more with the
labyrinthine city, into which Potter disappears in the last half of the *Life,*
than the two London chapters he later wrote (Chapters 24–25). Melville's
Craven Street lodgings lay between the Strand and the river, near Charing
Cross; and the Strand, according to Cruchley's *Picture of London* (an edition of which George Duyckinck supplied for the trip), was "a centre to a
greater variety of places and objects of curiosity than any other spot in the
Metropolis."[2] His journal records Melville's interest in the London slums:
entering "squalid lanes, alleys, & closes, till we got to a dirty blind lane",
pushing his way along with "a crowd of beggars" into the rear of Guildhall (November 10), joining the "brutish" mob at a public hanging (November 13), listening to his friend Davis on "the poverty & misery of so
large a portion of the London population" (November 27)—experiences,
one gathers, which might bear on his proposed "narrative of the beggar"
(though the Guildhall scenes will go into the English half of his magazine
story, "Poor Man's Pudding and Rich Man's Crumbs"). He was also
stirred by the view from the "river window" of his fourth-floor lodgings,
and he frequented the Thames bridges:

2. Which of the editions of George Frederick Cruchley's *Picture of London* was supplied
Melville by George Duyckinck is not known; there were fourteen between 1831 and 1849, of
which Sealts, *Melville's Reading,* No. 166, cites the eleventh, 1847.

> While on one of the Bridges, the thought struck me again that a fine thing might be written about a Blue Monday in November London—a city of Dis (Dante's)—clouds of smoke—the damned &c.—coal barges—coaly waters, cast-iron Duke &c.—its marks are left upon you, &c.&c.&c. [November 9]

This scene, fusing perhaps with another view from Primrose Hill of "clouds of smoke" hanging over the city "like a view of hell from Abraham's bosom," becomes the narrator's apocalyptic vision, "In the City of Dis" (Chapter 24), as Israel enters London. So too the city fogs that Melville frequently records in his journal (as, November 25: "Lost my way in the fog") spawned the invented episode of the second London chapter in which old Israel becomes fog-bewildered and experiences hallucination. Some of the London place-names that litter his journal—Holborn, Covent Garden, St. James's Park, and Barbican—reappear in *Israel Potter*. Melville's series of excursions beyond the city—to Hampton Court, Vauxhall, Dulwich, Greenwich Hospital, and Windsor Castle—gave him a sense of the kinds of villages and countryside through which his refugee will be pursued, as well as a sight of Kew Gardens where Israel will talk with the King. Before sailing from Portsmouth Melville took time for "a short stroll into the town" (December 25) where Israel will escape from the ale-house. Although *Israel Potter* would not become as much an English or London book as Melville probably anticipated in 1849, he was experiencing at first hand the backgrounds he might need. Thus *Israel Potter* will be in marked contrast to the section of *Redburn* in which the reader is whirled in and out of the city for "A Mysterious Night in London" (Chapter 46) without ever being shown London.

The Paris visit that followed Melville's London stay provided a second usable environment. His own Channel crossing, his ten days in France (November 28–December 7), and especially his lodgings in the Latin Quarter, gave him settings for Israel's secret mission to Franklin in Paris, barely sketched in the *Life*, but spun into high comedy for *Israel Potter* (Chapters 7–12). One passage from Melville's journal is so richly exploited in Chapter 9 as to warrant full quotation:

> After the lapse of a few days, I find myself this Thursday night [November 29], snugly *roomed* in the fifth story of a lodging house No. 12 & 14 Rue de Bussy, Paris. It is the first night that I have taken possession, & the "Bonne" or chambermaid has lighted a fire of wood, lit the candle, & left me alone, at 11 o'clock P.M. On first gazing around, I am struck by the apparition of a bottle containing a dark fluid, a glass, a decanter of water, & a paper package of sugar (loaf) with a glass basin next to it.—I protest all this was not in the

bond.—But though if I use these things they will doubtless be charged to me, yet let us be charitable,—so I ascribe all this to the benevolence of Madame Capelle, my most polite, pleasant, and Frenchified landlady below. I shall try the brandy before writing more.—And now to resume my Journal.

The brandy and the mood of mild irony here both served nicely when Melville was ready for the scene of Israel being duped by the man of "benevolent irony"—the good Dr. Franklin.

After coming home to New York, Melville renewed acquaintance with a third environment that would enter the novel. In the summer of 1850 he took his family from New York to western Massachusetts. Enchanted with the countryside of the Berkshire Hills he had known in boyhood and the lively literary and social life of the summer resort-season, he purchased a farm outside Pittsfield. Here at Arrowhead, his home for thirteen years, he settled into the writing of *Moby-Dick, Pierre,* magazine tales and sketches, and, in May, 1854, *Israel Potter.* His sensitivity to the Berkshire landforms and the impingement on his imagination of their seasonal changes gave him a theme and an enclosing structure for his "narrative of the beggar" (Chapters 1, 26).[3]

By reaching back into the adventure-years of his earlier life, Melville recovered a fourth environment for *Israel Potter:* naval life at sea. In direct departure from his basic source, he was to create a long sequence (Chapters 14–20) in which Israel serves under the flag of John Paul Jones during his boldest escapades; though historically possible, none of these events happened to Israel Potter of Cranston, Rhode Island. No doubt Melville's sailing through English waters in 1849 ("Through these waters Blake's & Nelson's ships once sailed"—journal, November 1) and the sight in England of Nelson mementos—portraits, busts, uniforms, and the *Victory* riding at anchor in Portsmouth harbor—contributed to Melville's urge to send Israel sailing these historic waters. But back of this recent experience, and back of the volumes of naval history that he would plunder for details, lay his own fourteen months (1843–44) as an ordinary seaman aboard the U.S. frigate *United States.* As in *White-Jacket,* he could count on firsthand familiarity with the language and lore of naval shipboard routine. The temptation became irresistible.

It may well be that when Melville was buying his old map in London he anticipated a simple rewrite job—a hedge against winter winds, a book

3. See Hershel Parker, "Melville and the Berkshires: Emotion-Laden Terrain, 'Reckless Sky-Assaulting Mood,' and Encroaching Wordsworthianism," in *American Literature: The New England Heritage,* ed. James Nagel and Richard Astro (New York: Garland, 1981), pp. 65–80.

merely fun to do if he ever got time, or simply a quick way to make money. It is interesting that he even contemplated, as early as 1849, composing a work whose major narrative line would be from another book, a writing method which would have anticipated his procedure with "Benito Cereno." All we know is that on his return from Europe any serious commitment to *Israel Potter* gave way to massive preoccupation with *Moby-Dick* and *Pierre*. After that, in a period of readjustment and while working on his magazine pieces, the "Revolutionary narrative of the beggar" resurfaced. Then London, Paris, the Berkshire Hills, and the sea all became part of *Israel Potter*.

II

The two years between the publication of *Pierre* in the summer of 1852 and the first installment of *Israel Potter* in the summer of 1854 seem to have been a difficult and ambiguous time for Melville. Two books that he planned did not get published, if indeed they were ever completed. On the other hand, he found a new market, for tales and sketches in the magazines. Both circumstances bear directly on *Israel Potter*.

Pierre had complicated life for Melville as a writer and as a member of the ever watchful Melville-Shaw-Gansevoort clans. The "rural bowl of milk"—so Melville had described *Pierre* to Mrs. Hawthorne during his work on it—soured in the mouths of the critics. The reviewers were almost unanimously shocked by its style and themes, and some, as if personally insulted, directed rage against the author himself, charging Melville with moral depravity and even insanity. His family and relatives, united in believing that too close application to his work was endangering his health, as they diplomatically put it, massed their considerable energies and those of influential friends, including Hawthorne, towards seeking a consulship for Melville under the newly elected president, Franklin Pierce. But by the summer of 1853 these efforts had failed to secure one he could accept.

In 1852, meanwhile, even while *Pierre* was suffering universal castigation, Melville was getting ambiguously involved in the "Agatha story" which he had heard on Nantucket that July, and for which by mid-August he had a written account from the journal of the lawyer who had told it to him. In a curious gesture of affection, presumption, and self-doubt, he offered the materials to his friend Hawthorne in the first of his three "Agatha letters," with detailed suggestions for their development. In December when Melville visited him in Concord, Hawthorne (according to

Melville's letter to him soon after) "expressed uncertainty" about under-
taking it, whether because he was actually considering it or as a way of
extricating himself from Melville's possessive generosity—and properly in
the end urged Melville to write the story himself. Melville wrote to him, "I
have decided to do so, and shall begin it immediately upon reaching home;
and so far as in me lies, I shall endeavor to do justice to so interesting a
story of reality." In turn, he now asked Hawthorne to send *him* ideas on
how best to go about it. Whether when he got right down to it Melville
found that it really wasn't his kind of story, or as some evidence suggests
couldn't interest a publisher in whatever portions he may have written, no
published book or long magazine story came from the winter of 1852–53,
though the "story of Agatha" was most likely the manuscript he took to
the Harpers in the spring of 1853 but was "prevented from printing."[4]

Similarly, complications blocked Melville's efforts to get out a book
the following winter. He wrote the Harpers on November 24, 1853:

> In addition to the work which I took to New York last Spring, but
> which I was prevented from printing at that time; I have now in hand, and
> pretty well on towards completion, another book—300 pages, say—partly of
> nautical adventure, and partly—or, rather, chiefly, of Tortoise Hunting Ad-
> venture. It will be ready for press some time in the coming January. . . .

Melville asked and got an advance of $300 for the proposed work, but the
book was never published. The obvious but unclear relationship of the
book to the spring 1854 publication of "The Encantadas," in *Putnam's,*
suggests that Melville's gift for complicating business affairs, at least, was
in its normal, healthy condition. It also typifies his new commitment to
the magazines.

Harper's New Monthly Magazine, which began publication in 1850,
found itself with a serious competitor at the beginning of 1853 when the
first (January) number of *Putnam's Monthly Magazine of American Literature,
Science, and Art* appeared. *Harper's* offered commentaries on current politics at home and abroad, which *Putnam's* did not attempt, but the staple
fare of both magazines was history, biography, travel, and fiction, offered
in single articles or installments, supplemented by literary notices and
general news and gossip of the arts. Both magazines were printed in

4. See Harrison Hayford, "The Significance of Melville's 'Agatha' Letters," *ELH, A
Journal of English Literary History,* XIII (December, 1946), 299–310; Merton M. Sealts, Jr.,
"The Chronology of Melville's Short Fiction, 1853–1856," *Harvard Library Bulletin,* XXVIII
(October, 1980), 398.

double column, with uncomfortably small type; but frequent vignettes or full-page engravings, a fashionable feature of mid-century printing in which *Harper's* excelled, and a generally lively editorial air of a Victorian sort, made both of them attractive to subscribers. They were, in fact, somewhat livelier counterparts of the English and Continental reviews, which they consciously rivaled. Both magazines tried with considerable success for a middle ground between high performance and a popular but educated audience. *Harper's* took pride in its English contributors; *Putnam's* was after original materials from Americans. In retrospect, it was Melville's good fortune that at a time when he was subject to rather virulent criticism, and was experiencing uncertainties about his career and health, two magazines of such quality were available to him. They provided a regular market and reasonable pay. Even the anonymity both magazines preferred for their contributors was not without some advantages for Melville. *Putnam's* "Introductory" to its first number made a point of this anonymity, along with its main theme of seeing "through 'American spectacles' "; their reader would find

> poets, wits, philosophers, critics, artists, travellers, men of erudition and science, all strictly masked, as becomes worshippers of that invisible Truth which all our efforts and aims will seek to serve. And as he turns from us to accost those masks we remind the reader of the young worshipper of Isis. For in her temple at Säis, upon the Nile, stood her image, for ever veiled. And when an ardent neophyte passionately besought that he might see her, and would take no refusal, his prayer was granted. The veil was lifted, and the exceeding splendor of that beauty dazzled him to death. Let it content you, ardent reader, to know that behind these masks are those whom you much delight to honor—those whose names, like the fame of Isis, have gone into other lands.

This was Melville country even if somewhat flattened out, and the advantage of pseudo-anonymity—everybody played the unmasking game—was that Melville could have it both ways at a time when his reputation could use some disguise. It was also a protection for editors like the *Putnam's* team of George William Curtis, Charles F. Briggs, and Parke Godwin, whose enthusiasm for Melville at this period was real but guarded.

By May, 1854, Melville saw a special opportunity for serving up the Potter narrative. His difficulties with two book projects and his recent success with the magazines gave him a new idea: why not try for serialization? Having made the decision it was natural that he should turn first to

Harper's. The house after all held rights to all seven of his previous books and the magazine had published a *Moby-Dick* excerpt, "The Town-Ho's Story" (October, 1851), and more recently "Cock-A-Doodle-Doo!" (December, 1853). The June *Harper's* was printing "Poor Man's Pudding and Rich Man's Crumbs"—the writing of which, taking him back to the Guildhall beggars, may have reawakened interest in his Revolutionary beggar. On May 25 he made a proposal to the Harper brothers:

> When you write me concerning the "Tortoises" extract, you may, if you choose, inform me at about what time you would be prepared to commence the publication of another Serial in your Magazine—supposing you had one, in prospect, that suited you. . . . By writing soon, on the latter subject, you will greatly oblige.

Apparently their lack of interest left Melville free to turn to *Putnam's*.

Melville's standing with the new magazine was good. He had been one of the more than seventy American writers who had received a printed letter in October, 1852, announcing *Putnam's* and soliciting contributions. The first number (January, 1853), in an essay-review of *The Homes of American Authors,* gave Melville passing mention three times. The second number (February) featured Melville with a long anonymous piece (by Fitz-James O'Brien): "Our Young Authors—Melville." O'Brien's essay was highly laudatory about the first five books but curiously omitted any discussion of *Moby-Dick,* was repeatedly caustic about the "inexcusable insanity" of *Pierre,* and ended by advising Melville to stop feeding on Sir Thomas Browne and begin a diet of Addison. Nevertheless Melville was sufficiently pleased with these early numbers of *Putnam's* to send the editors "Bartleby" that fall, and "The Encantadas" soon after. Their refusal of "The Two Temples," though it must have angered Melville, may well have given him the opening for *Israel Potter*. Briggs wrote Melville (May 12) an elaborate defense of the refusal—he feared the pointed satire of New York's wealthy Grace Church—and attempted pacification through praise. Obviously anxious not to lose Melville to *Harper's*, Putnam himself, who had been the American publisher of *Typee,* wrote Melville the very next day with further explanations, a request for a drawing or daguerreotype of Melville for use in the magazine, and an invitation: "We hope you will give us some more of your good things." This was on May 13, 1854. Twelve days later Melville tried *Harper's* on the "Serial" without success. Then he turned to *Putnam's*.

Melville's letter to Putnam, June 7, 1854, is the key document on *Israel*

Potter. Unfortunately only a transcript is known,[5] which carries a tantalizing ellipsis:

> I send you prepaid by Express, to-day, some sixty and odd pages of MSS. The manuscript is part of a story called "Israel Potter," concerning which a more particular understanding need be had. . . .
>
> This story when finished will embrace some 300 or more MS. pages. I propose to publish it in your Magazine at the rate of five dollars per printed page, the copyright to be retained by me. Upon the acceptation of this proposition (if accepted) $100. to be remitted to me as an advance. After that advance shall have been cancelled in the course of publication of the numbers, the price of the subsequent numbers to be remitted to me upon each issue of the Magazine as long as the story lasts. Not less than the amount of ten printed pages (but as much more as may be usually convenient) to be published in one number.
>
> On my side, I guarantee to provide you with matter for at least ten printed pages in ample time for each issue. I engage that the story shall contain nothing of any sort to shock the fastidious. There will be very little reflective writing in it; nothing weighty. It is adventure. As for its interest, I shall try to sustain that as well as I can[.]

The passage cut from the first paragraph may be a serious loss, but a fair guess can be made as to its probable contents. First, the subject about which Melville felt "a more particular understanding need be had" would not seem to have been matters of payment or contract, for these are dealt with *ab ovo,* and with consummate clumsiness, in the next paragraph. Second, the one aspect of Melville's proposed work that was peculiar, and surely called for an "understanding" before publication, was that some of it was to be a virtual paraphrase of a previously published work, the *Life,* a matter different in kind and extent from Melville's habitual use of "sources" for some passages beginning with *Typee.* The portion of the manuscript enclosed—"some sixty and odd pages" of a proposed "300 or more MS. pages," roughly the first fifth—must have included that part of *Israel Potter* (Chapters 2–6) which in fact, as he said in the book dedication, "preserves, almost as in a reprint," the *Life;* it was a very close rewrite, as will be shown later. Third, the magazine version of *Israel Potter* (and presumably the enclosed manuscript) did not include the dedication added

---

5. *Letters* (p. 169) corrects to June the transcript's evident misdating as July while retaining 7 as the day. However, Bruce Bebb (letter to Bezanson, April 6, 1977) queries whether this letter may not be the same as the unlocated one of June 12 cited below (p. 212, from *Letters,* p. xx, n. 6)—in which case June 12, not June 7, may be its correct date.

to the book version of the following March; and it was only in the dedication that, among other things, Melville was to make clear his very substantive indebtedness to the original narrative. The time for George P. Putnam to learn that *Israel Potter* was to be basically a rewrite job was now rather than after the critical vultures could move in, and it is probable that in the passage omitted from the letter Melville explained his intentions. It is quite possible that Melville did not yet know that he would abandon sustained use of the *Life* in the next batch of manuscript.

The rate of payment Melville asked for and got—$5.00 per page—was actually less than the $150 he had recently received for twenty-five pages of "The Encantadas," but it was the same rate he had been given the previous winter for "Bartleby," and was the top standard rate with *Putnam's*. The request for an advance of $100 was not granted; though we do not have George P. Putnam's reply to Melville's letter, other records show that from the beginning monthly payments were made to Melville according to the count of his pages in each number. Nor did *Putnam's*, for five of the nine installments, hold to Melville's request for not less than ten pages per number (see tabulation, p. 207). But the arrangements on the whole were a good bargain for Melville, providing him, as it turned out, with an average of nearly $47 per month of steady income for a nine-month period. His total receipts for the magazine publication were to come to $421.50. And he still held the copyright (if Putnam at this point agreed to that) for future book publication.

The most interesting part of the letter, of course, is the last paragraph. Here Melville engages not only to get his copy in on time but draws some lines within which the tale will operate. When Melville promises "that the story shall contain nothing of any sort to shock the fastidious" he is surely recalling Briggs's and Putnam's recent letters on "The Two Temples" and his reply to Putnam on May 16 with a similar promise of "some other things, to which, I think, no objections will be made on the score of tender consciences of the public."[6] But the larger context of these promises is their mutual awareness of the shock Melville's last novel, *Pierre,* had provided. It was wise and probably necessary for Melville, peddling only the first section of an unfinished manuscript, to make his intentions clear. In effect he is responding to the critics' demands that he respect contemporary moral conventions, and that he write a Defoe-style narrative. His promise to rule out anything "weighty" and to minimize "reflective

6. Sealts, "Chronology," p. 379, n. 19.

writing," however, goes beyond the problem of *Pierre;* it is a promise not to mount the German horse—in the day's parlance, whatever was "metaphysical" and Carlylean, with *Mardi* and *Moby-Dick* perhaps as instances. The reader of *Israel Potter* can decide how well Melville kept that part of the bargain.

III

In constructing his historical novel Melville moved in and out of his sources so frequently that *Israel Potter* offers a rare opportunity to watch him at work. Four books were successively open beside him during the writing of thirteen of his twenty-six chapters: Henry Trumbull's *Life and Remarkable Adventures of Israel R. Potter* (Providence, 1824); Robert C. Sands's compiled *Life and Correspondence of John Paul Jones* (New York, 1830); James Fenimore Cooper's *History of the Navy of the United States of America* (New York, 1853);[7] and Ethan Allen's *A Narrative of Colonel Ethan Allen's Captivity* (first published in Philadelphia, 1779).

In addition he read widely in Benjamin Franklin's collected writings, made minor use of a few other books, and refreshed his memory of England and Paris with his own journal. About any section of *Israel Potter* we can say with assurance: here Melville is following a particular source closely, using much of the original language; or here he is merely picking up random facts or phrases from that source; or here he is amplifying that source by invention; or now he has laid aside that source and turned to another; or at this point he has pushed all sources aside and is engaged in full improvisation.

The *Life* is Melville's first source in point of order and importance.[8] Some familiarity with this characteristic document from American popular culture of the 1820's is almost requisite to an understanding of *Israel Potter*. The *Life* belongs to a long tradition of personal narratives such as the earlier accounts of Indian captivity and later narratives of escaped slaves.

---

7. Neither the copy nor imprint of Cooper's *History of the Navy* used by Melville is known; but R. D. Madison (*Melville Society Extracts,* No. 46, September, 1981, pp. 9–10) has shown that Melville's borrowings were drawn not from the first edition (1839) but from the revised text that appeared only in the editions of 1840 and 1846. The stereotyped plates of the 1846 edition were used by Melville's own publisher, G. P. Putnam & Co., in the three-volumes-in-one *History of the Navy* (New York, 1853) cited here.

8. See the account and photographic reproduction of the *Life* in the RELATED DOCUMENT section at the end of this volume. Full citations are given there for the American Experience Series paperback reprint and for the excerpts in Dorson's *America Rebels.* Sources of information about Trumbull are also cited.

Potter's sad tale was among the last to appear of the more than two hundred veterans' narratives of the American Revolution which Richard Dorson found to be in print following the War of 1812. Though written in the first person and presented as if every word were Potter's, the *Life* was the work of Henry Trumbull (1781–1842), about whom little is known. He seems to have been himself a versatile Yankee from a famous Connecticut family and the probable author, possibly at the age of seventeen, of a notably inaccurate history of early America, popularly known as "Trumbull's Indian Wars."[9] How true the *Life* is remains uncertain, for we are dependent on Trumbull for almost everything now known about his subject. When in June of 1823 old Potter came tottering into Providence (having set out from Boston on foot), he took lodgings, according to the *Life,* "at a public Inn in High-Street" (p. 103).[10] Trumbull ran a printing office near by. During the next seven months, apparently, while Potter was trying unsuccessfully to claim a veteran's pension to relieve his abject want, Trumbull hastily put together the *Life and Remarkable Adventures,* a twelvemo volume of 108 pages, crudely printed, to be sold in the streets for twenty-eight cents. The copyright notice firmly asserted Trumbull's authorship ("the right whereof he claims as author"). A deposition at the end offered a validation of Potter's war record by a local veteran who remembered him. In a brief foreword, "TO THE PUBLIC", Trumbull made the case for Potter's need, which he hoped his book would remedy; and then, promising a "concise and simple narration," the author stepped aside, presumably, as if to let Potter speak for himself.

Trumbull offered a narrative with a new twist. Though Potter had served his Country with Honor at Bunker Hill, endured Harsh Imprisonment, and escaped to serve as Courier for a Secret Mission to France, Fortune had consigned him to a Lifetime of Oblivion in the Enemy's Capital. Now home, broken and penniless, his country refused him a pension; as the *Life* phrased it in its one shrill passage, "on no other principle, than that *I was absent from the country when the pension law passed*—my Petition was REJECTED!!!" (p. 105). Trumbull must have

9. Trumbull's *History,* which was republished under different titles over several decades, was "vigorously denounced in Field's *Indian bibliography,*" and Peter Force "said that he found twenty-two chronological errors on a single page," as reported by J. N. Larned in *The Literature of American History* (Boston: Houghton Mifflin, 1902), p. 90.

10. References simply by number are to page (or page and line) in the present NN (Northwestern-Newberry) edition; those with "p." or "pp." are to the source under discussion.

felt it was a strong bid to lay before a country already aquiver with semicentennial celebration plans, including a huge monument to celebrate Bunker Hill.[11] A cute Yankee with a feel for the popular taste, Trumbull brought out in the same year as the *Life* of Potter a similar little book, *Life and Adventures of Colonel Daniel Boon.* Then five years later he exploited another "remarkable adventure" by interviewing a hermit who lived in a cave near the Massachusetts border, discovering (if it was true) that he was a fugitive slave, and publishing another similar little book about him—thereby leaping from the popular genre of one generation to a promising one for the next. (See further discussion and reproductions, pp. 277–401.)

Probably the major episodes of the *Life* are reasonably accurate, but the rhetorical devices—the air of aggrieved innocence, the bits of Yankee posturing, the pathetic apostrophes, the patriotic pietism—are very likely Trumbull's. The message is clear: Trumbull's *Life*—the "Revolutionary narrative of the beggar," as Melville had ungrammatically phrased it in London—however accurate as biography, was first of all a prime document of American popular culture. That Melville sensed this, perhaps was drawn to it for that very reason, is suggested by his enlargement of Israel into a partially mythic figure in the middle section of his own narrative.

As he began to write *Israel Potter* Melville made two important decisions: to take the narrative role away from Potter, and to change his birthplace from Cranston, Rhode Island, to the Berkshire region near Pittsfield. Together these decisions gave Melville the chance to write a prelude of "poetic reflection" on the Berkshire country (Chapter 1) quite beyond the imaginative or geographical range of his provincial hero. Melville's intimate knowledge of his own environment had been deepened by at least two books. In his first adult summer at Pittsfield he had acquired (July 16, 1850) *A History of the County of Berkshire, Massachusetts* (Pittsfield, 1829), edited by David Dudley Field. The book has several interesting connections with *Israel Potter.*[12] So too, in a general way, has Godfrey

11. The cornerstone was laid June 17, 1825, by Lafayette, and Daniel Webster's oration was a school classic for a century. The Monument, completed in 1843, was dedicated by President Tyler and his cabinet before a massive crowd. *"His Highness"* (Melville's dedicatory phrase) is 30 feet square at the base, 221 feet high.

12. Melville's copy, in the Berkshire Athenæum, Pittsfield, has numerous marks, annotations, and notes by Melville. (See Sealts, *Melville's Reading,* No. 216; also *Log,* I, 378–79; and Jay Leyda, "White Elephant vs. White Whale," *Town and Country,* CI [August, 1947], 69.) The *History* has an excellent folding map of the county which shows clearly the Otis-Windsor region and other landmarks referred to in Chapter 1. It also has sections on the weather and change of seasons, though Melville had no need to crib here, and a bird list that

Greylock's [J. E. A. Smith's] *Taghconic; or Letters and Legends about Our Summer Home* (Boston, 1852), about which Melville wrote to Hawthorne in October, 1852: "you figure in it, & I also." In fact he had been asked to contribute to it.[13] But Melville's eloquent first chapter in *Israel Potter* has no significant indebtedness to Field or Smith. Rather it establishes its own thematic motifs for the narrative as a whole—the sense of place, the passage of time, a tone of alienation, and mythical resonances. Melville's casual remark in his dedication about the "change in the grammatical person" implies mere substitution of "he" for "I"; to the contrary, the creation of a narrator of complex sensibility outside the simple account of the *Life* was the crucial compositional act.

For Chapter 2 Melville opened his copy of the *Life* and went to work. Through five chapters (2–6) he held himself to a relatively simple rewriting of the first half of Trumbull's narrative (pp. 5–50), staying remarkably close to its text. Melville's method in its simplest form can be seen by comparing his first four paragraphs in Chapter 2 with the opening lines of the *Life*. (In those opening lines, given here, words Melville borrowed verbatim are italicized; words he paraphrased are placed within brackets; the remaining words he did not use. For full comparison, see the photofacsimile of the *Life*, keyed marginally to the NN text, pp. 286–394.)

> I was born of reputable parents in the town of Cranston, State of Rhode Island, August 1st, 1744.—I *continued* with my parents there *in the* full *enjoyment of parental* [affection] and indulgence, un*til* I arrived at *the age of 18, when, having formed an* [acquaintance with the] *daughter* of a Mr. Richard Gardner, a near *neighbour,* for whom (in the opinion of my friends) entertaining too

includes six birds named in Chapter 1. On the front flyleaves Melville penciled thirty-four lines describing his three-day trip through the back country to the southwest with his cousin, Robert Melvill, surveying crops for the Agricultural Society. A newspaper clipping pasted in the book announces this trip and a second one a few days later "through the eastern towns to the north"; if Melville made the second trip (there is no evidence) it took him up through the Otis-Windsor region which he chose as Israel's birthplace. Two other links: a newspaper clipping from a local Fourth of July address, pasted on the front endpapers and entitled by Melville "Revolutionary Reminiscences of Pittsfield" (but not drawn upon); and, among several of Melville's reference notes on a back flyleaf: "Old man—soldier 118." Page 118 carries an account of the forming of Colonel John Patterson's local regiment of minutemen in 1774 and its rapid departure for Boston after the battle of Lexington; Melville borrowed several lines, partly verbatim, for his second and third paragraphs in Chapter 3, "Israel Goes to the Wars . . . ."

13. See Sealts, *Melville's Reading,* No. 478; *Letters,* p. 161; *Log,* I, 461–62; and Merton M. Sealts, Jr., *The Early Lives of Melville* (Madison: University of Wisconsin Press, 1974), pp. 29 ff.

great a degree of partiality, I *was repremanded and threatened* by them *with*
more *severe punishment,* [if my *visits* were not *discontinu*ed.] Disappointed in
my intentions of [forming an union (when of suitable age)] with one whom I
really loved, I *deemed* the *conduct* of [my parents] in this respect *unreasonable
and oppressive,* and *formed the determination to* [leave] *them, for* the purpose of
seeking *another home and other friends.*

    It was on Sunday, while the family were [at meeting,] *that* I *packed up as*
[many arti*c*les] *of* my *cloathing as* [could] *be contained in a* pocket *handkerchief,
which, with a small quantity of provision,* I conveyed to and [secreted] *in a piece
of woods in the rear of* my father's *house;* I *then returned and continued in the house
until about 9 in the evening, when* [with the *pretence* of retiring] *to bed,* I *passed*
into a back room and from thence *out of a back door and hastened to the* [spot
where I had deposited my cloathes, &c.]—*it was a* [warm summer's] *night,
and that* I *might* be enabled to *travel with the more* [facility] *the succeeding day,* I
lay down at the foot of a tree and *repose*d my*self un*til [about 4 in the morning]
when I *arose and* [commenced my journey], travelling *westward,* with an
intention of *reach*ing if possible *the new countries . . . .*

Trumbull's flat, ingenuous tone suggests problems for Melville, yet almost everything here Melville either borrowed verbatim or paraphrased.
Melville's prefatory lines are cool; the narrator means to keep his distance.
But he is introducing a theme not in Trumbull when he raises the king/
sire analogy, suggesting a link between personal and political rebellion
mildly reminiscent of Hawthorne's "My Kinsman, Major Molineux."
And in the course of the passage he heightens the discord between father
and son with the gratuitous phrases "oppressed by his father," "the desperate boy," and "the tyranny of his father." One other addition, the half
dozen lines about Israel's sensations on waking, suggests the narrator will
not hesitate to make a simile or two when so moved.

    Melville's close adherence to the *Life* in the example just cited is repre-
sentative of his method in Chapters 2–6, with exceptions presently to be
noted. Put bluntly but fairly, in these five chapters Melville transcribed
some words or phrases from Trumbull into at least half the lines of his
manuscript. Nor was he leaving out much: up to the midpoint of the *Life*
(p. 50—which he reached as he finished Chapter 6) he seldom ignored so
much as a whole sentence, and only five or six times jumped over as many
as a dozen lines. The most typical intrusions of the narrator are his brief
speculations on Israel's motives, or his recurrent foreshadowing of coming
tribulations. The narrator's generally mild tone and relaxed manner are
indicated by the phrase in the middle of Chapter 2 (9.9): "I suppose it
never entered his mind, that . . ." (Melville's only use of the first person

by his narrator). Only rarely does he let his narrator sound the Ishmael tone, as in a rhythmic short paragraph in Chapter 2:

> A hermitage in the forest is the refuge of the narrow-minded misan-thrope; a hammock on the ocean is the asylum for the generous distressed. The ocean brims with natural griefs and tragedies; and into that watery immensity of terror, man's private grief is lost like a drop (10.7–10).

Yet as he composed—one might almost say paraphrased—this first section of manuscript, Melville began to allow himself a little more freedom with each chapter. Thus he begins his third chapter with a longer prologue than his second. Allusions to Sicinius Dentatus (the much-wounded Roman hero) and to Jaffa and Jonah open the distance between the narrator and Israel. Trumbull's four-page account (pp. 14–17) of the Battle of Bunker Hill occasioned Melville's first indifference to his source: "But every one knows all about the battle," says the narrator, passing up the *Life*'s systematic description of the three waves of British attack for fragments of Israel's personal experience. Melville's image of the severed sword arm on the ground is a bold adaptation of Trumbull's punning account of how with a rusty cutlass Israel "dis-*armed*" a British officer forever. Potter's six weeks in the hospital (p. 18) become two weeks to let him see Washington take command on the third of July, but there is no dramatized scene. For the first time Melville constructs a bit of dialogue (17) not in the source (the exchanges with the drunken soldiers) and wholly invents two comic episodes: Israel's encounter with the boorish peasants (18), and his meeting while masquerading as a cripple with "a genuine cripple" (20). These inventions, slight as they are, suggest that as early as Chapter 3 Melville is getting restless with his source. He begins to strengthen the comic possibilities in the Yankee theme which appears intermittently in Trumbull's usually somber account. In the Yankee-jig scene (16) the narrator first notes Israel's "lank and flaxen hair"—the beginning of a motif, not in the *Life,* which will become Israel's mythic mark in the Jones chapters. But Melville is working rapidly. He mistakenly gives the date of June 17 to the day *before* the battle (13.13, emended in the present edition). He misreads as ten feet the width of the ditch across which Potter made his great leap of "upwards of 19 feet" (p. 31).[14]

14. In the first edition of the *Life* the reading is "upwards of 19 feet". Roger P. McCutcheon thought Melville's change to "ten" was a case of his "not wishing to try his reader too far" (p. 169); but McCutcheon was reasoning from a copy of the second or third edition (as indicated by his citing, p. 162, the title-page price of 31 cents) where the reading is "12 feet". See discussion of the NN emendation to "19" at 21.8 and p. 285.

In Chapter 4, though continuing the close paraphrase, Melville opens up two scenes—Israel's conversations with Sir John Millet—with far greater freedom than heretofore (24–26). Israel's insistent addressing of Sir John as "Mr. Millet" is a bit of social comedy constructed out of Trumbull's indiscriminate and unknowing mixture of both forms of address.[15] Israel's hair is again specially noticed: "See his long, yellow hair behind; he looks like a Chinaman," says one of the English gentlemen.

The primary scenes of Chapter 5 and 6 are elaborate expansions of the *Life*. Israel's meeting with the King is five times longer in Melville, and as he had with Sir John, Israel again plays the defiant Yankee game. Whereas Trumbull specifically describes Potter as "taking off my hat" (p. 44) and twice addressing the King as "your Majesty" (pp. 44, 45), Melville's Israel "touched his hat—but did not remove it," and at first bluntly refused to grant the King his majesty (30). The interview with the three English gentlemen and the business about the boots with the false heels (34–36) is a broad dramatization of Trumbull's account (pp. 47–50). Dialogue is introduced, Squire Woodcock calls Israel "a Yankee of the true blue stamp," and Israel, when he asks "Am I to steal from here to Paris on my stocking-feet?" begins a new style of Yankee retort not even hinted at in the original.

With the conclusion of Chapter 6, Melville pushed aside the *Life and Remarkable Adventures*. He had his central figure in mind now, and saw large sequences for Israel burgeoning out of Trumbull's simple facts. A paragraph on Potter's new role as secret courier to Franklin (pp. 50–51) grows into four chapters (Chapters 7–10). A merely honorific mention of John Paul Jones's exploits (pp. 59–60) flowers into major sequences which Captain Paul dominates (Chapters 10–11, 14–19). A dozen lines on Potter's return to England from Paris, and a passing remark—"I remained secreted in the house of 'Squire Woodcock a few days . . ." (p. 51)—open up into the elaborate adventures surrounding Israel's incarceration at the Squire's house (Chapters 12–13). Though Melville dipped back into the *Life* a few times for even lesser episodes or phrases, he did not return to Trumbull's long account of Potter's dismal London years (pp. 55–100) until his next-to-last chapter; there in summary he presented "Forty-five Years" (Chapter 25). From Chapter 7 on, Melville turned elsewhere for major sources, or improvised at will.

Melville's dedication to *Israel Potter* is misleading about his use of the

15. The joke is one of the oldest in the Brother Jonathan tradition; Melville had played it on himself (or caught himself in it) in his journal, December 13, 1849, by describing "a note sealed with a coronet" as "from Mr. Rutland—The Duke of Rutland I mean . . . ."

Life. By no standards could it be said truly of the book as a whole that "it preserves, almost as in a reprint, Israel Potter's autobiographical story," merely "retouched." The qualifications Melville offers—"with the exception of some expansions, and additions of historic and personal details, and one or two shiftings of scene"—nicely describe only Chapters 2–6. If Melville actually wrote the dedication on or near the Bunker Hill Day whose date he gave it—June 17, 1854—when he was still merely rewriting the *Life,* he never bothered to revise it when he sent it to Putnam's six or eight months later for inclusion in the book. If he wrote the dedication for the book early in 1855, back-dating it to Bunker Hill Day, 1854, for the historical and ironic effect, he was being literary rather than literal. Melville's intention would seem to have been to protect himself against charges from opposite sides that he expected (and did get) from the critics: that he had simply rewritten another work without acknowledgment, or that in rewriting a historical account he had taken undue fictional liberties. Writing his dedication, Melville obviously was more amused with the game of presenting his work "TO HIS HIGHNESS THE BUNKER-HILL MONUMENT" (the book's first Yankee joke), more bemused by certain pathetic ironies of Israel's fate, than concerned with being exact about how he had used the *Life.* What he meant by claiming "general fidelity to the main drift of the original narrative" is linked to his ironic pose—that the only reason his hero falls into misfortune in the tale that follows is that his source requires it. He cannot mitigate "the allotment of Providence" (perhaps a play on the city of publication). To that high source he will be true. Otherwise, as we have seen, his general fidelity to the *Life* (in his Chapters 2–6) gave out when he had used but half of it.

Melville's sources for the brilliant sequence on Franklin (Chapters 7–10, beginning of 12) are best conceived broadly. In London Melville lodged at 25 Craven Street, Strand; Franklin had lived eighteen years at 7 (later 36) Craven Street.[16] In Paris Melville noted seeing "Franklin's letter" at the Bibliothèque Royale. In mid-nineteenth-century America it was impossible to escape Franklin; only Washington, archetypal father of the Republic, surpassed him as cultural hero. If Parson Weems, who had planted Washington's cherry tree in the garden of national morals, was unable to do as much for Franklin with *The Life of Doctor Benjamin Franklin* (1815), it was because the shrewd Doctor had gotten there first. Poor Richard had been a folk hero for a hundred years, and the half-mythical

16. Carl Van Doren, *Benjamin Franklin* (New York: Viking, 1938), p. 272.

figure of the printer's apprentice who went to the top was everywhere, especially after a reasonably complete edition of the *Autobiography* became available (1818). Indefatigable publicists like Parson Weems, Noah Webster, Peter Parley (Samuel Goodrich), Jacob Abbott (author of the Rollo books for boys), and William Holmes McGuffey (compiler of the Readers) drenched the American mind with "choice anecdotes" of Franklin. Melville's primary resource, as he turned to creating his own complex image of "the man of wisdom" was contemporary American culture. He was a subscriber to *Harper's,* for example, when two issues (January, February, 1852) carried Abbott's life of Franklin, illustrated with seventy-seven woodcuts; not specifically a source, Abbott's version of the Franklin story—a kind of Rollo book for adults—was the popular one: that the good Doctor performed his duties in a way "to invest industry, and frugality, and all the other plain and unpretending virtues of humble life with a sort of poetic charm . . . ."

Melville's presentation of Franklin, though dominantly comic, is so complex and informed as to suggest considerable study of Franklin's life and writings. "The Way to Wealth" (1757), from which Israel reads aloud a passage and plucks the motto that will fire Captain Jones and shed its ironies on Israel's subsequent fate ("God helps them that help themselves"), was of course available everywhere. But if Melville copied these sayings of Poor Richard from the second volume of Jared Sparks's edition of Franklin's *Works,* he could not have missed Franklin's essay on Indian Corn, and so may have been led into the sage's words of greeting to Israel (40.1), on hearing his "How do you do, Doctor Franklin?"—"Ah! I smell Indian corn . . . ."[17] The same volume contains a rich variety of Franklin's essays on morals, economy, and politics, as well as the bagatelles; saturation in some such collection underlies Melville's detailed references to the sage's range of interests and the felicity with which Melville's narrator captures Franklin's tone throughout these chapters. Another volume of Sparks contains "Maritime Observations," in which Franklin discusses problems of over-ballasting, ship design, and "driving to leeward"—subjects the man

17. The original passage in "The Way to Wealth," which Israel slightly "misreads," runs: "So what signifies wishing and hoping for better times? We may make these times better, if we bestir ourselves. *Industry need not wish, and he that lives upon hopes will die fasting. There are no gains without pains; then help, hands, for I have no lands;* or, if I have, they are smartly taxed." *The Works of Benjamin Franklin,* ed. Jared Sparks (Boston, 1836–40), II, 96. See discussion at 53.38. The last paragraph of "The Way to Wealth" and the title, "Observations on Mayz, or Indian Corn," are on the same page: *Works,* II, 103.

of wisdom expounds to Captain Paul as rapt Israel listens in.[18] Sparks's
first volume, containing the *Autobiography* and a long "Continuation" by
Sparks, has many phrases that echo in the Franklin sequence; and an
uncommon fact, that for a short time Franklin lodged in the rue de
l'Université (near the Sorbonne) before taking up his famous residency at
Passy, enabled Melville legitimately to use some of his own Latin Quarter
experiences of 1849.[19] Personal experience, contemporary culture, and
Franklin's own writings merge in Melville's subtly ambiguous portrayal of
the man of wisdom. All he had from Trumbull was a dozen lines beginning: "My interview with Dr. Franklin was a pleasing one—for nearly an
hour he conversed with me in the most agreeable and instructive manner,
and listened to the tale of my sufferings with much apparent interest . . ."
(pp. 50–51). Perhaps Melville was teased into action by Trumbull's evalua-
tion of Franklin: "that great and good man (whose humanity and generosity
have been the theme of infinitely abler pens than mine) . . ." (p. 51). The
Franklin sequence marks a new sophistication in the narrator's rhetoric and
tone; his book never again quite settles back into a simple account.

Midway in the Franklin sequence Melville reached out for another
American hero with whom to involve Israel. In Trumbull's *Life,* Potter
pauses for a three-page historical digression on events leading to the surrender of Cornwallis. From nine lines of routine eulogy on the coastal
raids of "that bold adventurer capt. Paul Jones" (p. 60), whom Potter
never so much as laid eyes on, Melville took a cue. It was common
historical knowledge that Jones had worked through Franklin in getting
French support for his daredevil coastal raids and attacks on British shipping. Why not add to the Franklin sequence, then, a confrontation between the canny old sage and the impetuous young adventurer, with Israel
privileged to look on? And so the scene (Chapter 10) in which Captain

18. *Works,* VI, 463–504, especially pp. 481 ff. See also the passing reference to swimming
bladders (VI, 287), good for a simile in Chapter 9 (51.27). Franklin's letters on magic squares
and magic circles (VI, 100–105) were possibly germinal to Melville's fictional "conjuror's
robe" and "necromantic" surroundings in Chapter 7 (38), and the drawings and charts in this
volume are the kind Melville puts on the sage's walls.

19. *Works,* I, 419 n. Sparks quotes a French historian (I, 420–21) who says some imagined Franklin "a sage of antiquity," calls him "a venerable old man," and notes the "manly
frankness" with which he spoke to young officers who visited him (cf. the bemused word-
play on *frankness, frank,* and *Franklin* in Chapter 10—anticipating *The Confidence-Man*). Sparks
also quotes Franklin on his own comic tendencies (I, 122 n.) in a sentence that contains the
words "grave" and "serious" (cf. Melville's "his mind was often grave, but never serious,"
in Chapter 8, 48.13–14).

Paul bursts into the sage's lodgings, after pinching the French maid, demanding by God that he be given a decent ship with which to smash the enemy. It worked well enough to keep Paul overnight in what turned out to be a kind of Queequeg-Ishmael scene (Chapter 11), with a chance to exploit the paradoxes of a melodramatic character.

Melville's restlessness with the *Life* was now loosed. Israel's adventures as secret courier after he returns to England (Chapters 12–13) become an elaborate free fiction growing out of inconsequential details from Trumbull. In the center is the tale of Israel buried alive for four nights in the secret recess at Squire Woodcock's house, an idea which he could have easily picked up from other writers. Readers of Poe's *The Narrative of Arthur Gordon Pym* (1838) will note some parallels: the victim's nightmare sense of entombment, his re-emergence dressed in a dead man's clothes, the self-inspection in a mirror beforehand. Flanking either side of this Gothic digression are two comic scenes, wholly improvised, with Israel playing the stage Yankee: the boot-stealing episode on the Channel packet (Chapter 12), and the Israel-as-scarecrow sequence (Chapter 13). At the end, Israel finds himself stranded in Dover by the Channel closing (Chapter 13). So it had been with Trumbull's Potter, though after two French missions, not one. At this point Potter disappeared into the London labyrinth. But Melville decided that his Israel should be impressed into the English navy!

With this stroke Melville postpones indefinitely Israel's descent into beggarly anonymity. The very heart of the *Life,* the grimly ironic London aftermath to heroism which seems to have invoked Melville's interest in the first place, is thrust aside for a whole new mid-section of naval adventures (Chapters 14–20). Whether from boredom with the Potter story or from excitement at the "discovery" of Jones, Melville has a new book going. Now there will be no question about providing the "adventure" he had promised Putnam. We do not know whether he already had the Jones excursus in mind when he made that promise, or discovered it later. And we can only guess at the proportions of cynicism (giving in to a mass public) and relief (at not having to project Israel's degradation at length) which underlay Melville's decision. But there can be no doubt that Captain Paul has already generated a good bit of electricity in the narrator as well as in Israel. From Paul's first appearance Melville too seems impressed by the possibilities ahead.

Melville may have browsed in numerous books and articles on Jones, but two writers, Sands and Cooper, can account for everything he needed and used in the Jones chapters.[20] Every biographer, after praising Jones for his impetuous bravery, his insatiable determination to destroy the enemy or go down, raises questions about his character. Sands, the young poet and essayist who put together the rather heterogeneous collection of documents that make up *Life and Correspondence of John Paul Jones,* in a concluding eulogy admits Jones was "ardent, impatient, and irritable," but pushes aside "the extravagant stories and ridiculous legends, circulated orally and in print" as efforts to discredit a heroic figure (pp. 551, 554). Cooper is cooler, pausing in the course of his long *History of the Navy of the United States of America,* for a sizable footnote on John Paul Jones's life and character. He finds him "a remarkable man" with "an invincible resolution to conquer," but only "respectable" in reasoning, vain, too poorly educated to withstand "the flattery and seductions of Parisian society," and given to an "affectation of a literary taste."[21] Melville's version of Jones—his "Captain Paul"— responds to such polarities by swallowing up all arguments in a vigorous image of an insatiable fighter whose lust for battle, honor, and fame spills over into crude chivalric posturings. Melville combines the admiring and hostile views of Jones, with a touch of parody, into an oxymoronic figure of the civilized barbarian. "Much subtle casuistry has been expended upon the point," says the narrator, "whether Paul Jones was a knave or a hero, or a union of both. But war and warriors, like politics and politicians, like religion and religionists, admit of no metaphysics" (95–96). Preferring symbolism to argument, the narrator contrives the fiction that under "his laced coat-sleeve" Paul hides "mysterious tatooings . . . seen only on thoroughbred savages—deep blue, elaborate, labyrinthine, cabalistic" (62).

20. W. Sprague Holden assumed Melville also made considerable use of John Henry Sherburne's *The Life and Character of John Paul Jones* . . . (Washington, 1825, and New York, 1851), and Walter Jones also accepts this; but all the materials Holden found in Sherburne I have found in Sands, and the opposite is not true. Leon Howard, *Herman Melville,* p. 214, adds two more sources for which I find no hard evidence: Nathaniel Fanning's anonymous and hostile account of Jones, *Narrative of the Adventures of an American Navy Officer Who Served During Part of the American Revolution under the Command of Captain John Paul Jones, Esq.* (New York, 1806), and Alexander Slidell Mackenzie's *The Life of Paul Jones* (Boston, 1841). The problem arises because all the biographers drew on the same basic documents, which Sands prints. Howard thought Melville's use of Fanning's *Narrative* is shown by the similarity of his characterization of Jones and by his use of "a rather silly reference to the moon's emotions" by Fanning "which Melville made even sillier in his description of the fight." But Sands and Cooper also mention the moon prominently, though without personifying it; Fanning's whole account, moreover, is so graphic that Melville can scarcely have had it in hand, one would think, without availing himself of many more of its striking details.

21. *History of the Navy,* I, 117–18 n.

Melville's dependence on Sands for information, as well as for models of Jones's flamboyant rhetoric, is obvious from the beginning (Chapter 10). In Sands he could learn of Jones's "middling" stature and "swarthy" complexion (p. 177 n.), his addiction to poetry with samples provided (pp. 317–20), his image of himself as world citizen (p. 91), and the like. Franklin's speech to Captain Paul about the Jersey privateers (57) is largely verbatim from an actual letter the man of wisdom once wrote to Jones (pp. 105–6).[22] The three ships Captain Paul mentions in conversation with Israel (one is misspelled) are noted in Sands (pp. 39–41), as is the secret expedition of Count D'Estaing (also misspelled) that Doctor Franklin refers to (p. 75). For the Franklin sequence Melville had already opened Sands, the book that would be almost as useful to the middle chapters of *Israel Potter* as Trumbull's *Life* had been to the early ones.

Once Israel has been impressed, Melville's narrator by quick and sourceless conjuration moves him in one night from a British ship of the line to a revenue cutter to the deck of the *Ranger,* there joining Captain Paul, four days out of Brest on his historic cruise into the Irish Sea (Chapter 14).[23] The sound of Captain Paul's voice has roused Israel to mythic powers in his one-man seizure of the cutter (again reminiscent of Poe's *Pym*), completing a transformation away from the harassed Potter of the *Life* that will last as long as he serves with Captain Paul. Melville's grossest fictional liberty with the Jones story in events to follow is to make Israel the bosom companion of a man historically private and almost unapproachable. Potter was thirty-four in 1778, and Jones was thirty, but now Israel becomes the "lad" and "yellow lion" of Captain Paul. In a scene reminiscent of Pip and Ahab and marked by the highest rhetorical pitch thus far, Israel is taken into the Captain's cabin and confidence.[24]

Melville's version of the famous twenty-eight-day cruise of the *Ranger*

22. Except for an erroneous insertion by Melville (emended by NN at 57.13): "say, even your present ship, the 'Amphitrite.' " The plan for Jones to sail the *Amphitrite* from America to France (Sands, p. 67) was changed; he crossed in the *Ranger* (Sands, pp. 69–70).

23. The *Ranger*'s course was "between Scilly and Cape Clear" according to Jones (Sands, p. 79); Melville (85.21) uses the same phrase and course for the *Unprincipled*. Sailing home from England, December 25, 1849, Melville "passed the Land's End & the Scilly Isles" the next day, according to his journal.

24. The details of his life that Captain Paul tells Israel in the cabin are from Sands: sailing out of Whitehaven at age twelve (p. 16); the Mungo Maxwell affair (pp. 18–22); his refusal to sleep when cruising (p. 200). So too is his Scotch bonnet, edged with gold (pp. 177 n., 201 n.)—Paul's symbol in this section, comparable to Israel's yellow hair. The rest Melville imagined.

(Chapters 15–17) is based on Jones's own day-by-day record, as reported May 27, 1778, to the American Commissioners in Paris—Franklin, Arthur Lee, and Silas Deane.[25] He began by picking from it five encounters with vessels (April 17–20) to show Captain Paul's style of action, for much of the description helping himself to the language of Jones's report. From Jones's mere mention of a landfall on April 20 ("I pursued no farther than the Rock of Ailsa") he took a chapter title and constructed the ominously symbolic episode that ends Chapter 15, using as well the *Penny Cyclopædia* for details (as he did also on Whitehaven and the coast between Flamborough Head and the Spurn).

Melville's description of the first, unsuccessful try at encountering the *Drake* off Carrickfergus is based on Jones's action of April 21, and the dramatically rendered account of the firing of Whitehaven (Chapter 16) is a fictional enlargement of Jones's detailed record of April 23, Melville borrowing words or phrases from Sands some thirty to forty times. When during the dawn landing at Whitehaven the time came to spike the shore cannons, Jones reported that "I now took with me one man only, (Mr. Green,) . . . ." Presto, Israel gets the job. He gets, too, the Promethean-comic role of stealing fire, a full-page projection from Jones's passing remark that "a light was obtained at a house disjoined from the town . . . ."

The same kind of balloon method—free flight, but a strong cord back to the source—marks the St. Mary's Isle episode: the elaborate effort to kidnap the Earl of Selkirk (Chapter 17). In his report to the Commissioners Jones merely mentions the episode (April 23), referring them to a copy of his famous letter to Lady Selkirk, written the day he returned to port (May 8) in apology for his officers' having taken the family silver as prize. This letter and other postal exchanges between Jones and Lord and Lady Selkirk were notorious—Jones all pretentious chivalry, the Lady cool, the Earl cold.[26] From these letters Melville constructed his comedy, taking ample liberties with events but dipping into their language for tone, phrases, and facts. Captain Paul's absurd speech to Lady Selkirk (107.33), beginning "it cannot be too poignantly lamented . . . ," is two-thirds verbatim from the May 8 letter; and his "super-ardent note" scribbled at the beach before he leaves represents a fictional parallel to the May 8 letter, shortened, and the rhetoric heightened into parody it hardly needed. The major liberty Melville took with his materials, however, was to stage an

25. Printed in full in Sands, pp. 79–87.
26. Sands, pp. 83–84, 89–93, and 93–101, notes.

actual meeting between the Captain and the Lady. In fact, Jones wrote that "when I was informed, by some men whom I met at landing, that his lordship was absent, I walked back to my boat, determined to leave the island." He did so; the men went to the house alone. But Melville could not resist the chance to show Captain Paul in his full, rakish pretentiousness paying court to the Lady, while Israel makes strictly Yankee jokes on Scotch armor, the family plate, and inevitably "Mr. Selkirk" and even "Mister Butler" (the servant).[27] The same pattern of source plundering, comic invention, and language play marks Melville's version of Jones's capture of the *Drake* the next day (last half of Chapter 17).[28]

After a quick and inaccurate summary of events following the Brest cruise,[29] Melville turned to the story of the *Bon Homme Richard*'s bold descent on Leith (Chapter 18). In describing here the famous old Indiaman, formerly the *Duc de Duras,* Melville began to draw on Cooper's *History of the Navy* as well as on Sands.[30] Melville's "secret history" of how the *Richard* got her name—he gives the credit to Israel—is a fictional parallel to Sands's passing remark that at Jones's request it was "called *Le Bon Homme Richard,* in compliment to a saying of Poor Richard; 'If you

27. The mention of a "butler's pantry" and "the butler" in Lord Selkirk's letter (p. 101 n.) was all Melville needed.

28. Melville used thirty or more word clusters from Jones's letter to the Commissioners (pp. 84–87), invented a half-page comic episode from the sentence: "When the officer came on the quarter deck, he was greatly surprised to find himself a prisoner" (p. 84), and sowed a harvest of rhetoric around Jones's technical description of the mutilated *Drake* (pp. 84–85). Melville's tableau of Israel enveloped in the American flag (112) occasions Captain Paul's exultant recall that he was the first to fly that flag on a man-of-war (pp. 69–70, 555) and the first to get it saluted (p. 76).

29. Sands's account of the year and three months during which Jones was negotiating for a new command (pp. 96–166) bored or confused Melville; Melville's opening line, "Three months after anchoring at Brest . . . ," is one year off. It was August 14, 1779, when "the squadron sailed from Groix [cf. Melville's chapter title], consisting of seven sail, including the two privateers" (p. 166)—cf. Melville's "nine vessels" (114.5).

30. Melville turned to Cooper to get a more systematic account of the complex battle with the *Serapis* in preference to Sands's documents. In so doing he encountered descriptions of the *Richard*'s having "one of those high old-fashioned *poops,* that caused the sterns of the ships . . . to resemble *towers*" (I, 100), source of Melville's "poop like the leaning tower of Pisa"; and "*She was,* properly, *a single-decked ship; or carried her armament on one gundeck . . . .* Commodore Jones . . . caused twelve *ports* to be *cut* in the gun-room *below,* where *six old eighteen-pounders* were mounted . . ." (I, 100). And on the crew: "*Luckily a cartel arrived from England, at this* moment, bringing *with* her more than *a hundred exchanged American seamen,* most of whom joined the squadron" (I, 101). Words Melville used (115–16) are italicized here to establish his use of Cooper.

would have your business done, come yourself; if not, send' " (p. 149); Melville's substitute maxim ("God helps them that help themselves") of course links with the opening of Chapter 11, and other passages. Passing up the miscellaneous events of the *Richard*'s cruise, Melville moved directly to Sands's account of the September, 1779, attempted attack on Leith, the port city of Edinburgh (pp. 171–78). He stayed close to his source in describing the plan of action. Then he struck upon an entry in Jones's journal: "A member of the British Parliament sent off a boat from the north shore, to give information that he was greatly afraid of Paul Jones, and begging for some powder and shot. Captain Jones set his fears to rest, by sending him a barrel of powder with a kind message, but had no *suitable shot*" (p. 175). Taking off from the wee Scotch joke underlined by Jones's italics, Melville worked up one of the funniest comic routines of *Israel Potter,* the set-piece on "pickled powder" (117). Back-to-back with it he put his own burlesque version of Jones's encounter with "the Rev. Mr. Shirra, a worthy and very eccentric dissenting clergyman, remarkable for his quaint humour"—plucked from a footnote in Sands.[31]

The battle of the *Richard* and the *Serapis* (Chapter 19) is the climactic event of Israel's service under Captain Paul, as in fact it was of Jones's own career. Once again, as with Bunker Hill, the narrator denies he is equal to "any regular account" of the battle. To this sophism he adds two more: "The writer is but brought to mention the battle, because he must needs follow, in all events, the fortunes of the humble adventurer whose life he records" (120.20–121.1). It is hard to say which misrepresentation amused the narrator more—continuing to offer Israel, who under Captain Paul's tutelage has become a kind of rip-roaring Davy Crockett, as "the humble adventurer," or making believe that "the writer" is still trying to be faithful to Potter's real history. About Melville's elaborate version of the battle only two points need be made here. The first is that Melville worked closely with the accounts of both Sands and Cooper, doing his best not to violate the complex and partly uncertain facts, not inventing new episodes, and not clowning. Approximately one-third of his narration can be shown to be verbally close either to Sands or Cooper.[32] The second point, which the attentive reader will notice without source study, is that

31. Sands, pp. 176–77. Melville's Yankee ear probably affected his spelling: for "Shirra" he wrote "Shirrer", emended by NN at 118.29.

32. Since Cooper's account of the battle (I, 104–14) naturally draws on documents such as are in Sands (pp. 179–202) some language is common to both sources. It seems unnecessary to disentangle them, beyond noting there is clear evidence both were used. See footnote 21.

the narrator's chief interest in the chapter is neither naval history nor the death struggle of the two locked ships, but his own battle of the tropes, so to speak. The most baroque phase of this is the Man-in-the-Moon paragraph (123), a huge theatrical metaphor growing out of the statement by Sands that the battle was fought "under a bright and beautiful harvest moon, and its issue awaited by multitudes, (thousands it is said,) who watched the engagement from the shore" (p. 179). Cooper perhaps contributed to Melville's treatment of the moon: he reports its rising, saying "until the moon rose, objects at a distance were distinguished with difficulty, and even after the moon appeared, with uncertainty" (I, 106), a passage which may have led to Melville's sentence, "Objects before perceived with difficulty, now glimmered ambiguously" (123.20–21). The narrator's principal method, however, is to create a running drumfire of similitudes not present in the sources. The effect at times is almost as of two parallel stories. Similes and metaphors rain down on the helpless reader almost from beginning to end. Chapter 19 is above all a merciless linguistic broadside that has no counterpart in the sources.

Israel's adventures with Captain Paul having been brought to climax, Melville's problem now was how to return his hero to captivity. Still drawing on Sands and Cooper, he put Israel aboard the *Ariel* with Captain Paul, headed for America (Jones sailed December 18, 1780). By the second page of "The Shuttle" (Chapter 20) the *Ariel* has met and defeated an English man-of-war only to have her escape with the too-impetuous Israel trapped aboard her.[33] Israel's renewed captivity marks Melville's escape from Sands. The balance of "The Shuttle," the most brilliantly sustained Yankee tale in *Israel Potter,* brings Israel to the peak of his comic stance. If it has any other source than Melville's imaginings, some old sea yarn heard on the night watch may have served.

Still avoiding the narration of Israel's pathetic years, Melville now introduces a third American hero, one not even mentioned in the *Life,* Ethan Allen (Chapters 21–22). Every nineteenth-century schoolboy knew the story of the Green Mountain Boys, and how one midnight in May, 1775, their gigantic leader pounded on the British commander's door at Fort Ticonderoga demanding surrender "in the name of the great Jehovah, and the Continental Congress." Less was known about his thirty-two months of captivity, except to readers of his own brash account, *A Narrative*

---

33. All details and much of the language of the *Ariel*'s encounter with the English ship (the *Triumph*) come from Jones's own journal account (pp. 300–302). The thrusting of the *Triumph*'s spanker-boom across the *Ariel*'s quarter-deck is Melville's conjuration.

of Colonel Ethan Allen's Captivity. [34] Just when Israel, as "Peter Perkins," sails into the roadstead at Falmouth aboard the British letter of marque, Allen is being taken ashore for imprisonment and display at Castle Pendennis on the cliff above the town. Except for sweeping indifference to historical chronology—it is Christmas of 1775 for the Colonel and presumably some time in 1780 for Israel—Melville's narrator will be studiously faithful to the spirit and even letter of the *Narrative.*

Allen's *Narrative* is in form an early ancestor of Trumbull's *Life.* Though printed forty-five years apart, both are amateurish accounts of Revolutionary captivities told in the first person (Potter's story, however, constructed by Trumbull). Both narratives run to about 27,000 words, and both were issued in cheap format to attract popular audiences. There the similarities end, the disparate fates of the two patriots being striking. Colonel Allen, though constantly threatened with hanging, was released in an exchange of prisoners; he returned home to receive public praise at Valley Forge from General Washington, salutes from cannons, and punch bowls shared with his Green Mountain Boys. Allen's little book, written at the peak of his fame and in the heat of battle, is a kind of huzzah to "the rising States of America" (p. 46), full of coarse obloquy against all Britons and Tories. Poor Potter's book, alas, was an almost anonymous cry for help, long after battle. The two books had the same luck (if that's what it was) as their respective heroes. Allen's *Narrative* went through some twenty editions, half a dozen or more appearing in the decade before Melville used it. Potter's *Life,* as Melville poignantly put it in his book dedication, was by then out of print "like the crutch-marks of the cripple by the Beautiful Gate" (vii.20).

The section of the *Narrative* dealing with Allen's two weeks at Falmouth occupies but a few pages (pp. 14–19). In composing the disembarkation account and the major scene—Allen staked out on the parade grounds, while crowds of curious visitors taunt the big Yankee rebel—Melville took from his source the details of Allen's barbaric costume,

34. Melville's edition of the *Narrative* is not known. References here are to the original edition of 1779, *A Narrative of Colonel Ethan Allen's Captivity* (Philadelphia: Robert Bell). The edition in the American Experience Series (New York: Corinth Books, 1961), with an introduction by Brooke Hindle, does not follow the 1779 edition exactly. Jared Sparks wrote a life of Allen for his Library of American Biography (Boston, 1834), I, 227–356. When Melville in his dedication refers to "the volumes of Sparks" he means this famous series, but there is no evidence that he used it; perhaps he chose Allen's own *Narrative* as a livelier source. Sparks's concluding apology for Allen's "roughness of manners and coarseness of language" (I, 354) and his regrets about Allen's deism contrast with Melville's estimate of Allen's "peculiar Americanism" in Chapter 22 (149.12–13).

threats of the halter, the verbal exchange with the cleric (which he combines with Allen's brief account of the punch bowl episode), and the
encounter with the prosperous farmer (including the repartee on freedom
and the quip about conjuring and divinity). Allen's comic courtship of the
ladies, reminiscent of Captain Paul's pretenses to Lady Selkirk, is Melville's invention. Allen's opening harangue as Israel arrives on the scene is
a pastiche of several ranting passages in the *Narrative:*

> Vaunt no more Old England! consider you are but an island! . . . Order
> your broken and vanquished battalions to retire from America . . . . Go
> home and repent in dust and sackcloth . . . (p. 43).
> . . . In him [Burgoyne] the tories placed their confidence, "and forgot the
> Lord their God," and served Howe, Burgoyne and Knyphausen . . . (p. 35).
> I was told by the officer who put them on [leg irons, bars, shackles, hand
> cuffs], that it was the king's plate . . . (p. 10).[35]

As in his projections of Franklin and Jones, Melville is again using rhetorical style as a key to character, drawing on original documents to get
accurate tone. In the narrator's short essay on Allen (Chapter 22), comparable to the one on Franklin (Chapter 8) and the more scattered observations on Jones, he continues weaving together threads pulled from
throughout the *Narrative.*[36] This chapter and a half on Allen was popular
enough in its day to be reprinted at least twice.[37] If it seems oddly discursive to the modern reader, it is partly because Israel remains so passive a
spectator, even his "yellow hair" having been yielded to Allen. As
Chapter 22 ends, Israel seems about ready at last to drop back into the part
Henry Trumbull wrote for him.[38] After some fifteen chapters of diversions, the narrator is back on course: "Once more in beggar's garb, the
fugitive sped towards London . . ." (153.3).

35. Similarly, for Allen's rant against Lord Howe's attempt at bribery, Melville brings
together two passages from the *Narrative* (pp. 35, 39); they include the reference to Satan's
temptation of Jesus, and a sturdy consignment of Howe to Hell (p. 39).

36. The opening of Chapter 22 is original; the third paragraph is an intricate layering of
scattered scenes and phrases from some ten different pages of the *Narrative.* Melville is still
working hastily, for example attributing to Colonel McCloud actions which in the source are
clearly General Prescott's (p. 9)—emended by NN at 150.9.

37. Leyda (*Log,* II, 508) notes its condensation in the *Western Literary Messenger* (September, 1855), 21–23. Mailloux and Parker list also a second reprinting in the New York *Leader*
(June 8, 1856).

38. The Sergeant Singles episode (151–52) is from the *Life,* pp. 53–55. In using the scene
Melville moves it from London to Falmouth. Potter's exclamation is almost verbatim. That
Singles stole Israel's girl is Melville's idea.

Yet nothing could be more misleading than to assume that Melville's narrator really returns to Trumbull's *Life* in the final section (Chapters 23–26). To be sure some contacts with it are re-established, as will be shown; but on the whole the narrator refuses to be bound by its sequences, or even to be faithful to its major events or moods. The first two chapters (23,24) have, respectively, little and no relation to the *Life*. "Israel in Egypt" presents a scene, with high biblical and allegorical overtones, of Israel at work in a dismal brickyard "upon a wild waste moor, belted round by bogs and fens" (156.2–3). Potter merely records on two occasions that for five summers (not "thirteen weary weeks") he was a brick maker and gardener in London, and became "an expert workman" though at "very small wages."[39] Melville's facts and allegory, and especially the narrator's high style, contrast handsomely with what Trumbull says a man named Potter told him. And the apocalyptic vision from London Bridge, "In the City of Dis" (Chapter 24), as Israel stands watching the stream of lost humanity pass over it,[40] is wholly imagined from Melville's own 1849 London experience, as we have seen; there is no counterpart to it whatsoever in the *Life*.

For his two concluding chapters (25,26) Melville has obviously fanned through the last half of the *Life,* here and there picking out factual details and borrowing a few phrases.[41] But the narrator is correct in his own

39. *Life,* pp. 56, 68. Some other source, a technical article, or unrecorded visit by Melville to a brickyard, probably lies back of Chapter 23. Leyda (*Log,* I, 486) points out that Melville found a suggestion for this chapter in *Life of Benjamin Robert Haydon, Historical Painter, from His Autobiography and Journals,* edited and compiled by Tom Taylor (New York, 1853), I, 54–55. Haydon comments on the grandeur of the "sublime canopy" of smoke that shrouds London; he quotes Fuseli as comparing it to the smoke of the Israelites making bricks. This work was charged to Melville's Harper account on April 7, 1854 (Sealts, No. 262).

40. The short paragraph beginning "On they passed; two-and-two . . ." (160.5–9) occurs in the *Putnam's Monthly* printing but was cut from the book printing, and has never been restored until the present NN text. Who ordered it cut is not known; a fair guess is that the editors could not resist one stroke against the *Pierre*-like tendencies Melville allowed to emerge in the late chapters despite his promise to Putnam to avoid anything "weighty" that might "shock the fastidious." Melville may never have noticed the cut. The passage strikingly anticipates the "Via Crucis" canto in *Clarel* (IV.xxxiv).

41. Common to both, for example, are: chair-mending, rag-picking, making matches; the death of all but one child (nine dead in the *Life,* ten in Melville); the American consul's appointment and Potter's refusal to desert his family when they were denied passage; the return of beggars to London streets after the two wars. Two spoken lines from the *Life* are seized on: the false cry of fake cripples, "an honourable scar of a wound, received in Egypt, at Waterloo or at Trafalgar . . ." (p. 63), and the son's cry about going to America: "would to God it was to morrow!" (p. 95).

statement about the summary chapter (25), "Forty-five Years": that he will "skim events . . . omitting the particulars . . ." (161.22). His sober view—the comedy is over now—is that Potter's sufferings were too squalid to bear much repetition.[42] Instead, curiously, the narrator conjures up his own set of horrors such as fighting rats in the sewers, the doorless house with three dead men, the "crazy hovel" that fell "in phosphoric rottenness"; the whole business of living in sewers too is invented, or taken from an unknown source. Though he does not say so, the narrator is also trying to account for a curious gap in the *Life*.[43] American readers of Trumbull, at least, must have been baffled that so energetic a Yankee as Potter could get trapped in London for more than forty years. Potter's tale—was Potter's Yankee ingenuity *Trumbull's* invention?—never faces up to that. Melville's narrator, having made Israel twice the man that Potter may have been, brings him down by imposing two injuries on Israel, one of which affects his faculties. Thus Potter's mere nostalgia for home in the *Life* is rendered by two vivid hallucinations in which Israel, now an old man, acts "insanely" and suffers "monomaniac reminiscences."

Israel's eventual homecoming (Chapter 26) makes only such slight use of Trumbull's last pages as are to the narrator's own purposes. Potter landed in New York, met his son in Boston, made a quick visit to Bunker Hill, and headed for Cranston on foot to recover his share of the family property; but his brothers had divided it and gone. Trumbull concludes with Potter's plea for a pension, "unfeigned thanks to the Almighty" for bringing him home, and a hope to end his life "devoting myself sincerely to the duties of religion." Israel's ironic near-accident on the Fourth of July, the tableau of his meditation on Copp's Hill, and the deeply Hawthornesque final scene, are Melville's.

---

42. Among the squalid episodes Melville avoided: the execution of a man for stealing for his family (p. 72); the widow who fed her five children on roasted dog (p. 73); the hovel with seven starving children, a father, and the corpse of a mother who died in childbirth (p. 74); the autopsy that showed grass in the stomach of a man who died in the streets (pp. 81–82)— but cf. Melville's Israel, who in one extremity "chewed grass, and swallowed it" (23.18). He also bypassed Potter's imprisonment for debt (p. 70), and the long account of his wife's illness and death (pp. 84–89). Though Melville says pointedly that "Israel, the American, never sunk below the mud, to actual beggary" (165.31–32), Potter frequently accepted charity in the streets (pp. 85, 92–93, 94).

43. The initial reason supplied, that he spent on wedlock his savings for the voyage home, involves some curious associative cluster in Melville's mind that had surfaced in both *Omoo* (Chapter 14) and *Moby-Dick* (Chapter 34) before appearing here in *Israel Potter,* involving baking, nursing, wedlock, and bankruptcy.

Melville had presumably set out in all good conscience simply to re-write Henry Trumbull's *Life and Remarkable Adventures of Israel R. Potter*. After allowing himself the luxury of a lyric opening chapter, he had settled down into paraphrase, touching up the prose toward felicity of expression, granting his narrator mild rights of commentary on the course of events. But restlessness led to increasing invention, and then suddenly two things seem to have happened at once. Melville discovered that at its midpoint his source itself fell apart, its simple narrative line giving way to a tangled recital of random disasters and bathetic appeals. His interest in it waned. He would come back to Potter's last years, but the four decades of bleak back-city deprivation and crime, of starvation, beggary, and domestic tragedy, lost their powers of attraction, perhaps became repellent. But as his source failed him, Melville's fictional urgencies began to assert them-selves. In the presence of the Franklin he invented, the narrator of *Israel Potter* came alive. From here on Melville filled his magazine installments with pages of comedy, melodrama, meditation, and adventure of his own devising, mixed half-and-half with pages of his own hurry-up brand of history. Melville, after all, was no scrivener.

IV

Everything about the serial publication of *Israel Potter* in *Putnam's Magazine* seems to have gone rather well for Melville from the outset. Just when he began writing we cannot be sure. He may have written the opening Berkshire chapter as early as the first summer in Pittsfield (1850), when he was excitedly exploring the countryside, poring over *A History of the County of Berkshire,* edited by David Dudley Field, and perhaps that early making his note in it: "Old man—soldier 118." Then or at some point well before 1854 he may even have tried to rewrite part of the *Life* to see how it would go. But storing manuscript ahead was not characteristic of Melville, and it is more likely that he did not begin actual writing more than a few weeks before his inquiry to the Harpers on May 25, 1854. Even during May, Melville could readily have turned out all of the sixty-some pages of *Israel Potter* that he mailed to Putnam on June 7. He had been writing rapidly for several years now, as his critics often complained.

Two letters to Putnam tell us what we know of Melville's production of manuscript for the magazine printing. The first of these, that of June 7, anticipated a total manuscript of 300 or more pages, of which more than

60 were sent in at that time. The other reference to manuscript we have is Melville's letter to Putnam of November 3, 1854, by which time the fifth of the nine installments was in print. Putnam had recently returned some manuscript to Melville (probably not related to *Israel Potter*) with a note in which he apparently inquired about the amount of manuscript yet to come; to this inquiry Melville replied:

> Day before yesterday I wrote you [a now lost letter] on that subject. But there was an error in my note; which I now rectify, that it may not cause you future trouble.
>
> I said in my note that there would be some <u>25</u> more pages of M.S.—It should have been forty five—<u>45</u>.
>
> I will send it all down in a few days.

From Melville's wording this would seem to be the last batch of manuscript; together with the first batch it constitutes some 100–110 pages, or roughly one-third of the amount originally proposed. Between June and November other batches—say four if of the same size—were sent. No parts or even fragments of manuscript for *Israel Potter* are known to exist.

This minimal evidence on how Melville turned out manuscript, when combined with an examination of the actual installments as they appeared in *Putnam's,* tells us something about the aesthetic form of the magazine version of *Israel Potter.* Put severely, the question is whether Melville in any way responded to what Henry James, in his preface to *The Ambassadors,* called the "small compositional law": the sense that serial publication itself provides aesthetic demands and opportunities for rhythmic movement within the novel form. One-half the answer comes from the lack of any evidence whatsoever that Melville exercised control, or even tried to, over the contents of individual installments. Melville's June 7 letter to Putnam, asking only that ten pages per issue be printed, plus "as much more as may be usually convenient," sounds as if Melville were quite willing to leave to the editors all decisions about the shape of individual installments. The other half of the answer must be inferred from internal evidence, as to whether in fact the installments express visible formal effects. Here are the data from which any conclusion must be drawn (supplemented by payment records; chapter numbers are given in Roman numerals as in *Putnam's*):[44]

---

44. Both *Log* (I, 498) and *Letters* (p. 170, n. 9) mistakenly list the February pages as 5 instead of 7. Payments are taken from *Log* (I, 490; II, 499); they were recorded in the Putnam ledger, now unlocated.

Installment	Chapters	Pages	Payment
#1 July, 1854	I–III	9½	$50.
#2 August	IV–VII	11½	$55.
#3 September	VIII–XII	13½	$67.50
#4 October	XIII	7	$35.
#5 November	XIV[a]–XVI	10½	$52.50
#6 December	XVII–XIX	10	$50.
#7 January, 1855	XIX.Cont'd[b]–XX	8¾	$44.
#8 February	XXI–XXIII	7	$35.
#9 March	XXIV[c]–XXVII	6½	$32.50
		84¼	$421.50

a. Chapter XIV was incorrectly numbered XVI in *Putnam's*.
b. Chapter XIX was divided between two installments, the second part headed "CHAPTER XIX. CONTINUED."
c. Chapter XXIII was divided between two installments, the second part headed "CHAPTER XXIV. (CONTINUED.)"

In the magazine there was carelessness in the chapter numbering, whether due to Melville's manuscript or to poor copy editing or typesetting. The misnumbered chapter gave a XVI–XV–XVI sequence in a single installment. The two instances of divided chapters were inconsistently treated, the same chapter number being retained the earlier time (giving two Chapter 19's, the second as "CONTINUED") and a higher number being added the later (Chapter 23 becoming 24). It is not clear why they were split in the first place. Chapter 19 may have been broken up because of length, the two parts totaling over six magazine pages (only Chapter 13 is longer); but the two parts of Chapter 23 together printed out as less than two pages. Mechanical symmetry was not at stake, for the length of installments varies from 6½ to 13½ pages, and the number of chapters in each installment ranges from one to five. As to literary structure, the reader who goes through *Israel Potter* with attention to the eight pauses imposed by the serial form will note random endings as often as pointed ones, and few correspondences between the installments and the internal rhythms of the tale. In short, the evidence suggests that the dominant principle to which the installments respond are the space needs of magazine layout, that other correspondences are accidental, and that Melville, even if he cared, probably had nothing to do with such decisions. Melville's only instance of a serialized novel lacks regularity even in obvious plot climaxes of the Pearl White order, let alone Jamesian niceties of serial composition. Melville probably did not even suggest installment breaks as he wrote his manuscript; if he did, they would seem to have been lost on the editor or compositor. When Melville wrote Putnam that he would "try to sustain" interest as well as he could he was promising a lively tale rather than a conscious effort to exploit the demands of serialization as did Dickens and Thackeray. He was writing a book; that it was to be published first in installments was merely an economic bonus.

This is not to say that Melville was indifferent to the amounts of manuscript he submitted, or that there was no correlation between them and certain sequences of the tale as it developed. The first batch of "some sixty and odd pages" can be presumed to have gone at least through Chapter 6 (Chapters 2–6 are uniquely dependent on the *Life* as a source, and also reach a natural break when Israel first crosses the Channel). Even more likely is that this first batch went through Chapter 7, for if we assume that Melville's magazine experience to date had taught him the proportions between his kind of manuscript and the number of magazine pages—and he did write at so-much-per-page—then this first batch probably printed out at two installments (through Chapter 7) rather than at something short of the ten-page minimum he had asked for.[45] Melville seems to have had no trouble in keeping *Putnam's* supplied with manuscript, and he probably sent sequences closely allied to his changing sources.

A curiosity of the magazine publication is the single appearance, midway through Chapter 13, of an unnumbered title: "AN ENCOUNTER OF GHOSTS." This could have been Melville's intention, or Melville's carelessness (failing to number it as a chapter). It could also have been an inspiration of someone on the magazine staff, who either wished to break up the installment (the only one consisting of a single chapter), or simply to introduce an attention-getter.

The title of *Israel Potter* underwent a change during its serialization. The original title in the July, 1854, issue, repeated in August, was "ISRAEL POTTER; OR, FIFTY YEARS OF EXILE. *A FOURTH OF JULY STORY.*" Beginning with the third installment, in September, the

---

45. The final shipment of manuscript can also be translated into chapters. At a ratio of 3 manuscript pages to 1 printed page (on the grounds that 60-plus pages had printed up at 21 pages) the presumed 45 pages of the last shipment became the last 15 pages of the magazine printing. If so, the final batch of manuscript either began with Chapter 20 (previous manuscript having finished off the Jones section) or picked up after Chapter 20 (a separate interlude) with the Ethan Allen sequence. More simply, it may have consisted of the last five chapters, the final movement of the tale.

third part of the title was dropped, and it likewise was omitted from the book six months later. The decision both to supply the Fourth of July reference and later to omit it may have been made in the magazine offices, without consulting Melville.[46] Its topical reference is more obviously to its largely fortuitous initial appearance in the July issue of *Putnam's,* as a patriotic story, than to internal thematic matters, which are keyed to Bunker Hill Day, June 17, despite the Fourth of July allusion in the final chapter—which Melville can scarcely have had in mind at the outset. (See the DISCUSSIONS OF ADOPTED READINGS at v.2.)

In keeping with the magazine's policy, *Putnam's* newest serial was offered anonymously. However, the New York and New England newspapers often commented on the current issues of leading magazines, and it was here, in brief and random notices, that Melville's authorship was immediately disclosed and the first reactions to *Israel Potter* reached print. Of the eight papers so far known to have responded to the serial, one New York daily promptly singled out Melville's first installment as "the greatest literary attraction" of the July *Putnam's,* describing it as "an original American romance . . . understood to be written by Mr. Herman Melville. We think it much more interesting, and likely to be much more popular than even his admired narratives of South Sea adventures."[47] Another New York daily, the *Citizen,* by September, said that "Melville is reaping fresh honors in his 'Israel Potter,' " and responded enthusiastically to the January installment (in which the fight with the *Serapis* is concluded, followed by "The Shuttle") as "a stirring narrative,

46. The several *Putnam's* top "editors" —Putnam himself, Charles F. Briggs, George William Curtis, Frederick Law Olmsted—at one time or another during Melville's association with the magazine evidently intervened in various ways in his texts; see the GENERAL NOTE ON THE TEXT of the Northwestern-Newberry Edition of *THE PIAZZA TALES and Other Prose Pieces, 1839–1860.* Circumstances indicate that Melville did not plan *Israel Potter* with an eye to its opening in the July issue of *Putnam's;* he had first suggested it to the Harpers, and Sealts, in "Chronology," p. 397, says the timing was such that "a place was found for the first installment . . . in the issue then in press . . . ."

47. All such notices occurred in short reviews of a whole number of *Putnam's.* Citations from the following serial notices, and their dates, have been drawn from the originals, except when specifically designated as from the *Log;* several notices are newly discovered. Cited above: New York *Commercial Advertiser,* July 3, 1854, which also noted the continuation of "Melville's popular story" (October 31) and its conclusion (March 2). The New York *Evangelist* also assumed Melville's authorship: "Melville begins a new story, of the Revolution" (July 6), and noted "the continuation of Mr. Melville's fine tale of Israel Potter" (August 3).

and admirably written; so that if you begin you must finish it."[48] A third combined praise with retrospective chastisement: "It is whispered that it is by Herman Melville, but if the report be well founded," it went on rather disingenuously, "then indeed has the author effected a sudden and great improvement in his style, which in this tale is manly, direct and clear. 'Israel Potter's' story is told quite as if De Foe had undertaken to tell it, albeit it is more enlivened with dialogue . . . ." The same paper kept its guard up through the September installment, cautiously noting "the direct simplicity of style which has thus far marked it"; only with the October issue did it relax, simply acknowledging that the tale "continued with unflagging interest."[49] Across the Hudson a Newark paper with the same cautionary praise spoke of: "Israel Potter, commenced by Melville, and in his best, i.e. natural vein," and defined that vein, the next month, as having "all the power of description of real occurrences." The casual nature of such quick estimates is handsomely illustrated by the same paper's confession in mid-November that its writer had had time merely to glance at some of the *Putnam's* articles, but had "carefully read" several pieces including "Melville's Paul Potter." The Newark paper's praise of Melville was consistently part of a larger enthusiasm for a native magazine that could "creditably compare with any literary magazine in the world."[50] Up in Massachusetts an early notice, perhaps by J. E. A. Smith, appeared in Melville's local paper, the *Berkshire County Eagle,* which called its readers' attention to the July *Putnam's*— "This best of Magazines for men with minds"—and among pieces of "superior merit" singled out *Israel Potter:* "A Berkshire story, said— without doubt correctly—to be written by Herman Melville, will be of especial interest in this quarter." The third installment (by now, the Berkshire boy was escaping entombment at Squire Woodcock's) found the *Eagle* still absorbed in the adventures of "our old friend and fellow countryman, Israel Potter"—"strange adventures, with much result of

48. The *Citizen,* September 2 and December 30, 1854; this paper also noted the serial's continuation (November 4) and found the next-to-last installment "good, as usual" (February 3, 1855).

49. *Morning Courier and New-York Enquirer,* "after July 31 [1854]" (*Log*); August 29; and September 30 (*Log*).

50. Newark *Daily Advertiser,* July 15, 1854; August 16 (reading uncertain due to crease in newspaper); November 14; October 5, containing the encomium for *Putnam's,* and noting "Melville's Israel Potter is continued."

poetical thought and eccentric comment."[51] In summary, the serial notices suggest that Melville had amply carried out his promise to Putnam
to provide "adventure" and sustain "interest." At the same time, if he
saw many of these notices, Melville could not have escaped the sense of
pressure, while he was still writing, to keep his style toned down.

    With *Israel Potter* Melville established himself as one of the leading
contributors to *Putnam's*. Between November, 1853, when the first part of
"Bartleby, The Scrivener" appeared, and March, 1855, when *Israel Potter*
concluded, all but three of the seventeen issues carried work by Melville,
and the August, 1854, issue offered "The Lightning-Rod Man" as well as
the second installment of *Israel Potter*. Melville had become a steady con-
tributor, paid at the best rate, to a magazine that Thackeray said—so the
gossip ran in September, 1855—"was much the best Mag. in the world"
(even though his *The Newcomes* had been running in *Harper's*). Melville
had refused or ignored, however, George P. Putnam's urgent request for a
daguerreotype to be used in the magazine. During the serialization of *Israel
Potter* one author was featured each month with a full-page frontispiece
engraving (except for the November issue, a spot Melville could have
had); the group included George William Curtis, Bayard Taylor, John
Pendleton Kennedy, Parke Godwin, James Russell Lowell, and William
Cullen Bryant. One recalls Melville's letter to Evert A. Duyckinck (February 12, 1851) refusing a comparable request on the grounds that "almost
everybody is having his 'mug' engraved nowadays; so that this test of
distinction is getting to be reversed . . ." and his use of the episode in
Pierre (NN 253–54). Melville apparently still wanted his reversed distinction, perhaps for the very reason that his only serialized novel seemed to
threaten him with success.

V

    An account of the publication of *Israel Potter* in book form, its recep-
tion, subsequent editions, and modern reputation, begins with the question of the book contract. The publisher's agreement is lost; what we
know of it is circumstantial.

    Melville's letter to Putnam of June 7, in which he proposed terms for
the magazine publication, specifically noted: "the copyright to be retained

    51. July 7, 1854, and August 25, both cited in *Log*. Leyda also reports routine notices in
the Salem *Register*, July 31, 1854, and the Boston *Daily Advertiser*, March 7, 1855. Smith's
possible authorship of the *Eagle* items is pointed out both in *Log* and by Merton M. Sealts,
Jr., *The Early Lives of Melville*, pp. 32, 211, n. 5.

by me." Melville's intention was obviously to retain his freedom to negotiate separately for the book. Whether Melville or Putnam first proposed
that the book be done by G. P. Putnam & Company, and when, is not
certain, but it seems to have been agreed on early. The answer may well be
in an unlocated letter of Melville's sold at auction in 1941 with the following
catalogue description: "an A.L.S. of the author, Pittsfield, June 12 [n.y.] to
G. P. Putnam regarding cash advance and copyright matters for certain of
his writings." No year other than 1854 fits the given circumstances. Unless
a misdating of the June 7 letter has made two letters of one (see footnote
5), this would mean that Melville wrote Putnam about terms for the book
within five days of asking terms for the serial, possibly prompted by an
immediate reply from Putnam to the first letter. An exchange of missing
letters, about November 1, 1854 (both mentioned in Melville's letter of
November 3), may also have borne on the matter of the book contract.
Retrospective information on the *Israel Potter* contract is given in a letter of
Melville's (January 7, 1856) to Dix & Edwards, the publishers who bought
out *Putnam's Monthly Magazine* in the spring of 1855 just as Melville's
serial was finishing. Melville suggested a written agreement—

> of the same sort made concerning "I Potter" with Mr Putnam.
>   In your note you state *12 per cent* as the terms I mentioned. But I meant
> to say *12 & ½ per cent;* that is, the same terms as I had for "I Potter"; which
> was *12 & ½* as I now find *by reference to the Agreement.*

Curiously, there is some uncertainty about just what percentage Melville
had arranged with Mr. Putnam. When Melville wrote Putnam & Company (August 21, 1855) six months after publication that "by reference to
our Agreement about *Israel Potter,* I see there is to be a payment (by note)
during the present month," he received an accounting figured initially not
at twelve and one-half, nor twelve, but at ten percent; later, on his copy,
the account was refigured at twelve and one-half.

On February 1, 1855, the Pittsfield *Sun* published an announcement:
"*New Work by Melville.*—G. P. Putnam & Co. of New York announce
that 'Herman Melville's new Book, *Israel Potter,* will be ready March
1st.' " However, the copyright deposit of the title page (which, according
to the copyright law, was to take place before publication) did not occur
until March 10—the same date on which the book itself was also deposited
for copyright. It is likely, of course, that copies of the book may have
been available somewhat earlier (the Boston *Daily Advertiser* listed it
among the new books on March 7, though perhaps not on the basis of an

actual copy). The book differed from the magazine serial in several ways: the title became *Israel Potter: His Fifty Years of Exile;* Melville was named as author (and identified as "Author of 'Typee,' 'Omoo,' Etc."); the dedication and a table of contents were added; and one paragraph in Chapter 24 was deleted, as already noted (see footnote 40). The volume of 276 pages, priced at seventy-five cents, was available in various colors of cloth (green, blue, brown, dark purple), with the shortened title "Fifty Years Exile" stamped in gold on the spine above Melville's last name.

There is no evidence to suggest that Melville had much to do with the preparation of the book. When the cluster of *Putnam's Monthly* stories was put together for *The Piazza Tales* in 1856, Melville wrote Dix & Edwards (January 19) about having made "ordinary corrections" of the magazine pages and "some few other improvements" and having added "a desirable note or two"; he also discussed title page problems. Now, however, he seems to have largely left to the publishers the less complicated production of *Israel Potter*. He probably supplied the subtitle change "His" for "Or"; and he may have read proof on the dedication, since it was unpublished, but two circumstances suggest he otherwise did no proofreading. One is that his own copy of the third printing of *Israel Potter* contains eight minor changes of the sort he might well have made if he had read proofs; five of them are used for the first time in the present edition. The other is that the book printing carried over from the magazine the awkward split chapters, with the numbering treated two different ways, and even the XVI–XV–XVI error; although someone decided to cut one paragraph and made a few scattered corrections that took more than casual attention, it was more likely someone in the editorial office than Melville himself. The magazine pages presumably used as printer's copy got no identifiable authorial revisions (such as those Melville made for *The Piazza Tales*) and no thorough authorial or editorial correction. Both author and publisher seemed content simply to get the book out fast.

The book was launched with solid advertising. More than two dozen separate ads for *Israel Potter,* appearing between March 7 and March 28 in Boston and New York newspapers, have thus far been noted.[52] All were

52. One ad in the New York *Herald* (March 10); 6 in the New York *Daily Times* (March 9, 19, 21, 23, 26, 28); 8 in the New York *Daily Tribune* (March 10, 14, 15, 17, 20, 22, 24, 27); 11 in the New York *Commercial Advertiser* (March 9, 10, 15, 16, 17, 19–24); one in the Boston *Daily Advertiser* (March 7); and two in the Boston *Semi-Weekly Atlas* (March 7). A Putnam ad "To the Trade" appeared in *Norton's Literary Gazette* (April 2), but no further April ads have been noted so far.

single-column ads, ranging in vertical length from just over one inch, the first week, to nearly five inches late in the month. A common pattern, with variations, marked the major sequences appearing in the *Times, Tribune,* and *Commercial Advertiser.* On March 9 came a pre-publication notice. Saturday, March 10, came the announcement that "G. P. Putnam & Co./ publish this day/ ISRAEL POTTER . . ./ By Hermann Melville," followed by the inevitable "Author of 'Typee,' 'Omoo,' &c. &c.," and ending with "For sale by all Booksellers." About a week later the ad picked up two short quotations: "Melville's best work" (from an unlocated notice in the Reading [Pa.] *Gazette*), and "A stirring narrative, and admirably written" (from the *Citizen* serial notice already quoted). During the week of March 19 seven-line extracts from two book reviews were added. Late that same week the Putnam firm's biggest name nearly crowded Melville off the page: *Israel Potter* was cut to four lines at the bottom of a large advertisement featuring the forthcoming *Life of Washington* and other works by Irving. By March 27 *Israel Potter* received its largest layout, headed "AN EXCITING NARRATIVE" and containing six extracts from reviews.[53]

The pre-publication notice in the *Times* (and similar ones elsewhere) explained what may have been a change in publishing date: "In order to secure a good supply of this book, which seems likely to have a large sale, the trade are requested to send their orders early, the publishers having already been obliged twice to postpone the day of publication, to enable them to arrange for a large enough quantity." This may have been chiefly an advertising ploy, but it is true that a second printing followed very quickly, for as early as March 19 a *Times* advertisement stated, "Now Ready. Third Edition." (The second printing can be identified, among other ways, by the correct numeral "XIV" appearing at the head of the fourteenth chapter; the third is labeled *"THIRD EDITION"* on the title page—and the copies of it for England had a cancel title leaf with the imprint of Low, Son & Co. under that of Putnam.) The appearance of three printings in such rapid succession suggests that the publisher had reason to be encouraged by the initial reception of the book. After all, some of the serial notices had suggested not only that Melville was back on course, but that *Israel Potter,* with its stirring and strange adventures, might well be very popular. The generous advertising campaign suggests that Putnam decided to find out.

53. Extracts were from: *Norton's Literary Gazette* (7 lines); *Morning Courier and New-York Enquirer* (4 lines); Philadelphia *City Item* (8 lines); Boston *Puritan Recorder* (4 lines); New York *Evening Post* (5 lines); and New York *Albion* (1 line).

Some of the leading literary magazines that had previously followed
Melville's novels, including *Harper's, Graham's,* and the *Southern Literary
Messenger,* ignored the book altogether. Although serialization may have
undercut the book's impact and even encouraged the silence of rival magazines, the basic fact may have been G. W. Curtis's view in January, 1856:
"He has lost his prestige." Editors who did not assign reviews may have
become too disaffected to want re-engagement, or perhaps lost interest as
the chance for juicy castigation seemed to melt away.

Twenty American newspapers and periodicals are thus far known to
have printed responses to the 192 review copies that Putnam sent out.[54]
Most of these "reviews" were short, only five of them containing more
than twenty lines of commentary, and few rose above perfunctory critical
levels. But with only two exceptions they were favorable, finding *Israel
Potter* eminently readable, exciting, and destined to be popular. "A
downright good book," the *Albion* review began—a phrase that ended up
in the Putnam ads. It was good enough to win the capitulation of the
Boston *Post,* whose editor, Colonel Charles Gordon Greene, had been for
some time trying (with his own or his reviewers' pens) to knock some
common sense into Melville. The Colonel, or his reviewer, put *Israel
Potter* back-to-back with Kingsley's *Westward Ho!*—the current English
fashion in historical novels—and judged the contest a draw. Kingsley's
book he found "far superior to 'Israel Potter,' in scope, in brilliancy, in
tone and in character," but "the American book, after making every
proper deduction, is more truth-like, pithy, vigorous and readable than the
English" [C2]. It was probably the poet William Ellery Channing, Jr., one
of Melville's few steady admirers in the press, who spelled out the book's
readability in the New Bedford *Mercury* (March 12, 1855) as "a mixture of

54. The 20 are: [A] New Bedford *Mercury* (March 12, 1855); [B] *Norton's Literary Gazette*
(March 15); [C1] and [C2] Boston *Post* (March 15 and April 5); [D] *Morning Courier and
New-York Enquirer* (March 17); [E] New York *Albion* (March 17); [F] New York *Evening Post*
(March 17); [G] New York *Commercial Advertiser* (March 21); [H] Boston *Puritan Recorder*
(March 22); [I] New York *Evangelist* (March 15); [J] Newark *Daily Advertiser* (April 5); [K]
New York *Citizen* (April 7); [L] New York *Christian Intelligencer* (May 3); [M] New York
National Magazine (May); [N] Boston *Christian Examiner and Religious Miscellany* (May); [O1]
and [O2] *Putnam's Monthly,* pp. 545, 548 (May); [P] unknown Albany (?) paper (April 30);
[Q] Reading (Pa.) *Gazette* (date unknown); [R] Philadelphia *City Item* (date unknown); [S]
Hartford *Republican* (date unknown); [T] *New York Quarterly* (April). All citations above and
the dates are drawn from the originals, except that [C2] and [P] are from *Log;* [Q] and [R]
from *Times* ads, March 19, 28; and [S] from Meade Minnigerode, *Some Personal Letters of
Herman Melville and a Bibliography,* p. 170.

fun, gravity, romance and reality very taking from beginning to end."
The *Citizen* called it "a beautifully printed, racy volume, abounding with
lively sketches of character, and graphic scenes on land and sea." A Philadelphia paper's view that the tale was "told in a simple and direct, but
charming manner" [R] was exploited in the Putnam advertising. Melville's
cousin Kate Lansing sent down from Albany a clipping that praised the way
Melville gained his effects "with few words, selected with marvellous apt-
ness" [P]. And a Hartford reviewer thought the "descriptions . . . among
the finest in the language. Such splendid writing rarely issues from the
press" [S]. *Israel Potter* seemed headed for both popular and literary success.

Appreciation dropped into such clichés, no doubt welcome enough to
G. P. Putnam & Company, as "rich and novel entertainment" [B], "very
simple yet graphic recital of interesting adventure" [D], "a most charming
tale" [J]. The only outright dissents from this wave of enthusiasm were
one reviewer's blunt complaint that the story was "rather heavy reading. . . . the author fails to interest us very much in the fortunes of his
hero" [N] and another's that the "author of Israel Potter has to do with the
detail of a narrative not too interesting, and for purposes of romantic
interest not too well chosen" [T]. The representative view, however, was
that the book had "raciness of flavour" [E] and was "delightfully told" [F].
One reviewer was grateful for "the pleasure we have derived from its
perusal" [G]; another, "sorry to see the work hastened so rapidly to a
close," was ready like Oliver to "ask for more" [J].

Israel Potter won praise for its masculine style, Yankee wit, and alleged
patriotism. Colonel Greene's *Post* cherished its "curt, manly, independent
tone" [C1]. The *Morning Courier* noted its "manly and direct" style, and
then touched on the problem of vulgarity: to be sure, the book was
"occasionally somewhat coarse for the refinement of our day; but so are
Robinson Crusoe and *The Pilgrim's Progress*." Thus Melville had sufficiently
kept his promise to Putnam ("nothing of any sort to shock the fastidious")
so that the only reviewer to raise the question could make his own answer.
Whether Melville or his publishers had reduced the few bits of sailor
rhetoric to asterisks is not known; such pruderies and the rather touching
enthusiasm of reviewers for the book's masculinity remind one that
though men wrote the notices, literary tone was distinctly subject to the
ladies' review. The New Bedford *Mercury* reviewer, probably Channing,
relished Melville's "keen sense" for native scenery and "the peculiarities of
the Yankee character at the revolutionary period" [A]. *Norton's Literary
Gazette* promised the reader that when he was not "filled with horror at

the mad passions of fighting men" he would find himself "laughing at the Yankee shrewdness that is never outwitted"; for Israel always "preserves the unmistakable characteristics of a true son of New England." The *National Magazine* also liked the mix of Yankee character and stirring scenes in a "half-comic, half-patriotic vein," but concluded its dozen lines with a kind of astonished discovery: "A tinge of obscure sarcasm pervades the book, most apparent in its dedication to the Bunker Hill Monument!" The *Citizen,* however, thought the dedication merely "humorous," and the *Commercial Advertiser* judged it a "burlesque on certain European dedications." The common view was that the tale was "thoroughly saturated with American sentiment" [G], that it "will be, for its patriotic interest, most popular in the community" [J], and that it "will be greedily devoured by Young America!" [K].

Only one review saw political criticism in *Israel Potter.* The *Albion,* in perhaps the most acute notice Melville's book received at home, first praised its "masculine vigour, and even a certain fantastical ruggedness, that separate it from the herd of smoothly-written tales." Then it singled out the battle of the *Richard* and the *Serapis* as "a master-piece of writing; albeit some may deem its imagery too fanciful and far-fetched." The review ended thus:

> But Mr. Melville, though American enough to be a Know-Nothing, has a plain way of speaking. Thus, he says: "Sharing the same blood with England, and yet her proved foe in two wars—not wholly inclined at bottom to forget an old grudge—intrepid, unprincipled, reckless, predatory, with boundless ambition, civilized in externals but a savage at heart, America is, or may yet be, the Paul Jones of nations." Just contrast this short but expressive passage, with the terms wherein the famous "Ostend Conference" recently heralded a scheme of spoliation, with a set of fine phrases about "conscious rectitude" and "approbation of the world." Mr. Melville comes to the point.

The force of the remarks here about the infamous Ostend Manifesto of October 18, 1854,[55] is brilliantly appropriate and in contrast to the generally purblind claims for Melville's patriotism. No American review noted that Israel was nearly run down by the patriotic car near Faneuil Hall on the Fourth of July (Chapter 26).

55. The reviewer is quoting from the text of the Manifesto. The document had been drawn by the American ministers to Great Britain, France, and Spain, who declared in it that should Spain's refusal to sell Cuba to the United States seem to threaten us "we shall be justified in wresting it from Spain if we possess the power . . . ." (Henry Steele Commager, ed., *Documents of American History* [New York, 1948], pp. 333–35.)

The question of authenticity—an old problem for Melville's critics and publishers—came up only once, but most uncomfortably. Most reviewers seemed happy enough with Melville's dedicatory account of his source and his claim to "general fidelity to the main drift of the original narrative." They assumed that *Israel Potter* was history somewhat romanticized. In a friendly way, for example, *Norton's Literary Gazette* guessed that the intense reality of the scenes owed more to "the power of Mr. Melville's imagination"—citing *Typee* and *Omoo* as instances—than to his source. Reviewers even praised it as "a romance of history" [L] and "a most thrilling romance" [H]. The trouble came from—of all places—*Putnam's Monthly*. The "Editorial Notes" of the May issue [O1] opened with a page of self-congratulation that in its short two-year history no less than six of its serials had already become books. "The youngest of the tribe is named 'Israel Potter,' the earnest, indomitable, free-hearted, much suffering Israel, who having just made his bow to 'his Highness, the Bunker Hill Monument,' is about to make a patriotic progress, like a new President, over the nation. May he be everywhere received"—not well, or with huzzahs, but—"according to his deserts!" (V, 545). The reason for questioning the concluding tone of this generous *ave atque vale* appears three pages later in the same issue [O2]. For there the same editor, presumably, gave Melville the shaft, to speak rudely of the Monument: "It has sometimes been inquired whether Mr. MELVILLE'S *Israel Potter* is a romance or an authentic narrative; and in the dedication of the book (which did not appear in our Monthly), he explains." Thereupon he quoted the balance of the third paragraph of the dedication, and sprung his trap: "The original, however, is not so rare as Mr. Melville seems to think. At any rate, we have a copy before us, as we write . . . ." Next came full quotation of the title page of *Life and Remarkable Adventures*, right down to "Price 31 cents." For his own reasons the editor concluded with the question of historical fidelity rather than the charge of plagiarism: "Mr. Melville departs considerably from his original. He makes Israel born in Berkshire, Mass., and brings him acquainted with Paul Jones, as he was not. How far he is justified in the historical liberties he has taken, would be a curious case of literary casuistry" (V, 548). Why this exposure of its own author by *Putnam's* itself? Had Melville after all not forewarned Putnam? Or had Putnam not passed the word along? Was it perhaps a prudential protective gesture, to forestall outside critics? Or did someone on the staff, feeling that the magazine, or the public, had been duped, take this means to even the score? In any case, the American reviews were already written, and the subject died.

Many of the reviewers took occasion, if only in passing, to compare *Israel Potter* with Melville's earlier books. The current profile of his reputation clearly had two reference points: the successful early writings, recalled with pleasure; and his "recent writings" (presumably a euphemism for *Pierre*), about which the less said the better. The dissenter cited above thought the new work "scarcely sustains . . . [his] reputation" [N]. Otherwise *Israel Potter* was given a standing it has rarely had since: "far above . . . *Pierre* and some of its predecessors" [C1]; "not excelled by any thing which Herman Melville has ever before written" [B]; "equal to any thing which Mr. Melville's pen has produced" and "in pleasant contrast to . . . Mr. Melville's last book" [D]; "quite equal in a literary point of view to any of its author's previous works, and . . . much superior to some of them in other respects" [G]; "one of the most genuine of the author's numerous books" [J]; and "in some respects the best thing he has ever done" [I]. The bluntest praise—used by Putnam in the ads—was: "Melville's best work" [Q]. In short there was general feasting at the prodigal son's return. No doubt this gave Melville "confidence" for his next novel.

All this enthusiasm for *Israel Potter* and Melville's redemption somehow failed to translate into the popular success the American reviewers predicted. When Melville asked for an accounting from Putnam he received a statement (October 8) showing the book's status as of July 1. Putnam had printed 1400 copies, an additional 800, and then 1500 more (the "Third Edition" advertised on March 19), for a total of 3700 copies. Twenty-five shorts on the three printings left 3675 bound copies, of which 192, the account showed, were given to editors. With 906 copies still on hand, sales by July 1 amounted to 2577. At seventy-five cents per copy receipts were $1932.75. Melville's profit was figured at ten percent as $193.27. Another hand, possibly Allan Melville's, wrote the figure of $241.58 on the account; this was Melville's profit if he received the twelve and a half percent royalty he later claimed. Melville's total returns from Putnam on the serial and the book were $614.77 at a minimum, and on up to $748 at most (if he received the larger percentage, and further royalties on the remaining 906 copies). Compared to his usual earnings it was a good income for about six months' work.

As a venture into popular culture, however, if at any time either Melville or Putnam so conceived the project, neither had reaped the popular rewards. The column of the New York *Times* that announced the "Third Edition" of *Israel Potter* also advertised *The Lamplighter*—"The charming story of Uncle True and Little Gerty"; in its first year, the publisher reported, it had sold 75,000 copies. The big seller in March, 1855, was not *Israel Potter* but *The Life and Beauties of Fanny Fern,* and the March papers were awash with advertisements for and speculations about this anonymous and mysterious book having to do with the author of *Ruth Hall* (1854). Closer competition came from another novel, also a historical romance of the American Revolution, with a title strangely parallel to that of Melville's book: *Kate Aylesford: A Story of the Refugees.* On March 20, *Israel Potter* was advertised in the New York *Tribune,* on the front page, directly under the masthead. Three days later *Kate Aylesford* was announced in the same spot, with twice the space; it was published March 30, with a bold-print ad headed: "THE GREAT REVOLUTIONARY ROMANCE," and a Putnam ad of April 3 for new books listed *Kate Aylesford,* but not *Israel Potter.* The new romance was by Charles J. Peterson, publisher of *Peterson's Magazine,* whose three brothers published the book for the firm of T. B. Peterson, Philadelphia. Melville was to have a second encounter with the Petersons. But perhaps the truer perspective lies in the column of the *Times* (March 21) which ran ads for both *Israel Potter* and *Walden.* Thoreau's masterpiece had been published in August, 1854, by Ticknor & Fields in an edition of 2000 copies; the next reprinting was not until 1862, 280 copies.[56] The simple fact would seem to be that mid-nineteenth-century America was not very widely or deeply interested in good literature. Hawthorne's famous complaint, written to Ticknor from England in January, 1855, speaks directly to Melville's situation:

> America is now wholly given over to a d——d mob of scribbling women, and I should have no chance of success while the public taste is occupied with their trash—and should be ashamed of myself if I did succeed. What is the mystery of these innumerable editions of the "Lamplighter," and other books neither better nor worse?—worse they could not be, and better they need not be, when they sell by the 100,000. . . .[57]

In England *Israel Potter* received wider distribution in Routledge's unauthorized edition than in the form of the third American printing imported by Sampson Low, Son & Co. George Routledge & Co., which had published unauthorized editions of *Typee* and *Omoo* in 1850,

56. *The Annotated Walden,* ed. Philip Van Doren Stern (New York: Clarkson N. Potter, 1970), pp. 38–41.

57. Caroline Ticknor, *Hawthorne and His Publisher* (Boston: Houghton Mifflin, 1913), pp. 141–42.

brought out *Israel Potter* in the early summer of 1855 as No. 113 in its "Cheap Series" of one-shilling books in paper-covered boards (also available in slightly more expensive cloth covers). The Routledge edition was announced in the London *Atlas* on May 5 and was listed in Routledge's Wholesale Catalogue for May. Routledge's Paper and Print Book contains an entry for June, 1855, estimating the cost of printing and paper for 6000 copies to come to 3⅜ pence per copy. An edition of this size (more than half again as large as the American edition) was probably printed, for 6000 copies was Routledge's usual print run for fiction reprints. Many people therefore must have seen the decorated yellow-paper cover of the cheap issue, which bore on the front a nautical scene printed in black, showing a whaler among icebergs and, in the foreground, a whale surfacing beneath a whaleboat whose crew is leaping overboard; thus another hand improvised further adventures for Israel.

The three known English reviews, all elicited by the Routledge shilling edition, treated *Israel Potter* more severely than had the American ones, but in two instances with perception. George Henry Lewes, who may have been the author of a brilliant earlier review of *The Whale,* just possibly wrote the cogent critical estimate in the *Leader* (May 5, 1855), though the tone is quite different. The reviewer found it "a curiously unequal book," admirable in subject, and so artful in treatment that by Chapter 14 he "felt disposed to rank *Israel Potter* as incomparably the best work that Mr. Melville had yet written." The "curious falling off" at midpoint he attributed to two successive defects: "the least successful character," Jones, is the "most fully developed"; and toward the end, Melville's shift from particularity to generality is a disastrous reversal of novelistic principle. If only Melville had cut half the Jones scenes, and taken a second volume for Israel's life in London and return to America, the reviewer lamented, Melville would have had "not only his best book, but the best book that any American author has written for a long time past." Instead, "*Israel Potter* is the work of an original thinker and vigorous writer, damaged by want of constructive ability—or, in plainer and shorter words, by want of Art." Nevertheless he recommended the book, especially for the interview with Franklin, and quoted the shorter scene with the King as an instance of Melville's power. The other perceptive review appeared in the *Weekly Chronicle* (June 2), which also quoted the whole scene with the King as "one of the best parts," but took a hard, penetrating line: "The book leaves the impression of having been carefully and purposely rendered common-place. You feel that the author is capable of something much better, but for a freak is resolved to curb his fancy and adhere to the dustiest routine." As an example of the "abrupt, condensed style" the reviewer quoted the book's final paragraph.

These two London reviews raised serious questions of craft (the *Leader*) and commitment (the *Weekly Chronicle*) which relate hauntingly to Melville's method of composition, as described in the present study, and to Melville's self-imposed limits (and whether or not he held himself to them), as described in his letter to Putnam (June 7, 1854). Future critics may find them crucial. Not so with the review in the *Athenæum* (June 2). The reviewer, possibly Henry Chorley, who may have been the reviewer who had found *The Whale* "so much trash belonging to the worst school of Bedlam literature," thought *Israel Potter* not much better. His verdict was that "Mr. Melville . . . becomes wilder and wilder, and more and more turgid in each successive book," and he quoted from "In the City of Dis" (paragraphs 6–7) in evidence. As "a proficient in the 'earthquake' and 'alligator' style" Melville offered a Franklin who was "rather weak and very tiresome," a Jones who was "a melo-dramatic caricature," and hopelessly unreal scenes at Whitehaven and St. Mary's Isle. In contemptuous conclusion this reviewer suggested the book was "not a bad shilling's worth for any railway reader, who does not object to small type and a style the glories of which are nebulous."

Easily the longest and in many ways the most interesting response to *Israel Potter* came from a French critic. Emile Montégut took fifty-two pages of the *Revue des deux mondes* (July 1, 1855) to present Melville's latest work to an international audience. The *Revue* had twice before given Melville sustained attention. M. Montégut was the same critic whom Henry James was to take to task in his *Hawthorne* for his—to James—superficial view of Hawthorne as "Un Romancier Pessimiste" (*Revue*, August 1, 1860). All but six pages of "ISRAËL POTTER: Légende Démocratique Américaine" were given to a condensed translation of the novel. In the essay surrounding the translation Montégut's chief interest is in *Israel Potter* as a cultural document, seen in the perspectives of Michelet, Tocqueville, and his own impassioned commitment to romantic democracy. What fascinates him is the American capacity to mythologize its own history, within two generations turning the merely able leaders of the Revolution into giants, quite as the Greeks created their demigods. The special contribution of *Israel Potter* to this process of canonization is that Melville has chosen for sainthood an obscure and humble soldier of that Revolution. Israel "représente le caractère américain au moment où il était en formation," before fifty years of prosperity had corrupted it into the menacing energies of the Know-Nothing movement and adventurism toward Cuba (again, the relation between *Israel Potter* and the Ostend Manifesto). Montégut assumes that Melville's tattered source was mere pretense for his own myth (though, probably from the *Putnam's Monthly* editorial note, he knows there was an actual book which sold for thirty-one cents) and that it became "sous sa plume une sorte de légende à la fois démocratique et patriotique." He is sensitive to Melville's recovery of traditional techniques for mythologizing: "l'amour du héros poussé en quelque sorte jusqu'à la susceptibilité, la narration lente et détaillée, le calque fidèle et minutieux de la réalité, l'apothéose et la *sublimisation,* si nous pouvons ainsi parler, des faits les plus humbles." But what strikes him far more than method is Melville's presumed motive—"le naïf orgueil qui anime . . . . L'esprit démocratique peut seul expliquer cette glorification d'un mort inconnu, humble soldat et simple citoyen . . . ." The meaning of the tale to Montégut is not Israel's ultimate victimization but his capacity for survival, and he assumes that is Melville's message too. In eloquent coda Montégut hymns the "foules anonymes" of history, first reborn in the American Revolution: "il représente, ce soldat de Bunker-Hill, le moment de l'histoire où la foule a perdu son antique caractère, et où les êtres qui la composent . . . ont compris qu'ils existaient réellement . . . ." All that Israel suffered falls away before one fact: "Il peut rester obscur et ignoré, car il *existe* et il a le sentiment de son existence."

Montégut's translation should not be ignored. As the presentation of *Israel Potter* under the distinguished banner of the *Revue* may well have affected the shape of Melville's continental reputation for some time, it seems fair to ask what version of Melville its readers received. The translation, in spite of some amusing ineptitudes at rendering Yankee dialect,[58] was generally skillful and verbally accurate. In cutting the book to one-fourth its length of course Montégut was performing a critical act quite as much as when writing his essay. Yet nothing in the essay or the format of the translation tells the reader he is not getting the whole book. Furthermore the text is presented as continuous prose, not as selections, and the lack of chapter indications leads the reader to assume any condensation has retained the original shape of the tale. In fact, though typically chapters

58. Franklin's marvelous "Ah! I smell Indian corn" becomes "Oh! je sens l'odeur des champs américains," and his " 'Pears to me you have rather high heels to your boots" becomes "Oh! Oh! il me semble que vos bottes . . . ." For whatever reason Israel is given "cheveux roux" in place of his yellow mane.

have been cut by a third or a half, eight chapters have been reduced to a half-dozen lines each.[59] In cutting, Montégut tended to keep portions that Israel dominates, minimizing the Franklin sequence and cutting heavily into the Jones section. He obviously preferred the narrator's simpler *récit* (Chapters 1–5 become one-third of his text) and scenes dramatizing Israel's Yankee encounters (with Sir John, with the King, with British sailors— "The Shuttle"). In turn he condensed or cut passages or chapters in which the narrator theorizes (on Franklin or Jones) or engages in rhetorical medita- tion (the dedication, the brickyard, on the bridge). In one notable instance he goes so far as to pervert the text: Melville's "the old man narrowly escaped being run over by a patriotic triumphal car in the procession" (Chapter 26) becomes "le viellard eut en débarquant la joie de voir écrits sur une bannière flottante, portée sur un char de triomphe . . . ." Thus through the tactics of translation, *si nous pouvons ainsi parler,* the reader gets the "légende à la fois démocratique et patriotique" that the good M. Montégut argues for in his essay.

In 1865 *Israel Potter* was reprinted in Philadelphia as *The Refugee* under circumstances that enraged Melville and his family. During the panic of 1857 Putnam had sold the plates to T. B. Peterson for $218.66. Peterson waited until the spring of 1865, when the war was grinding to a halt, to capitalize on a revitalized market; then T. B. Peterson & Brothers issued *The Refugee* and gave it publicity.[60] The tradition of referring to the Peter- son printing as a "pirated edition" is misleading. Peterson was within his rights in reprinting a work whose plates he had purchased. But it was another matter, at least to Melville, that the publisher took it on himself to re-title the book, to drop the dedication and table of contents, and for unknown reasons to attribute to Melville on the title page two nonexistent works—all without consulting Melville. Thus the *Times* advertisement and the book's title page both announced: "THE REFUGEE, by Herman Melville, Author of 'Typee,' 'Omoo,' 'The Two Captains,' 'The Man of the World,' etc. etc." That Peterson was after a popular market is clear from the three binding styles in which he issued *The Refugee,*[61] and from the puff he printed on the title page:

59. Chapters 8–9, 15–16, 18–19, 23–24.
60. Peterson pushed sales with an advertisement in the New York *Times* of March 11, 1865; he sent notice of the book to *Godey's Lady's Book and Magazine* which they ac- knowledged with brief comment in May; and he was still advertising the book as late as October 15, 1866, in the *American Literary Gazette and Publishers' Circular.*
61. *The Refugee* appeared in paper at $1.50 and in two distinctive cloth bindings. One of them, priced at $1.75, was in dark brownish cloth, blind-stamped front and back with the

"Written with a life-like power. We advise no one to take up 'The Refugee' until he has the leisure to finish it; for when he has once dipped into its fascinating and adventurous pages, he will not be disposed to leave them until he has reached the very last."

"This is really a delightful book, in which one may find food for laughter and sterling information into the bargain. It is written in a pleasant off-hand style, such as will be enjoyed by everybody. There are portions of the work, infinitely superior to any thing of the kind we ever before read."

Since neither the advertisements nor the book in any way suggested that this was simply a reprint of *Israel Potter,* one guesses that Peterson changed the title in order to imply that it was a new work, and made up two additional titles in order to suggest a "new Melville." It was indeed as if "something further" had followed from *The Confidence-Man.*

We know of four reactions on the part of Melville. First, by his own testimony, he wrote a letter of "remonstrance" to Peterson (date unknown); some twenty years later he claimed this letter "arrested the publication." Second, he made a public protest of Peterson's actions through a letter to the editor of a New York paper, the *World*:

Permit me through your columns to make a disavowal. T. B. Peterson & Brothers, of Philadelphia, include in a late list of their publications "The Refugee; by Herman Melville."

I have never written any work by that title. In connection with that title Peterson Brothers employ my name without authority, and notwithstanding a remonstrance conveyed to them long ago.

This letter, undated and surviving only in a newspaper clipping, was probably written in the late 1860's (see *Letters,* pp. 304 and 383, footnote 265). Third, in one of his letters (April 7, 1888) to his young English admirer, James Billson, Melville wrote:

As for the "Two Captains" and "Man of the World" they are books of the air—I know of none such. The names appear, tho', on the title-page of a book of mine—"Israel Potter" which was republished by a Philadelphia house some time ago under the unwarrantably altered title of "The Refugee." A letter to the publisher arrested the publication.

Fourth, in his own copy of *The Refugee,* Melville wrote on the title page in ink, in a small crabbed hand, beneath the two fake titles: "these books

<hr />

publisher's insignia, with a gilt spine panel for the title and Melville's name. (Minnigerode, p. 167, is the sole source for the report of a paper edition and of the prices.) A second, more garish binding, that of the Peterson Dollar Series, was of red cloth with black and gold stamping; Melville's name does not appear on the covers or the spine, which read: "The Refugee By Author of 'Omoo,' 'Typee,' &c.&c." (See the NOTE ON THE TEXT, footnotes 7 and 14.)

were not written by Herman Melville as alleged—"; and his wife wrote in pencil beneath the title: "Fraud by # on Israel Potter," with a line drawn from the symbol down to the publisher's name.[62] Melville's anger at the liberties taken by Peterson obviously exceeded whatever pleasure he felt in seeing *Israel Potter* suddenly popular ten years after its first publication. His anger would scarcely have been soothed by the news that the updated edition (1875) of the Duyckincks' *Cyclopædia of American Literature,* edited to date by M. Laird Simons, in a supplement to the 1855 entry which included *Israel Potter,* said: "In 1865 he wrote *The Refugee,* a tale of the Revolution, which sketched the daring deeds of Paul Jones in the *Bon Homme Richard*"—thus failing to identify *The Refugee* as *Israel Potter.*

Except for the episode of *The Refugee,* the short story of *Israel Potter*'s reputation from 1856 to 1921 might well be titled "Sixty-five Years of Exile." The Duyckincks' own 1855 *Cyclopædia* entry had commented that Melville's "reproduction, with various inventions and additions, of the adventures of *Israel Potter,* an actual character of the Revolution," has "met with deserved success," and in a note had cited as the original source Potter's *Life and Adventures,* "written from the narrative of Potter, by Mr. Henry Trumbull, of Hartford, Ct." But such fragments of record as we have clearly indicate how short-lived that success was. An essay in the *Dublin University Magazine* (January, 1856) on Cooper, Dana, and Melville remarked of Melville's books: "we have read them all carefully (excepting his last production, 'Israel Potter,' which is said to be mediocre)"; the English reviews may have spoiled sales. In a *Putnam's Monthly* essay on Curtis and Melville (April, 1857) Fitz-James O'Brien again offered the picture of a man of genius who "has been going wrong"; from this perspective *Israel Potter* seemed "a comparatively reasonable narrative." It was "a coherent story . . . told with considerable clearness and force"; but it lacked Melville's characteristic "animation" and the portraits of Franklin and Jones were "somewhat fantastic." A tiny but welcome tribute of consequence to Melville appeared in Hawthorne's *Our Old Home* (1863), a copy of which Melville obtained in 1868. In the section on his consular experiences, Hawthorne described "an old man, who . . . had been wandering about England more than a quarter of a century . . . , and all the while doing his utmost to get home again. Herman Melville, in his excellent novel or biography of 'Israel Potter,' has an idea somewhat similar

62. On the page facing the title page of his own "third" edition of *Israel Potter* (1855) Melville also wrote: "Re issued by T. B. Peterson & Bros. Phil." To this Mrs. Melville added: "fraudulently [underlined] under another title 'The Refugee' ."

to this."[63] A little piece on Berkshire authors by Henry T. Tuckerman (November, 1863) cited "Life of Israel Potter" as "more casual" than *Moby-Dick,* but "indicative of great versatility." In 1886 an artist friend gave Melville a watercolor of Flamborough Head, scene of the *Serapis-Richard* fight. When J. W. Barrs wrote Melville, January, 1890, sending him H. S. Salt's Melville essay from the *Scottish Art Review* (November, 1889), one of Barrs's regrets was that "Israel Potter ought not to have been passed over, although Salt may not have read it." So it went until the centennial year, 1919, when Professor Frank Jewett Mather of Princeton did his good essay in the *Review* (August); among his miscellaneous remarks, this one: " 'Israel Potter' contains the best account of a seafight in American fiction." By then the "Melville renaissance" was at the door.[64]

Modern criticism and scholarship relating to *Israel Potter* began slowly in the 1920's, virtually disappeared in the 1930's, then steadily increased in the next three decades. Among the ten books Melville wrote from 1846 to 1856 perhaps only *Omoo* has received as scant commentary. The present discussion examines the kinds of attention given *Israel Potter* in the major critical and biographical studies of the past sixty years.

With all the riches before him, Raymond Weaver, in *Herman Melville: Mariner and Mystic* (1921), found room only for noting three journal episodes as sources—a staple of subsequent commentary—and a hope that this "spirited narrative" might in due time find recognition. John Freeman, the English critic, began the first serious criticism in his *Herman Melville* (1926). Although Freeman found *Israel Potter* "a delightful picaresque story," he was sensitive to its "grim texture" and a disturbing tone of constraint in the writing. "The irony is not confined to the story," Freeman suggested; "it extends to the habit assumed by the author in writing it." He theorized that the attacks on Melville's "natural exuberance" seemed to have reached home, leading to a curiously dry rhetoric, and "putting an unnatural constraint upon his genius. In part this constraint brings a benefit to the reader, but it makes *Israel Potter* a much less characteristic book than its predecessors." It is only when he writes of Captain Paul that "Melville's style rises to the familiar exaltation." To Freeman here is "a story chiefly remarkable for what is suppressed, and

63. *Our Old Home* (Boston, 1863), p. 17; Sealts, No. 249.

64. For the period 1856 to 1921, the pieces cited from the *Dublin University Magazine,* by O'Brien in *Putnam's,* and by Mather in the *Review* are reprinted in *The Recognition of Herman Melville: Selected Criticism Since 1846,* ed. Hershel Parker (Ann Arbor: University of Michigan Press, 1967). For twentieth-century editions of *Israel Potter,* see pp. 244–45.

the difficult restraint of its telling." Lewis Mumford's widely-read study, *Herman Melville* (1929), viewed *Israel Potter* as "many removes from Melville at his best," but found in it "some of the fine qualities of his art, the mixture of tradition and fresh experience, the purification and heightening of actuality, with a loss of realism and a gain in reality." He took issue with Percy H. Boynton's contention that the novel was less interesting than its source (which Mumford read) and thought Melville's Jones superior to Cooper's in *The Pilot*. Mumford introduced a telling negation: "what it chiefly lacks is centrality." The question of whether or not the book has "centrality," and if so, its nature, is at the heart of most subsequent studies.

Two source studies came next—Roger P. McCutcheon's article (1928) on how Melville used the original *Life,* and W. Sprague Holden's massive, unpublished Master's thesis (1932), a discursive examination of possible sources. The most remarkable edict on *Israel Potter* during the 1930's came from Yvor Winters. In "Herman Melville and the Problems of Moral Navigation" (1938), an astonishing collection of dicta on the Melville canon, he issued a one-sentence decree: "*Israel Potter,* the life of an American patriot of the Revolutionary War, is one of the few great novels of pure adventure in English; it comes after *Moby Dick* in point of time, and probably surpasses all the works preceding *Moby Dick,* save, possibly, *Mardi.*" In contrast, F. O. Matthiessen's powerful study, *American Renaissance* (1941), found the novel's only strength in the biographical sketches, which show "how much Melville had reflected on the American character." Matthiessen saw Melville writing *Israel Potter* (and *The Confidence-Man*) "under a miserable compulsion"; he had set out "to portray the tragedy of exile, but when he came to the ex-soldier's destitution in London, his own sense of suffering was so great that he could not bear to dwell on Potter's, and slurred over what was to have been his main subject in a couple of short chapters." A similarly psychographic approach led William Ellery Sedgwick, in *Herman Melville: The Tragedy of Mind* (1945), to assert that Potter, for Melville, "became an image of his own soul," so that "Israel, uprooted and alone, was such a one as Melville felt himself to be." Sedgwick thought the central image one of "heroic stoicism," and that "other stories of the same period . . . group themselves around *Israel Potter.*" Rating the book "a brilliant historical novel," Sedgwick thought "nothing is better of its kind" than the Franklin sequence. Easily the most significant and influential study of *Israel Potter* thus far came in Richard Chase's *Herman Melville: A Critical Study* (1949). Chase urged accepting the immediate period after *Pierre* as one of Melville's most brilliant, when he was well in control of matured talents. *Israel Potter* is "a lighthearted and unpretentious book" in the picaresque tradition, and one of the "superior works" of that period. At least as important was Chase's focus on comedy, growing out of his own book on myth and folklore, and exploiting his absorption of the brilliant possibilities opened up by Constance Rourke's *American Humor* (1931). Chase set another major line for future criticism—*Israel Potter* as an inquiry into folk types and popular culture. The concept has been extended and enriched in various and significant ways, not discussed here, by Rosenberry (1955), Leary (1957), Hoffman (1961), Fussell (1965), and Browne (1968). Chase saw Israel, with his "lank and flaxen hair," as the very essence of the hero-peddler, kin to Brother Jonathan, Major Jack Downing, and Sam Slick. The same tone of comic myth underlies the portraits of Franklin, half sage and half con-man (a recurrent theme of later criticism); Jones, a Scot transformed into a frontier folk hero, at once Promethean (like Ahab) and risking all disorder (like Melville); and Ethan Allen, the powerful, enchained figure toward whom Israel unsuccessfully strives. "After *Moby-Dick*," Chase writes, "*Israel Potter* contains the completest array of heroes, true and false. Seen in this way, it is a sort of light and playful redaction of *Moby-Dick*, but lacking *Moby-Dick's* terrific energy and vision . . . ." The mythical import of Israel's disappearance into the City of Dis is that the new child of Space and "the forever youthful heavens and the earth"—quoting Melville, "has been swallowed up by Time." Mythic criticism, with emphasis on the comic, gave Chase one kind of answer to Mumford's demand for "centrality."

Two critics of the 1950's raised sober questions about the fictional craft of *Israel Potter*. Newton Arvin's widely influential *Herman Melville* (1950), saw "hardly more than a heap of sketches, some of them brilliant ones." Arvin thought Melville had not been up to the very things that most touched his imagination—the circumstances of the rebel, fugitive, and exile, and the themes of "poverty and oblivion." *Israel Potter* "could have been a masterpiece," but Melville got caught: "he follows his source either too closely or not closely enough." Thus Israel becomes "an almost featureless *recipient* of experience," and the book is betrayed by "radical aimlessness and disunity." Charles Feidelson, Jr., in the perspective of his rich study, *Symbolism and American Literature* (1953), argued that "most of the symbolism in *Israel Potter* . . . is mechanical and labored." This is so because Melville has reached a late phase of his preoccupation with "the metaphysical journey." Israel is "an unwilling exile . . . not a seeker, and he lives in a state of passive wonder." Israel's journey is simply "man's fate," with the result that "he is passive; his life accretes no meaning." For Israel the only "significance" left is "the evaporation of significance." Presumably the narrator sufficiently shares this emptiness in a way that cripples his symbolic resources. Contemporary with the criticism of Arvin and Feidelson, the standard biography, *Herman Melville,* by Leon Howard (1951), took the view that "the author of *Israel Potter* found nothing in his sources to inspire him to treat his material in any way other than that of the 'magazinist,' " except perhaps in the "imaginative and intellectual alertness" of the concluding chapters.

Four critics in the 1960's amplified the aesthetic problems and raised new perspectives. Warner Berthoff, studying aspects of Melville's craft rather than whole books in *The Example of Melville* (1962), added depth to a cliché of the early reviews—Melville's talent for "scene." Using Melville's Chapter 1 for his own chapter on "The Melvillean Setting," and quoting more than half of it, Berthoff stresses that "the scene is both composed and interpreted" as it proceeds. Though both *Israel Potter* and "Benito Cereno" were constructed from documents, each is "most notable for scene and atmosphere, and most expertly pictorial." It is "the succession of mood-asserting tableaux" which Berthoff finds impressive. Nevertheless, he agrees strongly with Arvin's view that *Israel Potter* consists of " 'sketches . . . for a masterpiece that never got composed.' " In Chapter 1 of *Israel Potter* (and also *The Confidence-Man*) Melville is "at the top of his form." But the initial momentum is wasted, the story becoming "impromptu to the point of negligence in its narrative sequence and correspondingly erratic in emphasis and detail." We are left with "individual scenes," offered in "casual order of their occurrence." Thus the book, like *The Confidence-Man,* gives "an impression of exceptional imaginative power scattering its effects more or less at random." It remains "an odd item in the Melville canon." Simultaneously a counter-argument was being published by John T. Frederick in his essay, "Symbol and Theme in Melville's *Israel Potter*" (1962). Returning to the techniques of New Criticism, Frederick examines the way themes of "solitude, immurement and confinement" are represented by symbolic images of smoke and fog, stone and mud, height and depth. He sees these key images, strategically placed at the beginning, middle, and end, in chapters not dependent on sources (Chapters 1, 12, and 23–24–25), providing a "symbolic structure" which lifts the tale to "a vision of the life of man." By the late 1960's however, criticism took radically new turns. Edgar A. Dryden's book on *Melville's Thematics of Form: The Great Art of Telling the Truth* (1968) finds *Israel Potter* non-visionary, but rather a significant stage in Melville's losing battle to use art to tell unbearable truths. Taking his cue from Melville's dedication, Dryden sees a "disinterested narrator" who "stands removed from the fiction . . . and comically calls attention to its meaninglessness." *Israel Potter,* like *Pierre,* is a book about "the emptiness behind everything," but in it "the narrator is never drawn into the masquerade." The famous sea-fight of the *Richard* and the *Serapis,* often singled out merely for vividness, exemplifies to Dryden a central image of "a stage-like world absurdly created by an invisible and hollow hand." The biblical allusions in *Israel Potter* had been previously studied by Nathalia Wright in *Melville's Use of the Bible* (1949); she had noted seven references to the "Israel" theme, backed by some twenty more used to "deepen the Biblical tone." But Dryden sees all such allusions in *Israel Potter* as ironic, as is the mock "burial and resurrection" of Israel at Squire Woodcock's. To Dryden *Israel Potter* is not an oddity of the Melville canon, but a significant bridge between the unresolved despair of *Pierre* and the apocalyptic laughter of *The Confidence-Man.* Turning away from aesthetics and psychology, Frederick W. Turner, III, in a provocative article, "Melville and Thomas Berger: The Novelist as Cultural Anthropologist" (1969), sees *Israel Potter* as a projection of the American dilemma in the nineteenth century: the lost, restless agrarian (Israel) fares better under vital barbarism (Jones) than under dehumanizing industrialism (London). Turner compares Melville's novel with Berger's recent meditations on frontier violence in *Little Big Man* (1964).

Thus the criticism of the 1960's, whether looking for social relevance or sounding tones from existential and absurdist doctrines, often operates beyond the heroic-tragic frame of earlier Melville criticism. John Seelye, in *Melville: The Ironic Diagram* (1970), finds Israel unlike Melville's earlier heroes, and rather than handwringing, Seelye seems positively to enjoy Israel's "solitary hegira to nowhere," his "onrush [that] is backward," his "tumbling down the stairs of life." Seelye finds that Israel "becomes many things without becoming anybody," and is "whirled through a kaleidoscope of costume changes signifying nothing." Appropriately he selects for study "The Shuttle," a chapter no contemporary of Melville ever cited, I believe, viewing it as a kind of parable of the misfit who becomes "recognized as unrecognizable" and survives "by adapting to the absurdity of the situation." Israel's "many identities add up to no identity at all."

The "featureless" quality of Israel, which Arvin lamented as a failure in craft, has now become a meaningful construct to another generation of critics.

The appearance of four studies devoted wholly to *Israel Potter* (two are unpublished dissertations: see Jones and Henchey entries in "Sources") suggests that interest in the book has come full circle since Weaver, sixty years ago, gave it one short paragraph. Arnold Rampersad's book, *Melville's ISRAEL POTTER: A Pilgrimage and Progress* (1969), seems excessive in pronouncing the novel second only to *Moby-Dick,* a judgment that would require firmer critical techniques than he provides. His view that Israel is an Everyman figure, though not new, fits his thesis that Melville in the 1850's moved from projections of the heroic ideal to studies of the common man's world, turning the quest allegory of the earlier romances to new ends. Alexander Keyssar, in his separately published essay of some fifty pages, *Melville's ISRAEL POTTER: Reflections on the American Dream* (1969), searches for "internal coherence" in "a deceptive and often confusing book." Keyssar sees Israel caught in the basic existential dilemma of unrealizable personal expectations, and simultaneously trapped in the unfulfilled promises of the American dream. The narrative line of captivities, escapes, disguises, and betrayals is "punctuated by symbolic episodes" such as "The Shuttle" and "Israel in Egypt"; these serve as interpolated commentary, "paradigms and explanations" of Israel's common-man's fate. To a talented young critic formed by the 1960's, for this piece was an undergraduate Honors Essay at Harvard, Israel seemed to enact "the pathetic plight of the faceless hero."

After the flurry of attention *Israel Potter* had just received, the 1970's offered no major studies. Charles N. Watson, Jr., linked the book to what he sees as the Timonism theme dominant in Melville's work from *Pierre* through *The Confidence-Man* and in another article picked out the father-son aspects of the tale, finding connections between parental authority and state sovereignty. Robert Zaller, too, took up the problem of authority and rebellion in his study of "Melville and the Myth of Revolution." Alfred Kazin, in his brief introduction to the third modern paperback edition of *Israel Potter* (Warner Paperback Library, 1974, preceded by volumes from Sagamore Press, 1957, and Dolphin Books, 1965), offered an uneven but "often richly comic book," full of "adventure, risk, deception." Satire mixes with Melville's unabashed admiration for an older, more heroic time. Through this "very personal and positive novel about masculine force" Israel moves haplessly, "the perpetual victim and wanderer. . . . the man things happen to . . . ." Joyce Sparer Adler's book, *War in Melville's Imagination* (1981), sees *Israel Potter* repeating the *White-Jacket* themes: that "war is butchery, and that the fame it holds out as a lure is not for the common man." To Adler the central irony in this story of the American Revolution is that "in the lives of the poor no revolution whatsoever has occurred."

Whether *Israel Potter* will win its future readers for its fictional power, as a cultural document of the mid-nineteenth century, as a mirror for new social and metaphysical perspectives, or merely because Melville wrote it, is for those readers to decide.

SOURCES

REFERENCES TO DATES, events, and documents that are not foot-noted or otherwise documented in the NOTE are to be found in the following printed sources: *The Letters of Herman Melville,* ed. Merrell R. Davis and William H. Gilman (New Haven: Yale University Press, 1960), of which a revised edition will appear as Volume Fourteen of the Northwestern-Newberry Edition of *The Writings of Herman Melville; Journal of a Visit to London and the Continent by Herman Melville, 1849–1850,* ed. Eleanor Melville Metcalf (Cambridge: Harvard University Press, 1948), of which a revised edition will also appear, in Volume Fifteen of the *Writings;* Jay Leyda, *The Melville Log* (New York: Harcourt, Brace, 1951; and New York: Gordian Press, 1969, with a new supplementary chapter), 2 vols.; Leon Howard, *Herman Melville: A Biography* (Berkeley and Los Angeles: University of California Press, 1951); Merton M. Sealts, Jr., *Melville's Reading: A Check-List of Books Owned and Borrowed* (Madison, Milwaukee, and London: University of Wisconsin Press, 1966), and "The Chronology of Melville's Short Fiction, 1853–1856," *Harvard Library Bulletin,* XXVIII (October, 1980), 391–403, whose substance will appear in the HISTORICAL NOTE to Volume Nine of the *Writings.* Documents may show slight differences in detail as transcribed in these and other sources. The editors of the present edition have supplied me with information about nineteenth-century American printings, sales, and profits, from Melville's accounts with G. P. Putnam & Co., now at the Houghton Library of Harvard University and summarized in G. Thomas Tanselle, "The Sales of Melville's Books," *Harvard Library Bulletin,* XVII (April, 1969), 195–215, and from the Routledge Wholesale Catalogues and the Routledge Paper and Print Book (for the latter they are indebted to Professor James J. Barnes and Routledge & Kegan Paul, Ltd.). I have completely restudied against the original texts all Melville sources and borrowings cited in this NOTE; my findings have been verified in detail by members of the Northwestern-Newberry Edition editorial staff, as acknowledged on page 172. My list of periodicals that published reviews of *Israel Potter* was drawn initially from Hugh W. Hetherington, *Melville's Reviewers: British and American, 1846–1891* (Chapel Hill: University of North Carolina Press, 1961), and from Jay Leyda's *Log,* supplemented by discoveries of my own; it has since been supplemented by Steven Mailloux and Hershel Parker, *Checklist of Melville Reviews* (Los Angeles: The Melville Society of America, 1975); in reading and citing these reviews I have used Xerox copies supplied from the Melville Collection of The Newberry Library and through the courtesy of Hershel Parker. My study of Melville's use of details from Cooper's *History of the Navy* and from the *Penny Cyclopædia* (London: Charles Knight, 1833–43), 27 vols. plus Supplement, 2 vols. (1841–46), has been aided by the use of an unpublished paper by Mary K. Madison. I wish to thank Tom Wolfe for research assistance in the early stages of this project.

The following articles and books are referred to in the NOTE without full bibliographical information: Joyce Sparer Adler, *War in Melville's Imagination* (New York: New York University Press, 1981); Newton Arvin, *Herman Melville* (New York: William Sloane, 1950); Warner Berthoff, *The Example of Melville* (Princeton: Princeton University Press, 1962); Percy H. Boynton, *More Contemporary Americans* (Chicago: University of Chicago Press, 1927), p. 45; Watson G. Branch, ed., *Melville: The Critical Heritage* (London and Boston: Routledge & Kegan Paul, 1974)—for six *Israel Potter* reviews; Ray B. Browne, "*Israel Potter:* Metamorphosis of a Superman," in *Frontiers of American Culture,* ed. Ray B. Browne et al. (Lafayette: Purdue University Studies, 1968), pp. 88–98; Richard Chase, *Herman Melville: A Critical Study* (New York: Macmillan, 1949); Edgar A. Dryden, *Melville's Thematics of Form: The Great Art of Telling the Truth* (Baltimore: Johns Hopkins University Press, 1968); Charles Feidelson, Jr., *Symbolism and American Literature* (Chicago: University of Chicago Press, 1953); Robert N. Farnsworth, "*Israel Potter:* Pathetic Comedy," *Bulletin of the New York Public Library,* LXV (1961), 125–32; John T. Frederick, "Symbol and Theme in Melville's *Israel Potter,*" *Modern Fiction Studies,* VIII (Autumn, 1962), 265–75; John Freeman, *Herman Melville* (New York: Macmillan, 1926); Edwin Fussell, *Frontier: American Literature and the American West* (Princeton: Princeton University Press, 1965); Richard Francis Henchey, "Herman Melville's *Israel Potter:* A Study in Survival," Ph.D. dissertation, University of Massachusetts, 1970; Daniel G. Hoffman, *Form and Fable in American Fiction* (New York: Oxford University Press, 1961); W. Sprague Holden, "Some Sources for Herman Melville's *Israel Potter*," M.A. thesis, Columbia University, 1932; Walter Dickinson Jones, "A Critical Study of Herman Melville's *Israel Potter*," Ph.D. dissertation, University of Alabama, 1962; Michael Kammen, *A Season of Youth: The American Revolution and the Historical Imagination* (New York: Alfred A. Knopf, 1978); Alfred Kazin, "Introduction," *Israel Potter* (New York: Warner Paperback Library, 1974); Alexander Keyssar, *Melville's ISRAEL POTTER: Reflections on the American Dream* (Cambridge: Harvard University Press, 1969); Lewis Leary, "Introduction," *Israel Potter* (New York: Sagamore Press, 1957); Roger P. McCutcheon, "The Technique of Melville's *Israel Potter*," *South Atlantic Quarterly*, XXVII (April, 1928), 161–74; F. O. Matthiessen, *American Renaissance* (New York: Oxford University Press, 1941); Meade Minnigerode, *Some Personal Letters of Herman Melville and a Bibliography* (New York: Brick Row Bookshop, 1922); Lewis Mumford, *Herman Melville* (New York: Harcourt, Brace, 1929); Arnold Rampersad, *Melville's ISRAEL POTTER: A Pilgrimage and Progress* (Bowling Green: Bowling Green University Popular Press, 1969); Edward H. Rosenberry, *Melville and the Comic Spirit* (Cambridge: Harvard University Press, 1955); William Ellery Sedgwick, *Herman Melville: The Tragedy of Mind* (Cambridge: Harvard University Press, 1944); John Seelye, *Melville: The Ironic Diagram* (Evanston: Northwestern University Press, 1970); Frederick W. Turner, III, "Melville and Thomas Berger: The Novelist as Cultural Anthropologist," *The Centennial Review*, XIII (Winter, 1969), 101–21; Charles N. Watson, Jr., "Melville and the Theme of Timonism: From *Pierre* to *The Confidence-Man*," *American Literature*, XLIV (November, 1972), 398–413; Charles N. Watson, Jr., "Melville's *Israel Potter*: Fathers and Sons," *Studies in the Novel*, VII (Winter, 1975), 563–68; Charles N. Watson, Jr., "Premature Burial in *Arthur Gordon Pym* and *Israel Potter*," *American Literature*, XLVII (March, 1975), 105–7; Raymond M. Weaver, *Herman Melville: Mariner and Mystic* (New York: George H. Doran, 1921); Yvor Winters, *Maule's Curse: Seven Studies in the History of American Obscurantism* (Norfolk: New Directions, 1938); Nathalia Wright, *Melville's Use of the Bible* (Durham: Duke University Press, 1949); Robert Zaller, "Melville and the Myth of Revolution," *Studies in Romanticism*, XV (Fall, 1976), 607–22.

Note on the Text

THIS EDITION of *Israel Potter* presents an unmodernized critical text, prepared according to the theory of copy-text formulated by Sir Walter Greg.[1] Central to that theory is the distinction between substantives (the words of a text) and accidentals (spelling and punctuation). Persons involved in the printing and publishing of texts have often taken it upon themselves to alter accidentals; and authors, when examining or revising printed forms of their work, have often been relatively unconcerned with accidentals.[2] An author's failure to change certain accidentals altered by a copyist, publisher, or compositor does not amount to an endorsement of those accidentals. Because the aim of a critical edition is to establish a text that represents as nearly as possible the author's intentions,

---

1. "The Rationale of Copy-Text," *Studies in Bibliography*, III (1950–51), 19–36. For an application of this method to the period of Melville, see the Center for Editions of American Authors, *Statement of Editorial Principles and Procedures* (rev. ed.; New York: Modern Language Association of America, 1972) and the various discussions recorded in *The Center for Scholarly Editions: An Introductory Statement* (New York: Modern Language Association of America, 1977; also printed in *PMLA*, XCII [1977], 586–97).

2. Accidentals can affect the meaning (or substance) of a text, and Greg's distinction is not meant to suggest otherwise; rather, its purpose is to emphasize the fact that those involved in the transmission of texts have habitually behaved differently in regard to the two categories.

it follows that—in the absence of contrary evidence—the formal texture of the work will be most accurately reproduced by adopting as copy-text[3] either the fair-copy manuscript or the first printing based on it. The printed form is chosen if the manuscript does not exist or if the author worked in such a way that corrected proof became in effect the final form of the manuscript. This basic text may then be emended with any later authorial alterations (whether substantive or accidental) and with other obvious corrections. Following this procedure maximizes the probability of keeping authorial readings when evidence is inconclusive as to the source of an alteration in a later authorized edition. The resulting text is *critical* in that it does not correspond exactly to any single authorized edition, but it is closer to the author's intentions—insofar as they are recoverable—than any such edition.

As the preceding HISTORICAL NOTE has shown, the edition of *Israel Potter* published serially in *Putnam's Monthly* between July, 1854, and March, 1855, was the one set directly from the manuscript Melville furnished the publisher; in the absence of that manuscript, the *Putnam's Monthly* text becomes the copy-text for the present edition.[4] Any impressions or editions published during Melville's lifetime are a potential source for emendations in this copy-text, since theoretically it would have been possible for Melville to make corrections or changes in them. The 1855 edition of George Routledge can be ruled out, however, since it was pirated and any textual variants in it have no connection whatever with the author. The authorized editions—the magazine and book editions published by G. P. Putnam & Co. (along with the later printing of T. B. Peterson & Brothers)[5]—have been fully collated in the following pattern:

    1. Putnam's Magazine against Putnam's Book Edition
       a. One complete sight collation[6] of the magazine edition (1854–1855) against the first impression of the book edition (1855)

---

3. "Copy-text" is the text accepted as the basis for an edition.

4. The particular copy of the *Putnam's Monthly* text which served (in the form of a marked photocopy) as printer's copy is Newberry A5.765.

5. The Peterson impression is authorized only in the sense that it is a later printing of an authorized edition, printed from plates purchased from the original publisher; its use of the title *The Refugee,* however, was not authorized. (See the HISTORICAL NOTE, p. 224.)

6. Collations between two *editions,* which (because they are printed from different settings of type) cannot be performed on the Hinman Collator, are "sight collations." Those

    b. One substantive sight collation of the magazine edition (1854–1855) against the first impression of the book edition (1855)

    c. One complete sight collation of the magazine edition (1854–1855) against the third impression of the book edition (1855)

2. Copies of Putnam's Magazine Edition

Two machine collations of copies of the magazine edition (1854–1855) against each other

3. Impressions of Putnam's Book Edition

    a. One machine collation of the first impression of this edition (1855) against the third (last Putnam) impression (1855)

    b. Two machine collations of the first impression of this edition (1855) against the fourth (the first issued by T. B. Peterson, 1865)

    c. One machine collation of the fourth impression of this edition (the first issued by T. B. Peterson, 1865) against the presently known sheets of a possible fifth (the second issued by Peterson, 1865)[7]

---

between *impressions* of the same edition are "machine collations"—so called because that machine, by superimposing page images, enables the human collator's eye to see differences, including minute changes not otherwise easily detected, such as resettings and type or plate damage. A "complete sight collation" is one in which both substantive and accidental variants are recorded; a "substantive sight collation" is one in which only substantive variants are recorded. The terms *edition, impression (printing), issue,* and *state,* as used here, follow the definitions of Fredson Bowers in *Principles of Bibliographical Description* (Princeton: Princeton University Press, 1949), pp. 379–426, supplemented by G. Thomas Tanselle, "The Bibliographical Concepts of *Issue* and *State*," *Papers of the Bibliographical Society of America,* LXIX (1975), 17–66.

7. The copies used for these collations are here recorded by identification number (for books in the Melville Collection of The Newberry Library) or by library name and call number (for books not in the Melville Collection): (1a) Northwestern O51P99 *vs.* M67-1603-2; (1b) Northwestern O51P99 *vs.* M67-103-16 (lacking pp. 201–208) and M67-722-19 (pp. 201–208 only); (1c) Newberry A5.764 *vs.* M67-722-201; (2) Northwestern O51P99 (wrappers) *vs.* Newberry A5.765 (wrappers); M69-316-18 (vol. IV) and M69-316-26 (vol. V) *vs.* M67-722-75 (vol. IV) and M67-722-294 (vol. V); (3a) Northwestern 813.3M531i (now M78-41457-32) *vs.* Newberry Y255M512; (3b) M67-722-265 *vs.* M66-2471-57; M67-722-19 *vs.* Gift M69-31 (Leon Howard copy); (3c) M68-796 *vs.* M66-3576-1. Of the two copies with the Peterson imprint recorded under 3b, the first is bound in dark purple or brown hexagon-grain cloth with the Peterson device on the front and back, while the second is in smooth red cloth with the device of Peterson's Dollar Series; no evidence was turned up in the collations, however, to suggest that the sheets bound these two ways represent more than a single impression. (See footnote 14 below.)

The text was thus collated for record nine times.[8] In addition, routine procedures in the process of compiling, checking, and preparing the information for publication have resulted in a larger total number of collations.[9]

Analysis of the variants (in both substantives and accidentals) disclosed by these collations has resulted in the adoption of 58 emendations in the copy-text; five further emendations derive from Melville's marked copy of the Putnam book edition; and 64 other emendations have been made by the present editors. In order to make clear the evidence and rationale on which these decisions rest, an account of the textual history of the work is given below, followed by a discussion of the treatment in this text of substantives and accidentals, and an explanation of the editorial apparatus through which the evidence is presented.

THE TEXTS

NO MANUSCRIPT of *Israel Potter* survives, and the closest text to Melville's final manuscript (i.e., to the printer's copy, which was copied from his own final draft, probably by his wife and sisters) is the one published first, as a serial in *Putnam's Monthly* (July, 1854–March, 1855). Examination of a number of copies of each of the issues involved has not revealed any textual variants or any conclusive evidence of more than one impression.[10] A few variations resulting from plate damage have been noted—examples occur in the last letters of the words "But" at 48.21

8. The number of collations which must be performed in order to detect all significant variations in a given text can never be prescribed with certainty, since chance determines, at least to some extent, the particular copies available for collation. Whether or not variant states of a first impression are detected, for example, depends largely upon whether or not at least one copy of an earlier state is present in the collection of copies assembled for collation; regardless of the size of this collection, there is always the chance that an unknown earlier state is missing. To reduce the element of chance somewhat, the present editors have checked many points in every copy of *Israel Potter* in the Melville Collection of The Newberry Library and have examined numerous copies in other collections. For making copies of *Israel Potter* available, the editors are indebted to William M. Gibson, Leon Howard, and M. Douglas Sackman.

9. Proofreading provided the chief opportunity for making these additional collations.

10. Copies in their original wrappers have been examined as well as copies in library bindings without wrappers. Since Putnam's issued bound volumes of the magazine upon the completion of each semiannual volume, it is conceivable that the sheets of certain issues bound in this way might represent a later impression and that presently rebound volumes might in some cases be the same volumes which were originally issued in publisher's cloth.

(P278.45a)[11] and "closed" at 60.7 (P284.49a), in various words in the first column of P65 (January, 1855), along the right margin of P66, and in several words at P481.34b–38b and P482.47a–48a (see footnote 31 below). None of these instances of damage, however, creates any textual problem. The copy-text for the present edition may therefore be defined simply as the installments of *Israel Potter* in the successive numbers of *Putnam's Monthly* from July, 1854, through March, 1855 (IV, 66–75, 135–46, 277–90, 371–78, 481–91, 592–601; V, 63–71, 176–82, 288–94).[12] (These installments correspond to the following page numbers in the present edition: 3–21, 22–45, 46–72, 73–84, 85–105, 106–125.25, 125.26–141, 142–156.19, 156.20–169.)

The first (and the only authorized) separate edition of the book was published in New York by G. P. Putnam & Co. in the spring of 1855 (it was deposited for copyright on March 10, 1855). Three impressions of this edition were issued during 1855 under the Putnam imprint, and in 1865 the book was again printed from the same plates and published by T. B. Peterson & Brothers of Philadelphia (Peterson had purchased the plates from Putnam in the fall of 1857). The first two of these impressions cannot be distinguished by the title page but can be differentiated by two instances of resetting: (1) in one impression, the heading for the fourteenth chapter reads "CHAPTER XVI.", while in the other it reads correctly; (2) in one, dashes are used to stand for "God" and the middle letters of "damned" (in "by ——!" at 144.20 and 145.12 and "d——d soul" at 144.27), while in the other asterisks are substituted for the entire expressions. Since the correct chapter number and the asterisks appear in later impressions, the setting with these readings is the later of the two. In addition, several examples of plate damage occur in copies with the later setting, but only three of them create textual differences—the loss of line-end hyphens after "any" (in "anything" at 59.3), "some" (in "something" at 91.13), and "White" (in "Whitehaven" at 91.14).

The third Putnam impression exists in two issues, which can be

11. Reference numbers with prefixed letters refer to page and line of the *Putnam's Monthly* edition (P) or the first American book edition (A); the letters "a" and "b," appended when necessary to the P numbers, designate the column. When the prefixed letters do not appear, reference is to the Northwestern-Newberry Edition.

12. Facts about the dates, sizes, and background of the various printings and editions are given in the Historical Note; precise physical descriptions will appear in the full-scale bibliography to be published in conjunction with the Northwestern-Newberry Edition. The present discussion is not concerned with bibliographical details discovered in the process of collation, unless they bear on textual questions.

identified by the title page: in the first the title page is integral and bears the phrase *"THIRD EDITION"*, while in the second the title page is a cancel and bears the imprint of the London distributor, Low, Son & Co., beneath the Putnam imprint. All of the slight variations in this impression result from plate damage.[13] The only remaining impression from the Putnam plates is that published by Peterson in 1865 under the title of *The Refugee*.[14] Aside from the alteration of the headlines to incorporate different page numbers as well as the new title, no deliberate changes were made in the plates after their purchase by Peterson; again, what differences there are simply result from plate damage.[15] Therefore none of the variations between any of the impressions from the Putnam plates—except the obvious correction of a chapter number—carries any textual authority.

The text of this Putnam book edition differs substantively from the magazine edition at 81 points (there are scores of other differences in spelling, punctuation, and capitalization). Some of these book variants are

13. Of the many instances of plate damage in the third impression, only the following three might create textual ambiguity: the damage to the semicolon after "elated" at 42.11 during the course of the impression which causes it to look like a comma in some copies; the loss of the line-end hyphen after "chamber" (in "chambermaid") at 53.24; and the failure to print of the comma after "erect" at 79.3. In this NOTE, when changes are listed within the Putnam book edition, the many instances of battered type or plates and missing letters are not included when it is clear what letter is intended; missing end-punctuation is not mentioned when the absent mark is a period; and missing hyphens at the ends of lines are not reported when the divided word is not a possible compound. However, missing commas are listed, since they might pass unnoticed. In other words, type or plate wear is noted only when it could pass unnoticed or be mistaken for intentional revision.

14. Possibly there were two Peterson impressions, for in some copies with the Peterson imprint (bound in pebbly rather than smooth red cloth) gatherings 9, 10, 13, 14, and 17 are of thinner paper and exhibit many new instances of plate damage. Although none of these characteristics taken individually would be convincing evidence of a new impression, the conjunction of all three—the different cloth, the thinner paper, and the new plate damage— along with the fact that very few instances of in-press plate damage have been discovered in the thicker Peterson sheets, may indicate a second Peterson impression. However, since only five thin-paper gatherings have been located, there is no conclusive evidence available to determine whether a second Peterson printing, if indeed it took place, involved the entire book or only certain sheets which happened to be in short supply. (See also footnote 7 above.)

15. Among the occurrences of plate damage, only the following nine create possible textual ambiguity: the loss of commas after "much" (92.14), "last" (131.17), and "charity" (164.6); the disappearance of line-end hyphens after "him" (in "himself", 57.21), "*White*" (in "*Whitehaven*", 98.2), and "main" (in "main-mast", 129.27); and the absence in some copies of the hyphen in "half-past eleven" (65.2), the line-end hyphen after "hood" (in "hoodwinking", 131.16), and the lower part of the semicolon after "bands" (133.40).

obviously the result of careless typesetting and proofreading,[16] but 18 are corrections of obvious substantive errors in the magazine edition.[17] Most of the variant readings, however, are neither obvious errors nor corrections of obvious errors. Of these, the most substantial are the omission of an entire paragraph of 57 words at 160.5–9, the omission of one phrase (the magazine subtitle, *"A FOURTH OF JULY STORY"*), and the addition of one clause (at 138.28 the words "take him away" appear three times rather than twice). All the other differences involve single words[18] and for the most part could have resulted from casual compositorial substitutions, though a few suggest a conscious attempt at improvement.

The only other edition of *Israel Potter* which appeared during Melville's lifetime[19] was the one published in the summer of 1855 in London by George Routledge. It was based on the text of the Putnam book, not the

16. Among such errors in the book edition are "off" for "of" (7.6), "its" for "it's" (17.17), "ought" for "out" (22.15), "of" for "or" (93.7), and "lock" for "loch" (96.30).

17. Such errors as incorrect letters which create different words ("night" for "right" at 18.32, or "essayest" for "essayist" at 48.17), misplaced or omitted apostrophes ("rascals' " for "rascal's" at 66.2, or "Its" for "It's" at 61.18), and repeated words ("the the" for "the" at 86.12, or "a a" for "a" at 160.14). See the variants recorded in the LIST OF EMENDATIONS at 15.34, 18.32, 25.18, 44.26, 48.17, 61.18, 66.2, 86.12, 92.10, 93.21, 102.8, 122.38, 126.20, 129.2, 132.12, 151.34, 159.10, and 160.14.

18. Among these variants are roughly a dozen differences in the forms of nouns and verbs (principally shifts in number, as "day" in the book for "days" in the magazine at 7.3, or shifts in tense, as "enter" for "entered" at 116.27); three which could be said to involve the choice of pronouns or verbs ("those" for "these" at 39.17, "causing" for "creating" at 118.23, and "ejected" for "rejected" at 136.12); about a dozen affecting other parts of speech (especially slight shifts in adjectives and adverbs, and the substitution of "of" for "in" twice, at 59.3 and 104.39); two in phrasing (the reversal of the order of words—"do so" for "so do" at 40.18 and "there was" for "was there" at 56.13); and, finally, slightly more than a dozen involving the addition or omission of single words (such as the insertion of "as" before "respectable" at 7.13 or the omission of "all" at 113.25). Comment on the authority of certain individual readings will be found below in the DISCUSSIONS OF ADOPTED READINGS.

19. A short extract from *Israel Potter* (consisting of the first three paragraphs of Chapter 22, followed—after a supplied transition—by all of Chapter 21 except the first seven paragraphs) appeared in the *Western Literary Messenger* (Buffalo) for September, 1855 (XXV, 21–23) under the title "Ethan Allen's Captivity"; its source was specified as *"Putnam's Magazine,"* but Melville's name was not given. In all probability Melville knew nothing of the appearance of this extract and had no opportunity to make revisions in it or the one in the New York *Leader* (June 8, 1856). A collation of the *Western Literary Messenger* text against the Putnam magazine text supports this view, for the large number of variants both in punctuation and in substantives is not of a kind to suggest authorial revision. Many of the variants are obvious compositorial errors, and others are additions or deletions of a word or two and minor shifts in punctuation, diction, and the forms of words which could be either editorial

magazine, edition, but it departed from that text frequently in punctuation and spelling and occasionally in substantives.[20] Since it was pirated, these alterations cannot stem from any communication with the author, and the Routledge edition therefore has no bearing on textual decisions.

Since the Melville revival, *Israel Potter* has been set in type at least seven times.[21] The Constable edition of *Israel Potter* (1923)—in the collected *Works*—is significant because it was the first edition of the book after Melville's death and because it is part of the only complete set of his work that has been available in the past (and is therefore often cited as standard); however, its text—which is based on the Putnam book, not the magazine, edition—departs widely from that edition in spelling (substitution of British forms), punctuation, and capitalization, as well as in occasional substantives, and it offers no explanation of its editorial policy.[22] Three more editions of the book were published in the 1920's: by Albert & Charles Boni in 1924 (issued in England by Jarrolds); by the St. Botolph Society in 1925 (reprinted by Jonathan Cape, D. D. Nickerson, and L. C. Page); and by Pickwick Publishers in 1928 (reprinted by Tudor Publishers). No further editions appeared until those of the Sagamore Press in 1957, the Doubleday Dolphin Books in 1965, and the Warner Paperback Library in 1974. Only the Dolphin edition makes any explicit comment on its text: a prefatory note points out that the edition is "set from a copy of *The Refugee*" and goes on to say that the text is "therefore a faithful reproduction of the original *Israel Potter* except for the correction of

or compositorial (such as "forth" for "further" at 144.39); the few which show some ingenuity in emendation (such as the substitution of "sword—" for "vowed" at 146.2, "chain" for "china" at 147.14, and "as" for the semicolon after "convivial" at 149.11) are not unquestionable improvements and, occurring among a large number of trivial changes and outright errors, do not furnish evidence of Melville's attention. (Copies used for collation: Chicago Historical Society *vs.* Newberry A5.765.)

20. This generalization about the Routledge edition is based on a partial collation of M67-1603-2 against M67-3407.

21. Details of all these editions will be included in the forthcoming descriptive bibliography. The Melville Collection of The Newberry Library contains these later editions. Charles Roberts Anderson, in *Melville in the South Seas* (New York: Columbia University Press, 1939), states that twelve "new editions" of *Israel Potter* had been published by 1938 (p. 439); but he is not using "edition" in the sense employed here, as a technical bibliographical term which encompasses all the impressions from a given setting of type.

22. This generalization is based on a partial collation of a copy of the Putnam book edition (M67-1603-2) with a copy of the Constable edition (London, 1923; M66-2758). For some background relating to the Constable texts, see Philip Durham, "Prelude to the Constable Edition of Melville," *Huntington Library Quarterly*, XXI (1957–58), 285–89.

obvious typographical errors and the alteration of typography and design"
(p. 7). All these editions have been based on the Putnam book text; the
present edition is thus the first twentieth-century edition to employ as
copy-text the earlier magazine text.

TREATMENT OF SUBSTANTIVES

THE TEXT of *Israel Potter* presents no complications, since the Putnam
book edition follows the wording of the magazine edition except for
the addition of a dedication and table of contents, the omission of one
paragraph, and a scattering of largely inconsequential variants, and since
Melville made no later revisions (other than the correction of four words).
An editor, after adopting some obvious corrections from the book variants, has only two problems. The first is to determine whether any of the
remaining book variants are authorial. The second is to find and correct
any readings that are corrupt in both editions—readings, that is, where the
book text follows the magazine in printing words that cannot be the ones
Melville intended. Neither problem is particularly difficult in *Israel Potter*.

Eighteen of the book variants are corrections obviously called for (see
p. 243, footnote 17). Whether compositors' errors or slips of the author's
or copyist's pen, the magazine readings can hardly have been intended by
Melville, and whether the correction was made by Melville or by someone
at Putnam's is immaterial.

In determining whether any of the remaining variants in the book
edition are authorial, an editor must consider, first, whether the book
could have been set from the same manuscript rather than from the
magazine text and thus reflect authorial readings at points where the
compositors or editors of the magazine introduced changes; second,
whether Melville had the opportunity to make revisions between the
time of the appearance of the magazine text and that of the book; and,
third, whether the nature of the variants themselves suggests authorial
attention. As to the first question, standard procedure would have been
for Putnam's to set the book from sheets of the magazine rather than to
preserve and use a second time the less legible manuscript. Some indica-
tion that this procedure was followed is offered by the repetition, in the
first printing of the book, of an error in chapter numbering that appeared
in the magazine ("XVI" is printed for "XIV"), as well as by the retention in the book of two chapter breaks from the magazine that were
surely introduced by the magazine editors, not by Melville, to make the

text fit the space for those installments. (Even the inconsistency in the manner of numbering the two additional chapters thus created—labeled simply "CONTINUED"—is followed in the book: the first has the same number, "XIX", as the preceding chapter, whereas the second, split off from Chapter "XXIII", is numbered "XXIV". The other odd chapter division—the inclusion of the sectional title "AN ENCOUNTER OF GHOSTS" in Chapter 13—offers no evidence here, since it does not coincide with an installment break and may well have been in Melville's manuscript. See the DISCUSSIONS OF ADOPTED READINGS at 77.19 and 125.26.) Although such evidence is perhaps not conclusive, it does suggest that the book was set from the magazine; and no evidence has come to light indicating a departure from this customary routine. One must proceed, therefore, on the assumption that the usual circumstances obtained; to do otherwise would be to give considerable weight to numerous indifferent variants which not only might be compositorial or editorial changes after all but also might be earlier readings superseded by authorial revisions in the magazine proof.

Once the book text is taken to have been set from the magazine text, the next question is whether there was opportunity for authorial revision between the setting of the two editions. Since the first installment appeared in *Putnam's* in July, 1854, and the book not until March, 1855, there is no question but that Melville had considerable time during which he could conceivably have made revisions in at least the early parts of the book. However, he was evidently still writing the book during a large part of this period and may not have been able to give much thought to the revision of the already published installments; in any event, there was practically no opportunity for revision of the last chapters between the publication of the magazine and the book, since the final magazine installment did not appear until the March, 1855, issue and the entire book was printed in time to be deposited for copyright on March 10.

Despite the difference in the time available for revising the early and the late chapters, there is no discernible difference between the number and kind of variants found in the early part of the book and those found in the last. Neither is the nature of the variants themselves such as to suggest an author's revision of his work. A few of the corrections of errors clearly demanded considerable attentiveness and insight (for example, correcting "least" to "last" at 25.18, or "wandering" to "wondering" at 159.10); but none is certainly authorial, and they do not provide sufficient grounds for believing that Melville made revisions for the book publication. Aside from the eighteen variants which correct obvious errors, the remaining five dozen or so are for the most part indifferent readings or omissions and insertions of single words that could easily be compositorial alterations; even the few that are arguably better than the magazine readings are of a kind that someone at Putnam's or an alert compositor would have been able to make. That intentional alteration of the text did occur at Putnam's is particularly suggested by the omission of a paragraph in Chapter 24 (160.5–9)—an omission surely to be accounted for by the publisher's caution and desire to avoid anything that might give offense. The same concern for propriety and an inclination to make alterations in texts are exhibited in the treatment of the tales Melville was sending to *Putnam's* during the same period; surviving letters from Charles F. Briggs (editor of the magazine) and George William Curtis refer to deletions in "The Encantadas" and "The Bell-Tower," and Briggs (seconded by Putnam himself) rejected "The Two Temples" in consideration of the feelings of "some of our church readers." Melville's recognition of this pressure is reflected in his letter to Putnam on June 7, 1854, asserting that *Israel Potter* will contain "nothing of any sort to shock the fastidious." (For a fuller discussion of this situation, see the GENERAL NOTE ON THE TEXT to the Northwestern-Newberry Edition of *THE PIAZZA TALES and Other Prose Pieces, 1839–1860.*) In the light of these considerations, the present editors have seen no sufficient reason to adopt any of the book variants in the body of the text except those that correct obvious errors.

One other authoritative source for emendations exists, however—a copy of the third impression of the book edition in which Melville noted certain corrections.[23] Inside the front cover of this copy Melville listed six page numbers, and each of the pages indicated contains one correction. Four of the alterations consist of striking the "y" from "illy" (see "ill" at 27.29, 41.2, 57.3, and 120.17); another is the change of "birth" to "berth" (listed as variant spellings in Worcester's 1847 dictionary) at 94.11; and the remaining one is the shift of "wild" to "mild" (54.13). In addition, though no other page numbers are listed, the word "boquets" is twice corrected to "bouquets" (68.8, 17).[24] Exactly when Melville made these corrections

---

23. This copy is now in the Melville Collection of the Houghton Library of Harvard University, catalogued as *AC85M4977.855ic(A).

24. All these corrections are almost certainly in Melville's hand, since the page numbers and the word "mild" are in his hand; but the nature of most of the corrections, involving simply a slash mark, eliminates the possibility of positive identification of individual marks apart from the pattern of the markings as a whole.

is not certain;[25] but another notation in his hand—"Friday 2½ PM, / J. Harper"—suggests that the occasion for the corrections may conceivably have been a meeting with one of the Harpers, perhaps to discuss the possibility of Harper & Brothers' taking over the book. In any case, these corrections clearly seem to represent Melville's final intention, and consequently they are adopted here. Since "berth" and "bouquets" were present in the original magazine edition, only five emendations of the copy-text from this marked copy of the book are required—the four instances of "illy" and the incorrect "wild".

Reference to the sources Melville used provides a basis for some further emendations. As the HISTORICAL NOTE has shown, Melville drew heavily on Henry Trumbull's *Life and Remarkable Adventures of Israel R. Potter* (Providence, 1824) and also used other books, such as Robert C. Sands's *Life and Correspondence of John Paul Jones* (New York, 1830), James Fenimore Cooper's *History of the Navy of the United States of America* (New York, 1853), and Ethan Allen's *A Narrative of Colonel Ethan Allen's Captivity* (Philadelphia, 1779). Comparison of passages in Melville's work with the source passages on which they were based often enables one to detect erroneous readings and to know what they should be replaced with; in short, it provides additional evidence for reconstructing what was present (or intended to be present) in Melville's manuscript. Of course, there are instances where one can argue that Melville intentionally changed the wording or information from his source; and in these cases no emendations are made, for the editorial goal is fidelity to Melville's intention rather than to the sources themselves. (Melville's treatment of numbers frequently falls into this category; see the DISCUSSIONS OF ADOPTED READINGS at 10.12 and 100.15.) But in many other cases it seems clear that Melville intended no alteration of his source; and whether the slip originated with him as he copied from the source, or with someone later reading his or a copyist's handwriting, the mistaken word should be corrected. Thus on the basis of Trumbull's *Life* "pulling" is corrected to "poling" (8.24), "cash" to "skins" (9.18), and "cutting" to "collecting"

25. The fact that four instances of "illy" in the American edition of *The Confidence-Man* (1857) were changed to "ill" in the English is not necessarily related to this alteration of "illy" in *Israel Potter*. It is possible, of course, that Melville (who was not himself responsible for changes in the English edition of *The Confidence-Man*) happened to notice this change after the book was published and then marked the same change in a copy of *Israel Potter*. But the changes could equally well have been made independently, stemming in each case from the point of view reflected in the 1847 Worcester's that "illy" is "rarely used by good writers" and in the 1848 Webster's that it is used "improperly" for "ill."

(163.2), for example. Among the changes based on Sands, Cooper, and Allen are, respectively, the correction of "disjointed" to "disjoined" (102.25), of "man" to "a man" (126.7), and of "Colonel McCloud" to "General Prescott" (150.9). Altogether some dozen and a half emendations (as well as other decisions not to emend) result from the examination of Melville's sources. (For further discussion of this general problem, see G. Thomas Tanselle, "External Fact as an Editorial Problem," *Studies in Bibliography*, XXXII [1979], 1–47.)

The only other substantive emendations in this edition are of corrupt readings in which the book edition follows the magazine in scribal or compositorial misreadings of Melville's manuscript (or in errors of his manuscript itself). In these instances, the emendations restore what Melville must originally have written or at least intended to write.[26] No substantive emendations have been made under any other circumstances.

TREATMENT OF ACCIDENTALS

IN THE ABSENCE of a final manuscript, the degree to which the author was responsible for the accidentals—the punctuation and spelling—of a printed text is a matter impossible to settle conclusively. Greg's theory of copy-text provides a method for playing the odds to advantage: adhering to the printed text closest to the manuscript will allow a maximum number of characteristic authorial usages to be retained, since each successive impression or edition offers further opportunities for corruption, in the form of publishers' changes, compositors' errors, or plate damage. Even though changes in the spelling and punctuation of *Israel Potter* were undoubtedly made in the magazine text at Putnam's, the magazine edition was nevertheless set directly from the manuscript Melville supplied and inevitably preserves more of its accidentals than Putnam's book edition, another step removed, could possibly do. Even if

26. Such changes are of course made only when the copy-text reading is unsatisfactory. The emendation must produce wording that Melville would have used in the context (judging from his literary practice); it must improve the sense and fit the tone of the context; and, if a substitution, it must be a word that in Melville's hand could have been misread as the word in the copy-text (or that Melville himself could mistakenly have written). Under these three criteria, for example, "seventy-two" is emended to "seventy-eight" (44.35, 44.37, 44.39); "foremost" to "foremast" (86.9); "severe" to "serene" (113.23); "three" to "four" (142.20); "its" to "their" (160.7); and "things" to "throngs" (153.6).

some of the variants in accidentals in the book edition are changes that Melville made in the magazine text, it is impossible to determine just which ones; to accept the book variants which appear to be improvements would be to risk adopting many instances of nonauthorial spelling and punctuation on the chance of acquiring a few authorial alterations—and to defeat the purpose of selecting a copy-text on Greg's principles.

Accordingly, the accidentals of the magazine edition of *Israel Potter* have been retained in the present edition except in a few unusual instances, even when the spelling and punctuation may appear incorrect or inconsistent by late-twentieth-century standards. Some of the inconsistencies in the spelling and punctuation may have been in the manuscript, and, although Melville may not have been aware of them, they constitute a suggestive part of his total expression, since patterns of accidentals do affect the texture of a literary work. On the other hand, some of the inconsistencies in accidentals may have resulted either from an imperfectly realized attempt to make the manuscript conform to a house style or from compositorial alterations. To regularize the punctuation and spelling would be to risk choosing nonauthorial forms.[27] Therefore no attempt has been made to impose general consistency on either spelling or punctuation,[28] and any changes have been made sparingly, according to the following guidelines:

SPELLING. The general rule adopted here is to retain any spellings (even when inconsistent) that were acceptable by the standards of 1854, as well as any obsolete variants that may have been intended by Melville or that may reflect his reading in earlier material; spellings are corrected only when they do not fall into these categories. One available guide for decisions about spelling is the 1847 revision of Webster's *American Dictionary of the English Language* (Springfield, Mass., 1848). Webster's was the dictionary used by Harper & Brothers, publishers of most of Melville's earlier books, for Melville remarked, in his letter to John Murray, the English publisher, on January 28, 1849, that "my printers here 'go for' Webster."

27. Melville's habits in the extant manuscripts and letters are not definite enough to offer grounds to emend for consistency (and in any case the letters, not intended for publication, do not provide a parallel situation). Neither is the Putnam house styling consistent enough to be helpful in determining precisely what elements of the punctuation of *Israel Potter* resulted from it.

28. For example, no emendations are made to secure consistency in the use (or nonuse) of capital letters; of apostrophes in contractions; of italics or of quotation marks (or both at once) for such items as foreign words, the first (or otherwise emphasized) occurrence of special terms, names of ships, and titles of books.

The Harper accounts show that Melville ordered at least three copies of Webster's (on April 10 and November 15, 1847, and on November 16, 1848), the third of which could have been the 1848 edition. In any case, the 1848 Webster's can be taken as a generally accepted standard in use in 1854, when Melville was writing *Israel Potter*. (In considering spellings that appear in *Putnam's,* one must also take into account the adoption of some of Webster's spelling reforms there; see Laura Wood Roper, " 'Mr. Law' and *Putnam's Monthly Magazine:* A Note on a Phase in the Career of Frederick Law Olmsted," *American Literature,* XXVI [March, 1954], 88–93.) Recourse to Webster's and to other contemporary dictionaries, such as Worcester's *A Universal and Critical Dictionary of the English Language* (Boston, 1847), with its list of "Words of Doubtful Orthography," to mid-nineteenth-century editions of American novels, biographies, and autobiographies, and to such sources for the historical study of spelling as the *Oxford English Dictionary* and the *Dictionary of American English,* has resulted in the retention of a good many anomalous-appearing copy-text forms, such as "augurs" (for "augers"), "baling" (for "bailing"), "befal", "brouse", "canvass" (for "canvas"), "Cœur de Lion", "dosing" (for "dozing"), "Dutchess", "grizzets", "jackall", "jams" (for "jambs"), "Louisbergh", "lounging" (for "lunging"), "Malmsbury", "skuttle", "stilness", "tatoo", "tussel", and "uncompunctuous". A few other forms, not found in reliable parallels in such sources or in the source books Melville drew on, have been corrected (or made to conform with Melville's sources): "Bellgarde", "D'Estang", "Galoway", "Hughs", "Kniphausen", "Shirrer", "Soleby", "Spurm", "Suffrien", and "tyrranical". Any changes to bring spelling into conformity with an 1850's standard have been made cautiously so as to preserve the wide latitude allowed in contemporary usage, especially for proper names.

PUNCTUATION. Emendations in punctuation are made only to correct obvious typographical errors; no alterations are made in punctuation which is not manifestly wrong simply in an effort to bring it into conformity with some presumed standard. Most of the obvious errors, which have been emended, fall into two categories: (1) the absence of periods at the ends of sentences or the presence of periods within sentences;[29] and (2) the absence of quotation marks where they are required or the presence of

---

29. For example, the period in the present text after "race" at 30.23 is not present in the copy-text and the period after "men" at 140.3 is a comma, while the colon after "added" at 42.9 and the comma after "captain" at 88.28 are periods in the copy-text.

them where they are not needed.[30] It is perhaps unnecessary to point out that, in those instances in which a mark of punctuation has slipped out of position before plating (in such a manner, for example, that a comma appears in the position of an apostrophe), the mark is placed properly in the present text; such alterations merely correct the typography of the copy-text but do not emend the text itself, and they are not recorded in the LIST OF EMENDATIONS.[31] Since it is not the aim of the present edition to modernize and since contemporary practice did not demand accuracy in the use of accents on foreign words (indeed, contemporary dictionaries sometimes listed them without accents), such words as "chasseing" (124.35–36) are allowed to stand, without accents, as they appear in the copy-text.

30. Thus necessary quotation marks are absent at 6 points (see the LIST OF EMENDATIONS at 15.23, 26.30, 42.2, 50.37, 99.32, and 115.31), and superfluous ones are present at 3 points (see the emendations at 68.16, 116.1, and 145.2); in addition, there are several instances of misplaced quotation marks (see the emendations at 82.12, 128.38, and 144.27) and of errors involving the marking of quotations within quotations (see the emendations at 43.30 and 56.29). In none of these instances does the emendation involve a decision affecting the meaning, since in none does the misuse or omission of quotation marks call into question who is speaking or what is said. No attempt has been made here to regularize the punctuation (and capitalization) of phrases or clauses which introduce or interrupt direct quotations; neither have unspoken thoughts, when not placed between quotation marks in the copy-text, been marked as direct quotations here.

31. A related category of defects in the copy-text not reported in the LIST OF EMENDATIONS consists of plate damage which creates no textual problems. For example, as a result of apparent carelessness in the printing shop, several letters are wholly or partially obscured in two passages of some, but not all, copies of the November, 1854, installment in *Putnam's*. In such copies, a white streak cuts across the middle of five lines at P481.34b–38b, obliterating parts of "th" in "officer-of-the-deck" (86.4), "lin" in "hailing" (86.4), "ma" in "matter" (86.5), "m" in "from" (86.5), and "ty-f" in "seventy-four" (86.6). Several paragraphs later, at P482.47a–48a, a similar streak almost entirely obliterates two words, "the toes" (86.37), in one line, and the upper part of another word, "him" (86.38), in the next line. The missing matter is obvious enough, except in two places: one could not know from the defective copies that "seventy-four" contained a hyphen or that "the toes" were the two words of which only small traces are visible. The copy of the copy-text that provided printer's copy for NN is one of the copies defective in this way; although NN has supplied these readings by reference to a perfect copy, they are of course not emendations of the copy-text. Similarly, improper spacing in the copy-text which results in the running together of two words (or some of the letters of two words) is not reported unless the flaw creates new words; thus the obvious errors in spacing in the copy-text readings "mechanicallycontinuing" (77.17) and "day samong" (163.34) are here corrected without being noted in the LIST OF EMENDATIONS. Finally, line-end hyphens which fail to print in the copy-text (though there is space for them) are not reported here when the words involved are not possible compounds and therefore appear as single unhyphenated words in the present edition.

EDITORIAL APPARATUS

THE BASIC EVIDENCE for textual decisions in the present edition is given in the preceding sections of this NOTE and in the four lists which follow it and complete the TEXTUAL RECORD:[32]

DISCUSSIONS OF ADOPTED READINGS. These discussions take up any reading (whether a copy-text reading or an emendation) adopted in the Northwestern-Newberry text which seems to require discussion or explanation beyond the general guidelines already stated. Certain instances of decisions not to emend, as well as some actual emendations, are commented upon in this list.

LIST OF EMENDATIONS. This list records every change made in the copy-text for the present edition, accidentals as well as substantives. The left column gives the Northwestern-Newberry readings, the right column the rejected copy-text readings. Each emendation is followed by a symbol to indicate whether the source is the Putnam book edition (A), Melville's marked copy (HM), or the present editors (NN).[33] Items marked with an asterisk are commented on in the DISCUSSIONS OF ADOPTED READINGS.

63 emendations have been made in accidentals, 64 in substantives. Of the accidentals, 37 are corrections made in the book edition, and the other 26 have been made by the present editors; of the substantives, 21 come from the book edition, 5 from Melville's annotation in a copy of the book, and 38 from the present editors. No emendations of any sort have been made silently; using the LIST OF EMENDATIONS and the REPORT OF LINE-END HYPHENATION, one can reconstruct the copy-text in every detail.[34]

32. On file in the Melville Collection of The Newberry Library is a complete list of variants between the magazine and book editions, including both substantives (which are reported in the LIST OF SUBSTANTIVE VARIANTS) and accidentals (which are reported in the LIST OF EMENDATIONS only when they are adopted). Also on file is the evidence for the decisions in the first list of the REPORT OF LINE-END HYPHENATION.

33. The presence of an NN symbol signifies only that the reading does not occur in the two authorized texts or in Melville's marked copy; it does not imply that no one has ever thought of it before.

34. That is, every *textual* detail: features of the styling or design of the edition containing the copy-text—such as the length of lines, the form and content of the running titles, the typography and punctuation of chapter numbers and chapter titles, the display capitalization of chapter openings, and the use of the phrases "Continued from . . ." and "To be continued" at the beginning and end of installments—are not recoverable from these lists. (Nor are such typographic devices as the occasional use of two or more short dashes in the attempt to create a single dash.) Opening double and single quotation marks are omitted before the display capital at the beginning of Chapter 11, p. 61.

REPORT OF LINE-END HYPHENATION. Since some possible compound words are hyphenated at the ends of lines in the copy-text, the intended forms of these words become a matter for editorial decision. When such a word appears elsewhere in the copy-text in only one form, that form is followed; when its treatment is not consistent (and the inconsistency is an acceptable one, to be retained in the present text), the form which occurs more times in analogous situations is followed. If the word does not occur elsewhere in the copy-text, the form is determined by a survey of similar words, by the usage in the 1847 Worcester's and the 1848 Webster's, and by any relevant evidence in a Melville manuscript. The first list in the REPORT OF LINE-END HYPHENATION records these decisions, by listing the adopted Northwestern-Newberry forms of possible compounds which are hyphenated at the ends of lines in the copy-text. The second list is a guide to the established copy-text forms of compounds which are hyphenated at the ends of lines in the Northwestern-Newberry Edition. No editorial decisions are involved in this second list,[35] but the information recorded is essential for reconstructing the copy-text and making exact quotations from the present edition.

LIST OF SUBSTANTIVE VARIANTS. This list is a record of all variant substantive readings in the two editions authorized by Melville.[36] The left column gives the readings of the first American impression in *Putnam's Monthly* (and also the Northwestern-Newberry readings when they differ from the copy-text). The right column lists the substantive readings in the book edition which are at variance with the copy-text. Editions are designated by three symbols: P (*Putnam's Monthly*), A (Putnam's book edition, the first separate American edition), and NN (Northwestern-Newberry).

In these four lists readers have before them all the copy-text readings and all the substantive variations from those readings in authorized editions. With these lists they can examine and reconsider for themselves the textual decisions for the present edition and in the process see more clearly the relationships between the texts of *Israel Potter* available during Melville's lifetime and the one which is offered here as a more faithful representation of the author's intentions.

35. Except in the cases of words hyphenated at the ends of lines in the copy-text as well. These words, which also appear in the first list and are marked with daggers, are given in the forms which the present editors adopted but which are obscured by hyphenation at the ends of lines in this edition.

36. Such variants as "berth"/"birth", "enclose"/"inclose", and "subtile"/"subtle" are considered accidentals whenever the 1847 Worcester's, the 1848 Webster's, or other contemporary dictionaries classify them as interchangeable forms of the same word.

Discussions of Adopted Readings

I N THESE COMMENTS on emendations and on decisions not to emend, the following symbols are employed:

P *Putnam's Monthly* (1854–1855)
A Putnam's Book Edition (1855–1865)
NN Northwestern-Newberry Edition

v.2   *His*]   NN departs from the title in P (which has "OR," at this point) and follows the wording of the title page in A. One cannot be sure whether the exact form of the title in the magazine, with the "OR,", was supplied by Melville or by an editor for *Putnam's*. It seems likely, however, that the magazine did supply the second subtitle of the first two installments (not repeated in A), *"A FOURTH OF JULY STORY"*, to fit the July number in which the first installment appeared; and conceivably other aspects of the title may have been introduced in the magazine office as well. In any case, the likelihood that Melville was responsible for the title with "His" is suggested by its parallelism with *Redburn: His First Voyage* and *The Confidence-Man: His Masquerade;* in all three instances the relationship of the subtitle to the title is clearly genitive (the meaning is "Israel Potter's Fifty Years of Exile")—whereas in *White-Jacket; or, The World in a Man-of-War* and *Pierre; or, The Ambiguities* the subtitles must begin with "or," for they are true alternative titles, not genitive phrases. (Neither "His" nor "Or" appears in the head title to the first chapter nor in the running titles in A. NN design of course alters the typography and eliminates the end punctuation of the titles and subtitles as they appear in P and A.) See also the HISTORICAL NOTE, p. 209.

v.2   *Exile*]   NN styling eliminates the period that follows this word in A. For a fuller discussion of the text of the title, see the preceding note.

ix.1–x.23   Contents . . . Pace]   The NN table of contents is made up of the chapter titles in P (since no table of contents appears there), as styled for capitalization in NN (since chapter titles appear in full capitals in P). The table of contents in A is identical (aside from capitalization and the adoption of Roman numerals), except for the use of a comma, instead of a semicolon, after "Selkirk's" in Chapter 17, and the presence of two chapters labeled "CONTINUED" (a second Chapter "XIX", and a continuation of Chapter "XXIII", numbered "XXIV"—causing the final three chapters to be numbered "XXV", "XXVI", and "XXVII"). On the chapter divisions, see also the discussion at 125.26.

8.24   poling]   The P and A reading "pulling" loses the sense of the corresponding word, spelled "poling" in the first edition and "polling" in the second and third editions, in Melville's source, Henry Trumbull's *Life and Remarkable Adventures of Israel R. Potter* (Providence, 1824), p. 7, without substituting a plausible one: the canoe was not "pulled" (i.e., "rowed") but propelled by a pole pushed against the river bed. Presumably, following the *Life,* Melville wrote either "poling" (if he was using the first edition) or "polling" (if he was using the second or third) and his word was misread "pulling" by the copyist or compositor. See 159.21, where coal-scows are "poled" on the Thames; also p. 285.

9.18   skins]   The P and A reading "cash" is emended from Trumbull's *Life,* p. 9, which makes clear that Potter exchanged only "skins" and "furs", not his money; the misreading, whether or not Melville's own, was inadvertent and makes no sense.

10.12   tenth]   NN keeps the P and A reading although Melville's source (Trumbull's *Life,* p. 10) says "on the 15th day . . . ," which he possibly misread as "10th". However, Melville treated quite freely such numbers given in the *Life,* usually heightening whatever point or effect is involved for Israel. Thus at 19.31 he makes Israel look like an old man of "eighty" where *Life* had "seventy", increases his hours of sleepless imprisonment to "about three o'clock" from "about midnight" at 23.14–15, lengthens his work hours to "About noon" from "about 11 o'clock" at 25.21, emphasizes his independence by shortening to "Ere two months" the time of his departure from service of "about three months" at 27.37, multiplies to "some forty or more" from "fifteen" the number of American prisoners of war at 151.20, adds one to the number of his children born and buried at 162.38–39, and rounds out to half a century the period of his exile by making the year of his return 1826 rather than 1823 at 166.23. Other number changes seem more arbitrary, such as "about ten o'clock" for "about 11 o'clock" at 22.10, "some

six or seven miles" for "within six miles" at 23.16–17, and the reading "tenth" for
"15th" day here at 10.12. Since accurate transcription of such numerical details was
clearly not Melville's intention, NN emends numbers in only three instances: the
slip as to an important historical date at 13.13, the inadvertent halving of the
breadth of Israel's great jump at 21.8, and the confusion as to price and numbers of
rolls at 44.26, and 44.35, 37, 39.

12.21   Patterson]   Melville's spelling here of the name follows that of his
source, David Dudley Field's *History of the County of Berkshire* (Pittsfield, 1829), p.
118; the variant spelling "Paterson" is followed by *Appletons' Cyclopædia of American Biography* and the *Dictionary of American Biography*.

13.13   sixteenth]   NN emends the P and A reading "seventeenth" (evidently
Melville's own slip) from the source in Trumbull's *Life*, p. 14, which correctly
gives "the 16th June" as the day before the battle on June 17—a historic date that
became "the anniversary day we celebrate" of which Melville speaks in the dedication (viii.19), giving the correct date at viii.15 and viii.27.

13.29   marksmen's]   The sense of the passage requires this NN emendation of
the P and A evident misreading "marksman's".

15.23   what ship?"]   In P and A the hail "Ahoy!" is not followed by this
question (though Israel answers it), and there is no closing quotation mark in P (A
supplies one). NN adopts the question "what ship?" from Trumbull's *Life*, p. 21,
where it is asked and answered.

18.4   in very act]   Possibly this phrase in P should read "in the very act"; but
since it was not changed in A it may have been currently idiomatic without the
definite article.

18.20   lads]   Since the P and A reading "ladies" is clearly wrong (Israel must
be correcting his initial error, seven lines above, of so addressing the farm
workers), an emendation is called for which will correct the gender to masculine
but still cause the workers to stare "with added boorishness of surprise". Such an
available word of address is the NN emendation "lads" (more plausible than the
temptingly more similar "laddies") which continues Israel's half-roguish tone and
which might easily have been misread by the copyist or compositor. A soldier calls
Israel "lad" at 22.19, as does Paul Jones at 112.32 and 125.7, and a sailor at 134.22,
while Israel addresses sailors familiarly as "lad" or "lads" at 133.20, 133.25, and
135.20. Because the term implies comradeship or a shared occupation, the farm
workers might well be surprised to be so addressed by Israel, as they are when he
calls them "gentlemen" just below.

21.8   nineteen]   NN emends the P and A reading "ten" as the width in feet of
the "great ditch" Israel jumped, which the first edition of Trumbull's *Life*, p. 31,
states was "upwards of 19 feet". Probably Melville wrote "ten", but the reason he
did so with Trumbull's "19" before him (assuming his copy was the first edition)

was that most likely he misread Trumbull's "19", which is indistinct in some copies, as "10", not that he meant to cut Israel's great jump in half. If his copy was the second or third edition, which gave the width as "upwards of 12 feet" (presumably a misreading of the first edition's indistinct "19"), the same reason applies. The P and A misreading "ten" goes against Melville's evident intention throughout the book to magnify Israel's feats, and it is therefore emended by NN to the original figure Melville presumably would have kept had he read it correctly. See the discussion at 10.12 and the account of the editions of the *Life*, pp. 283–85.

23.32   directions] Trumbull's *Life*, p. 34, reads "agreeable to the directions which I had received"; the P and A reading "direction" seems less likely to be Melville's deliberate change of idiom than an instance in which his copyist or compositor failed to notice his often inconspicuous final "-s". At 37.5 the plural form is used.

24.4   man] NN keeps (from P) the singular generalized form, which conveys the intended meaning, expressed by a plural construction in the corresponding phrase in the source, Trumbull's *Life*, p. 36 ("the rich and purse-proud of England . . . were generally the lords of the manor . . ."); the A reading is "men".

25.18   last] NN follows the A correction of P "least" but without the comma supplied by A.

27.29   Ill] In a copy of *Israel Potter* now at Harvard Melville corrected the P and A reading "Illy" to "Ill" here and similarly at 41.2, 57.3, and 120.17. See the NOTE ON THE TEXT, p. 247. NN makes the emendation in each case, although Melville was inconsistent in his use of such hypercorrect adverbial forms as "illy" throughout his works; his correction in these instances is not grounds for emendation in similar cases. One wonders why and how Melville managed to find "illy" each time it occurs in the book when he overlooked so many other anomalies.

32.15   gardener] NN emends the P and A "gardeners" as a misreading. Trumbull's *Life*, p. 45, has "gardner" here and above (p. 44). Israel is employed by an individual, "the overseer" of the gardens, as Melville realized in paraphrasing "overseer" as "the chief gardener" (29.12–13). Melville's intended reference here, therefore, was to the one "gardener" not to several.

32.20   Yankee!] This anomalous placing of the exclamation point in P and A was possibly influenced by the frequent use in Trumbull's *Life* of exclamation points within sentences.

34.18   At that] Possibly a compositorial error for "All that", though the phrase makes sense as an ellipsis (as for "I'll arrive at that . . .").

41.2   ill] See the discussion at 27.29.

44.26   Three penny rolls]   NN adopts from A this emendation of P, where Israel's answer "Three two-penny rolls" is obviously incorrect. This correction seems somewhat awkward in its introduction of one-penny rolls (to the actual existence of which no reference is made elsewhere), when Franklin's continuing computations involve both two-penny rolls (equated with "loaves") and three-pence glasses of wine; but it is apparently the only way to make sense of the passage and correct Israel's error (without rewriting his answer to "One and a half two-penny rolls"). Granting the existence of penny rolls and Franklin's choosing to switch in his ensuing computation from one- to two-penny rolls, the only remaining error in the whole passage about the price of bread and wine (44.22–39) is the thrice repeated "seventy-two" in P (uncorrected by A) at 44.35, 37, 39, which is corrected each time by NN. The possibility that Melville intended the incorrect arithmetic (both by Israel and by Franklin) as a satiric comment on the calculating Dr. Franklin seems unlikely since the initial error not only is Israel's but is too elementary for him to make or Franklin to overlook, and the second error, thrice repeated, of "seventy-two loaves" cannot have been intended by Melville as Franklin's since Franklin first makes the computation ("seventy-eight") correctly in the previous sentence (44.33). Clearly somebody—Melville himself, his copyist, or the compositor—blundered in making both errors. Such blunders in computation occur repeatedly in Melville's works, notably in Flask's reckoning about cigars in Chapter 99, "The Doubloon," in *Moby-Dick*.

44.35   seventy-eight]   See the discussion at 44.26.

50.39   said, "Come]   The P paragraph break between the two words is an obvious compositorial error in spacing (since "said," falls at the end of a line in the double-column layout of P and the quotation mark and "Come" are simply placed directly under "Clapping" rather than at the left margin); following A, NN corrects the error. A reverse error, failure to indent for a new paragraph, is made twice in P and is corrected by NN at 57.28 (uncorrected by A) and at 169.23 (corrected by A).

53.38   *wishing*]   The P and A reading *"waiting"* is corrected from Franklin's text in Melville's probable source, Jared Sparks's edition of the *Works* (Boston, 1836–40), II, 96 (see the HISTORICAL NOTE, p. 192 and footnote 17). Whether it was Melville himself or a copyist or compositor who misread the word, it requires emendation (as does *"hope"* to *"hopes"* at 54.1 and the missing comma after *"help"* at 54.2), since the passage purports to be Israel's presumably accurate reading from Poor Richard in "The Way to Wealth." No point is made that Israel is misreading; nor does there seem to be any plausible reason why Melville would wish readers of his book to think that Franklin's text actually reads as it does with these three changes.

54.1   *hopes*]   See the discussion at 53.38.

54.2   *help,*]   See the discussion at 53.38.

54.13   mild]   Melville corrected "wild" (which appears here in both P and A) to "mild" in a copy of *Israel Potter*. See the discussion at 27.29.

57.3   ill]   See the discussion at 27.29.

57.13   Ranger,]   The name "Amphitrite", which appears in both P and A, is emended because the error in naming Jones's "present ship" is evidently a slip on Melville's part in reading his source (Robert Sands's *Life and Correspondence of John Paul Jones* [New York, 1830], pp. 67, 69–70), not an error he intentionally assigned Franklin in this speech addressed to Jones (who in that case would be shown correcting Franklin). The obvious error in P of a period for a comma after the ship's name is also emended (as it is in A).

57.28   "Everything]   The needed paragraph break did not occur here in P and A. See the discussion at 50.39.

57.28   shillyshallying,]   A omitted the comma, present in P, thus making "shillyshallying" an adjective modifying "timidity" (rather than a noun with which "timidity called prudence" is in apposition). The A reading is attractive, but in the absence of evidence that Melville made such corrections for the book text the change in punctuation is more likely compositorial than authorial.

58.10   Solebay]   NN corrects the P and A misspelling "Soleby"; the correct spelling occurs in both of Melville's sources: Sands, *Life and Correspondence of John Paul Jones,* p. 39; J. Fenimore Cooper, *History of the Navy of the United States of America* (New York, 1853), I, 56. See p. 184, footnote 7.

58.11   Louisbergh]   Although this P and A spelling departs from the "Louisbourg" spelling of Melville's source passage (Sands, *Life and Correspondence of John Paul Jones,* p. 44) and has not been located elsewhere, it is retained by NN because the spelling of this place name was not standardized and various endings occur (such as "-urg", "-urgh", and most commonly "-ourg"). Melville's handwriting was often difficult to make out, but it seems unlikely that if he had followed Sands's "-ourg" spelling his copyist could have misread it with the "-ergh" ending. For NN policy in such cases, see the NOTE ON THE TEXT, p. 251.

59.33   D'Estaing]   The P and A corrupt spelling "D'Estang" is emended here and at 59.35 to the correct form, which appears at 95.19 (as it does in Melville's source, Sands's *Life and Correspondence of John Paul Jones,* p. 75).

61.18   as]   To make sense of the sentence in the context (without assuming an unlikely metaphor), the addition of "as" to the P and A reading "good" seems required.

77.19   AN . . . GHOSTS]   This anomalous P and A section title, the only one in the book, though possibly due to error or oversight on Melville's or an editor's part, is retained by NN. It is not analogous to the division in P (followed by A) of Chapters 19 and 23 into two parts (see the discussion at 125.26), for in each of those cases the second part begins a new installment; someone on the magazine staff evidently made those chapter breaks because the original chapters were too long for the allotted space. But in this instance the sectional division falls within an installment; and though the magazine editors could still have been responsible for it (perhaps to break what was regarded as an unduly long chapter, filling the whole installment), the case is not as strong. The sectional title may well have been in the manuscript; possibly Melville meant for it to be given a chapter number. In any event, there is not sufficient evidence to justify deleting it from the copy-text.

85.1   14]   NN corrects the error in P that numbers this chapter "XVI" rather than "XIV"; the first impression of A also had the erroneous "XVI", but it was corrected to "XIV" in the second impression. (NN styling substitutes "14" for "XIV".)

88.26   of tiller]   The plausible A reading "of the tiller" is not a necessary correction if the P reading "of tiller" is taken to refer to the nature of the material that the "stump" consisted of rather than to a particular object.

90.2   swart]   The P and A reading "smart" is emended as a misreading. Paul Jones is not elsewhere described as "smart" but twice as "swarthy"—upon his first appearance at 56.6, and below at 96.34. In Sands, *Life and Correspondence*, p. 177 n., possibly Melville's source, Jones is described as "swarthy". See the HISTORICAL NOTE, p. 196.

100.15   six or seven]   Since the source Melville was following in general (Sands, *Life and Correspondence of John Paul Jones*) records the population of White- haven as fifty thousand (p. 108), not the more nearly correct six or seven as P and A state here and just below (100.18), Melville must have had access to a more accurate source for this figure.

101.38   north]   The P and A reading "south" is corrected from Melville's source (Sands, *Life and Correspondence of John Paul Jones,* p. 81), which reports "from the north"; the fact that 101.12 reads "north" indicates that the error here was a slip by Melville, his copyist, or the compositor.

102.25   disjoined]   This word, adopted by NN from Melville's source (Sands, *Life and Correspondence of John Paul Jones,* p. 82), is required by the sense of the passage; the P and A reading "disjointed" is a slip.

104.28   discretion]   Since Sands (*Life and Correspondence of John Paul Jones,* p. 83), whom Melville is following, here reads "direction", it is possible that Melville also wrote "direction" and that the word was misread by his copyist or the composi- tor. However, "discretion" (the P and A reading) also makes sense here, is idio- matic, and brings in a more rather than a less complex meaning than "direction".

113.23   serene]   The P and A reading "severe" is clearly an error for "serene" (see the description two paragraphs above, at 113.6–7: "The sky was serene").

118.29   Shirra's] The incorrect P and A spelling "Shirrer's" (the source, Sands, *Life and Correspondence of John Paul Jones,* p. 176, has "Shirra") must be an inadvertent ear-spelling, presumably Melville's own, reflecting a Northeast dialect pronunciation. His consistent similar spelling of Polynesian words in *Typee* and *Omoo* (e.g., "kannaker" for "kannaka") reflects the same dialect influence; see Harrison Hayford's explanation of Melville's rendition of Polynesian words, in the Hendricks House edition of *Omoo* (New York, 1969), pp. 343–47.

120.17   ill] See the discussion at 27.29.

121.8   crowding] P and A have "crowning", an evident misreading (though it makes some sense) of the clearly intended "crowding"—see the reference at 124.17 to the "crowds" of witnesses.

121.18   Spurn] The corrupt P and A reading "Spurm" is emended by NN to the correct form, which occurs in Melville's source (Sands, *Life and Correspondence of John Paul Jones,* p. 179).

122.23   *the comparatively squalid*] NN follows the P and A italics though no reason for such emphasis is apparent and italicization may not have been Melville's intention. (This point could possibly also be made about the italicized "You" at 26.27.)

122.35   lounging] Presumably a variant spelling (not a corrupt reading) of "lunging", of which the OED reports several nineteenth-century examples.

124.4   principal's] Although the plural form "principals' " might seem called for, the singular, retained from P and A, is also a quite possible construction here.

125.22   to enter to] Melville's phrasing compresses and obscures that of his source passage (Cooper, *History of the Navy,* I, 108) which reads, "and cases actually occurred in which the rammers had to be thrust into the ports of the opposite ship in order to be entered into the muzzles of their proper guns."

125.26   Ere] In P and A the first of two chapters numbered "XIX" ends with "fight.", and "CHAPTER XIX. CONTINUED." begins with "ERE". NN disregards that two-part division of Chapter 19 on the ground that it was less likely to have been made by Melville for literary purposes than by *Putnam's* for editorial convenience, since the December, 1854, installment ends with "fight." (at the end of a page) and the January, 1855, installment begins with "CHAPTER XIX. CONTINUED." Similarly, at 156.20, Chapter 23 is continued as a separate chapter at the beginning of the following installment; this time, however, the continuation is inconsistently assigned the next higher number, "XXIV". NN also on the same ground disregards this chapter division and includes P and A Chapter "XXIV" in NN Chapter 23; consequently P and A Chapters "XXV", "XXVI", and "XXVII" become NN Chapters 24, 25, and 26. See the HISTORICAL NOTE, pp. 207–208, and the NOTE ON THE TEXT, pp. 245–46.

126.7 a man] Although the P and A reading "man" makes sense as a generalized singular, the following parallel phrase "a corpse" calls for emendation of "man"
to "a man". The corresponding phrasing in Melville's source (Cooper, *History of the
Navy,* I, 108) refers to single men, not generalized man, in reporting so animated a
gunfire on the deck "as to drive nearly every man off it, that was not shot down."

129.2 involuntarily] NN follows A in correcting the evident compositorial
blunder "involuntary" in P. No such uncertainty as to the adjectival or the adverbial form seems involved as at the four points where Melville corrected "illy" to
"ill"—see the discussion at 27.29.

136.12 shove, once more] The P and A reading "shove once more," is mis-
punctuated, making "once more" modify "with a shove" rather than "rejected" as
Melville obviously intended. (Israel is not shoved each time but rejected; see the
parallel phrasing at 135.10 above, "Once more Israel decamped.")

142.20 four] The P and A reading "three" is emended by NN because it does
not agree with the statement just above at 142.15 that "four of the soldiers" drew
their swords. One or the other of the numbers requires emendation, and three
seems a less likely number of soldiers than four to do the job of forcing the passage
through the mob; also the confusion may have arisen because "three officers"
(142.8) and "four men" are involved.

143.22 Knyphausen] The P and A spelling "Kniphausen" is corrected by NN
from Ethan Allen's *A Narrative of Colonel Ethan Allen's Captivity* (Philadelphia,
1779), p. 96. See p. 201, footnote 34.

145.2 undress;] NN follows A here in dropping P's excrescent closing quotation mark but retains the semicolon of P (changed to a comma by A).

150.9 General Prescott] Here Melville's source (Allen's *Narrative,* p. 9) re-
lates, ". . . I met general Prescott . . . : Then he shook his cane . . . ; upon which
capt. M'Cloud . . . whispered to him . . . that it was inconsistent with his honour
to strike a prisoner." But P has "Colonel McCloud" in place of "general Prescott"
(uncorrected by A); NN emends because evidently Melville's confusion of the two
officers was inadvertent—no literary or other purpose seems served by the indeed
unfair switch. (NN capitalizes "general" as Melville's usage.)

150.27 Abbé Bellegarde] Both P and A have the corrupt reading "Albe Bell-
garde". Melville owned a copy of *Politeness of Manners and Behaviour in Fashionable
Society. From the French of the Abbé de Bellegarde* (Paris, 1817). See Hennig Cohen,
"Abbé Bellegarde and Melville's *Israel Potter:* An Emendation," *Direction Line,* No.
1 (Autumn, 1975), pp. 2–3; and Merton M. Sealts, Jr., *Melville's Reading: A Check-
List of Books Owned and Borrowed* (Madison: University of Wisconsin Press, 1966),
No. 57.

150.35 on a man] Possibly Melville wrote "in": his "in" and "on" were
sometimes difficult to distinguish.

156.20   All]   In P and A a new chapter, labeled "CONTINUED" and numbered "XXIV", begins here. For NN treatment, see the discussion at 125.26.

157.2   carted]   Possibly "the bricks" should be supplied before "carted"; but
the elliptical construction does not render the meaning unclear.

159.10   wondering]   NN follows A rather than the P reading "wandering",
which seems neither called for nor supported by the context; even though in the
book as a whole Israel is indeed a wanderer, here the controlling sequence is
"amazement" (159.9), "surprise" (159.10), "wondering" (159.10).

160.5–9   On . . . torture.]   This paragraph in P was omitted from A. NN
keeps it because it was certainly not omitted by Melville's intention for literary
reasons but by the Putnam firm's editorial interference for prudential reasons (see
the HISTORICAL NOTE, p. 203, footnote 40, and the NOTE ON THE TEXT, p. 247).
Even if Melville himself were thought to have excised it for those reasons NN
would retain it as expressing his true intention. (The GENERAL NOTE ON THE TEXT
to the NN edition of THE PIAZZA TALES and Other Prose Pieces, 1839–1860 discusses
in detail the editorial interference in Melville's works published by the Putnam
firm and by Dix & Edwards.)

160.7   their]   Some emendation is required by the P reading "its". The NN
substitution of "their" serves to clarify the reference not only of "its" but also of
"it" in the following clause; in addition, "their doom" is parallel with "their fate"
and "their torture".

163.2   collecting]   Emended by NN from the source, Trumbull's Life, p. 265;
the P and A reading "cutting" makes no sense and is evidently a misreading.

166.23   1826]   Although this date is two years after the publication date of
Trumbull's Life (1824), which Melville purports to be following, he clearly altered
deliberately the date 1823 given in the Life, p. 100, as the year of Israel's return, in
order to round out the half-century of his exile to 1826, which was also themati-
cally appropriate as the fiftieth anniversary of the Declaration of Independence and
the year in which both Thomas Jefferson and John Adams died.

169.23   " 'Father]   NN (following A) corrects the compositorial failure in P to
make the required paragraph indentation (the preceding word comes at a right
margin in P). See the discussion at 50.39.

List of Emendations

I N THIS LIST of changes made in the copy-text by the present editors, the following abbreviations are used to designate the sources
of readings:

> P *Putnam's Monthly* (1854–1855)
> A Putnam's Book Edition (1855)
> HM Melville's Marginal Corrections (see pp. 247–48)
> NN Northwestern-Newberry Edition

For further comment on this list, see p. 253 above; for discussions of the
emendations marked with an asterisk (*), see the Discussions of Adopted
Readings, pp. 255–64. The wavy dash (~) stands for the word cited in the
left column and signals that only a punctuation mark is emended. The
caret ($_\wedge$) indicates the absence of a punctuation mark. Empty brackets ([ ])
indicate space where a mark of punctuation failed to print.

	NN Reading	Copy-Text (P) Reading
*v.2	*His* A	OR,
*v.2	*Exile* A	EXILE./A FOURTH OF
		JULY STORY.

	NN Reading	Copy-Text (P) Reading
vii.1–viii.27	TO . . . 1854. A	[*not present*]
*ix.1–x.23	Contents . . . Pace NN	[*not present*]
*8.24	poling NN	pulling
*9.18	skins NN	cash
*13.13	sixteenth NN	seventeenth
*13.29	marksmen's NN	marksman's
*15.23	what ship?" NN	[*not present*]
15.34	he A	[*not present*]
*18.20	lads NN	ladies
18.32	right A	night
*21.8	nineteen NN	ten
*23.32	directions NN	direction
*25.18	last A	least
26.30	all." NN	~·ᴧ
*27.29	Ill HM	Illy
30.23	race. A	~[ ]
30.33	me, NN	~.
*32.15	gardener NN	gardeners
38.34	different A	kifferent
39.22	gravelyᴧ NN	~,
40.14	lift A	lfit
*41.2	ill HM	illy
42.2	lips." A	~·ᴧ
42.9	added: A	~.
43.30	hither." A	~.'
*44.26	penny A	two-penny
*44.35	seventy-eight NN	seventy-two
44.37	seventy-eight NN	seventy-two
44.39	seventy-eight NN	seventy-two
47.36	of NN	in
48.17	essayist A	essayest
50.37	Hark!" A	~!ᴧ
*50.39	[*no*¶]"Come A	[¶]"Come

	NN Reading	Copy-Text (P) Reading
*53.38	*wishing* NN	*waiting*
*54.1	*hopes* NN	*hope*
*54.2	*help,* NN	~ˌ
*54.13	mild HM	wild
56.29	'Indien,' NN	"~,"
*57.3	ill HM	illy
*57.13	Ranger, NN	Amphitrite.
*57.28	[¶]"Everything NN	[*no*¶]"Everything
*58.10	Solebay NN	Soleby
*59.33	D'Estaing NN	D'Estang
59.35	D'Estaing NN	D'Estang
61.18	It's A	Its
*61.18	as NN	[*not present*]
66.2	rascal's A	rascals'
68.16	Israel.ˌ A	~."
69.20	griffins' A	~ˌ
74.33	household A	hous-/hold
75.12	piece-meal NN	piece[ ]/meal
77.24	namely: A	~;
82.12	friend," A	~,ˌ
82.12	Israel,ˌ A	~,"
82.12	"that A	ˌ~
82.36	Tristram NN	Tristam
84.22	Hughes NN	Hughs
84.24–25	Suffren's NN	Suffrien's
*85.1	14 NN	XVI
86.9	foremast NN	foremost
86.12	the A	the the
88.28	captain, A	~.
*90.2	swart NN	smart
91.8	tyrannical A	tyr-/ranical
92.10	it's A	its
93.21	trey A	treize

	NN READING	COPY-TEXT (P) READING
96.24	Galloway NN	Galoway
97.16	cone NN	cove
99.32	spikes?" A	~?∧
99.39	Bees NN	Bee's
101.24	to. A	~,
*101.38	north NN	south
102.8	were A	where
*102.25	disjoined NN	disjointed
110.31	Countess A	Countes
*113.23	serene NN	severe
113.28	anchorage A	anhcorage
115.31	Franklin." NN	~·∧
116.1	∧Now A	"~
116.17	descried NN	described
*118.29	Shirra's NN	Shirrer's
119.4	stubborn A	stupborn
*120.17	ill HM	illy
*121.8	crowding NN	crowning
*121.18	Spurn NN	Spurm
122.13	twenty A	tweny
122.38	within A	with
125.17	smoothness A	smoothess
*125.26	[no chapter break]Ere NN	[chapter heading CHAPTER XIX. CONTINUED.] ERE
*126.7	a man NN	man
126.20	belligerents A	belligerent's
128.37–38	quarter!" A	~!∧
128.38	Serapis.∧ A	~."
*129.2	involuntarily A	involuntary
132.12	boom A	boon
133.15	Frenchman NN	Frenchman's
*136.12	shove, once more∧ NN	~∧~~,
139.31	away! A	~?

	NN Reading	Copy-Text (P) Reading
139.32	sir? A	~!
140.3	men. A	~,
*142.20	four NN	three
*143.22	Knyphausen NN	Kniphausen
144.13	leaves NN	leases
144.27	earth!' NN	~!ᴧ
144.27	on!ᴧ" NN	~!' "
*145.2	undress;ᴧ A	~;"
*150.9	General Prescott NN	Colonel McCloud
*150.27	Abbé Bellegarde NN	Albe Bellgarde
151.34	Singles A	Shingles
153.6	throngs NN	things
155.14	disinterring A	disinter-/ing
*156.20	[no chapter break]All NN	[chapter heading CHAPTER XXIV. (CONTINUED.)] ALL
158.1	24 NN	XXV
*159.10	wondering A	wandering
*160.7	their NN	its
160.14	a A	a a
161.1	25 NN	XXVI
161.14	truthfulest A	truthfullest
*163.2	collecting NN	cutting
164.32	Barbican A	Bartican
165.2	Barbican A	Bartican
165.38	keeping A	keep./ing
167.1	26 NN	XXVII
167.11	Copp's NN	Copps'
*169.23	[¶]" 'Father A	[no¶]" 'Father

Report of Line-End Hyphenation

THE FIRST LIST below records the forms adopted in the present edition (NN) for possible compound words which were hyphenated at line-ends in the copy-text (P) and which the editors had to decide whether to print as single-word compounds without hyphens or as hyphenated compounds. The second list enables one to determine the established reading (present in P or established by the editors) of compounds which happen to be hyphenated at the ends of lines in NN; any possible compound hyphenated at the end of a line in NN should be transcribed as one unhyphenated word unless it appears in this list. Those words coincidentally hyphenated between the same elements at line-ends in both P and NN are marked with daggers (†); in the first list they are given in the forms which would have been adopted if they had fallen within a line in NN. A slash (/) indicates the line-end break in P in a word which might possibly be hyphenated in more than one place. For further comment on these lists, see p. 254 above.

I. NN *forms of possible compounds which were hyphenated at copy-text line-ends*

3.13	township	4.24	frame-work
4.7	charcoal-burner	5.17	two-steepled
4.15	well-known	5.32	stronghold

6.20	†intercommunication	80.16	good-natured
8.15	westward	81.11	earthenware
8.35	brave-hearted	81.38	outskirts
10.1	†countermined	82.9	crown-pieces
13.28	deer-skin	82.36	good-natured
15.33	landlord	82.37	good-natured
16.32	thenceforth	83.3	haystack
19.1	public-house	83.24	likewise
20.13	perverse-minded	83.33	seaman's
22.16	look-out	86.22	stern-sheets
23.12	handcuffs	86.23	oarsmen
23.36	fire-brand	87.15	overboard
24.20	Chinaman	87.17	Meantime
25.1	carriage-house	88.15	shipmates
25.21	workmen	89.1	hatchway
26.35	sea-faring	89.15	alongside
27.14	workmen	90.18	white-squall
27.16	bareheaded	92.9	mankind
30.20	half-stammering	92.10	state-room
33.15	well-known	92.20	Scotchman
34.38	cross-questions	93.4	state-room
41.1	undergone	96.17	merchantman
41.8	sometimes	96.22	hail-storm
41.12	blacking-men	99.12	chain-shot
41.31	ill-advised	100.21	lighthouses
43.30	cook-shops	101.39	day-sparks
45.24	household	103.16	windward
47.17	lodging-houses	104.4	madman
48.19	housewifery	109.36	red-cheeked
51.6	landladies	111.8	high-born
59.8	playthings	115.10	†gun-deck
61.19	crosstrees	115.13	cellar-way
62.25	midnight	122.1	Meantime
63.16	nose-rings	123.26	trap-door
67.15	weather-stained	124.19	merchantmen
74.10	overhead	124.29	water-spout
74.33	household	125.3	jib-boom
76.10	withdrawing	125.27	eighteen-pounders
77.18	scarecrow	125.32	Thenceforth
77.28	tobacco-box	126.28	corposant-ball
78.4	daylight	127.10	pike-wise
78.11	scarecrow's	127.14	long-handled

128.5	foremost	146.18	Whereupon
130.10	daylight	152.11	countryman
131.3	otherwise	155.12	grave-digger
132.2	knock-down	155.17	cast-off
132.8	mankind	156.11	brick-yard
134.5	forecastle	157.12	bondsman
135.6	shipmate	158.12	gulf-stream
135.36	broken-nosed	159.21	broadside
135.37	death-rattle	159.35	tomb-stones
137.18	mizen-top	160.6	long-drawn
138.25	main-top	161.18	knuckle-bone
139.17	sailing-master	162.14	shop-girl
139.18	spanker-boom	163.26	huckster-women
140.32	midship/man	165.9	upland
140.38	mid/shipman	166.14	to-morrow
141.5	sheep-walks	167.13	grave-yard
143.6	nightfall	168.37	oversight
144.31	†lick-spittle	169.14	†hearth-stone
146.4	overcoming	169.17	half-buried

II. *Compounds containing line-end hyphens in* NN *which should be retained in transcription*

12.18	minute-men	127.14	death-dealing
33.20	evil-minded	133.32	jewel-block
44.5	decanter-like	134.19	gun-carriages
47.19	small-clothes	134.25	stern-looking
48.19	herb-doctor	141.5	hen-tracks
56.8	self-possessed	141.8	signal-gun
63.15	finger-rings	141.18	good-humored
65.36	half-lengthwise	142.6	sight-seers
71.1	second-story	144.7	half-rotten
80.16	corn-loft	144.31	†lick-spittle
87.5	cabin-boy	154.5	brick-yard
91.28	self-command	155.18	half-burst
95.14	mizzen-shrouds	155.26	helter-skelter
98.6	ship-of-war	155.38	grave-digger's
115.10	†gun-deck	163.28	blood-beets
115.12	water-line	164.38	ghost-like
118.1	fish-barrel	166.6	well-remembered
126.14	yard-arms	168.36	sledging-time
126.15	hand-grenades	169.14	†hearth-stone

List of Substantive Variants

I N THIS LIST, which is a record of the substantive variants in the authorized editions during Melville's lifetime, the following abbreviations are used to designate the sources of readings:

> P *Putnam's Monthly Magazine* (1854–1855)
> A Putnam's Book Edition (1855–1865)
> NN Northwestern-Newberry Edition

Copy-text (P) readings are listed in the left column and readings differing from them in the right. (In the instances of emendations made by the present editors, the NN reading also appears in the left column to provide a reference to the text.) If a reading does not remain constant throughout all the impressions of an edition, a date or inclusive dates are appended to the symbol to show the period during which new impressions carried the reading in question; superscript numbers indicate impressions within a given year. Features of the styling or design of the copy-text (P) are not necessarily followed in the present edition, and such deviations are not recorded here (see the NOTE ON THE TEXT, p. 253, footnote 34).

v.2   *His* NN
             OR, P   His A

v.2	*Exile* NN	
	EXILE./*A FOURTH OF JULY STORY.* P	Exile. A
vii.1–viii.27	TO . . . 1854. NN	
	[*not present*] P	TO . . . 1854. A
ix.1–x.23	Contents . . . Pace NN	
	[*not present*] P	CONTENTS . . . pace A
7.3	days P	day A
7.6	of P	off A
7.13	respectable P	as respectable A
15.34	he NN	
	[*not present*] P	he A
15.39	of a P	of A
17.17	it's P	its A
17.22	backwards P	back A
18.32	right NN	
	night P	right A
22.15	out P	ought A
24.4	man P	men A
25.18	last NN	
	least P	last A
26.40	hereabouts P	hereabout A
31.17	ye P	you A
35.29	objections P	objection A
39.17	these P	those A
39.27	the time P	that time A
40.18	so do P	do so A
44.26	penny NN	
	two-penny P	penny A
48.1	last P	[*not present*] A
48.17	essayist NN	
	essayest P	essayist A
54.20	refer to P	refer to it A
55.10	patriarchi-/cally P	patriarchially A
56.13	was there P	there was A
59.3	in P	of A

61.18	It's NN	
	Its P	It's A
65.19	hens' P	hen's A
66.2	rascal's NN	
	rascals' P	rascal's A
66.15	that P	[*not present*] A
67.35	a P	[*not present*] A
69.19	slanted P	slanting A
74.12–13	intently P	instantly A
77.28	open P	opened A
83.33	seaman's P	seamen's A
84.16	Englishmen P	Englishman A
85.1	14 NN	
	XVI P	XVI A1855[1]
		XIV A1855[2]–A1865
86.12	the NN	
	the the P	the A
87.17	Meantime P	Meanwhile A
88.20	bull P	hull A
88.26	tiller P	the tiller A
90.12	had P	[*not present*] A
92.10	it's NN	
	its P	it's A
93.7	or P	of A
93.21	trey NN	
	treize P	trey A
96.30	loch P	lock A
99.24	simultaneously P	as simultaneously A
100.27	its P	the A
102.8	were NN	
	where P	were A
104.39	in P	of A
107.28	decided P	a decided A
112.10	draw P	drew A
113.25	all P	[*not present*] A
115.36	Gad P	'Gad A

116.27	entered P	enter A
118.23	creating P	causing A
122.38	within NN	
	with P	within A
126.20	belligerents NN	
	belligerent's P	belligerents A
128.17	received P	[*not present*] A
129.2	involuntarily NN	
	involuntary P	involuntarily A
130.18	well P	[*not present*] A
132.12	spanker boom NN	
	spanker boon P	spanker-boom A
132.39	sank P	sunk A
136.12	rejected P	ejected A
138.28	"Take him away, take him	"Take him away, take him
	away— P	away, take him away— A
144.20	by —— P	by —— A1855¹
		* * * A1855²–A1865
144.27	d——d soul P	d——d soul A1855¹
		* * * * * A1855²–A1865
145.12	by —— P	by —— A1855¹
		* * * A1855²–A1865
151.20	other P	[*not present*] A
151.34	Singles NN	
	Shingles P	Singles A
155.37	taskmasters P	task-/master A
156.16	the P	[*not present*] A
159.7	first P	first time A
159.10	wondering NN	
	wandering P	wondering A
159.12	funereal P	funeral A
160.5–9	On . . . torture. P	[*not present*] A
160.14	a NN	
	a a P	a A
161.3	years' P	years A
168.3	Potters' P	Potter's A

Melville's Basic Source

MELVILLE'S BASIC SOURCE for his *Israel Potter*—Trumbull's *Life and Remarkable Adventures of Israel R. Potter*—is included here so that the ways he used it may be studied in conjunction with the analysis by Walter E. Bezanson in the HISTORICAL NOTE.[1] A copy of the first of the three contemporary editions is presented in photographic reproduction, along with the title pages and frontispieces of two other little "life and adventures" books similarly brought out by the same enterprising Yankee, Henry Trumbull, in Providence, Rhode Island—one on Daniel Boone in 1824, the same year as the *Life* of Potter, and one on Robert Voorhis, a hermit living in a cave near the Massachusetts border, in two printings with variant titles in 1829. The title page and frontispiece of the third edition of the *Life* (from which those of the second do not differ) are also reproduced here. (See pp. 395–401.)

Beyond the account in the *Life*, little is known about either Israel

1. The editorial staff of the Northwestern-Newberry Edition collaborated with R. D. Madison in the preparation of this document and compilation of the headnote, which was written by Harrison Hayford. Information supplied by Bezanson has also been included, particularly the substance of the third paragraph, some of which was communicated to him by Stuart C. Sherman, whose search for vital records on Potter located the entry in the 1824 *Providence Directory* (letter to Bezanson, August 15, 1969). Michael Lofaro also supplied helpful information about Trumbull's version of the life of Daniel Boone.

Potter or Henry Trumbull. Remarkably indeed, an account—all too brief—and an engraved portrait sketch of Israel Potter, the obscure old crier of "Old chairs to mend," were prepared in London by John Thomas Smith several years before Israel's return to his homeland in 1823 and the appearance of Trumbull's book in 1824. This account and portrait became known to Melville scholars only as the present volume was about to go to press.[2] They were published in 1839, after a long delay, in *The Cries of London: Exhibiting Several of the Itinerant Traders of Antient and Modern Times. Copied from Rare Engravings, or Drawn from the Life, by John Thomas Smith, Late Keeper of the Prints in the British Museum* (London: John Bowyer Nichols and Son, 1839). A note explains that "the present work was some years since prepared for the press by its late ingenious author, who engraved all the plates for it himself, thirteen of which are copied from early prints, and the rest sketched from the life. . . . The descriptions of the plates were also prepared by Mr. Smith . . . ." According to the biographical memoir, John Thomas Smith (1766–1833) was a student in the Royal Academy, a pupil of the engraver John Keyse Sherwin, a drawing-master, and from 1816 Keeper of Prints and Drawings in the British Museum; he compiled various works on antiquarian subjects. Fortunately, Israel Potter was among the "Itinerant Traders" whose portraits this trained artist "sketched from the life" then engraved himself. Unlike the two crude woodcuts in Trumbull's editions, Smith's fine portrait engraving, dated 1819 on its plate, brings us face to face with old Israel himself (see original size reproduction opposite). His account, so far as it goes, is gratifyingly specific and unsentimental about its humble subject:

> The Plate exhibits the figure of Israel Potter, one of the oldest menders of chairs now living, who resides in Compton's Buildings, Burton Crescent, and sallies forth by eight o'clock in the morning, not with a view of getting chairs to mend; for, from the matted mass of dirty rushes which have sometimes been thrown across his shoulders for months together, without ever being once opened, it must be concluded that his cry of "Old chairs to mend" avails him but little; the fact is, that like many other itinerants, he goes his rounds and procures broken meat and subsistence thus early in the morning for his daily wants.

2. Ian Jackson, of Berkeley, California, kindly called Richard Colles Johnson's attention to Smith's volume, with its portrait and account of Israel Potter; they were first reported, and the portrait was reproduced, in an article by Alma A. MacDougall in *Melville Society Extracts*, No. 47 (February, 1982).

Courtesy of Special Collections Department, Northwestern University Library.

This account shows that Smith had observed Israel Potter for some while, but since his interest was in Potter's street cry, not in Potter himself, he stops short in his report of the street crier's ways and goes into six paragraphs on the trade of chair-bottoming and the history of the cry. Alas for vital autobiographical details Israel may have poured out to him as he did later to Trumbull! Even so, Smith confirms Trumbull's book in a major way, although he makes Israel more of a scavenger than an active chair-mender. We may speculate that Melville, had he known of this book, would not only have seized upon and made much of the striking portrait of Israel and the side glimpse of his scavenging routine but might well have ironically dramatized the remarkable incident of the learned antiquarian Keeper of Prints sketching his portrait and finding his traditional London street cry more worthy of interest than his American tale of woe.

The next known record of Israel Potter, after Trumbull's book, is the 1824 *Providence Directory* (its first number), which lists both Potter and Trumbull, Israel R. Potter as an active chair-mender at 10 High Street, and Henry Trumbull as a printer at 26 and 34 High Street. The thirteen-line entry for Trumbull in *Printers and Printing in Providence: 1762–1907* (Providence: Typographical Union, 1907) reports his birth in Stonington, Connecticut, November 16, 1781, where "probably he learned printing . . . with a kinsman who conducted a printing office there when Mr. Trumbull was of an age to be apprenticed." It goes on to cite the 1824 *Providence Directory* entry, identifying High Street as "now Westminster street," and adds only that "between 1836 and 1838 he removed to Brooklyn, N.Y., where he died Aug. 14, 1842. He was buried in Stonington."[3]

Amusingly enough, the next entry we find for the historical Israel Potter uses Melville's book as an authority: the article on "Potter, Israel Ralph, patriot," in *Appletons' Cyclopædia of American Biography* (New York, 1888) is based wholly on the *Life,* with two exceptions, both drawn from *Israel Potter.* First, Potter, who in fact served in a Rhode Island regiment under Edmund Johnson (*Life,* p. 13), is said by the article to have served under Colonel John Patterson (i.e., in a Berkshire regiment)—a

3. There is an entry for Trumbull in *A Directory of Printing, Publishing, Bookselling & Allied Trades in Rhode Island to 1865* by H. Glenn Brown and Maude O. Brown (New York: The New York Public Library, 1958), p. 170; in addition to the 1824 *Providence Directory,* this entry cites the 1826, 1828, 1830, 1832, and 1836 directories, which list Trumbull's address as 25 High Street. The entry also notes that Trumbull's name appears in an incomplete manuscript list of imprints for 1829 in the Rhode Island Historical Society.

fiction from Melville's novel![4] Second, the article says (drawing on Melville's book dedication), "his memoirs . . . were sold by peddlers, and finally were entirely lost until a tattered copy fell into the hands of Herman Melville and was made the basis of his 'Israel Potter' . . . ."

Charles Edward Potter's *Genealogies of the Potter Families and Their Descendants in America* (Boston, 1888) cites the *Appletons'* piece almost in its entirety without correcting any of its errors; it does, however, add the detailed information (nowhere indicated in Israel's own account) that Israel was the "natural son of Captain Joseph Potter and a Miss Ralph" and that he was brought up from infancy by his paternal grandparents, John and Phebe Potter, Quaker preachers. Israel's father subsequently married Mary Low, served in the French War, and died at Crown Point, New York, before 1762. If this account of Israel's parentage and upbringing is right, his (or Trumbull's) possible reasons for not spelling out such details in the *Life* are understandable; and though misleading, his more general references there to his "parents" and particularly to his oppressive father may be true as far as they go.

Another entry, in the *National Cyclopædia of American Biography* (New York, 1892), refers to *Israel Potter* but avoids the error of drawing on any of its "facts"; it discusses Israel's upbringing by his grandparents but not his parentage. Finally, a biography of one of Israel's more illustrious relations, *Henry Codman Potter, Seventh Bishop of New York,* by George Hodges (New York: Macmillan, 1915), devotes two paragraphs, drawn mostly from the *Life* and the Potter genealogy, to this "wild young grandson, whose parents named him Israel; if they had foreseen his career they might have called him Esau."

4. There is a proof copy of this article in the Melville Collection of the Houghton Library of Harvard University, donated by Eleanor Melville Metcalf (*AC85M4977.2939e). On it in the hand of Elizabeth Shaw Melville, Herman Melville's wife, is the ink notation, "From Appleton's Cyclopedia of American Biography   Office 63 Bleecker st New York." In the last sentence of the article she revised "His memoirs published in Providence" by inking out "published" and writing "issued" below. Finally, she made an ink "X" after "Providence" and added, below, "X written by Henry Trumbull". Why the proof was sent to Melville does not appear, nor does the purpose or source (presumably Melville) of her changes. Perhaps Melville was consulted for the *Appletons'* article but did not point out the fictional element in it from his own book, or perhaps for some reason he was sent the proof but could or did not make the correction (Mrs. Melville's changes were never incorporated in the printed article). Least likely is the possibility that he wrote the article and received proof as its author.

In the twentieth century two complete editions of the *Life* have appeared. The first, with the imprint "New York, Reprinted William Abbatt 1911," was Extra No. 16 of *The Magazine of History with Notes and Queries*, Volume IV (1911); examination shows that its text is based on the third edition, and it includes a photofacsimile of the title page (with only vestiges of the erased price line). The other new edition, following the first edition text, was included in the paperback American Experience Series (New York: Corinth Books, 1962), with an introduction by Leonard Kriegel and an appendix that reproduces the 1855 title page, dedication, and last two chapters of *Israel Potter*. Also Richard Dorson, in *America Rebels: Narratives of the Patriots* (New York: Pantheon Books, 1953), prints editorially revised extracts from fourteen narratives including the *Life* (pp. 289–339).

It may be added that in a twentieth-century literary rewriting of Trumbull's *Life* of Potter, William Doreski renders it imaginatively into a long narrative poem, *The Testament of Israel Potter* (New York: Seven Woods Press, 1976). In this poem Israel at the age of 80, back in America, dictates his autobiography to Henry Trumbull, addressing it to his beloved dead English wife whom he imagines is with him—somewhat as Melville's "Bridegroom Dick" in *John Marr* reminisces to his old wife, though Doreski's Israel does so in a more frank and modern idiom. The poem is more faithful to the *Life* than to Melville's *Israel Potter* but takes from the latter some of Israel's conversations with King George and Benjamin Franklin.

A few facts about Trumbull's relation to Potter and about the little autobiographical book can be pieced together from the facts just reported and from an examination of multiple copies in The Newberry Library of the *Life* itself, which, incidentally, is even now by no means so rare a book as Melville's dedication (echoed by the *Appletons'* article) dramatically makes out. Sometime soon after Israel's return to Providence in 1823, he told his story to Trumbull, who saw a good commercial venture (as well as a chance to help Israel's claims), wrote it up in simple, straightforward fashion more or less as Israel "dictated" it, printed it as reproduced here, and on January 30, 1824, deposited the title for copyright, "the right whereof he claims as author" (see p. 288, following). He offered it for sale at "Price 28 Cents." Melville's dedication seems to be the only source for the report that it was distributed through peddlers, though that seems likely enough.

The copies examined show that the *Life* was brought out in three successive duodecimo editions in the same year, 1824—suggesting that the work sold better than had been anticipated (otherwise more would have been printed in the first place to avoid the cost of resetting). Whether it was Trumbull who brought out the second and third editions is not clear from their imprints. The second edition was reset nearly line-for-line from the first edition, correcting the two errata it had listed (p. 108) but omitting its preface "TO THE PUBLIC." Its price (given on the title page) was raised from twenty-eight to thirty-one cents. For some reason this second edition was not printed by Trumbull but, as its title page states, "Printed by J. HOWARD, for I. R. POTTER", also in Providence. Curiously, we find no entry for J. Howard in the *Providence Directory* for that year, or in any other source.

Another edition, presumably the third, identical with the second in its title-page details (such as printer and price) and in its omission of the preface, seems to have been set from the second edition with the exception of the first gathering (A) and the last two (H and I). The first (pp. 3–12) was not reset (apparently copies of this gathering were available in second-edition sheets); the last two (pp. 85–108) were set from the first edition, possibly indicating that near the end of the volume two compositors were simultaneously setting the type, one from a copy of the second edition and the other from a copy of the first. Although the second and third editions are not distinguishable by their title pages, there are many points of variation by which they may be identified, such as the placement of signature B on page 13 (under "to" in the second edition and under "quit" in the third) or the substitution of "Kew" in the third edition for "Quew" in the second on pages 43 and 45. The first edition frontispiece woodcut showed Israel walking to the right carrying a caneless chair and accompanied by a boy; both the second and third editions replaced this by a different woodcut showing Israel walking to the left carrying a bundle of rushes and accompanied by a boy and a girl. Examined copies of the three editions have bindings that are apparently original; they are all cheaply bound in marbled paper over boards with leather spines.[5]

Disappointingly, we have not yet been able to determine which of the three editions of the *Life* Melville owned and used. The copy of the first edition now in the Melville Collection of the Houghton Library of Harvard University (accession number 41-6047), donated in 1941 by Eleanor

5. An item in *Putnam's Monthly* (May, 1855) says, "The original . . . is not so rare as Mr. Melville seems to think. At any rate, we have a copy before us which is clearly printed and neatly bound, with a coarse wood-cut frontispiece, representing Israel as he trudged about London, with his two children, crying 'old chairs to mend.' " Since Israel has two children in the frontispiece, the copy referred to was from the second or third edition.

Melville Metcalf, his granddaughter, is evidently not the same one. Only its coming from her suggests that it may be; but such physical evidence as it offers does not support that inference. Strongly negative is the fact that the Harvard copy does not contain either Melville's signature or any other markings by him; it seems dubious indeed that without marking the book at all (contrary to his usual treatment of his source books) he could have used this copy either for his initial readings around 1849 (during which he was considering whether to "serve up the Revolutionary narrative of the beggar") or through the several months in 1854–55 when he was writing *Israel Potter* from it. The erased lines of writing scrawled in pencil on the verso of the frontispiece are certainly not in Melville's hand. Less to the point, perhaps, because Melville's literary descriptions of books are often more fancifully appropriate than bibliographically faithful, the Harvard copy does not resemble his description of his copy in the dedication as "tattered." The Harvard copy, except for its frontispiece, the top inch of which has been torn off and neatly replaced by other paper, and for a few minor repairs elsewhere, shows no sign that it can ever have been "tattered." (It had already been repaired, trimmed to 162 × 103 mm, and rebound with the spine title "REMARKABLE ADVENTURES ▪ POTTER", in the twentieth century, before Mrs. Metcalf presented it to the Houghton Library.[6]) A final and convincing piece of negative evidence is that its twentieth-century endpapers (added in the rebinding) bear two separate coded prices in pencil ("atf / 7^{00}"—or possibly "7^{50}"—on the front pastedown; and "5^{00} / wef" on the front free endpaper, verso); the obvious interpretation is that these are booksellers' prices, that after its rebinding it was on sale, perhaps twice, and, therefore, that it came to Eleanor Melville Metcalf not through family inheritance but through purchase, whether by herself or another person.

Although textual variants among the three editions do not, as might be hoped, reveal conclusively which edition Melville used, by his retention of wording or spelling that occurs in only one of them, an interesting variant

6. So Carolyn Jakeman, of the Houghton Library staff, informed Harrison Hayford, January 5, 1977, from her firsthand knowledge. In 1981, William H. Bond, librarian of the Houghton Library, confirmed her information to Hayford, and separately to Robert C. Ryan; he agreed that no evidence at hand indicates that it was Melville's own copy, and pointed out that the call number assigned it by the cataloguer in 1942 (*AC85M4977R824p) does not so classify it but (by the letter "R" rather than "ZZ") as a book Melville used as a source; what evidence guided the cataloguer is not known. The book is listed by Merton M. Sealts, Jr., in *Melville's Reading* (Madison: University of Wisconsin Press, 1966), No. 407, with no comment on this problem of provenience and without attributing its erased writing on the frontispiece verso to Melville.

does occur that points to the first edition. In the first line of page 31 of the first edition only, the type in the figure "9" in the phrase "upwards of 19 feet"—describing the breadth of the ditch Israel jumped—is imperfect, and the impression, unless carefully scrutinized, is unclear in all copies examined. This fact points to the most plausible explanation of Melville's stating the breadth as "ten feet" rather than "upwards of 19": that he was using a first-edition copy and misread its indistinct "19" as "10". In the second and third editions the breadth given at this point is "upwards of 12 feet"—a figure probably occasioned by the second-edition compositor's misreading of the indistinct "19" as "12" in the first-edition copy from which he was setting. It seems unlikely that Melville, using a copy of the second or third edition with the reading "12", would have reduced Israel's jump from "upwards of 12" to simply "ten" feet. (See the DISCUSSIONS OF ADOPTED READINGS at 21.8.)

On the other hand, two variants point, less strongly, rather to Melville's use of the second or third edition of the *Life*. In both of these editions in line nine of page 7 the spelling "poling" in the first edition becomes "polling"—a spelling which could more easily have induced the misreading "pulling" that occurs in Melville's *Israel Potter* at the corresponding point. (See the DISCUSSIONS OF ADOPTED READINGS at 8.24.) Also, in both the second and the third edition the reading "a month" replaces "one month" from the first edition (in the ninth line of page 20), and likewise in *Israel Potter* (15.5) the corresponding reading is also "a month". However, both the spelling difference and the difference in wording are too slight, even taken together, to justify identifying the edition Melville used on their evidence alone. Conservatively, in sum, we must say that Melville's edition remains uncertain. In any case, substantive variants among the three editions are slight, and the matter proves to be of no textual consequence for *Israel Potter*.[7]

The copy of the *Life* reproduced here in its original size is a first edition copy in The Newberry Library (Case E5P8522). Accompanying this reproduced text are marginal page and line numbers to indicate the corresponding passages of Melville's *Israel Potter* in the present Northwestern-Newberry edition.

7. There are only about a dozen substantive variants between the first and second editions, most of which—other than those already referred to, and "west"/"east" (p. 11.25)—are differences in number, tense, or preposition.

"OLD CHAIRS TO MEND"

ISRAEL R. POTTER

Born in Cranston, R.I. August 1st 1744.

LIFE

AND

REMARKABLE ADVENTURES

OF

ISRAEL R. POTTER,

(A NATIVE OF CRANSTON, RHODE-ISLAND.)

WHO WAS A SOLDIER IN THE

AMERICAN REVOLUTION,

And took a distinguished part in the Battle of Bunker
Hill (in which he received three wounds.) after
which he was taken Prisoner by the British, conveyed to England, where for 30 years he obtained a
livelihood for himself and family, by crying " *Old
Chairs to Mend*" through the Streets of London.—
In May last, by the assistance of the American Con
sul, he succeeded (in the 79th year of his age) in
obtaining a passage to his native country, after an
absence of 48 years.

PROVIDENCE:
Printed by HENRY TRUMBULL—1824.
(Price 28 Cents.)

DISTRICT of RHODE ISLAND, to wit:

BE it remembered, That on the thirtieth day of January one Thousand eight hundred and twenty four and in the forty eighth year of the Independence of the United States of America, HENRY TRUMBULL, of said District, deposited in this office the title of a book, the right whereof he claims as author, in the following words to wit:—" Life and Remarkable Adventures of Israel R Potter, a native of Cranston Rhode Island—who was a soldier in the American Revolution, and took a distinguished part in the battle of Bunker Hill (in which he received three wounds) after which he was taken Prisoner by the British, and conveyed to England where for thirty years he attained a livelihood for himself and family by crying " old Chairs to mend" through the Streets of London—In May last by the assistance of the American Consul he succeeded in (the 79th year of his age) in obtaining a passage to his native Country after an absence of 48 years."

In conformity to an Act of Congress entitled " An Act for the encouragement of learning, by securing the copies of maps, charts, and books to the authors and proprietors of such copies, during the time there in mentioned" and also to an act entitled "An Act for the encouragement of learning by securing the copies of maps, charts, and book, to the authors and proprietors of such copies during the time therein mentioned, and extending the benefit thereof to the Art of designing, engraving, and etching, historical, and other prints."

             Witness,—Benjamin Cowell,
                 Clerk of the Rhode Island District.

TO THE PUBLIC.

IN the foregoing pages we have attempted a simple narrative of the life and extraordinary adventures of one of the few survivors who fought and bled for American Independence. There is not probably another now living who took an equally active part in the Revolutionary war, whose life has been marked with more extraordinary events, and who has drank deeper of the cup of adversity, than the aged veteran with whose History we now beg liberty to present the American public. Doomed by the fate of War to be early seperated from kindred and friends, and to be conveyed by a foreign foe a prisoner of war from his native land, to a far distant country, where after having for 48 years experienced almost every hardship and deprivation of which adverse fortune is productive, providence appears at length to have so far interfered in his behalf, as to provide means whereby he has been enabled at an advanced age once more to visit and inhale the pure air of his native land. At the age of Seventy-Nine, an age in which it cannot be expected that the lamp of human life can long remain unextinguished, he has arrived among us, in a state of penury and want, to seek in common with his countrymen the enjoyment of a few of the blessings produced by Amer-

ican valour, in her memorable conflict with the
mother country, and in which he took a distinguished part.

As it yet remains doubtful whether (in consquence
of his long absence) he will be so fortunate as to be
included in that number to whom Government has
granted pensions for their Revolutionary services, it
is to obtain if possible a humble pittance as a remuneration, in part, for the unprecedented privations
and sufferings of which he has been the unfortunate
subject, that he is now induced to present the public with the following concise and simple narration
of the most extraordinary incidents of his life.

LIFE AND ADVENTURES

OF

ISRAEL R. POTTER,

———

I WAS born of reputable parents in the town of
Cranston, State of Rhode Island, August 1st, 1744.
—I continued with my parents there in the full enjoyment of parental affection and indulgence, until I arrived at the age of 18, when, having formed
an acquaintance with the daughter of a Mr. Richard
Gardner, a near neighbour, for whom (in the opinion of my friends) entertaining too great a degree
of partiality, I was repremanded and threatened by
them with more severe punishment, if my visits
were not discontinued. Disappointed in my intentions of forming an union (when of suitable age)
with one whom I really loved, I deemed the conduct of my parents in this respect unreasonable and

7.7

7.10

7.14

6   LIFE AND ADVENTURES

7.20
oppressive, and formed the determination to leave
them, for the purpose of seeking another home and
other friends.

8.1
It was on Sunday, while the family were at meeting, that I packed up as many articles of my cloathing as could be contained in a pocket handkerchief,
which, with a small quantity of provision, I conveyed to and secreted in a piece of woods in the rear
of my father's house ; I then returned and continued in the house until about 9 in the evening, when
8.4
with the pretence of retiring to bed, I passed into
a back room and from thence out of a back door and
hastened to the spot where I had deposited my
cloathes, &c.—it was a warm summer's night, and
8.6
that I might be enabled to travel with the more fa-
cility the succeeding day, I lay down at the foot of a
tree and reposed myself until about 4 in the morning
when I arose and commenced my journey, travelling
westward, with an intention of reaching if possible
the new countries, which I had heard highly spoken
8.14
of as affording excellent prospects for industrious
and enterprizing young men—to evade the pursuit
of my friends, by whom I knew I should be early
missed and diligently sought for, I confined my trav-
8.17
el to the woods and shunned the public roads, until
I had reached the distance of about 12 miles from
my father's house.
At noon the succeeding day I reached Hartford,
8.20
in Connecticut, and applied to a farmer in that town
for work, and for whom I agreed to labour for one

month for the sum of six dollars Having completed my month's work to the satisfaction of my employer. I received my money and started from Hartford for Otter Creek ; but, when I reached Springfield, i met with a man bound to the Cahos country, and who offered me four dollars to accompany him, of which offer I accepted, and the next morning we left Springfield and in a canoe ascended Connecticut river, and in about two weeks after much hard labor in paddling and poling the boat against the current, we reached Lebanon, (N. H.) the place of our destination. It was with some difficulty and not until I had procured a writ, by the assistance of a respectable innkeeper in Lebanon, by the name of Hill, that I obtained from my last employer the four dollars which he had agreed to pay me for my services.

From Lebanon I crossed the river to New-Hartford (then N. Y.) where I bargained with a Mr. Brink of that town for 200 acres of new land, lying in New Hampshire, and for which I was to labour for him four months. As this may appear to some a small consideration for so great a number of acres of land, it may be well here to acquaint the reader with the situation of the country in that quarter, at that early period of its settlement —which was an almost impenetrable wilderness, containing but few civilized inhabitants, far distantly situated from each other and from any considerable settlement ; and whose temporary habitations with a few exceptions were constructed of logs in their natural state —the

8.20

8.23

8.24

8.25

8.28
8.29

8.28

woods abounded with wild beasts of almost every
description peculiar to this country, nor were the
few inhabitants at that time free from serious apprehension of being at some unguarded moment sud-

8.30

denly attacked and destroyed, or conveyed into captivity by the savages, who from the commencement
of the French war, had improved every favourable
opportunity to cut off the defenceless inhabitants of

8.32

the frontier towns.

After the expiration of my four months labour the
person who had promised me a deed of 200 acres
of land therefor, having refused to fulfill his engagements I was obliged to engage with a party of his Ma-

8.39

jesty's Surveyors at fifteen shillings per month, as an
assistant chain bearer, to survey the wild unsettled
lands bordering on the Connecticut river, to its
source. It was in the winter season, and the snow
so deep that it was impossible to travel without
snow shoes—at the close of each day we enkind-

9.6

led a fire, cooked our victuals and erected with the
branches of hemlock a temporary hut, which served us for a shelter for the night. The Surveyors
having completed their business returned to Lebanon, after an absence of about two months. Receiv-

9.7

ing my wages I purchased a fowling-piece and ma-
munition therewith, and for the four succeeding
months devoted my time in hunting Deer, Beavers,

9.8

&c. in which I was very successful, as in the four
months I obtained as many skins of these animals
as produced me forty dollars—with my money I pur-

chased of a Mr. John Marsh, 100 acres of new land, lying on Water Quechy River, (so called) about five miles from Hartford, (N Y.) on this land I went immediately to work, erected a small log hut thereon, and in two summers without any assistance, cleared up thirty acres fit for sowing—in the winter seasons I employed my time in hunting and entraping such animals whose hides and furs were esteemed of the most value. I remained in possession of my land two years, and then disposed of it to the same person of whom I purchased it, at the advanced price of 200 dollars, and then conveyed my skins and furs which I had collected the two preceding winters, to NO. 4, (now Charlestown,) where I exchanged them for Indian blankets, wampeag, and such other articles as I could conveniently convey on a hand sled, and with which I started for Canada, to barter with the Indians for furs.— This proved a very profitable trip, as I very soon disposed of every article at an advance of more than two hundred per cent, and received payment in furs at a reduced price, and for which I received in NO. 4. 200 dollars, cash. With this money, together with what I was before in possession of, I now set out for home, once more to visit my parents after an absence of two years and nine months, in which time my friends had not been enabled to receive any correct information of me. On my arrival, so greatly effected were my parents at the presence of a son whom they had considered dead, that

1*

9.13

9.15

9.16

9.20

9.30

9.33

9.36

it was sometime before either could become sufficiently composed to listen to or to request me to
furnish them with an account of my travels.

Soon after my return, as some atonement for the
anxiety which I had caused my parents, I presented
them with most of the money that I had earned in
my absence, and formed the determination that I
would remain with them contented at home, in consequence of a conclusion from the welcome reception that I met with, that they had repented of their
opposition, and had become reconciled to my intended union— but, in this, I soon found that I was
mistaken ; for, although overjoyed to see me alive,
whom they had supposed really dead, no sooner did
they find that my long absence had rather increased
than diminished my attachment for their neighbor's
daughter, than their resentment and opposition appeared to increase in proportion—in consequence of
which I formed the determination again to quit them,
and try my fortune at sea, as I had now arrived at
an age in which I had an unquestionable right to
think and act for myself.

After remaining at home one month, I applied for
and procured a birth at Providence, on board the
Sloop —— Capt. Fuller, bound to Grenada—having completed her loading (which consisted of stone
lime, hoops, staves, &c.) we set sail with a favorable wind, and nothing worthy of note occurred until
the 15th day from that on which we left Providence,
when the sloop was discovered to be on fire, by a

9.38

10.1

10.5

10.11

10.12

smoke issuing from her hold—the hatches were immediately raised, but as it was discovered that the
fire was caused by water communicating with the   10.13
lime, it was deemed useless to make any attempts
to extinguish it—orders were immediately there-
upon given by the captain to hoist out the long   10.14
boat, which was found in such a leaky condition as
to require constant bailing to keep her afloat : we
had only time to put on board a small quantity of
bread, a firkin of butter and a ten gallon keg of wa-   10.16
ter, when we embarked, eight in number, to trust
ourselves to the mercy of the waves, in a leaky   10.17
boat and many leagues from land. As our provi-
sion was but small in quantity, and it being uncertain how long we might remain in our perilous situation, it was proposed by the captain soon after
leaving the sloop, that we should put ourselves on
an allowance of one buiscuit and half a pint of water
per day, for each man, which was readily agreed
to by all on board—in ten minutes after leaving the
sloop she was in a complete blaze, and presented an
awful spectacle. With a piece of the flying-jib,   10.19
which had been fortunately thrown into the boat, we
made shift to erect a sail, and proceeded in a south
west direction in hopes to reach the spanish maine,
if not so fortunate as to fall in with some vessel in
our course—which, by the interposition of kind prov-   10.22
idence in our favour, actually took place the second
day after leaving the sloop—we were discovered
and picked up by a Dutch ship bound from Eusta-   10.23

12   LIFE AND ADVENTURES

10.24

tia to Holland, and from the captain and crew met
with a humane reception, and were supplied with
every necessary that the ship afforded—we continued on board one week when we fell in with an A-
merican sloop bound from Piscataqua to Antigua,
which received us all on board and conveyed us in
safety to the port of her destination. At Antigua I
got a birth on board an American brig bound to Porto
Rico, and from thence to Eustatia. At Eustatia I
received my discharge and entered on board a Ship
belonging to Nantucket, and bound on a whaling
voyage, which proved an uncommonly short and
successful one— we returned to Nantucket full of
oil after an absence of the ship from that port of
only 16 months. After my discharge I continued
about one month on the island, and then took passage for Providence, and from thence went to Cranston, once more to visit my friends, with whom I
continued three weeks, and then returned to Nantucket. From Nantucket I made another whaling
voyage to the South Seas, and after an absence of
three years, (in which time I experienced almost
all the hardships and deprivations peculiar to Whale-
men in long voyages) I succeeded by the blessings
of providence in reaching once more my native
home, perfectly sick of the sea, and willing to return to the bush and exchange a mariner's life for
one less hazardous and fatiguing.

I remained with my friends at Cranston a few
weeks, and then hired myself to a Mr. James Wa-

10.29

10.31

10.34

10.35

11.5
11.6

terman, of Coventry, for 12 months, to work at
farming. This was in the year 1774, and I continued with him about six months, when the difficulties which had for some time prevailed between the
Americans and Britons, had now arrived at that
crisis, as to render it certain that hostilities would
soon commence in good earnest between the two nations; in consequence of which, the Americans at
this period began to prepare themselves for the e-
vent—companies were formed in several of the
towns in New-England, who received the appellation of "minute men," and who were to hold themselves in readiness to obey the first summons of
their officers, to march at a moment's notice;—a
company of this kind was formed in Coventry, into
which I enlisted, and to the command of which
Edmund Johnson, of said Coventry, was appointed.

It was on a Sabbath morning that news was received of the destruction of the provincial stores at
Concord, and of the massacre of our countrymen
at Lexington, by a detached party of the British
troops from Boston: and I immediately thereupon received a summons from the captain, to be prepared
to march with the company early the morning ensuing—and, although I felt not less willing to obey
the call of my country at a minute's notice, and to
face her foes, than did the gallant Putnam, yet, the
nature of the summons did not render it necessary
for me, like him, to quit my plough in the field; as

2

12.15
12.16
12.17
12.19
12.23
12.23
13.4
13.3

14   LIFE AND ADVENTURES

having the day previous commenced the ploughing
of a field of ten or twelve acres, that I might not leave
my work half done, I improved the sabbath to complete it.

By the break of day Monday morning I swung
my knapsack, shouldered my musket, and with the
company commenced my march with a quick step
for Charlestown, where we arrived about sunset, and
remained encamped in the vicinity until about noon
of the 16th June; when, having been previously
joined by the remainder of the regiment from Rhode
Island, to which our company was attached, we
received orders to proceed and join a detachment
of about 1000 American troops, which had that
morning taken possession of Bunker-Hill, and which
we had orders immediately to fortify, in the best
manner that circumstances would admit of. We
laboured all night without cessation and with very
little refreshment, and by the dawn of day succeeded in throwing up a redoubt of eight or nine rods
square. As soon as our works were discovered by
the British in the morning, they commenced a heavy
fire upon us, which was supported by a fort on
Copp's hill; we however (under the command of
the intrepid Putnam) continued to labour like be-
vers until our breast-work was completed.

About noon, a number of the enemy's boats and
barges, filled with troops, landed at Charlestown,
and commenced a deliberate march to attack us—
we were now harangued by Gen. Putnam, who re-

minded us, that exhausted as we were, by our incessant labour through the preceding night, the most
important part of our duty was yet to be performed,
and that much would be expected from so great a
number of excellent marksmen—he charged us to
be cool, and to reserve our fire until the enemy approached so near as to enable us to see the white of
their eyes—when within about ten rods of our works
we gave them the contents of our muskets, and
which were aimed with so good effect, as soon to
cause them to turn their backs and to retreat with a
much quicker step than with what they approached us. We were now again harangued by " old
General Put," as he was termed, and requested by
him to aim at the officers, should the enemy renew
the attack—which they did in a few moments, with
a reinforcement—their approach was with a slow
step, which gave us an excellent opportunity to
obey the commands of our General in bringing
down their officers. I feel but little disposed to
boast of my own performances on this occasion,
and will only say, that after devoting so many
months in hunting the wild animals of the wilderness, while an inhabitant of New Hampshire, the
reader will not suppose me a bad or unexperien-
ced marksman, and that such were the fare shots
which the epuletted red coats presented in the two
attacks, that every shot which they received from
me, I am confident on another occasion would have
produced me a deer skin.

13.17

13.20

13.23

13.25

13.26

13.28

16   LIFE AND ADVENTURES

So warm was the reception that the enemy met
with in their second attack, that they again found it
necessary to retreat, but soon after receiving a fresh
reinforcement, a third assault was made, in which,
in consequence of our ammunition failing, they too
well succeeded—a close and bloody engagement
now ensued—to fight our way through a very considerable body of the enemy, with clubbed muskets
(for there were not one in twenty of us provided with
bayonets) were now the only means left us to escape;—the conflict, which was a sharp and severe
one, is still fresh in my memory, and cannot be forgotten by me while the scars of the wounds which I
then received, remain to remind me of it!—fortunately for me, at this critical moment, I was armed
with a cutlass, which although without an edge, and
much rust-eaten, I found of infinite more service to
me than my musket—in one instance I am certain it
was the means of saving my life—a blow with a cutlass was aimed at my head by a British officer, which
I parried and received only a slight cut with the
point on my right arm near the elbow, which I was
then unconscious of, but this slight wound cost my
antagonist at the moment a much more serious one,
which effectually dis-*armed* him, for with one well
directed stroke I deprived him of the power of very
soon again measuring swords with a " yankee rebel !"
We finally however should have been mostly cut off,
and compelled to yield to a superiour and better e-
quipped force, had not a body of three or four hun'

13.29
13.29
13.31
13.35
14.2
13.39

dred Connecticut men formed a temporary breast
work, with rails &c and by which means held the
enemy at bay until our main body had time to ascend the heights, and retreat across the neck;—in
this retreat I was less fortunate than many of my
comrads—I received two musket ball wounds, one
in my hip and the other near the ancle of my left leg
—I succeeded however without any assistance in
reaching Prospect Hill, where the main body of the
Americans had made a stand and commenced fortifying—from thence I was soon after conveyed to the
Hospital in Cambridge, where my wounds were
dressed and the bullet extracted from my hip by one
of the Surgeons; the house was nearly filled with
the poor fellows who like myself had received wounds
in the late engagement, and presented a melancholly
spectacle.

Bunker-Hill fight proved a sore thing for the British, and will I doubt not be long remembered by
them; while in London I heard it frequently spoken
of by many who had taken an active part therein,
some of whom were pensioners, and bore indelible
proofs of American bravery—by them the Yankees
by whom they were opposed, were not unfrequently
represented as a set of infuriated beings, whom nothing could daunt or intimidate: and who, after their
ammunition failed, disputed the ground, inch by inch,
for a full hour with clubbed muskets, rusty swords,
pitchforks and billets of wood, against the British
bayonets.

2*

14.6

14.9

14.10

13.32

18   LIFE AND ADVENTURES

14.11

I suffered much pain from the wound which I received in my ancle, the bone was badly fractured and
several pieces were extracted by the surgeon, and it
was six weeks before I was sufficiently recovered to
be able to join my regiment quartered on Prospect-

14.14

Hill, where they had thrown up entrenchments within the distance of little more than a mile of the enc-
my's camp, which was full in view, they having en-

14.15

trenched themselves on Bunker hill after the engagement.

14.17

On the 3d July, to the great satisfaction of the A-
mericans, General WASHINGTON arrived from the
south to take command—I was then confined in the
Hospital, but as far as my observations could extend,

14.18

he met with a joyful reception, and his arrival was
welcomed by every one throughout the camp—the
troops had been long waiting with impatience for his
arrival as being nearly destitute of ammunition, and
the British receiving reinforcements daily, their prospects began to wear a gloomy aspect.

14.19

The British quartered in Boston began soon to suffer much from the scarcity of provisions, and General Washington took every precaution to prevent their
gaining a supply—from the country all supplies
could be easily cut off, and to prevent their receiving
any from Tories, and other disaffected persons by

14.22

water, the General found it necessary to equip two
or three armed vessels to intercept them---among
these was the brigantine Washington of 10 guns,

14.24

commanded by capt. Martindale,—as seamen at this

time could not easily be obtained, as most of them
had enlisted in the land service, permission was giv-
en to any of the soldiers who should be pleased to accept of the offer, to man these vessels—consequently
myself with several others of the same regiment went
on board of the Washington, then lying at Plymouth,
and in complete order for a cruize.

14.25

14.26

We set sail about the 8th December, but had been
out but three days when we were captured by the
enemy's ship Foy, of 20 guns, who took us all out and
put a prize crew on board the Washington—the Foy
proceeded with us immediately to Boston bay where
we was put on board the British frigate Tartar and
orders given to convey us to England.—When two
or three days out I projected a scheme (with the assistance of my fellow prisoners, 72 in number) to take
the ship, in which we should undoubtedly have succeeded, as we had a number of resolute fellows on
board, had it not been for the treachery of a renegado
Englishman, who betrayed us—as I was pointed out
by this fellow as the principal in the plot, I was ordered in irons by the Officers of the Tartar, and in
which situation I remained until the arrival of the
ship at Portsmouth (Eng) when I was brought on
deck and closely examined, but protesting my innocence, and what was very fortunate for me in the
course of the examination, the person by whom I had
been betrayed, having been proved a British deserter,
his story was discredited and I was relieved of my i-
rons.

14.30

14.33

14.34

14.36

14.39

20   LIFE AND ADVENTURES

The prisoners were now all thoroughly cleansed
and conveyed to the marine hospital on shore, where
many of us took the small-pox the natural way, by
some whom we found in the hospital effected with
that disease, and which proved fatal to nearly one
half our number. From the hospital those of us who
survived were conveyed to Spithead, and put on
board a Guard Ship, and where I had been confined
with my fellow prisoners about one month, when I
was ordered into the boat, to assist the bargemen (in
consequence of the absence of one of their gang) in
rowing the lieutenant on shore. As soon as we
reached the shore and the officer landed, it was proposed by some of the boat's crew to resort for a few
moments to an ale-house, in the vicinity, to treat
themselves to a few pots of beer; which being agreed
to by all, I thought this a favourable opportunity and
the only one that might present, to escape from my
Floating Prison, and felt determined not to let it pass
unimproved; accordingly, as the boat's crew were a-
bout to enter the house, I expressed a necessity of my
seperating from them a few moments, to which they
(not suspecting any design,) readily assented. As
soon as I saw them all snugly in and the door closed, I gave speed to my legs, and ran, as I then concluded, about four miles without once halting— I
steered my course toward London as when there
by mingling with the crowd, I thought it probable
that I should be least suspected.

When I had reached the distance of about ten

15.1

15.3

15.7

15.11

15.13

15.16

15.20

miles from where I quit the bargemen and beginning to think myself in little danger of apprehension, should any of them be sent by the lieutenant in
pursuit of me, as I was leisurely passing a public
house, I was noticed and hailed by a naval officer at
the door with "ahoi, what ship ?"---"no ship," was
my reply, on which he ordered me to stop, but on
which I took no other notice than to observe to him
that if he would attend to his own business I would
proceed quietly about mine---this rather increasing
than diminishing his suspicions that I was a deserter, garbed as I was, he gave chase---finding myself closely persued and unwilling again to be made
a prisoner of, if it was possible to escape, I had
once more to trust to my legs, and should have a-
gain succeeded had not the officer, on finding himself likely to be distanced, set up a cry of "stop-
thief !" this brought numbers out of their houses
and work shops, who, joining in the pursuit, succeeded after a chace of nearly a mile in overhaul-
ing me.

Finding myself once more in their power and a
perfect stranger to the country, I deemed it vain to
attempt to deceive them with a lie, and therefore
made a voluntary confession to the officer that I was
a prisoner of war, and related to him in what manner I had that morning made my escape. By the
officer I was conveyed back to the Inn, and left in
custody of two soldiers—the former (previous to retiring) observing to the landlord that believing me

15.22

15.23

15.26

15.27

15.30

15.31

15.33

32   LIFE AND ADVENTURES

15.34   to be a true blooded yankee, requested him to supply me at his expence with as much liquor as I
should call for.

The house was thronged early in the evening by
many of the " good and faithful subjects of King
George," who had assembled to take a peep at the
15.37   " yankee rebel," (as they termed me) who had so
recently taken an active part in the rebellious war,
then raging in his Majesty's American provinces—
while others came apparently to gratify a curiosity
in viewing, for the first time, an " American Yan-
15.38   kee!" whom they had been taught to believe a kind
of non descripts—beings of much less refinement
than the ancient Britains, and possessing little more
humanity than the Buccaniers.

As for myself I thought it best not to be reserved,
but to reply readily to all their inquiries; for while
16.5   my mind was wholly employed in devising a plan to
16.3   escape from the custody of my keepers, so far from
manifesting a disposition to resent any of the insults
offered me, or my country, to prevent any suspicions
of my designs, I feigned myself not a little pleased
with their observations, and in no way dissatisfied
with my situation. As the officer had left orders
16.8   with the landlord to supply me with as much liquor
as I should be pleased to call for, I felt determined
16.10   to make my keepers merry at his expence, if possible, as the best means that I could adopt to effect
my escape.

The loyal group having attempted in vain to irri-

tate me by their mean and ungenerous reflections,
by one (who observed that he had frequently heard
it mentioned that the yankees were extraordinary
dancers,) it was proposed that I should entertain
the company with a jig! to which I expressed a
willingness to assent with much feigned satisfaction,
if a fiddler could be procured—fortunately for them,
there was one residing in the neighborhood, who
was soon introduced, when I was obliged (although
much against my own inclination) to take the floor
—with the full determination, however that if John
Bull was to be thus diverted at the expence of an
unfortunate prisoner of war, uncle Jonathan should
come in for his part of the sport before morning,
by showing them a few *Yankee steps* which they then
little dreamed of.

By my performances they were soon satisfied
that in this kind of exercise, I should suffer but
little in competition with the most nimble footed
Britain among them : nor would they release me
until I had danced myself into a state of perfect
perspiration ; which, however, so far from being any
disadvantage to me, I considered all in favour of
my projected plan to escape—for while I was pleased to see the flowing bowl passing merrily about,
and not unfrequently brought in contact with the
lips of my two keepers, the state of perspiration
that I was in, prevented its producing on me any
intoxicating effects.

The evening having become now far spent and

16.12

16.11

16.13

16.16

16.18

16.21

16.22

24   LIFE AND ADVENTURES

16.23   the company mostly retiring, my keepers (who,
to use a sailor's phrase I was happy to discover
" half seas over") having much to my dissatisfaction
furnished me with a pair of handcuffs, spread a blank-
16.24   et by the side of their bed on which I was to repose for the night. I feigned myself very grateful to them for having humanely furnished me with
so comfortable a bed, and on which I stretched myself with much apparent unconcern, and remained
16.26   quiet about one hour, when I was sure that the
family had all retired to bed. The important moment had now arrived in which I was resolved to
carry my premeditated plan into execution, or die
in the attempt—for certain I was that if I let this
16.29   opportunity pass unimproved, I might have cause
to regret it when it was too late---that I should
most assuredly be conveyed early in the morning
back to the floating prison from which I had so recently escaped, and where I might possibly remain confined until America should obtain her in-
16.32   dependence, or the differences between Great-Britain
and her American provinces were adjusted. Yet
should I in my attempt to escape meet with more
opposition from my keepers, than what I had calculated from their apparent state of inebriaty, the
contest I well knew would be very unequal---they
16.36   were two full grown stout men, with whom (if
they were assisted by no others) I should have to
16.37   contend, handcuffed! but, after mature delibera-
tion, I resolved that however hazardous the attempt,
it should be made, and that immediately.

After remaining quiet, as I before observed, until
I thought it probable that all had retired to bed in
the house, I intimated to my keepers that I was un-
der the necessity of requesting permission to retire   17.12
for a few moments to the back yard ; when both instantly arose and reeling toward me seized each an
arm, and proceeded to conduct me through a long
and narrow entry to the back door, which was no   17.20
sooner unbolted and opened by one of them, than I
tripped up the heels of both and laid them sprawling,   17.22
and in a moment was at the garden wall seeking a
passage whereby I might gain the public road—a
new and unexpected obstacle now presented, for I
found the whole garden enclosed with a smooth brick-
en wall, of the heighth of twelve feet at least, and   17.26
was prevented by the darkness of the night from
discovering an avenue leading therefrom—in this
predicament, my only alternative was either to scale
this wall handcuffed as I was, and without a moment's   17.27
hesitation, or to suffer myself to be made a captive
again by my keepers, who had already recovered
their feet and were bellowing like bullocks for assistance—had it not been a very dark night, I must certainly have been discovered and re-taken by them ;—
fortunately before they had succeeded in rallying the
family, in groping about I met with a fruit tree sit-   17.26
uated within ten or twelve feet of the wall, which I
ascended as expeditiously as possible, and by an extraordinary leap from the branches reached the top
of the wall, and was in an instant on the opposit side.   17.28
3

26   LIFE AND ADVENTURES

17.32

The coast being now clear, I ran to the distance of
two or three miles, with as much speed as my situation would admit of;—my next object now was to rid
myself of my handcuffs, which fortunately proving

17.33

none of the stoutest, I succeeded in doing after much
painful labour.

It was now as I judged about 12 o'clock, and I had
succeeded in reaching a considerable distance from
the Inn from which I had made my escape, without

17.32

hearing or seeing any thing of my keepers, whom I

17.31

had left staggering about in the garden in search of
their "Yankee captive!"—it was indeed to their in-
toxicated state, and the extreme darkness of the night;
that I imputed my success in evading their pursuit.

17.35

—I saw no one until about the break of day, when I

19.10

met an old man, tottering beneath the weight of his

19.11

pick-ax, hoe and shovel, clad in tattered garments,

19.12

and otherwise the picture of poverty and distress ; he
had just left his humble dwelling, and was proceeding thus early to his daily labour ;—and as I was now

19.8

satisfied that it would be very difficult for me to

19.6

travel in the day time garbed as I was, in a sailor's
habit, without exciting the suspicions of his Royal
Majesty's pimps, who (I had been informed) were

19.13

constantly on the look-out for deserters, I applyed to
the old man, miserable as he appeared, for a change

19.14

of cloathing, offering those which I then wore for a
suit of inferior quality and less value—this I was induced to do at that moment, as I thought that the
proposal could be made with perfect safety, for what-

ever might have been his suspicions as to my motives in wishing to exchange my dress, I doubted not,
that with an object of so much apparent distress, self-
interest would prevent his communicating them.——
The old man however appeared a little surprised at
my offer, and after a short examination of my pea-
jacket, trowsers, &c. expressed a doubt whether I
would be willing to exchange them for his " Church
suit," which he represented as something worse for
wear, and not worth half so much as those I then
wore—taking courage however from my assurances
that a change of dress was my only object, he deposited his tools by the side of a hedge, and invited
me to accompany him to his house, which we soon
reached and entered, when a scene of poverty and
wretchedness presented, which exceeded every thing
of the kind that I had ever before witnessed—the
internal appearance of the miserable hovel, I am
confident would suffer in a comparison with any of
the meanest stables of our American farmers—there
was but one room, in one corner of which was a bed
of straw covered with a coarse sheet, and on which
reposed his wife and five small children. I had
heard much of the impoverished and distressed situation of the poor in England, but the present presented an instance of which I had formed no conception—little indeed did I then think that it would be
my lot, before I should meet with an opportunity to
return to my native country, to be placed in an infinitely worse situation ! but, alas, such was my hard
fortune !

19.16

19.16

28   LIFE AND ADVENTURES

The first garment presented by the poor old man, of his best, or "church suit," as he termed it, was a coat of very coarse cloth, and containing a number of patches of almost every colour but that of the cloth of which it was originally made—the next was a waistcoat and a pair of small cloathes, which appeared each to have received a bountiful supply of patches to correspond with the coat—the coat I put on without much difficulty, but the two other garments proved much too small for me, and when I had succeeded with considerable difficulty in putting them on, they set so taught as to cause me some apprehension that they might even stop the circulation of blood!—my next exchange was my buff cap for an old rusty large brimmed hat.

The old man appeared very much pleased with his bargain, and represented to his wife that he could now accompany her to church much more decently clad—he immediately tried on the pea-jacket and trowsers, and seemed to give himself very little concern about their size, although I am confident that one leg of the trowsers was sufficiently large to admit his whole body—but, however ludicrous his appearance, in his new suit, I am confident that it could not have been more so than mine, garbed as I was, like an old man of seventy!—From my old friend I learned the course that I must steer to reach London, the towns and villages that I should have to pass through, and the distance thereto, which was between 70 and 80 miles. He likewise represented to me that the

19.27

19.23

19.21
19.20

19.31,34

19.35

country was filled with soldiers, who were on the
constant look-out for deserters from the navy and army, for the apprehension of which they received a
stipulated reward.

After enjoining it on the old man not to give any
information of me, should he meet on the road any
one who should enquire for such a person, I took my
leave of him, and again set out with a determination
to reach London, thus disguised, if possible;—I travelled about 30 miles that day, and at night entered
a barn in hopes to find some straw or hay on which
to repose for the night, for I had not money sufficient
to pay for a night's lodging at a public house, had I
thought it prudent to apply for one—in my expectation to find either hay or straw in the barn I was sadly disappointed, for I soon found that it contained not
a lock of either, and after groping about in the dark
in search of something that might serve for a substitute, I found nothing better than an undressed sheep-
skin—with no other bed on which to repose my wearied limbs I spent a sleepless night; cold, hungry and
weary, and impatient for the arrival of the morning's
dawn, that I might be enabled to pursue my journey.

By break of day I again set out and soon found myself within the suburbs of a considerable village, in
passing which I was fearful there would be some risk
of detection, but to guard myself as much as possible
against suspicion, I furnished myself with a crutch,
and feigning myself a cripple, hobled through the
town without meeting with any interruption. In two

3*

19.36

19.38
19.40

20.4

20.5

20.7

20.10

20.12

80   LIFE AND ADVENTURES

20.17
20.32
20.34
20.40

20.35

20.37

hours after, I arrived in the vicinity of another still
more considerable village, but fortunately for me, at
the moment, I was overtaken by an empty baggage
waggon, bound to London—again feigning myself
very lame, I begged of the driver to grant a poor
cripple the indulgence to ride a few miles, to which
he assenting, I concealed myself by lying prostrate on
the bottom of the waggon, until we had passed quite
through the village ; when, finding the waggoner disposed to drive much slower than what I wished to
travel, after thanking him for the kind disposition
which he had manifested to oblige me, I quite the
waggon, threw away my crutch and travelled with a
speed, calculated to surprise the driver with so sudden a recovery of the use of my legs—the reader will
perceive that I had now become almost an adept at
deception, which I would not however have so frequently practiced, had not self preservation demanded it.

21.3

21.4

21.4

    As I thought there would be in my journey to
London, infinitely more danger of detection in passing through large towns or villages, than in con-
fining myself to the country, I avoided them as
much as possible ; and as I found myself once more
on the borders of one, apparently of much larger
size than any that I had yet passed, I thought it
most expedient to take a circuitous route to avoid
it; in attempting which, I met with an almost insurmountable obstacle, that I little dreamed of—
when nearly abreast of the town, I found my route

obstructed by a ditch, of upwards of 19 feet in
breadth, and of what depth I could not determine;
as there was now no other alternative left me, but
to leap this ditch, or to retrace my steps and pass
through the town, after a moment's reflection I determined to attempt the former, although it would
be attempting a fete of activity, that I supposed myself incapable of performing ; yet, however incredible it may appear, I assure my readers that I did
effect it, and reached the opposite side with dry
feet !

I had now arrived within about 16 miles of London, when night approaching, I again sought lodgings in a barn ; which containing a small quantity
of hay, I succeeded in obtaining a tolerable comfortable night's rest. By the dawn of day I arose
somewhat refreshed, and reasumed my journey
with the pleasing prospect of reaching London before night—but, while encouraged and cheered by
these pleasing anticipations, an unexpected occurrence blasted my fair prospects—I had succeeded
in reaching in safety a distance so great from the
place where I had been last held a prisoner, and
within so short a distance of London, the place of
my destination that I began to think myself so far
out of danger, as to cause me to relax in a measure, in the precautionary means which I had made
use of to avoid detection ;—as I was passing through
the town of Staines, (within a few miles of London)
about 11 o'clock in the forenoon, I was met by

21.7
21.8

22.4

22.7

22.8

22.9

22.10

22.11

22.11
22.17
22.15

22.13
22.21

three or four British soldiers, whose notice I attracted, and who unfortunately for me, discovered
by the collar (which I had not taken the precaution
to conceal) that I wore a shirt which exactly cor-
responded with those uniformly worn by his Majesty's seamen—not being able to give a satisfactory
account of myself, I was made a prisoner of, on
suspicion of being a deserter from his Majesty's
service, and was immediately committed to the

22.23

the Round House ; a prison so called, appropriated
to the confinement of runaways, and those convicted of small offences—I was committed in the evening, and to secure me the more effectually, I was

23.2

handcuffed, and left supperless by my unfeeling jail-
or, to pass the night in wretchedness.

I had now been three days without food (with
the exception of a single two-penny loaf) and felt
myself unable much longer to resist the cravings
of nature—my spirits, which until now had armed

23.5

me with fortitude began to forsake me—indeed I
was at this moment on the eve of despair ! when,
calling to mind, that grief would only aggravate
my calamity, I endeavoured to arm my soul with

23.8

patience ; and habituate myself as well as I could,
to woe.—Accordingly I roused my spirits ; and ban-
ishing for a few moments, these gloomy ideas, I
began to reflect seriously on the methods how to

23.10

extricate myself from this labyrinth of horror.

My first object was to rid myself of my hand-

23.11

cuffs, which I succeeded in doing after two hours

hard labour, by sawing them across the grating of
the window; having my hands now at liberty, the
next thing to be done was to force the door of my
apartment, which was secured on the outside by a
hasp and padlock ; I devised many schemes but for
the want of tools to work with, was unable to carry
them into execution---I however at length succeeded, with the assistance of no other instrument than
the bolt of my handcuffs ; with which, thirsting my
arm through a small window or aperture in the
door, I forced the padlock, and as there was now
no other barrier to prevent my escape, after an
imprisonment of about five hours, I was once more
at large.

It was now as I judged about midnight, and although enfeebled and tormented with excessive
hunger and fatigue, I set out with the determination of reaching London, if possible, early the ensuing morning. By break of day I reached and passed through Brintford, a town of considerable note
and within six miles of the Capital---but so great
was my hunger at this moment, that I was under
serious apprehension of falling a victim to absolute
starvation, if not so fortunate soon to obtain something to appease it. I recollected of having read in
my youth, accounts of the dreadful effects of hunger, which had led men to the commission of the
most horrible excesses, but did not then think that
fate would ever thereafter doom me to an almost
similar situation.

23.11

23.12

23.13

23.17

23.17

34   LIFE AND ADVENTURES

23.18

23.20

23.24

23.24,25

23.28

23.31

23.33

23.38

23.34

When I made my escape from the Prison ship, six English pennys was all the money that I possessed—with two I had purchased a two penny loaf the day after I had escaped from my keepers at the Inn, and the other four still remained in my possession, not having met with a favourable opportunity since the purchase of the first loaf to purchase food of any kind. When I had arrived at the distance of one and an half miles from Brintford, I met with a labourer employed in building a pale fence, to whom my deplorable situation induced me to apply for work ; or for information of any one in the neighborhood, that might be in want of a hand to work at farming or gardening. He informed me that he did not wish himself to hire, but that Sir John Millet, whose seat he represented but a short distance, was in the habit of employing many hands at that season of the year (which was in the spring of 1776) and he doubted not but that I might there meet with employment.

With my spirits a little revived, at even a distant prospect of obtaining something to alleviate my sufferings, I started in quest of the seat of Sir John, agreeable to the directions which I had received ; in attempting to reach which, I mistook my way, and proceeded up a gravelled and beautifully ornamented walk, which unconsciously led me directly to the garden of the Princess Amelia—I had approached within view of the Royal Mansion when a glimpse of a number of "red coats" who thronged the yard, satisfied me of my mistake, and caused me to make an

instantaneous and precipitate retreat, being determined not to afford any more of their mess an opportunity of boasting of the capture of a "Yankee Rebel,"
—indeed, a wolf or a bear, of the American wilderness, could not be more terrified or panic-struck at
the sight of a firebrand, than I then was at that of a
British red coat !

Having succeeded in making good my retreat
from the garden of her highness, without being discovered, I took another path which led me to where
a number of labourers were employed in shovelling
gravel, and to whom I repeated my enquiry if they
could inform me of any in want of help, &c.—" why
in troth friend (answered one in a dialect peculiar to
the labouring class of people of that part of the
country) me master, Sir John, hires a goodly many,
and as we've a deal of work now, may-be he'll hire
you ; 'spose he stop a little with us until work is
done, he may then gang along, and we'll question
Sir John, whither him be wanting another like us or
no !"

Although I was sensible that an application of this
kind, might lead to a discovery of my situation,
whereby I might be again deprived of my liberty,
and immured in a loathsome prison ; yet, as there
was now no other alternative left me but to seek in
this way, something to satisfy the cravings of hunger, or to yield a victim to starvation, with all its
attending horrors : of the the two evils I preferred
the least, and concluded as the honest labourer had

23.35

23.36

23.39
23.39

proposed, to await until they had completed their work, and then to accompany them home to ascertain the will of Sir John.

24.3

As I had heard much of the tyrannical and domineering disposition of the rich and purse-proud of England, and who were generally the lords of the manor, and the particular favourites of the crown; it was not without feeling a very considerable degree of diffidence, that I introduced myself into the presence of one whom I strongly suspected to be of that class—but, what was peculiarly fortunate for me, a short acquaintance was sufficient to satisfy me that as regarded this gentleman, my apprehensions were without cause. I found him walking in his front yard in company with several gentlemen, and on being made acquainted with my business, his first enquiry was whether I had a hoe, or money to purchace one, and on being answered in the negative, he requested me to call early the ensuing morning, and he would endeavour to furnish me with one.

24.5

24.2
24.3

24.14,16

24.28
24.29

24.31

It is impossible for me to express the satisfaction that I felt at this prospect of a deliverance from my wretched situation. I was now by so long fasting reduced to such a state of weakness, that my legs were hardly able to support me, and it was with extreme difficulty that I succeeded in reaching a baker's shop in the neighborhood, where with my four remaining pennys, which I had reserved for a last resource, I purchased two two-penny loaves.

24.32
24.33

After four days of intolerable hunger, the reader may judge how great must have been my joy, to find myself in possession of even a morsel to appease it—well might I have exclaimed at this moment with the unfortunate Trenck—" O nature! what delight hast thou combined with the gratification of thy wants! remember this ye who rack invention to excite appetite, and which yet you cannot procure ; remember how simple are the means that will give a crust of mouldy bread a flavour more exquisite than all the spices of the east, or all the profusion of land or sea; remember this, grow hungry, and indulge your sensuality."

Although five times the quantity of the " staff of life" would have been insufficient to have satisfied my appetite, yet, as I thought it improbable that I should be indulged with a mouthful of any thing to eat in the morning, I concluded to eat then but one loaf, and to reserve the other for another meal; but having eaten one, so far from satisfying, it seemed rather to increase my appetite for the other—the temptation was irresistable—the cravings of hunger predominated, and would not be satisfied until I had devoured the remaining one.

The day was now far spent and I was compelled to resort with reluctance to a carriage house, to spend another night in misery; I found nothing therein on which to repose my wearied limbs but the bare floor, which was sufficient to deprive me of sleep, however much exhausted nature required

4

24.34

24.35

24.37

24.39

25.4

88 LIFE AND ADVENTURES

it ; my spirits were however buoyed up by the pleasing consolation that the succeeding day would bring
relief ;—as soon as day light appeared. I hastened
to await the commands of one, whom, since my first
introduction, I could not but flatter myself would
prove my benefactor, and afford me that relief which
my pitiful situation so much required—it was an
hour much earlier than that at which even the domestics were in the habit of arising, and I had been a
considerable time walking back and fourth in the
barn yard, before any made their appearance. It
was now about 4 o'clock, and by the person of whom
I made the enquiry, I was informed that 8 o'clock
was the usual hour in which the labourers commenced their day's work—permission was granted me
by this person (who had the care of the stable) to
repose myself on some straw beneath the manger,
until they should be in readiness to depart to commence their day's work—in the four hours I had a
more comfortable nap than any that I had enjoyed
the four preceding nights. At 8 o'clock precisely
all hands were called, and preparations made for a
commencement of the labours of the day—I was
furnished with a large iron fork and a hoe, and ordered by my employer to accompany them, and although my strength at this moment was hardly sufficient to enable me to bear even so light a burthen, yet was unwilling to expose my weakness, so
long as it could be avoided—but, the time had now
arrived in which it was impossible for me any long-

25.5

25.6

25.9

25.8

25.13

25.14

25.15

25.17

er to conceal it, and had to confess the cause to my
fellow labourers, so far as to declare to them, that
such had been my state of poverty, that (with the
exception of the four small loaves of bread) I had
not tasted food for four days! I was not I must
confess displeased nor a little disappointed to witness
the evident emotions of pity and commiseration,
which this woeful declaration appeared to excite in
their minds: as I had supposed them too much accustomed to witness scenes of misery and distress,
to have their feelings much effected by a brief recital of my sufferings and deprivations—but in justice
to them I must say, that although a very illiterate,
I found them (with a few exceptions) a humane
and benevolent people.

About 11 o'clock we were visited by our employer, Sir John: who, noticing me particularly, and
perceiving the little progress I made in my labour,
observed, that although I had the appearance of being a stout hearty man, yet I either feigned myself
or really was a very weak one! on which it was
immediately observed by one of my friendly fellow
labourers, that it was not surprising that I lacked
strength, as I had eaten nothing of consequence for
four days! Mr. Millet, who appeared at first little disposed to credit the fact, on being assured
by me that it was really so, put a shilling into my
hand, and bid me go immediately and purchase to
that amount in bread and meat—a request which
the reader may suppose I did not hesitate to comply
with.

25.18

25.19

25.21

25.23

25.26

25.28

40.   LIFE AND ADVENTURES

Having made a tolerable meal, and feeling somewhat refreshed thereby, I was on my return when I
was met by my fellow labourers on their return home,
four o'clock being the hour in which they usually
quit work.   As soon as we arrived, some victuals
was ordered for me by Sir John, when the maid presenting a much smaller quantity, than what her benevolent master supposed sufficient to satisfy the appetite of one who had been four days fasting, she was
ordered to return and bring out the platter and the
whole of its contents, and of which I was requested
to eat my fill, but of which I eat sparingly to prevent
the dangerous consequences which might have resulted from my voracity in the debilitated state to
which my stomach was reduced.

My light repast being over, one of the men were
ordered by my hospitable friend to provide for me a
comfortable bed in the barn, where I spent the night
on a couch of clean straw, more sweetly than ever I
had done in the days of my better fortune. I arose
early much refreshed, and was preparing after breakfast to accompany the labourers to their work, which
was no sooner discovered by Sir John, than smiling,
he bid me return to my couch and there remain until I was in a better state to resume my labours ; indeed the generous compassion and benevolence of
this gentleman was unbounded. After having on
that day partook of an excellent dinner, which had
been provided expressly for me, and the domestics
having been ordered to retire, I was not a little sur-

25.29

25.34

25.36

25.35

25.39

25.40

26.3

prised to hear myself thus addressed by him —" my
honest friend, I perceive that you are a sea-faring
man, and your history probably is a secret which you
may not wish to divulge; but, whatever circumstances may have attended you, you may make them
known to me with the greatest safety, for I pledge
my honour I will never betray you."

Having experienced so many proofs of the friendly disposition of Mr Millet, I could not hesitate a
moment to comply with his request, and without attempting to conceal a single fact, made him acquainted with every circumstance that had attended me
since my first enlistment as a soldier—after expressing his regret that there should be any of his countrymen found so void of the principles of humanity,
as to treat thus an unfortunate prisoner of war, he assured me that so long as I remained in his employ
he would guarantee my safety—adding, that notwithstanding (in consequence of the unhappy differences
which then prevailed between Great Britain and her
American colonies) the inhabitants of the latter were
denominated Rebels, yet they were not without their
friends in England, who wished well to their cause,
and would cheerfully aid them whenever an opportunity should present—he represented the soldiers
(whom it had been reported to me, were constantly
on the look out for deserters) as a set of mean and
contemptible wretches, little better than a lawless
banditti, who, to obtain the fee awarded by government, for the apprehension of a deserter, would betray their best friends.

4*

26.16
26.23

26.25

26.37

27.2

27.3

27.4

27.4

27.8

27.14
27.26

27.23

27.28

27.29

27.32

27.38

28.1

Having been generously supplyed with a new suit of cloathes and other necessaries by Mr. M. I contracted with him for six months, to superintend his strawbury garden, in the course of which so far from being molested, I was not suspected by even his own domestics of being an American—at the expiration of the six months, by the recommendation of my hospitable friend, I got a birth in the garden of the Princes, Amelia, where although among my fellow labourers the American Rebellion was not unfrequently the topic of their conversation, and the " d—d Yankee Rebels" (as they termed them) frequently the subjects of their vilest abuse, I was little suspected of being one of that class whom they were pleased thus to denominate—I must confess that it was not without some difficulty, that I was enabled to suppress the indignant feelings occasioned by hearing my countrymen spoken so disrespectfully of, but as a single word in their favour might have betrayed me, I could obtain no other satisfaction than by secretly indulging the hope that I might before the conclusion of the war, have an opportunity to repay them, in their own coin, with interest.

I remained in the employ of the Princess about three months, and then in consequence of a misunderstanding with the overseer, I hired myself to a farmer in a small village adjoining Brintford, where I had not been three weeks employed before rumour was afloat that I was a Yankee Prisoner of war! from whence the report arose, or by what occcasioned, I

never could learn—it no sooner reached the ears of   28.1
the soldiers, than they were on the alert, seeking an
opportunity to seize my person—fortunately I was
apprised of their intentions before they had time to
carry them into effect; I was however hard pushed,   28.3
and sought for by them with that diligence and perseverance that certainly deserved a better cause—I
had many hair breadth escapes, and most assuredly
should have been taken, had it not been for the friend-   28.5
ship of those whom I suspect felt not less friendly to
the cause of my country, but dare not publicly avow
it--I was at one time traced by the soldiers in pursuit
of me to the house of one of this description, in whose
garret I was concealed, and was at that moment in   28.10
bed; they entered and enquired for me, and on be-
ing told that I was not in the house, they insisted on
searching, and were in the act of ascending the chamber stairs for that purpose, when seizing my cloathes,
I passed up through the scuttle, and reached the roof   28.10
of the house, and from thence half naked passed to
those of the adjoining ones to the number of ten or
twelve, and succeeded in making my escape without   28.12
being discovered.

  Being continually harrassed by night and day by   29.3
the soldiers, and driven from place to place, without
an opportunity to perform a day's work, I was advised by one whose sincerity I could not doubt, to
apply for a birth as a labourer in a garden of his
Royal Majesty, situated in the village of Quew, a   29.7
few miles from Brintford; where, under the pro-.

44   LIFE AND ADVENTURES

29.8

29.12

29.14

29.12

tection of his Majesty, it was represented to me that I should be perfectly safe, as the soldiers dare not approach the royal premises, to molest any one therein employed—he was indeed so friendly as to introduce me personally to the overseer, as an acquaintance who possessed a perfect knowledge of gardening, but from whom he carefully concealed the fact of my being an American born, and of the suspicion entertained by some of my being a prisoner of war, who had escaped the vigilance of my keepers.

29.22

29.17

30.11

31.11

31.12

31.37

31.33

30.12

30.13

30.14

30.19

The overseer concluded to receive me on trial; —it was here that I had not only frequent opportunities to see his Royal Majesty in person, in his frequent resorts to this, one of his country retreats, but once had the honour of being addressed by him. The fact was, that I had not been one week employed in the garden, before the suspicion of my being either a prisoner of war, or a Spy, in the employ of the American Rebels, was communicated, not only to the overseer and other persons employed in the garden, but even to the King himself! As I was one day busily engaged with three others in gravelling a walk, I was unexpectedly accosted by his Majesty: who, with much apparent good nature, enquired of me of what country I was—" an American born, may it please your majesty." was my reply (taking off my hat, which he requested me instantly to replace on my head,)— " ah! (continued he with a smile) an American, a

stubborn, a very stubborn people indeed !--and what
brought you to this country, and how long have you
been here ?" "the fate of war, your Majesty—I
was brought to this country a prisoner about eleven
months since,"—and thinking this a favourable opportunity to acquaint him with a few of my grievances, I briefly stated to him how much I had been
harassed by the soldiers—"while here employed
they will not trouble you," was the only reply he
made, and passed on. The familiar manner in
which I had been interrogated by his majesty, had
I must confess a tendency in some degree to pre-
possess me in his favour—I at least suspected
him to possess a disposition less tyrannical, and capable of better views than what had been imputed
to him ; and as I had frequently heard it represented in America, that uninfluenced by such of his
ministers, as unwisely disregarded the reiterated
complaints of the American people, he would have
been foremost to have redressed their grievances,
of which they so justly complained.

I continued in the service of his Majesty's gardner
at Qeuw, about four months, when the season having
arrived in which the work of the garden required less
labourers I with three others was discharged ; and
the day after engaged myself for a few months, to a
farmer in the town and neighborhood where I had
been last employed—but, not one week had expired
before the old story of my being an American prisoner of war &c. was revived and industriously circu-

30.23

30.25

31.17

31.29,38

31.39

32.4

32.2

32.15

32.17

32.19

46   *LIFE AND ADVENTURES*

lated, and the soldiers (eager to obtain the proffered bounty) like a pack of blood-hounds were again on the track seeking an opportunity to surprise me—the house wherein I had taken up my abode, was several times thoroughly searched by them, but I was always so fortunate as to discover their approach in season to make good my escape by the assistance of a friend—to so much inconvenience however did this continual apprehension and fear subject me, that I was finally half resolved to surrender myself a prisoner to some of his Majesty's officers, and submit to my fate, whatever it might be, when by an unexpected occurrence, and the seasonable interposition of providence in my favour, I was induced to change my resolution.

I had been strongly of the opinion by what I had myself experienced, that America was not without her friends in England, and those who were her well wishers in the important cause in which she was at that moment engaged; an opinion which I think no one will disagree with me in saying, was somewhat confirmed, by a circumstance of that importance, as entitles it to a conspicuous place in my narrative. At a moment when driven almost to a state of despondency by continual alarms and fears of falling into the hands of a set of desperadoes, who for a very small reward would willingly have undertaken the commission of almost any crime; I received a message from a gentleman of respectability of Brintford (J. Woodcock Esq.) requesting me to repair imme-

32.21
32.22
32.26
32.27
32.28
33.7
33.16
33.24

diately to his house—the invitation I was disposed to
pay but little attention to, as I viewed it nothing more
than a plan of my pursuers to decoy and entrap me
—but, on learning from my confidential friend that
the gentleman by whom the message had been sent,
was one whose loyalty had been doubted, I was induced to comply with the request.

    I reached the house of 'Squire Woodcock about 8
o'clock in the evening, and after receiving from him
at the door assurances that I might enter without fear
or apprehension of any design on his part against me,
I suffered myself to be introduced into a private
chamber, where were seated two other gentlemen,
who appeared to be persons of no mean rank, and
proved to be no other than Horne Tooke and James
Bridges Esquires—as all three of these gentlemen
have long since paid the debt of nature, and are placed beyond the reach of such as might be disposed
to persecute or reproach them for their disloyalty, I
can now with perfect safety disclose their names—
names which ought to be dear to every true American.

    After having (by their particular request) furnish-
ed these gentlemen with a brief account of the most
important incidents of my life, I underwent a very
strict examination, as they seemed determined to satisfy themselves, before they made any important advances or disclosures, that I was a person in whom
they could repose implicit confidence. Finding me
firmly attached to the interests of my country, so

33.19

33.21

33.24

34.4

34.10

34.28

34.38

35.3
35.4

48   LIFE AND ADVENTURES

much so as to be willing to sacrifice even my life if
necessary in her behalf, they began to address me with
less reserve ; and after bestowing the highest encom-
iums on my countrymen, for the bravery which they
had displayed in their recent engagements with the
British troops, as well as for their patriotism in publicly manifesting their abhorrence and detestation of
the ministerial party in England, who to alienate their
affections and to enslave them, had endeavoured to
subvert the British constitution ; they enquired of me
if (to promote the interests of my country) I should
have any objection to take a trip to Paris, on an
important mission, if my passage and other expences were paid, and a generous compensation allowed me for my trouble ; and which in all probability would lead to the means whereby I might
be enabled to return to my country—to which I
replied that I should have none.   After having enjoined upon me to keep every thing which they
had communicated, a profound secret, they presented me with a guinea, and a letter for a gentleman in White Waltam (a country town about 30
miles from Brintford) which they requested me to
reach as soon as possible, and there remain until
they should send for me, and by no means to fail
to arrive at the precise hour that they should appoint.

After partaking of a little refreshment I set out
at 12 o'clock at night, and reached White Waltam at half past 11 the succeeding day, and imme-

diately waited on and presented the letter to the
gentleman to whom it was directed, and who gave
me a very cordial reception, and whom I soon
found was as real a friend to America's cause as the
three gentlemen in whose company I had last been.
It was from him that I received the first information
of the evacuation of Boston by the British troops, and
of the declaration of INDEPENDENCE, by the American Congress—he indeed appeared to possess a
knowledge of almost every important transaction in
America, since the memorable battle of Bunker-Hill,
and it was to him that I was indebted for many particulars, not a little interesting to myself, and which
I might otherwise have remained ignorant of, as I
have always found it a principle of the Britains, to
conceal every thing calculated to diminish or tarnish
their fame, as a " great and powerful nation!"

I remained in the family of this gentleman about
a fortnight, when I received a letter from 'Squire
Woodcock, requesting me to be at his house without fail precisely at 2 o'clock the morning ensuing—
in compliance of which I packed up and started immediately for Brintford, and reached the house of
'Squire Woodcock at the appointed hour—I found
there in company with the latter, the two gentlemen
whose names I have before mentioned, and by whom
the object of my mission to Paris was now made
known to me—which was to convey in the most secret manner possible a letter to Dr. FRANKLIN ; every thing was in readiness, and a chaise ready harness-

5

36.2

36.5

36.5

36.8

36.10

35.11

36.18

36.20

36.34

36.35
36.36

ed which was to convey me to Charing Cross, waiting at the door—I was presented with a pair of boots,
made expressly for me, and for the safe conveyance
of the letter of which I was to be the bearer, one of
them contained a false heel, in which the latter was
deposited, and was to be thus conveyed to the Doctor. After again repeating my former declarations,
that whatever might be my fate, they should never
be exposed, I departed, and was conveyed in quick
time to Charing Cross, where I took the post coach
for Dover, and from thence was immediately conveyed in a packet to Calais, and in fifteen minutes after
landing, started for Paris ; which I reached in safety,
and delivered to Dr. Franklin the letter of which I
was the bearer.

What were the contents of this letter I was never
informed and never knew, but had but little doubt
but that it contained important information relative to
the views of the British cabinet, as regarded the affairs of America ; and although I well knew that a
discovery (while within the British dominions) would
have proved equally fatal to me as to the gentlemen
by whom I was employed, yet, I most solemnly declare, that to be serviceable to my country at that important period, was much more of an object with me,
than the reward which I had been promised, however considerable it might be. My interview with Dr.
Franklin was a pleasing one—for nearly an hour he
conversed with me in the most agreeable and instructive manner, and listened to the tale of my sufferings

39.38 ff.
42.3

with much apparent interest, and seemed disposed to
encourage me with the assurance that if the Americans should succeed in their grand object, and firmly establish their Independence, they would not fail
to remunerate their soldiers for their services—but,
alas! as regards myself, these assurances have not
as yet been verified!—I am confident, however, that
had it been a possible thing for that great and good
man (whose humanity and generosity have been the
theme of infinitely abler pens than mine) to have lived to this day, I should not have petitioned my country in vain for a momentary enjoyment of that provision, which has been extended to so great a portion
of my fellow soldiers ; and whose hardships and deprivations, in the cause of their country, could not I
am sure have been half so great as mine !

After remaining two days in Paris, letters were delivered to me by the Doctor, to convey to the gentlemen by whom I had been employed, and which for
their better security as well as my own, I deposited
as the other, in the heel of my boot, and with which
to the great satisfaction of my friends I reached Brintford, in safety, and without exciting the suspicion of
any one as to the important, (although somewhat dangerous) mission that I had been engaged in. I remained secreted in the house of 'Squire Woodcock
a few days, and then by his and the two other gentlemen's request, made a second trip to Paris, and in
reaching which and in delivering my letters, was e-
qually as fortunate as in my first. If I should suc-

83.25

64.4
64.7

64.16

67.3
65.27

67.11

83.23

83.13

eed in returning in safety to Brintford this trip, I
was (agreeable to the generous proposal of Doctor
Franklin) to return immediately to France, from
whence he was to procure me a passage to America;
—but, although in my return I met with no difficulty, yet, as if fate had selected me as a victim to endure the miseries and privations which afterward attended me, but three hours before I reached Dover
to engage a passage for the third and last time to Calais, all intercourse between the two countries was
prohibited!

My flattering expectations of being enabled soon
to return to my native country, and once more to
meet and enjoy the society of my friends, (after an
absence of more than twelve months) being thus by
an unforeseen circumstance completely destroyed, I
returned immediately to the gentlemen by whom I
had been last employed to advise with them what it
would be best for me to do, in my then unpleasant
situation—for indeed, as all prospects were now at an
end, of meeting with an opportunity very soon to return to America, I could not bear the idea of remaining any longer in a neighborhood where I was so
strongly suspected of being a fugitive from justice
and under continual apprehension of being retaken,
and immured like a felon in a dungeon.

By these gentlemen I was advised to repair immediately to London, where employed as a labourer, if I
did not imprudently betray myself, they thought there
was little probability of my being suspected of being

an American. This advice I readily accepted as the
plan was such a one as exactly accorded with my o-
pinion, for from the very moment that I first escaped
from the clutches of my captors, I thought that i1
the city of London I should not be so liable to be suspected and harrassed by the soldiers, as I should to
remain in the country. These gentlemen supplied
me with money sufficient to defray my expences and
would have willingly furnished me with a recommendation had they not been fearful that if I should
be so unfortunate as to be recognised by any one acquainted with the circumstance of my capture and escape, those recommendations (as there loyalty was
already doubted) might operate much against them;
in as much as they might furnish a clue to the discovery of some transactions which they then felt unwilling to have exposed. I ought here to state that
before I set out for London, I was entrusted by these
gentlemen with Five Guineas, which I was requested to convey and distribute among a number of A-
mericans, then confined as prisoners of war, in one of
the city prisons

I reached London late in the evening and the next
day engaged board at Five Shillings per week, at a
public house in Lombard Street, where under a ficti-
cious name I passed for a farmer from Lincolnshire—
my next object was to find my way to the prison where
were confined as prisoners of war a number of my
countrymen, and among whom I was directed to distribute the 5 guineas with which I had been entrust-
5*

54   LIFE AND ADVENTURES

ed for that purpose by their friends at Brintford.—I
found the prison without much difficulty, but it was
with very considerable difficulty that I gained admittance, and not until I had presented the turnkey with
a considerable fee would he consent to indulge me.
The reader will suppose that I must have been very
much surprised, when, as soon as the door of the prisoner's apartment was opened, and I had passed the
threshold, to hear one of them exclaim with much
apparent astonishment, " Potter! is that you! how in
the name of heaven came you here !"—an exclamation like this by one of a number to whom I supposed myself a perfect stranger, caused me much un-
easiness for a few moments, as I expected nothing
less than to recognize in this man, some one of my
old shipmates, who had undoubtedly a knowledge of
the fact of my being a prisoner of war, and having
been confined as such on board the guard ship at spithead—but, in this I soon found to my satisfaction
that I was mistaken, for after viewing for a moment
the person by whom I had been thus addressed. I
discovered him to be no other than my old friend
seargent Singles, with whom I had been intimately
acquainted in America—as the exclamation was in
presence of the turnkey, least I should have the key
turned upon me, and be considered as lawful a prisoner as any of the rest, I hinted to my friend that
he certainly mistook me (a Lincolnshire farmer) for
another person, and by a wink which he received from
me at the same moment gave him to understand that

151.25
151.25

151.30

152.3

152.10

a renewal of our acquaintance or an exchange of ci-
vilities would be more agreeable to me at any other
time. I now as I had been requested divided the money as equally as possible among them, and to prevent the suspicions of the keeper, I represented to
them in a feigned dialect peculiar to the labouring
people of the Shire-towns, that, " me master was owing a little trifle or so to a rebel trader of one of his
Majesty's American provinces, and was quested by
him to pay the ballance and so, to his brother yankee
rebels here imprisoned."

I found the poor fellows (fifteen in number) confined in a dark filthy apartment of about 18 feet
square; and which I could not perceive contained
any thing but a rough plank bench of about 10 feet
in length, and a heap of straw with one or two tattered, filthy looking blankets spread thereon, which was
probably the only bedding allowed them—although
their situation was such as could not fail to excite my
pity, yet, I could do no more than lament that it was
not in my power to relieve them—how long they remained thus confined or when exchanged, I could never learn, as I never to my knowledge saw one of
them afterwards.

For four or five days, after I reached London, I did
very little more than walk about the city, viewing
such curiosities as met my eye ; when, reflecting
that remaining thus idle, I should not only be very
soon out of funds, but should run the risk of being
suspected and apprehended as one belonging to one

151.28

151.29

of the numerous gangs of pick pockets &c. which infest the streets of the city; I applied to an Intelligence Office for a coachman's birth, which I was so
fortunate as to procure, at 15 shillings per week—
my employer (J. Hyslop, Esq.) although rigid in
his exactions, was punctual in his payments, and by
my strict prudence and abstinence from the numerous diversions of the city, I was enabled in the six
months which I served him, to lay up more cash
than what I had earned the twelve months preceding. The next business in which I engaged was
that of brick making, and which together with that
of gardening. I pursued in the summer seasons almost exclusively for five years; in all which time
I was not once suspected of being an American,
yet, I must confess that my feelings were not unfrequently most powerfully wrought upon, by hearing my countrymen dubbed with cowardice, and by
those too who had been thrice flogged or frightened by them when attempting to ascend the heights
of Bunker Hill! and to be obliged to brook these
insults with impunity, as to have resented them
would have caused me to have been suspected directly of being attached to the American cause,
which might have been attended with serious consequences.

    I should now pass over the five years that I was
employed as above mentioned, as checquered by
few incidents worth relating, was it not for one or
two circumstances of some little importance that

154.12

155.37

31.1

either attended me, or came within my own personal knowledge. The reader has undoubtedly heard
that the city of London and its suburbs, is always
more or less infested with gangs of nefarious wretches, who come under the denomination of Robbers,
Pickpockets, Shoplifters, Swindlers, Beggars, &c.
who are constantly prowling the streets in disguise,
seeking opportunities to surprise and depredate on
the weak and unguarded—of these the former class
form no inconsiderable portion, who contrive to e-
lude and set at defiance the utmost vigilance of
government—they are a class who in the day time
disperse each to his avocation, as the better to blind
the scrutinizing eye of justice, they make it a principle to follow some laborious profession, and at
night assemble to proceed on their nocturnal rounds,
in quest of those whose well stored pockets promise
them a reward, equal to the risk which they run in
obtaining it. As I was one evening passing through
Hyde Park, with five guineas and a few pennys in
my pockets, I was stopped by six of these lawless
footpads; who, presenting pistols to my breast, demanded my money—fortunately for me I had previously deposited the guineas in a private pocket of
my pantaloons, for their better security; thirsting
their hands into my other pockets and finding me in
possession of but a few English pennys, they took
them and decamped. I hastened to Bow Street and
lodged information of the robbery with the officers,
and who to my no little surprise informed me that

162.16

mine was the fifth instance, of information of similar robberies by the same gang, which had been
lodged with them that evening! —runners had been
sent in every direction in pursuit of them, but with
what success I could never learn.

Despairing of meeting with a favourable opportunity to return to America, until the conclusion of
peace, and the prospects of a continuation of the
war being as great then (by what I could learn) as
at any period from its commencement, I became
more reconciled to my situation, and contracted an
intimacy with a young woman whose parents were
poor but respectable, and who I soon after married.
I took a small ready furnished chamber, in Red
Cross street, where with the fruits of my hard
earnings, I was enabled to live tolerable comfortable for three or four years—when, by sickness and
other unavoidable circumstances, I was doomed to
endure miseries uncommon to human nature.

In the winter of 1781, news was received in London of the surrender of the army of Lord Cornwallis, to the French and American forces!—the
receipt of news of an event so unexpected operated
on the British ministers and members of Parliament, like a tremendous clap of thunder—deep sorrow was evidently depicted in the countenances of
those who had been the most strenuous advocates
for the war—never was there a time in which I
longed more to exult, and to declare myself a true
blooded yankee—and what was still more pleasing

to me, was to find myself even surpassed in expressions of joy and satisfaction by my wife, in consequence of the receipt of news, which, while it went to establish the military fame of my countrymen, was so calculated to humble the pride of her own! greater proofs of her regard for me and my country I could not require.

The ministerial party in Parliament who had been the instigators of the war, and who believed that even a view of the bright glistening muskets and bayones of John Bull, would frighten the leather apron Yankees to a speedy submission, began now to harbour a more favourable opinion of the courage of the latter. His Majesty repaired immediately to the house of peers, and opened the sessions of parliament—warm debates took place, on account of the ruinous manner in which the American war was continued; but Lord North and his party appeared yet unwilling to give up the contest. The capitulation of Cornwallis had however one good effect, as it produced the immediate release of Mr. Laurens from the Tower, and although it did not put an immediate end to the war, yet all hopes of conquering America from that moment appeared to be given up by all except North and his adherents.

There was no one engaged in the cause of America, that did more to establish her fame in England, and to satisfy the high boasting Britains of the bravery and unconquerable resolutions of the Yan-

56.6 ff.

IOI.II
IO3.16
IOI.38

60   LIFE AND ADVENTURES

kees, than that bold adventurer capt. Paul Jones ; who, for ten or eleven months kept all the western coast of the island in alarm—he boldly landed at Whitehaven, where he burnt a ship in the harbour, and even attempted to burn the town ;—nor was this to my knowledge the only instance in which the Britains were threatened with a very serious conflagration, by the instigation of their enemies abroad—a daring attempt was made by one James Aitkin, commonly known in London by the name of John the Painter, to set fire to the royal dock and shipping at Portsmouth, and would probably have succeeded, had he not imprudently communicated his intentions to one, who, for the sake of a few guineas, shamefully betrayed him—poor Aitkin was immediately seized, tried, condemned, executed and hung in chains---every means was used to extort from him a confession by whom he had been employed, but without any success---it was however strongly suspected that he had been employed by the French, as it was about the time that they openly declared themselves in favour of the Americans.

With regard to Mr. Laurens, I ought to have mentioned that as soon as I heard of his capture on his passage to Holland, and of his confinement in the Tower, I applied for and obtained permission to visit him in his apartment, and (with some distant hopes that he might point out some way in which I might be enabled to return to America) I stated to him every particular as regarded my situation. He seemed not only to lament very much my hard fortune, but (to use his own words) " that America should be deprived of the services of such men, at the important period too when she most required them."—He informed me that he was himself held a prisoner, and knew not when or on what conditions he would be liberated, but should he thereafter be in a situation to assist me in obtaining a passage to America, he should consider it a duty which he owed his country to do it.

Although I succeeded in obtaining by my industry, a tolerable living for myself and family, yet so far from becoming reconciled to my situation, I was impatient for the return of Peace, when (as I then flattered myself) I should once more have an opportunity to return to my native country. I became every day less attached to a country where I could not meet with any thing (with the exception of my little family) that could compensate me for the loss of the pleasing society of my kindred and friends in America—born among a moral and humane people, and having in my early days contracted their habits, and a considerable number of their prejudices, it would be unnatural to suppose that I should not prefer their society, to either that of rogues, thieves, pimps and vagabonds, or of a more honest but an exceedingly oppressed and forlorn people.

I found London as it had been represented to me, a large and magnificent city, filled with inhabitants of almost every description and occupation—and such

6

162.11
162.10
162.11

62   LIFE AND ADVENTURES

an one indeed as might be pleasing to an Englishman, delighting in tumult and confusion, and accustomed to witness scenes of riot and dissapation, as
well as those of human infliction; and for the sake of
variety, would be willing to imprison himself within
the walls of a Bedlam, where continual noise would
deafen him, where the unwholesomeness of the air
would effect his lungs, and where the closeness of
the surrounding buildings would not permit him to
enjoy the enlivening influence of the sun!   There is
not perhaps another city of its size in the whole
world, the streets of which display a greater contrast
in the wealth and misery, the honesty and knavery,
of its inhabitants, than the city of London.   The eyes
of the passing stranger (unaccustomed to witness
such scenes) is at one moment dazzled by the appearance of pompous wealth, with its splendid equip-
page—at the next he is solicited by one apparently
of the most wretched of human beings, to impart a
single penny for the relief of his starving family!
Among the latter class, there are many; however,
who so far from being the real objects of charity that
they represent themselves to be, actually possess
more wealth than those who sometimes benevolently
bestow it—these vile imposters, by every species of
deception that was ever devised or practiced by man,
aim to excite the pity and compassion, and to extort
charity from those unacquainted with their easy circumstances—they possess the faculty of assuming a-
ny character that may best suit their purpose—some-

times hobbling with a crutch and exhibiting a wood-
en leg—at other times "an honourable scar of a
wound, received in Egypt, at Waterloo or at Trafalgar, fighting for their most gracious sovereign and
master King George!"

165.23
165.24
165.20

Independent of these there is another species of
beggars (the gypsies) who form a distinct clan, and
will associate with none but those of their own tribe
—they are notorious thieves as well as beggars, and
constantly infest the streets of London to the great
annoyance of strangers and those who have the appearance of being wealthy—they have no particular
home or abiding place, but encamp about in open
fields or under hedges, as occasion requires—they
are generally of a yellow complexion, and converse
in a dialect peculiar only to themselves—their thieving propensities does not unfrequently lead them to
kidnap little children, whenever an opportunity presents; having first by a dye changed their complexion to one that corresponds with their own, they represent them as their own offspring, and carry them
about half naked on their backs to excite the pity and
compassion of those of whom they beg charity. An
instance of this species of theft by a party of these
unprincipled vagabonds, occurred once in my neighborhood while an inhabitant of London—the little
girl kidnapped was the daughter of a Capt. Kellem
of Coventry Street—being sent abroad on some business for her parents, she was met by a gang of Gypsies, consisting of five men and six women, who seiz-

64   LIFE AND ADVENTURES

ed her, and forcibly carried her away to their camp,
in the country, at a considerable distance, having
first stripped her of her own cloathes, and in exchange
dressed her in some of their rags—thus garbed she
travelled about the country with them for nearly 7
months, and was treated as the most abject slave, and
her life threatened if she should endeavour to escape
or divulged her story ;—she stated that during the
time she was with them they entrapped a little boy
about her own age, whom they also stripped and carried with them, but took particular care he should
never converse with her, treating him in the like savage manner ; she said that they generally travelled
by cross roads and private ways, ever keeping a
watchful eye that she might not escape, and that no
opportunity offered until when, by some accident,
they were obliged to send her from their camp to a
neighboring farm house, in order to procure a light,
which she took advantage of ; and scrambling over
hedges and ditches, as she supposed for the distance
of 8 or 9 miles, reached London worn out with fatigue and hunger, her support with them being always scanty, and of the worst sort ; to which was added the misery of sleeping under hedges, and exposure to the inclemency of the weather—it was the intention of the gypsies she said to have coloured her
and the boy when the walnut season approached.

The streets of London and its suburbs are also infested with another and a still more dreadful species
of rogues, denominated Footpads, and who often mur-

der in the most inhuman manner, for the sake of only a few shillings, any unfortunate people who happen to fall in their way—of this I was made acquainted with enumerable instances, while an inhabitant of
London ; I shall however mention but two that I have
now recollection of :—

A Mr Wylde while passing through Marlborough
Street, in a chaise, was stopped by a footpad, who,
on demanding his money, received a few shillings,
but being dissatisfied with the little booty he obtained,
still kept a pistol at Mr. Wylde's head, and on the
latter's attempting gently to turn it aside, the villain
fired, and lodged seven slugs in his head and breast,
which caused instant death—Mr. W. expired in the
arms of his son and grandson without a groan. A
few days after as a Mr. Greenhill was passing through
York-Street in a single horse chaise, he was met and
stopped by three footpads, armed with pistols one of
them seized and held the horse's head, while the o-
ther two most inhumanely dragged Mr. G. over the
back of his chaise, and after robbing him of his notes,
watch and hat gave him two severe cuts on his head
and left him in that deplorable state in the road.—
The above are but two instances of hundreds of a
similar nature, which yearly occur in the most public
streets of the city of London. The city is infested
with a still higher order of rogues, denominated pickpockets or cutpurses, who to carry on their nefarious
practices, garb themselves like gentlemen, and introduce themselves into the most fashionable circles :
6*

many of them indeed are persons who once sustained respectable characters, but who, by extravagance
and excesses, have reduced themselves to want, and
find themselves obliged at last to have recourse to
pilfering and thieving.

Thus have I endeavoured to furnish the reader
with the particulars of a few of the vices peculiar to a
large portion of the inhabitants of the city of London
—to these might be added a thousand other misde-
meanors of a less criminal nature, daily practiced by
striplings from the age of six, to the hoary headed of
ninety!—this I assure my readers is a picture correctly deliniated and not too highly wrought of a city famous for its magnificence, and where I was doomed to spend more than 40 years of my life, and in
which time pen, ink, and paper would fail, were I to
attempt to record the various instances of misery and
want that attended me and my poor devoted family.

In September 1783, the glorious news of a defin-
itive treaty of Peace having been signed between the
United States and Great-Britain, was publicly announced in London—while on the minds of those
who had been made rich by the war, the unwelcom-
ed news operated apparently like a paralytic stroke,
a host of those whose views had been inimical to the
cause of America, and had sought refuge in England,
attempted to disguise their disappointment and dejec-
tion under a veil of assumed cheerfulness. As regarded myself, I can only say, that had an event so
long and ardently wished for by me taken place but

153.7

a few months before, I should have hailed it as the epoch of my deliverance from a state 'of oppression and privation that I had already too long endured.

An opportunity indeed now presented for me to return once more to my native country, after so long an absence, had I possessed the means ; but such was the high price demanded for a passage, and such had been my low wages, and the expences attending the support of even a small family in London, that I found myself at this time in possession of funds hardly sufficient to defray the expence of my own passage, and much less that of my wife and child—hence the only choice left me was either to desert them, and thereby subject them (far seperated from me) to the frowns of an uncharitable people, or to content myself to remain with them and partake of a portion of that wretchedness which even my presence could not avert. When the affairs of the American Government had become so far regulated as to support a Consul at the British court, I might indeed have availed myself individually, of the opportunity which presented of procuring a passage home at the Government's expence ; but as this was a priviledge that could not be extended to my wife and child, my regard for them, prevented my embracing the only means provided by my country for the return of her captured soldiers and seamen.

To make the best of my hard fortune, I became as resigned and reconciled to my situation as cir-

162.23

162.20
162.21

162.22

cumstances would admit of ; flattering myself that
fortune might at some unexpected moment so far
decide in my favour, as to enable me to accomplish
my wishes—I indeed bore my afflictions with a degree of fortitude which I could hardly have believed myself possessed of I had become an expert
workman at brick making, at which business and
at gardening I continued to work for very small
wages, for three or four years after the Peace---but
still found my prospects of a speedy return to my
country, by no ways flattering. The peace had
thrown thousands who had taken an active part in
the war, out of employ ; London was thronged with
them---who, in preference to starving. required no
other consideration for their labour than a humble
living, which had a lamentable effect in reducing
the wages of the labouring class of people ; who,
previous to this event were many of them so extremely poor, as to be scarcely able to procure the
necessaries of life for their impoverished families
—among this class I must rank myself, and from
this period ought I to date the commencement of
my greatest miseries, which never failed to attend
me in a greater or less degree until that happy moment, when favoured by providence, I was permitted once more to visit the peaceful shores of the
land of my nativity.

When I first entered the city of London, I was
almost stunned, while my curiosity was not a little
excited by what is termed the " cries of London"

162.25

162.26
162.28

162.29

—the streets were thronged by persons of both sexes and of every age, crying each the various articles which they were exposing for sale, or for jobs of work at their various occupations;—I little then thought that this was a mode which I should be obliged myself to adopt to obtain a scanty pittance for my needy family—but, such indeed proved to be the case. The great increase of labourers produced by the cessation of hostilities, had so great an effect in the reduction of wages, that the trifling consideration now allowed me by my employers for my services, in the line of business in which I had been several years engaged, was no longer an object, being insufficient to enable me to procure a humble sustenance. Having in vain sought for more profitable business, I was induced to apply to an acquaintance for instruction in the art of chair bottoming, and which I partially obtained from him for a trifling consideration.

162.33

It was now (which was in the year 1789) that I assumed a line of business very different from that in which I had ever before been engaged—fortunately for me, I possessed strong lungs, which I found very necessary in an employment the success of which depended, in a great measure, in being enabled to drown the voices of others (engaged in the same occupation) by my own—" Old Chairs to Mend," became now my constant cry through the streets of London, from morning to night; and although I found my business not so profitable as I

162.34

70   LIFE AND ADVENTURES

could have wished, yet it yielded a tolerable support
for my family some time, and probably would have
continued so to have done, had not the almost constant illness of my children, rendered the expences
of my family much greater than they otherwise
would have been—thus afflicted by additional cares
and expence, (although I did every thing in my
power to avoid it) I was obliged, to alleviate the
sufferings of my family, to contract some trifling
debts which it was not in my power to discharge.

I now became the victim of additional miseries—
I was visited by a biliff employed by a creditor, who
seizing me with the claws of a tyger, dragged me
from my poor afflicted family and inhumanly thurst
me into prison! indeed no misery that I ever before endured equalled this—seperated from those
dependent on me for the necessaries of life, and
placed in a situation in which it was impossible for
me to afford them any relief!—fortunately for me
at this melancholly moment, my wife enjoyed good
health, and it was to her praise worthy exertions
that her poor helpless children, as well as myself,
owed our preservation from a state of starvation!—
this good woman had become acquainted with many
who had been my customers, whom she made acquainted with my situation, and the sufferings of my
family, and who had the humanity to furnish me
with work during my confinement--the chairs were
conveyed to and from the prison by my wife---in
this way I was enabled to support myself and to

contribute something to the relief of my afflicted
family. I had in vain represented to my unfeeling
creditor my inability to satisfy his demands, and in
vain represented to him the suffering condition of
those wholly dependent on me; unfortunately for
me, he proved to be one of those human beasts,
who, having no soul, take pleasure in tormenting
that of others, who never feel but in their own
misfortunes, and never rejoice but in the afflictions
of others of such beings, so disgraceful to human nature, I assure the reader London contains
not an inconsiderable number.

After having for four months languished in a
horrid prison, I was liberated therefrom a mere
skeleton; the mind afflicted had tortured the body;
so much is the one in subjection to the other—I
returned sorrowful and dejected to my afflicted family, whom I found in very little better condition.
We now from necessity took up our abode in an
obscure situation near Moorfields; where, by my
constant application to business, I succeeded in
earning daily a humble pittance for my family,
bearly sufficient however to satisfy the cravings
of nature; and to add to my afflictions, some one
of my family were almost constantly indisposed.

However wretched my situation there were many
others at this period, with whom I was particularly
acquainted, whose sufferings were greater if possible
than my own; and whom want and misery drove to
the commission of crimes, that in any other situation

162.39

they would probably not have been guilty of. Such was the case of the unfortunate Bellamy, who was capitally convicted and executed for a crime which distresses in his family, almost unexampled, had in a moment of despair, compelled him to commit. He was one who had seen better days, was once a commissioned officer in the army, but being unfortunate he was obliged to quit the service to avoid the horrors of a prison, and was thrown on the world, without a single penny or a single friend. The distresses of his family were such, that they were obliged to live for a considerable time deprived of all sustenance except what they could derive from scanty and precarious meals of potatoes and milk—in this situation his unfortunate wife was confined in child bed —lodging in an obscure garret, she was destitute of every species of those conveniences almost indespensable with females in her condition, being herself without clothes, and to procure a covering for her new born infant, all their resources were exhausted. In this situation his wife and children must inevitably have starved, were it not for the loan of five shillings which he walked from London to Blackheath to borrow. At his trial he made a solemn appeal to heaven, as to the truth of every particular as above stated—and that so far from wishing to exaggerate a single fact, he had suppressed many more instances of calamity scarcely to be parralleled— that after the disgrace brought upon himself by this single transaction, life could not be a boon he would be anxious to solicit, but that nature pleaded in his breast for a deserving wife and helpless child—all however was ineffectual, he was condemned and executed pursuant to his sentence.

I have yet one or two more melancholly instances of the effects of famine to record, the first of which happened within a mile of my then miserable habitation —a poor widow woman, who had been left destitute with five small children, and who had been driven to the most awful extremities by hunger, overpowered at length by the pitiful cries of her wretched offspring, for a morsel of bread, in a fit of despair, rushed into the shop of a baker in the neighborhood, and seizing a loaf of bread bore it off to the relief of her starving family, and while in the act of dividing it among them, the baker (who had pursued her) entered and charged her with the theft—the charge she did not deny, but plead the starving condition of her wretched family in palliation of the crime !—the baker noticing a platter on the table containing a quantity of roasted meat, he pointed to it as a proof that she could not have been driven to such an extremity by hunger—but, his surprize may be better imagined than described, when being requested by the half distracted mother to approach and inspect more closely the contents of the platter, to find it to consist of the remains of a roasted dog ! and which she informed him had been her only food, and that of her poor children, for the three preceding days !—the baker struck with so shocking a proof of the poverty

7

74   LIFE AND ADVENTURES

and distress of the wretched family, humanely contributed to their relief until they were admitted into
the hospital.

I was not personally acquainted with the family,
but I well knew one who was, and who communicated to me the following melancholly particulars of its
wretched situation ; and with which I now present
my readers, as another proof of the deplorable situation of the poor in England, after the close of the A-
merican war :—The minister of a parish was sent
for to attend the funeral of a deceased person in his
neighborhood, being conducted to the apartment
which contained the corpse (and which was the only
one improved by the wretched family) he found it so
low as to be unable to stand upright in it—in a dark
corner of the room stood a three legged stool, which
supported a coffin of rough boards, and which contained the body of the wretched mother, who had the
day previous expired in labour for the want of assistance. The father was sitting on a little stool over
a few coals of fire, and endeavouring to keep the infant warm in his bosom ; five of his seven children,
half naked, were asking their father for a piece of
bread, while another about three years old was standing over the corpse of his mother, and crying, as he
was wont to do, "take me, take me, mammy !"—
"Mammy is asleep," said one of his sisters with
tears in her eyes, "mammy is asleep, Johnny, don't
cry, the good nurse has gone to beg you some bread
and will soon return !"—In a few minutes after, an

old woman, crooked with age, and clothed in tatters
came hobbling into the room, with a two-penny loaf
in her hand, and after heaving a sigh, calmly set
down, and divided the loaf as far as it would go a-
mong the poor half famished children ; and which
she observed was the only food they had tasted for
the last 24 hours! By the kind interposition of the
worthy divine, a contribution was immediately raised
for the relief of this wretched family.

I might add many more melancholly instances of
the extreme poverty and distress of the wretched
poor of London, and with which I was personally acquainted ; but the foregoing it is presumed will be
sufficient to satisfy the poorest class of inhabitants of
America, that, if deprived of the superfluities, so long
as they can obtain the necessaries of life, they ought
not to murmer, but have reason to thank the Almighty that they were born Americans. That one half the
world knows not how the other half lives, is a common and just observation ;--complaints and murmers
are frequent I find among those of the inhabitants of
this highly favoured country, who are not only blessed with the liberty and means of procuring for themselves and their families, the necessaries and comforts, but even many of the luxuries of life !--they
complain of poverty, and yet never knew what it was
to be really poor ! having never either experienced
or witnessed such scenes of distress and woe as I
have described, they even suppose their imaginary
wants and privations equal to those of almost any of
the human race !

76   LIFE AND ADVENTURES

Let those of my countrymen who thus imagine themselves miserable amid plenty, cross the atlantic and visit the miserable habitations of real and unaffected woe—if their hearts are not destitute of feeling, they will return satisfied to their own peaceful and happy shores, and pour fourth the ejaculations of gratitude to that universal parent, who has given them abundance and exempted them from the thousand ills, under the pressure of which a great portion of his children drag the load of life. Permit me to enquire of such unreasonable murmerers, have you compared your situation and circumstances of which you so much complain, with that of those of your fellow creatures, who are unable to earn by their hard labour even a scanty pittance for their starving families? have you compared your situation and circumstances, with that of those who have hardly ever seen the sun, but live confined in lead mines, stone quarries, and coal pits?—before you call yourselves wretched, take a survey of the goals in Europe, in which wretched beings who have been driven to the commission of crimes by starvation, or unfortunate and honest debtors (who have been torn from their impoverished families) are doomed to pine.

So far from uttering unreasonable complaints, the hearts of my highly favoured countrymen ought rather to be filled with gratitude to that Being, by whose assistance they have been enabled to avert so many of the miseries of life, so peculiar to a portion of the oppressed of Europe at the present day—and who, after groaning themselves for some time under the yoke of foreign tyranny, succeeded in emancipating themselves from slavery and are now blessed with the sweets of liberty, and the undisturbed enjoyment of their natural rights. Britain, imperious Britain, who once boasted the freedom of her government and the invincible power of her arms—now finds herself reduced to the humiliating necessity of receiving lessons of liberty from those whom till late she despised as slaves!—while our own country on the other hand, like a phenix from her ashes, having emerged from a long, an expensive and bloody war, and established a constitution upon the broad and immovable basis of national equality, now promises to become the permanent residence of peace, liberty, science, and national felicity.— But, to return to the tale of my own sufferings---

While hundreds were daily becoming the wretched victims of hunger and starvation, I was enabled by my industry to obtain a morsel each day for my family ; although this morsel, which was to be divided among four, would many times have proved insufficient to have satisfied the hunger of one---I seldom ever failed from morning to night to cry "old chairs to mend," through the principal streets of the city, but many times with very little success---if I obtained four chairs to rebottom in the course of one day, I considered myself fortunate indeed, but instances of such good luck were very rare ; it was more frequent that I did not obtain a single one, and after cry-

7*

ing the whole day until I made myself hoarse, I was obliged to return to my poor family at night empty handed.

So many at one time engaged in the same business, that had I not resorted to other means my family must inevitably have starved—while crying " old chairs to mend," I collected all the old rags, bits of paper, nails and broken glass which I could find in the streets, and which I deposited in a bag, which I carried with me for that purpose—these produced me a trifle, and that trifle, when other resources failed, procured me a morsel of bread, or a few pounds of potatoes, for my poor wife and children—yet I murmered not at the dispensation of the supreme Arbiter of allot- ments, which had assigned to me so humbled a line of duty ; although I could not have believed once, that I should ever have been brought to such a state of humiliating distress, as would have required such means to alleviate it.

In February 1793, War was declared by Great Britain against the republic of France—and although war is a calamity that ought always to be regretted by friends of humanity, as thousands are undoubted- ly thereby involved in misery ; yet, no event could have happened at that time productive of so much benefit to me, as this—it was the means of draining the country of those who had been once soldiers, and who, thrown out of employ by the peace, demanded a sum so trifling for their services, as to cause a re- duction in the wages of the poor labouring class of

163.2
163.3

163.12

163.12

people, to a sum insufficient to procure the necessaries of life for their families ;—this evil was now removed—the old soldiers preferred an employment more in character of themselves, to doing the drudgery of the city—great inducements were held out to them to enlist, and the army was not long retarded in its operations for the want of recruits My prospects in being enabled to earn something to satisfy the calls of nature, became now more flattering ;—the great number that had been employed during the Peace in a business similar to my own, were now reduced to one half, which enabled me to obtain such an extra number of jobs at chair mending, that I no longer found it necessary to collect the scrapings of the streets as I had been obliged to do for the many months past. I was now enabled to purchase for my family two or three pounds of fresh meat each week, an article to which (with one or two exceptions) we had been strangers for more than a year—having subsisted principally on potatoes, oat meal bread, and salt fish, and sometimes, but rarely however, were enabled to treat ourselves to a little skim milk.

Had not other afflictions attended me, I should not have had much cause to complain of very extraordinary hardships or privations, from this period, until the conclusion of the war in 1817 ;—my family had increased, and to increase my cares there was scarcely a week passed but that some one of them was seriously indisposed—of ten children of which I was the father, I had the misfortune to bury seven

163.25

162.39

80   LIFE AND ADVENTURES

under five years of age, and two more after they had
arrived to the age of twenty —my last and only child
now living, it pleased the Almighty to spare to me,
to administer help and comfort to his poor afflicted
parent, and without whose assistance I should (so
far from having been enabled once more to visit the
land of my nativity) 'ere this have paid the debt of
nature in a foreign land, and that too by a death no
less horrible than that of starvation !

As my life was unattended with any very extraordinary circumstance (except the one just mentioned)
from the commencement of the war, until the re-es-
tablishment of monarchy in France, and the cessation
of hostilities on the part of Great Britain, in 1817, I
shall commence on the narration of my unparalleled sufferings, from the latter period, until that when
by the kind interposition of Providence, I was enabled
finally to obtain a passage to my native country ; and
to bid an adieu, and I hope and trust a final one, to
that Island, where I had endured a complication of
miseries beyond the power of description.

The peace produced similar effects to that of 1783
—thousands were thrown out of employ and the
streets of London thronged with soldiers seeking
means to earn a humble subsistence. The cry of
" Old Chairs to Mend," (and that too at a very reduced price) was reiterated through the streets of London by numbers who but the month before were at
Waterloo fighting the battles of their country— which,
so seriously effected my business in this line, that to

obtain food (and that of the most humble kind) for
my family, I was obliged once more to have recourse
to the collecting of scraps of rags, paper, glass, and
such other articles of however trifling value that I
could find in the streets.

It was at this distressing period, that, in consequence of the impossibility of so great a number who
had been discharged from the service procuring a
livelihood by honest means, that instances of thefts,
and daring robberies, increased throughout Great
Britain three fold. Bands of highwaymen and robbers hovered about the vicinity of London in numbers which almost defied suppression ; many were
taken and executed or transported ; but this seemed
to render the rest only the more desperately bold
and cruel, while house-breaking and assassination
were daily perpetrated with new arts and outrages
in the very capital. Nor were the starving condition
of the honest poor, who were to be met with at all
times of day and in every street, seeking something
to appease their hunger, less remarkable—unable to
procure by any means within their power sustenance
sufficient to support nature, some actually became
the victims of absolute starvation, as the following
melancholly instance will show :—a poor man exhausted by want ; dropped down in the street—those
who were passing unacquainted with the frequency
of such melancholly events, at first thought him in-
toxicated ; but after languishing half an hour, he expired. On the following day, an inquest was held

82   LIFE AND ADVENTURES

on the body, and the verdict of the jury not giving
satisfaction to the Coroner, they adjourned to the
next day.—In the interim, two respectable surgeons
were engaged to open the body, in which not a particle of nutriment was to be found except a little yellow substance, supposed to be grass, or some crude
vegetable ; which the poor man had swallowed to appease the cravings of nature !—this lamentable proof
confirmed the opinion of the jury, that he died for
want of the necessaries of life, and gave their verdict accordingly.

Miserable as was the fate of this man and that of
many others, mine was but little better, and would
ultimately have been the same, had it not been for
the assistance afforded me by my only remaining
child, a lad but six years of age. I had now arrived to an advanced age of life, and although possessing an extraordinary constitution for one of my
years, yet by my incessant labours to obtain subsistence for my family, I brought on myself a severe
fit of sickness, which confined me three weeks to
my chamber ; in which time my only sustenance
was the produce of a few half pennys, which my
poor wife and little son had been able to earn each
day by, disposing of matches of their own make,
and in collecting and disposing of the articles of
small value, of which I have before made mention;
which were to be found thinly scattered in the streets.
In three weeks it was the will of providence so far
to restore to me my strength, as to enable me once

23.18

166.4

163.1

more to move abroad in search of something to
support nature.

The tenement which I at this time rented and
which was occupied by my family, was a small and
wretched apartment of a garret, and for which I
had obligated myself to pay sixpence per week,
which was to be paid at the close of every week ;
and in case of failure (agreeable to the laws or customs of the land) my furniture was liable to be
seized. In consequence of my illness, and other
misfortunes, I fell six weeks in arrears for rent ;
and having returned one evening with my wife and
son, from the performance of our daily task, my
kind readers may judge what my feelings must
have been to find our room stripped of every article (of however trifling value) that it contained !—
alas, oh heavens ! to what a state of wretchedness
were we now reduced ! if there was any thing wanting to complete our misery, this additional drop to
the cup of our afflictions, more than sufficed. Although the real value of all that they had taken
from me, or rather robbed me of, would not if
publicly disposed of, have produced a sum probably
exceeding five dollars ; yet it was our all, except
the few tattered garments that we had on our backs,
and were serviceable and all-important to us in our
impoverished situation. Not an article of bedding
of any kind was left us on which to repose at night;
or a chair or stool on which we could rest our
wearied limbs ! but, as destitute as we were, and

162.38

84   LIFE AND ADVENTURES

naked as they had left our dreary apartment, we
had no other abiding place.

With a few half penny's which were jointly our
hard earnings of that day, I purchased a peck of
coal and a few pounds of potatoes; which while
the former furnished us with a little fire, the latter
served for the moment to appease our hunger—by
a poor family in an adjoining room I was obliged
with the loan of a wooden bench, which served as
a seat and a table, from which we partook of our
homely fare. In this woeful situation, hovering o-
ver a few half consumed coals, we spent a sleepless
night. The day's dawn brought additional afflic-
tions···my poor wife who had until this period borne
her troubles without a sigh or a murmur, and had
passed through hardships and sorrows, which nothing but the Supreme Giver of patience and fortitude, and her perfect confidence in him, could have
enabled her to sustain; yet so severe and unexpected a stroke as the last, she could not withstand···
I found her in the morning gloomy and dejected,
and so extremely feeble as to be hardly able to
descend the stairs.

We left our miserable habitation in the morning,
with hopes that the wretched spectacle that we presented, weak and emaciated as we were, would
move some to pity and induce them to impart that
relief which our situations so much required···it
would however be almost endless to recount the
many rebuffs we met with in our attempts to crave

assistance. Some few indeed were more merciful, and whatever their opinion might be of the cause of our misery, the distress they saw us in excited their charity, and for their own sakes were induced to contribute a trifle to our wants. We alternately happened among savages and christians, but even the latter, too much influenced by appearances, were very sparing of their bounty.

With the small trifle that had been charitably bestowed on us, we returned at night to our wretched dwelling, which, stripped as it had been, could promise us but little more than a shelter, and where we spent the night very much as the preceding one.— Such was the debilitated state of my poor wife the ensuing morning, produced by excessive hunger and fatigue, as to render it certain, that sinking under the weight of misery, the hand of death in mercy to her, was about to release her from her long and unparalelled sufferings. I should be afraid of exciting too painful sensations in the minds of my readers, were I to attempt to describe my feelings at this moment, and to paint in all their horror, the miseries which afterward attended me ; although so numerous had been my afflictions, that it seemed impossible for any new calamity to be capable of augmenting them ; — men accustomed to vicissitudes are not soon dejected, but there are trials which human nature alone cannot surmount—indeed to such a state of wretchedness was I now reduced, that had it not been for my suffering family, life would have been no lon-

8

86   LIFE AND ADVENTURES

ger desirable. The attendance that the helpless situation of my poor wife now demanded, it was not
within my power to afford her, as early the next day
I was reluctantly driven by hunger abroad in search
of something that might serve to contribute to our
relief. I left my unfortunate companion, attended by
no other person but our little son, destitute of fuel
and food, and stretched on an armful of straw, which
I had been so fortunate as to provide myself with the
day preceding ;—the whole produce of my labours
this day (which I may safely say was the most melancholly one of my life) amounted to no more than
one shilling ! which I laid out to the best advantage
possible, in the purchase of a few of the necessaries,
which the situation of my sick companion most required.

I ought to have mentioned, that previous to this
melancholly period, when most severely afflicted, I
had been two or three times driven to the necessity
of making application to the Overseers of the poor, of
the parish in which I resided, for admittance into the
Almshouse, or for some assistance, but never with a-
ny success ; having always been put off by them with
some evasive answer or frivolous pretence—sometimes charged by them with being an imposter, and
that laziness more than debility and real want, had
induced me to make the application—at other times
I was told that being an American born, I had no lawful claim on the government of that country for support ; that I ought to have made application to the

American Consul for assistance, whose business it was to assist such of his countrymen whose situations required it.

But such now was my distress, in consequence of the extreme illness of my wife, that I must receive that aid so indispensably necessary at this important crisis, or subject myself to witness a scene no less distressing, than that of my poor wretched wife, actually perishing for the want of that care and nourishment which it was not in my power to afford her! Thus situated I was induced to renew my application to the Overseer for assistance, representing to him the deplorable situation of my family, who were actually starving for the want of that sustenance which it was not in my power to procure for them; and what I thought would most probably effect his feelings, described to him the peculiar and distressing situation of my wife, the hour of whose dissolution was apparently fast approaching—but, I soon found that I was addressing one who possessed a heart callous to the feelings of humanity—one, whose feelings were not to be touched by a representation of the greatest misery with which human nature could be afflicted. The same cruel observations were made as before, that I was a vile imposture who was seeking by imposition to obtain that support in England, which my own country had withheld from me—that the American Yankees had fought for and obtained their Independence, and yet were not independent enough to support their own poor!—that

88   LIFE AND ADVENTURES

Great Britain would find enough to do, was she to afford relief to every d—d yankee vagabond that should apply for it!—fortunately for this abusive british scoundrel, I possessed not now that bodily strength and activity, which I could once boast of, or the villian (whether within his majesty's dominions or not) should have received on the spot a proof of " Yankee Independence" for his insolence.

Failing in my attempts to obtain the assistance which the lamentable situation of my wife required, I had recourse to other means—I waited on two or three gentlemen in my neighborhood, who had been represented to me as persons of humanity, and in-treated them to visit my wretched dwelling, and to satisfy themselves by occular demonstration, of the state of my wretchedness, especially that of my dying companion—they complied with my request, and were introduced by me to a scene, which for misery and distress, they declared surpassed every thing that they had ever before witnessed !—they accompanied me immediately to one in whom was invested the principal government of the poor of the parish, and represented to him, the scene of human misery which they had been an eye witness to—whereupon an or-der was issued to have my wife conveyed to the Hospital, which was immediately done and where she was comfortably provided for—but, alas, the re-lief which her situation had so much required, had been too long deferred—her deprivation and suffer-ings had been too great to admit of her being now

restored to her former state of health, or relieved by
any thing that could be administered —after her re-
moval to the Hospital, she lingered a few days in a
state of perfect insensibility, and then closed her eyes
forever on a world, where for many years, she had
been the unhappy subject of almost constant afflic-
tion.

I felt very sensibly the irreparable loss of one who
had been my companion in adversity, as well as in
prosperity; and when blessed with health, had afforded me by her industry that assistance, without
which, the sufferings of our poor children would
have been greater if possible than what they were.
My situation was now truly a lonely one, bereaved of
my wife, and all my children except one; who, although but little more than seven years of age, was a
child of that sprightliness and activity, as to possess
himself with a perfect knowledge of the chair bottoming business, and by which he earned not only enough
(when work could be obtained) to furnish himself
with food, but contributed much to the relief of his
surviving parent, when confined by illness and infir-
mity.

We continued to improve the apartment from
which my wife had been removed, until I was so fortunate as to be able to rent a ready furnished apartment (as it was termed) at four shillings and sixpence
per week. Apartments of this kind are not uncommon in London, and are intended to accommodate
poor families, situated as we were, who had been so

8*

unfortunate as to be stripped of every thing but the cloathes on their backs by their unfeeling landlords. These "ready furnished rooms" were nothing but miserable apartments in garrets, and contain but few more conveniences than what many of our common prisons in America afford—a bunk of straw, with two or three old blankets, a couple of chairs, and a rough table about three feet square, with an article or two of iron ware in which to cook our victuals (if we should be so fortunate as to obtain any) was the contents of the "ready furnished apartment" that we was now about to occupy—but even with these few conveniences, it was comparatively a palace to the one we had for several weeks past improved.

When my health would permit, I seldom failed to visit daily the most public streets of the city, and from morning to night cry for old chairs to mend—accompanied by my son Thomas, with a bundle of flags, as represented in the Plate annexed to this volume. If we was so fortunate as to obtain a job of work more than we could complete in the day, with the permission of the owner, I would convey the chairs on my back to my humble dwelling, and with the assistance of my little son, improve the evening to complete the work, which would produce us a few half pennys to purchase something for our breakfast the next morning—but it was very seldom that instances of this kind occurred, as it was more frequently the case that after crying for old chairs to mend, the whole day, we were obliged to return,

hungry and weary, and without a single half penny
in our pockets, to our humble dwelling, where we
were obliged to fast until the succeeding day ; and
indeed there were some instances in which we were
compelled to fast two or three days successively,
without being able to procure a single job of work.
— The rent I had obligated myself to pay every night,
and frequently when our hunger was such as hardly
to be endured, I was obliged to reserve the few pennys that I was possessed of to apply to this purpose.

    In our most starving condition, when every other
plan failed, my little son would adopt the expedient
of sweeping the public cause-ways (leading from one
walk to the other) where he would labour the whole
day, with the expectation of receiving no other reward than what the generosity of gentlemen, who had
occasion to cross, would induce them to bestow in
charity, and which seldom amounted to more than
a few pennys—sometime the poor boy would toil
in this way the whole day, without being so fortunate
as to receive a single half penny—it was then he
would return home sorrowful and dejected, and while
he attempted to conceal his own hunger, with tears
in his eyes, would lament his hard fortune in not being able to obtain something to appease mine.—
While he was thus employed I remained at home,
but not idle, being as busily engaged in making
matches, with which (when he returned home empty handed) we were obliged as fatigued as we were,
to visit the markets to expose for sale, and where we

163.1

were obliged sometimes to tarry until eleven o'clock at night, before we could meet with a single purchaser

Having one stormy night of a Saturday, visited the market with my son for this purpose, and after exposing ourselves to the chilling rain until past 10 o'clock, without being able either of us to sell a single match, I advised the youth (being thinly clad) to return home feeling disposed to tarry myself a while longer, in hopes that better success might attend me, as having already fasted one day and night, it was indispensably necessary that I should obtain something to appease our hunger the succeeding day (Sunday) or what seemed almost impossible, to endure longer its torments! I remained until the clock struck eleven, the hour at which the market closed, and yet had met with no better success! It is impossible to describe the sensation of despondency which overwhelmed me at this moment! I now considered it as certain that I must return home with nothing wherewith to satisfy our craving appetites—and with my mind filled with the most heart-rending reflections, I was about to return, when, Heaven seemed pleased to interpose in my behalf, and to send relief when I little expected it;—passing a beef stall I attracted the notice of the butcher, who viewing me, probably as I was, a miserable object of pity, emaciated by long fastings, and clad in tattered garments, from which the water was fast dripping, and judging no doubt by my appearance that on no one could charity be more properly bestowed, he threw into my basket a beeve's heart, with the request that I would depart with it immediately for my home, if any I had!—I will not attempt to describe the joy that I felt on this occasion, in so unexpectedly meeting with that relief, which my situation so much required. I hastened home with a much lighter heart than what I had anticipated; and when I arrived, the sensations of joy exhibited by my little son on viewing the prize that I bore, produced effects as various as extraordinary; he wept, then laughed and danced with transport.

The reader must suppose that while I found it so extremely difficult to earn enough to preserve us from starvation, I had little to spare for cloathing and other necessaries; and that this was really my situation, I think no one will doubt, when I positively declare that to such extremeties was I driven, that being unable to pay a barber for shaving me, I was obliged to adopt the expedient for more than two years, of clipping my beard as close as possible with a pair of scissors, which I kept expressly for that purpose!—as strange and laughable as the circumstance may appear to some, I assure the reader that I state facts, and exaggerate nothing. As regarded our cloathes, I can say no more than that they were the best that we could procure, and were such as persons in our situations were obliged to wear—they served to conceal our nakedness, but would have proved insufficient to have protected our bodies, from the in-

94   LIFE AND ADVENTURES

clemency of the weather of a colder climate. Such indeed was sometimes our miserable appearance, clad in tattered garments, that while engaged in our employment in crying for old chairs to mend, we not only attracted the notice of many, but there were instances in which a few half pennys unsolicited were bestowed on us in charity--an instance of this kind happened one day as I was passing through thread-needle street; a gentleman perceiving by the appearance of the shoes that I wore, that they were about to quit me, put a half crown in my hand, and bid me go and cry " old shoes to mend !"

In long and gloomy winter evenings, when unable to furnish myself with any other light than that emitted by a little fire of sea-coal, I would attempt to drive away melancholly by amusing my son with an account of my native country, and of the many blessings there enjoyed by even the poorest class of people--of their fair fields producing a regular supply of bread--their convenient houses, to which they could repair after the toils of the day, to partake of the fruits of their labour, safe from the storms and the cold, and where they could lay down their heads to rest without any to molest them or to make them afraid. Nothing could have been better calculated to excite animation in the mind of the poor child, than an account so flattering of a country which had given birth to his father, and to which he had received my repeated assurances he should accompany me as soon as an opportunity should present--after expres-

166.4

166.8

166.11

sing his fears that the happy day was yet far distant, with a deep sigh he would exclaim " would to God it was to morrow !".

166.14
166.14

About a year after the decease of my wife, I was taken extremely ill, insomuch that at one time my life was despaired of, and had it not been for the friendless and lonely situation in which such an event would have placed my son, I should have welcomed the hour of my dessolution and viewed it as a consummation rather to be wished than dreaded ; for so great had been my sufferings of mind and body, and the miseries to which I was still exposed, that life had really become a burthen to me—indeed I think it would have been difficult to have found on the face of the earth a being more wretched than I had been for the three years past.

During my illness my only friend on earth was my son Thomas, who did every thing to alleviate my wants within the power of his age to do—sometimes by crying for old chairs to mend (for he had become as expert a workman at this business as his father) and sometimes by sweeping the cause-ways, and by making and selling matches, he succeeded in earning each day a trifle sufficent to procure for me and himself a humble sustenance. When I had so far recovered as to be able to creep abroad, and the youth had been so fortunate as to obtain a good job, I would accompany him, although very feeble, and assist him in conveying the chairs home—it was on such occasions that my dear child would manifest his tenderness and affection for me, by insisting (if there were four chairs) that I should carry but one, and he would carry the remaining three, or in that proportion if a greater or less number.

From the moment that I had informed him of the many blessings enjoyed by my countrymen of every class, I was almost constantly urged by my son to apply to the American Consul for a passage—it was in vain that I represented to him, that if such an application was attended with success and the opportunity should be improved by me, it must cause our seperation, perhaps forever; as he would not be permitted to accompany me at the expence of government—"never mind me (he would reply) do not father suffer any more on my account; if you can only succeed in obtaining a passage to a country where you can enjoy the blessings that you have described to me, I may hereafter be so fortunate as to meet with an opportunity to join you—and if not, it will be a consolation to me, whatever my afflictions may be, to think that yours have ceased!" My ardent wish to return to America, was not less than that of my son, but could not bear the thoughts of a seperation; of leaving him behind exposed to all the miseries peculiar to the friendless poor of that country;—he was a child of my old age, and from whom I had received too many proofs of his love and regard for me, not to feel that parental affection for him to which his amiable disposition entitled him.

I was indeed unacquainted with the place of resi-

dence of the American Consul—I had made frequent
enquiries, but found no one that could inform me
correctly where he might be found ; but so anxious
was my son that I should spend the remnant of my
days in that country where I should receive (if nothing more) a christian burial at my decease, and bid
adieu forever to a land where I had spent so great a
portion of my life in sorrow, and many years had endured the lingering tortures of protracted famine;
that he ceased not to enquire of every one with whom
he was acquainted, until he obtained the wished for
information. Having learned the place of residence
of the American Consul, and fearful of the consequences of delay, he would give me no peace until
I promised that I would accompany him there the
succeeding day, if my strength would admit of it ;
for although I had partially recovered from a severe
fit of sickness, yet I was still so weak and feeble as
to be scarcely able to walk.

My son did not forget to remind me early the next
morning of my promise, and to gratify him more than
with an expectation of meeting with much success,
I set out with him, feeble as I was, for the Consul's.
The distance was about two miles, and before I had
succeeded in reaching half the way, I had wished
myself a dozen times safe home again, and had it not
been for the strong persuasions of my son to the contrary, I certainly should have returned.—I was never
before so sensible of the effects of my long sufferings—which had produced that rdegree of bodily

weakness and debility, as to leave me scarcely
strength sufficient to move without the assistance of
my son; who, when he found me reeling or halting
through weakness, would support me until I had
gained sufficient strength to proceed.

Although the distance was but two miles, yet such
was the state of my weakness, that although we started early in the morning, it was half past 3 o'clock
P. M. when we reached the Consul's office, when I
was so much exhausted as to be obliged to ascend
the steps on my hands and knees. Fortunately we
found the Consul in, and on my addressing him and
acquainting him with the object of my visit, he seemed at first unwilling to credit the fact that I was an
American born—but after interrogating me sometime, as to the place of my nativity, the cause which
first brought me to England, &c. he seemed to be
more satisfied; he however observed (on being informed that the lad who accompanied me was my son)
that he could procure a passage for me, but not for
him, as being born in England, the American government would consider him a British subject, and
under no obligation to defray the expence of his passage—and as regarded myself, he observed, that he
had his doubts, so aged and infirm as I appeared to
be, whether I should live to reach America, if I
should attempt it.

I cannot say that I was much surprised at the observations of the Consul, as they exactly agreed with
what I had anticipated—and as anxious as I then felt

to visit once more my native country, I felt determined not to attempt it, unless I could be accompanied by my son, and expressed myself to this effect
to the Consul—the poor lad appeared nearly over-
come with grief when he saw me preparing to return
without being able to effect my object; indeed so
greatly was he affected, and such the sorrow that he
exhibited, that he attracted the notice (and I believe
I may add the pity) of the Consul—who, after making some few enquiries as regarded his disposition,
age, &c. observed that he could furnish the lad with
a passage at his own expence, which he should have
no objection to do if I would consent to his living
with a connexion of his (the Consul,) on his arrival
in America—"but (continued he,) in such a case you
must be a while seperated, for it would be imprudent
for you to attempt the passage until you have gained
more strength—I will pay your board, where by better living than you have been latterly accustomed to,
you may have a chance to recruit—but your son
must take passage on board the London Packet,
which sails for Boston the day after to-morrow."

Although but a few moments previous, my son
would have thought no sacrifice too great, that would
have enabled us to effect our object in obtaining passages to America; yet, when he found that instead of
himself, I was to be left for a while behind, he appeared at some loss how to determine—but on being
assured by the Consul that if my life was spared I
should soon join him, he consented; and being fur-

nished by the Consul with a few necessary articles of
cloathing, I the next day accompanied him on board
the packet which was to convey him to America—
and after giving him the best advice that I was capable of as regarded his behaviour and deportment
while on his passage, and on his arrival in America,
I took my leave of him and saw him not again until
I met him on the wharf on my arrival at Boston.

When I parted with the Consul he presented me
with half a crown, and directions where to apply for
board—it was at a public Inn where I found many
American seamen, who, like myself, were boarded
there at the Consul's expence, until passages could
be obtained for them to America—I was treated by
them with much civility, and by hearing them daily
recount their various and remarkable adventures, as
well as by relating my own, I passed my time more
agreeably than what I probably should have done in
other society.

In eight weeks I was so far recruited by good living, as in the opinion of the Consul, to be able to endure the fatigues of a passage to my native country,
and which was procured for me on board the ship
Carterian, bound to New-York. We set sail on the
5th April, 1823, and after a passage of 42 days, arrived safe at our port of destination. After having experienced in a foreign land so much ill-treatment from
those from whom I could expect no mercy, and for
no other fault than that of being an American, I could
not but flatter myself that when I bid adieu to that

country, I should no longer be the subject of unjust persecution, or have occasion to complain of ill treatment from those whose duty it was to afford me protection. But the sad reverse which I experienced while on board the Carterian, convinced me of the incorrectness of my conclusions. For my country's sake, I am happy that I have it in my power to say that the crew of this ship, was not composed altogether of Americans—there was a mixture of all nations; and among them some so vile, and destitute of every humane principle, as to delight in nothing so much as to sport with the infirmities of one, whose grey locks ought at least to have protected him. By these unfeeling wretches (who deserve not the name of sailors) I was not only most shamefully ill-used on the passage, but was robbed of some necessary articles of cloathing, which had been charitably bestowed on me by the American Consul.

We arrived in the harbour of New-York about midnight, and such were the pleasing sensations produced by the reflection that on the morrow I should be indulged with the priviledge of walking once more on American ground after an absence of almost 50 years, and that but a short distance now seperated me from my dear son, that it was in vain that I attempted to close my eyes to sleep. Never was the morning's dawn so cheerfully welcomed by me. I solicited and obtained the permission of the captain to be early set on shore, and on reaching which, I did not forget to offer up my unfeigned thanks to that Almighty Being, who had not only sustained me during my heavy afflictions abroad, but had finally restored me to my native country. The pleasure that I enjoyed in viewing the streets thronged by those, who, although I could not claim as acquaintances, I could greet as my countrymen, was unbounded, I felt a regard for almost every object that met my eye; because it was American.

Great as was my joy on finding myself once more among my countrymen, I felt not a little impatient for the arrival of the happy moment when I should be able to meet my son. Agreeable to the orders which I received from the American Consul, I applied to the Custom House in New-York for a passage from thence to Boston, and with which I was provided on board a regular packet which sailed the morning ensuing—in justice to the captain, I must say that I was treated by him as well as by all on board, with much civility. We arrived at the Long Wharf in Boston after a short and pleasant passage. I had been informed by the Consul, previous to leaving London, of the name of the gentleman with whom my son probably lived, and a fellow passenger on board the packet was so good as to call on and inform him of my arrival—in less than fifteen minutes after receiving the information my son met me on the wharf! Reader, you will not believe it possible for me to describe my feelings correctly at this joyful moment! if you are a parent, you may have some conception of them; but a faint one however unless

you and an only and beloved child have been placed
in a similar situation.

After acquainting myself with the state of my
boy's health, &c. my next enquiry was whether he
found the country as it had been described by me,
and how he esteemed it—" well, extremely well (was
his reply) since my arrival I have fared like a Prince,
I have meat every day, and have feasted on American
puddings and pies (such as you used to tell me about)
until I have become almost sick of them !"   I was
immediately conducted by him to the house of the
gentleman with whom he lived, and by whom I was
treated with much hospitality—in the afternoon of
the day succeeding (by the earnest request of my
son) I visited Bunker-Hill, which he had a curiosity
te view, having heard it so frequently spoken of by
me while in London, as the place where the memorable battle was fought and in which I received my
wounds.

I continued in Boston about a fortnight, and then
set out on foot to visit once more my native State.
My son accompanied me as far as Roxbury, when I
was obliged reluctantly to part with him, and proceeded myself no farther on my journey that day
than Jamaica plains, where at a public house I tarried all night—from thence I started early the next
morning and reached Providence about 5 o'clock in
the afternoon, and obtained lodgings at a public Inn
in High Street.

It may not be improper here to acquaint my rea-

ders that as I had left my father possessed of very
considerable property, and of which at his decease I
thought myself entitled to a portion equal to that of
the other children, which (as my father was very e-
conomical in the management of his affairs) I knew
could not amount to a very inconsiderable sum ; it
was to obtain this if possible, that I became extremely anxious to visit immediately the place of my nativity—accordingly the day after I arrived in Provi-
idence, I hastened to Cranston, to seek my connex-
ions if any were to be found ; and if not to seek among
the most aged of the inhabitants, some one who had
not forgotten me, and who might be able to furnish
me with the sought for information.   But, alas, too
soon were blasted my hopeful expectations of finding
something in reserve for me, that might have afforded me a humble support, the few remaining years
of my life.   It was by a distant connexion that I was
informed that my brothers had many years since removed to a distant part of the country—that having
credited a rumour in circulation of my death, at the
decease of my father had disposed of the real estate
of which he died possessed, and had divided the proceeds equally among themselves !   This was another instance of adverse fortune that I had not anticipated !—it was indeed a circumstance so foreign
from my mind that I felt myself for the first time,
unhappy, since my return to my native country, and
even believed myself now doomed to endure, among
my own countrymen (for whose liberties I had fought

168.9
168.11

and bled) miseries similar to those that had attended me for many years in Europe.   With these gloomy forebodings I returned to Providence, and contracted for board with the gentleman at whose house I had lodged the first night of my arrival in town, and to whom for the kind treatment that I have received from him and his family, I shall feel till death under the deepest obligations that gratitude can dictate; for I can truly say of him, that I was a stranger and he took me in, I was hungry and naked, and he fed and cloathed me.

As I had never received any remuneration for services rendered, and hardships endured in the cause of my country, I was now obliged, as my last resort, to petition Congress to be included in that number of the few surviving soldiers of the Revolution, for whose services they had been pleased to grant pensions—and I would to God that I could add, for the honour of my country, that the application met with its deserving success—but, although accompanied by the deposition of a respectable gentleman (which deposition I have thought proper to annex to my narrative) satisfactorily confirming every fact as therein stated—yet, on no other principle, than that *I was absent from the country when the pension law passed*—my Petition was REJECTED !!!   Reader, I have been for 30 years (as you will perceive by what I have stated in the foregoing pages) subject, in a *foreign* country, to almost all the miseries with which poor human nature is capable of being inflicted—yet, in no

one instance did I ever feel so great degree of a depression of spirits, as when the fate of my Petition
was announced to me! I love too well the country
which gave me birth, and entertain too high a respect
for those employed in its government, to reproach
them with ingratitude; yet, it is my sincere prayer
that this strange and unprecedented circumstance, of
withholding from me that reward which they have
so generally bestowed on others, may never be told
in Europe, or published in the streets of London, least
it reach the ears of some who had the effrontery to
declare to me personally, that for the active part that
I had taken in the "rebellious war" misery and starvation would ultimately be my reward!

To conclude—although I may be again unfortunate in a renewal of my application to govenment, for
that reward to which my services so justly entitle
me—yet I feel thankful that I am priviledged (after
enduring so much) to spend the remainder of my
days, among those who I am confident are possessed of too much humanity, to see me suffer; and
which I am sensible I owe to the divine goodness,
which graciously condescended to support me under my numerous afflictions, and finally enabled me
to return to my native country in the 79th year of
my age---for this I return unfeigned thanks to the
Almighty; and hope to give during the remainder
of my life, convincing testimonies of the strong impression which those afflictions made on my mind,
by devoting myself sincerely to the duties of religion.

DEPOSITION OF JOHN VIAL.

I JOHN VIAL of North Providence, in the county of Providence, in the State of Rhode Island, on oath certify and say, that sometime in the latter part of November or the beginning of December A.D. 1775. I entered as gunner's mate on board the Washington, a public armed vessel in the service of the United States, and under the command of S. Martindale, Esq.—said vessel was sent out by order of General WASHINGTON, from Plymouth (Mass.) to cruize in Boston harbour to intercept supplies going to Boston, then in the possession of the British troops. After we had been out a short time, we were captured by a British 20 gun ship, called the " Foy," and were carried to Boston, where we remained about a week and were then put on board the frigate Tartar, and sent to England as prisoners—and I the said John further testify and say, that I well remember Israel R. Potter, now residing in Cranston, who was a mariner on board the Washington also—said Potter entered about the time I did and was captured and carried to England with me. We arrived in England in January 1776, we were then put into the Hospital, the greater part of the crew being sick in consequence of the confinement during the voyage, where many died—I remained in imprisonment about sixteen months when I made my escape—what became of said Potter afterwards I do not know but I have not the least doubt he remained a prisoner until the peace 1783 as he

108   LIFE AND ADVENTURES OF &c.

stated in his application for a pension—I have no doubt he suffered a great deal during his captivity. According to my best recollection nearly one third of the crew died in the hospital—I do remember an affair which took place during our voyage to England which caused Potter to suffer a great deal more than perhaps he otherwise would—a number of the crew of the Washington formed a plan to rise and take the Frigate but was defeated in their purpose, among whom I believe Potter was one, and in consequence, put in irons for the remaining part of the voyage with a number of others. And I the said John do further testify that I do not know of any of the said crew of the Washington now being alive except said Potter and myself—and that I do not believe it to be in the power of said Potter to procure any other testimony of the above mentioned facts except mine.

JOHN VIAL.

Rhode Island District—Providence Aug 6, 1823.

The said John Vial, who is well known to me and is a creditable witness, made solemn oath to the truth of the foregoing deposition by him subscribed in my presence.   DAVID HOWELL.
DISTRICT JUDGE.

ERRATA.

In page 82, 15th line from the top for "a child but six years of age" read "a child but seven years of age"—In page 82, sixth line from the top, for "sixpence per week" read "sixpence per day".—In addition to the above some few typographical errors of words improperly spelled, escaped the notice of the publisher, until too late to correct them.

LATER TRUMBULL "LIVES"

Life and Remarkable Adventures of Israel R. Potter (Third Edition, 1824)

This frontispiece and title page are reproduced approximately original size from a third edition copy in the Melville Collection of The Newberry Library (Melville 76-24869). The frontispiece, showing Israel walking to the left carrying a bundle of rushes and accompanied by a boy and a girl, and the title page are the same as in the second edition.

Life and Adventures of Colonel Daniel Boon, the First White Settler of the State of Kentucky (1824)

Trumbull's book is one of many versions of Boone's life which are based on John Filson's 1784 narrative. The frontispiece and title page reproduced here in their original size are those of a first edition copy in The Newberry Library (Graff 1324).

Life and Adventures of Robert, the Hermit of Massachusetts (1829)

Trumbull also published this work in the same year with a slightly variant title, *Life and Adventures of Robert Voorhis.* . . . Reproductions (approximately original size) of the frontispiece and title page are from a copy in The Newberry Library (E5.9 Rin-San).

"OLD CHAIRS TO MEND."

ISRAEL R. POTTER,
Born in Cranston (Rhode Island) August 1st. 1744.

LIFE

AND

REMARKABLE ADVENTURES

OF

ISRAEL R. POTTER,

(A NATIVE OF CRANSTON, RHODE-ISLAND,)

WHO WAS A SOLDIER IN THE

AMERICAN REVOLUTION,

And took a distinguished part in the Battle of Bunker
Hill (in which he received three wounds,) after
which he was taken Prisoner by the British, conveyed to England, where for 30 years he obtained a
livelihood for himself and family, by crying "*Old
Chairs to Mend,*" through the Streets of London.—
In May last, by the assistance of the American Consul, he succeeded (in the 79th year of his age) in
obtaining a passage to his native country, after an
absence of 48 years.

PROVIDENCE:
Printed by J. HOWARD, for I. R. POTTER—1824.
(Price 31 Cents.)

COL. DANIEL BOON,

The first settler of the State of Kentucky

LIFE AND ADVENTURES

OF

Colonel DANIEL BOON,

THE FIRST WHITE SETTLER OF THE STATE OF
KENTUCKY.

— COMPRISING —

An account of his first excursion to Kentucky in
1769, then a wild Wilderness, inhabited by no
other human beings but Savages—his remove
there with his family in 1773—and of his various
encounters with the Indians, from the year 1769
to 1782.

WRITTEN BY HIMSELF.

TO WHICH IS ADDED,

A narration of the most important incidents of his
life from the latter period, until the period of his
death, June 27, 1821, at the advanced age of 90
years—comprising an account of his many extraordinary excursions and hair-breath escapes,
while in pursuit of the wild beasts of the forest,
his favorite amusement until the day of his death.

ANNEXED,

Is an Eulogy on Col. Boon, and choice of life, by

LORD BYRON

PROVIDENCE—Printed by H. Trumbull. 1824.

ROBERT THE HERMIT.

LIFE AND ADVENTURES

OF

ROBERT,

THE

HERMIT OF MASSACHUSETTS,

Who has lived 14 Years in a Cave, secluded from human society.

COMPRISING,

An account of his Birth, Parentage, Sufferings, and
providential escape from unjust and cruel Bond-
age in early life—and his reasons for becoming a Recluse.

Taken from his own mouth, and published for his
benefit.

PROVIDENCE :

Printed for H. TRUMBULL---1829.

Price 12 1-2 Cents.

COLOPHON

THE TEXT of the *Northwestern-Newberry Edition* of THE WRITINGS OF HERMAN MELVILLE *is set in eleven-point Monophoto Bembo, two points leaded. This exceptionally handsome type face is a modern rendering of designs made by Francesco Griffo for the office of Aldus Manatius in Venice and first used for the printing, in 1495, of the tract* De Aetna *by Cardinal Pietro Bembo. The display face is Bruce Rogers's Centaur, a twentieth-century design based on and reflective of the late-fifteenth-century Venetian models of Nicolas Jenson.*

This volume was composed by William Clowes & Sons, Ltd., of Beccles, Suffolk, England. It was printed and bound by Bookcrafters, Inc., of Chelsea, Michigan. The typography and binding design of the edition are by Paul Randall Mize.